J. P. Carter is the pseudonym of a bestselling author who has also written sixteen books under the names Jaime and James Raven. Before becoming a full-time writer he spent a career in journalism as a newspaper reporter and television producer. He was, for a number of years, director of a major UK news division and co-owned a TV production company. He now splits his time between homes in Hampshire and Spain with his wife.

AT YOUR DOOR

J. P. CARTER

avon.

Published by AVON
A division of HarperCollins*Publishers* Ltd
1 London Bridge Street
London SE1 9GF

www.harpercollins.co.uk

A Paperback Original 2019

First published in Great Britain by HarperCollins*Publishers* 2019

A catalogue copy of this book is available from the British Library.

ISBN: 978-0-00831-330-2

Typeset in Minion Pro by Palimpsest Book Production Limited, Falkirk, Stirlingshire
Printed and bound in UK by CPI Group (UK) Ltd, Croydon CR0 4YY

To my three wonderful daughters.

PROLOGUE

He was a bag of nerves because he had never disposed of a body before.

He knew that if he made a mistake, or was simply unlucky, then he could be caught red-handed or leave clues for the police to find.

He'd briefly considered driving out of London into the countryside, but had decided against it the moment he'd got behind the wheel. The longer he was in the car the greater the risk of something unforeseen happening. It wasn't beyond the realms of possibility that he'd be pulled over by a couple of bored coppers working the night shift.

And then there were the ubiquitous traffic cameras to take into account. All the routes out of the capital were packed with them, and it was essential he avoided as many as possible.

Having taken all this into consideration he had opted to drive to a spot he was familiar with. It was on the edge of a wooded area on Barnes Common. He would only have to travel another mile or so and he'd be there. By then it'd be well after midnight and the area would hopefully be deserted.

His heart was pumping furiously and beads of sweat pulsed on his forehead. He was struggling to focus and he needed to. He couldn't afford to slip up. Dumping the body would be the easy part. He knew exactly what he was going to do. The important thing was not to leave any traces of himself behind such as fingerprints, DNA and incriminating fibres. But after she was found things would hot up, become ever more dangerous.

If he had known what was going to happen earlier this evening he would have made plans. And they would have included finding somewhere to bury the corpse. But that was out of the question now. It would take ages to dig a grave even if he had a shovel and the inclination to do so. And he would first have to find a suitable spot that didn't require him to haul the body any great distance.

Luckily the roads were quiet and the weather calm. But according to the Met Office there would be showers later in the morning to welcome in the first Wednesday of September. He hoped the forecasters were right because it would mess things up for the forensics team when they eventually arrived to examine the ground around the body.

He was past Putney now and the common was up ahead. He could feel the panic rising inside him and he tried to push it down. Hold your nerve, he told himself. Just concentrate and this will soon be over.

A bout of trembling gripped him when he reached the common and turned onto the road that led to his chosen spot. Trees pressed in on either side. He drove for half a mile and passed only two cars coming in the opposite direction.

When he arrived at his destination he slowed down and made sure there were no cars approaching from behind. Then he stopped before reversing onto a short patch of gravel that formed the entrance to a field with dense woodland on one side. In doing so his headlights picked out the gates to an old cemetery on the opposite side of the road.

Once the car was stationary he switched off the engine and the darkness descended. He sat for a full minute as the adrenalin surged through him. Only one car passed during that time and he saw no sign of life around him.

Eventually he sucked in a lungful of air through gritted teeth and put his gloves back on. Then he got out of the car. He had parked at a slight angle so that passing motorists wouldn't be able to see his number plate. The back of the car was a few feet away from a metal gate that blocked vehicular access to the field. But on one side of it was another smaller gate that opened onto a narrow walking trail.

He walked around and opened the boot, confident that he wasn't visible from the road. Inside, the body was wrapped in black plastic bin bags that had been taped together.

She only weighed about eight stone so it was easy enough for him to lift her out. He carried her through the small gate and along the trail to the right into the woods. The vegetation between the trees was high and thick and he found the perfect spot after only a short distance. He dropped her onto a bed of ferns and then carefully removed the bin bags so she was lying there naked, her skin pale against the dark undergrowth.

As he stared down at her he realised there were tears in his eyes and a voice inside his head was telling him to stay with her for a while so that he could get off his chest the things he wanted to say to her. But another voice told him not to be stupid and to get away from there as quickly as possible. And it was that voice he listened to.

He gathered up some leaves and branches and threw them on top of her, and while doing so he wondered if the body would be discovered before the animals and insects feasted on it.

Finally, he picked up the bin bags and used the torch on his phone to make sure he'd left nothing behind.

Then he returned to the car and put the blood-soaked bin bags into an unused bag. He then placed this in the boot alongside her clothes, handbag and purse. Seconds later he was back behind the wheel.

But his work wasn't finished. On the way home he stopped next to half a dozen different street bins into which he deposited her belongings along with the bin bags. As a precaution everything had already been wiped clean, her phone had been smashed and all her credit cards cut up into small pieces.

The only item he intended to keep was her driving licence, which he took from his pocket after he pulled the car to a stop in front of his home. He stared at it for almost half a minute, and was careful not to touch the spatter of blood on the back. Then he blew a kiss at her photograph, and said, 'I'm so very, very sorry. You really didn't deserve this.'

CHAPTER ONE

Anna was glad that nobody in the office had realised it was her birthday. The last thing she wanted was any kind of fuss.

It was depressing enough knowing that she was another year older. She didn't want to be teased about reaching the ripe old age of forty-three.

It was scary how quickly the time had passed, and how many milestones she had clocked up. A lot of tears had been shed during those four decades, and she didn't feel inclined to celebrate the fact that September the sixth had come around again.

The only reason she was going out for dinner tonight was because Tom had insisted.

'You've had a tough year, Anna,' he'd said this morning just before they left her house and went their separate ways. 'And I wouldn't be a very good boyfriend if I let your birthday pass without making it at least a little different to every other day.'

He was right about it having been a tough year, especially

on the work front. She and her colleagues in the Major Investigation Team had been swamped by the biggest tidal wave of serious crime ever to hit South London. The murder rate was up, along with knife attacks, shootings, robberies and gang violence. The last case they'd dealt with had been the most challenging, though. It had involved the abduction of nine small children from a nursery school in Rotherhithe, and the murder of one of their teachers.

The investigation had ended dramatically two weeks ago, but the paperwork was still piled up on the desk in front of her. She'd been wading through it all afternoon and her eyes were tired from reading the case notes, interview transcripts, forensics reports and briefing documents that were being prepared for the Crown Prosecution Service.

Still, in another forty-five minutes it'd be five o'clock and that was when she'd decided to call it a day. It was only a short drive from the Wandsworth HQ to her home in Vauxhall so she'd have plenty of time to shower and get dressed before Tom arrived.

He was getting ready at his own flat, which was only a mile away, and coming over by taxi. He'd booked a table at their favourite Italian restaurant for seven-thirty and she was hoping he hadn't done something daft like ordered a cake or arranged for someone to sing 'Happy Birthday' to her.

The more she thought about tonight the less she felt like going. But if she cried off without having a really good excuse it would upset Tom and give him another reason to believe that she was no longer committed to their relationship. The issue had taken root in his mind and she'd been struggling to convince him that it wasn't true.

But she knew it would take more than just words to banish

his insecurities. The main thing he wanted was for them to live together and she simply wasn't ready for that.

A burst of activity out in the main office seized her attention suddenly. She watched through the open door as several detectives gathered around the desk of DI Max Walker, who was holding a phone to his ear with one hand while scribbling frantically on a notepad with the other.

Instinct told Anna that something had happened and that Walker was being fed the details by an operator at central control. If so then it could well be the start of a new investigation.

That was usually how it began. A single phone call that prompted a collective rush of adrenalin and then a dash to the scene of whatever crime had been committed.

Anna was on her feet and out of her tiny office in a flash. By the time she reached Walker's desk he'd finished the call and was tearing a page from his notebook. He looked up at her but when he spoke it was loud enough so that everyone could hear.

'A body has been found on the edge of Barnes Common,' he said. 'A young woman. She's naked and has a stab wound to the throat. And it seems she hasn't been there very long. Uniform have just arrived and a forensics team are only minutes away.'

CHAPTER TWO

Anna told DI Walker and DC Megan Sweeny that she wanted them to go with her to the common. She then issued various instructions to the rest of the detectives.

'Check missing persons to see if any young women have been added to the database recently. And I want us to locate all the street cameras within a half-mile radius of where the body's been found.'

Anna hurried back into her office to collect her jacket and shoulder bag. As she was stepping back out her mobile rang. She answered it without checking the caller ID.

'DCI Tate,' she said.

'Hello, detective. This is Jan Groves in the Media Liaison Department. Can you spare a moment?'

'Not really. I'm on my way out of the office. And if you're calling to ask about the body found on Barnes Common then I don't have any information yet. We've only just got wind of it.'

'Actually it's got nothing to do with that,' Groves said. 'This is more of a personal matter.'

Anna paused in the doorway and frowned.

'In that case I'll let you satisfy my curiosity,' she said. 'I can give you sixty seconds. So fire away.'

'Well, we've been contacted by a producer at Channel Four,' Groves said. 'He just finished the second instalment of the feature about you that's been published in the *Evening Standard*. He said it blew his mind and he'd like to do a programme on it for their true crime series. He wants to know if you'd be willing to cooperate.'

Anna's heart skipped a beat. 'Of course I'm up for it. And the sooner it happens the better.'

'I thought that would be your reaction,' Groves said. 'I'll get back to him right away. Your superiors will need to sign off on it, but I don't think that will be a problem. We're working closely with several TV channels on a whole bunch of programmes at present.'

Anna was well aware of that. True crime documentaries were all the rage with broadcasters these days. Viewers were lapping them up, and that was good for the force because they often shed new light on unsolved cases going back years.

'As a matter of interest have you had any other response to the article in the *Standard*?' Groves asked.

'Nobody has contacted me yet,' Anna said. 'I checked with the paper a few hours ago but they said they hadn't received any calls or emails either.'

'That's a shame. I thought it was a really well-written piece, and the story itself is just extraordinary. Hopefully you'll have better luck if we can get this doco off the ground.'

'I'll be keeping my fingers crossed,' Anna said.

'And I'll keep you updated on where we are with it.'

After ending the call, Anna took a moment to reflect on

this latest news. In the ten years she'd been searching for her daughter she had never felt so close to finding her. Now, for the first time, the full story of Chloe's abduction, including the recent shocking developments, was going to be aired on a mainstream TV channel. With luck it would be seen by someone who had information that could end Anna's long-running nightmare.

It was hard for her to contain her excitement, but she knew she had to, at least for now. If she didn't squeeze it to the back of her mind it would become a distraction, and she couldn't allow that to happen at the start of what might prove to be a major new investigation.

She needed to focus all her attention on the job at hand. She owed that to the family of the young woman whose body had turned up on Barnes Common.

Anna travelled across South London in a pool car with DI Walker and DC Sweeny.

Walker, who was in his late thirties, had been part of the team for four years and was Anna's most trusted wingman. Sweeny, who was several years younger, had joined only three months ago and Anna was keen for her to have plenty of crime scene experience.

Walker was driving and Sweeny was in the back Googling the location of the body on her phone browser.

'It's right next to the road that passes between Barnes Common and Putney Lower Common,' she was saying. 'Just opposite there's a cemetery that's been closed to new burials for years. But it's quite well known because it contains some Commonwealth war graves.'

Anna was familiar with the area, which had more open

spaces than any other part of London. To the south of Barnes Common was Richmond Park, Putney Heath and Wimbledon Common. To the north was the Thames and the London Wetland Centre, an urban oasis for wildlife, with lakes, ponds and gardens.

The area contained hundreds of acres of woods and heathland, but very few bodies had ever been found there, which was perhaps surprising given the capital's high murder and suicide rates. That wasn't to say there weren't dozens buried beneath the topsoil or lying undiscovered amidst thick hedgerows.

Anna was already wondering about the woman whose corpse they were going to see. Was she married or single? Did she have children? Did she die on the common or elsewhere? Who found her? And why was she naked?

The questions would pile up as per usual and it would be their job to seek out the answers. They would also have to break the news to those with whom the woman had a relationship. The next of kin, be it mother, father, husband, son or daughter. It was a thankless task that Anna had carried out far too many times during her seventeen years on the force.

Her thoughts were interrupted by another call on her mobile. This time she checked the caller ID before answering. It was her boss, DCS Bill Nash.

'I can guess why you're ringing, guv,' she said. 'We're on our way to Barnes Common now. Traffic's pretty heavy but we should be there in ten minutes or so.'

'Well, I won't be back in London until tomorrow,' he responded. 'But I want you to keep me updated. This sounds like a nasty one.'

Anna had forgotten that Nash had been attending a

two-day conference in Newcastle with other senior police officers from all over the country.

'Everything is in hand,' she said. 'Uniform are already at the scene and forensics should have arrived by now too.'

'Well, don't hesitate to call me if there are any problems.'

It was only about two miles from MIT HQ to Barnes Common, but it was rush hour and therefore slow going even with the blue light flashing.

They finally arrived at their destination at five-thirty. It was a rural setting that should have been deserted and peaceful. Instead it was a scene of frenzied activity.

On one side of the road three patrol cars, a fast-response ambulance and a forensics van were parked in front of the wall to the cemetery that Sweeny had mentioned. On the opposite side a small group had gathered on a rough patch of gravel leading to a field. They included four officers in hi-vis jackets, a paramedic and a woman with a small dog on a lead.

Walker parked up next to the ambulance and Anna was the first out. The sky had clouded over and she was glad because it had taken the heat out of the day. It meant she could leave her jacket on without sweating buckets.

'Well, it's time to find out what we have here,' she said as she led the way across the road.

The detectives flashed their warrant cards and one of the uniforms quickly put them in the picture.

'We've just been informed that the pathologist will be here any minute,' he said.

He gestured to a metal gate behind him that blocked any vehicles driving onto the field, but there was a smaller gate to one side which led to an unpaved walking trail.

'We're trying to find out who owns the land so we can get them to open the gate,' he went on. 'The body is about forty yards into those woods over to the right. The SOCOs arrived ten minutes ago and are getting themselves sorted.'

'So who found it?' Anna asked.

The officer nodded towards the woman with the dog, who was speaking to the paramedic.

'Her name's Joyce Connor. Her mutt sniffed it out and she called it in. But understandably she's in a bit of a state.'

'We'll talk to her in a moment,' Anna said. 'First we'll see the body for ourselves.'

'Well, you need to brace yourselves,' the officer said. 'It really isn't a pretty sight.'

CHAPTER THREE

Anna and her two detectives followed the walking trail and saw the scene of crime officers as soon as they entered the wood. There were five of them. They had already unpacked their equipment and were starting to do their job with grim-faced determination.

Anna knew that it wasn't going to be easy for them. Crime scenes that were open to the elements were always more difficult to control and process. Contamination of evidence was inevitable and dead bodies usually fell prey to insects and animals. Much would depend on how long the woman had been here and that was for the pathologist to determine with any degree of accuracy.

The three detectives were greeted by a SOCO wearing a white paper suit. Anna had never met him before so she introduced herself and the others and then they all signed the crime scene log.

The officer pointed to a large cardboard box containing overalls, masks and shoe covers.

'You'll need to get suited up,' he said. 'And for your information another team will be here shortly. There's a lot of ground to be covered and it's pretty messy.'

Once they had the gear on they followed the officer into the wood along a narrow, uneven trail that looked as though it didn't get used much.

'So what have we got then?' Anna asked him.

'Female, probably in her early twenties,' he said. 'Looks as though she's been stabbed in the throat and I very much doubt that she did it to herself. She's also naked and there are no clothes or other belongings in the immediate vicinity of the body. And as yet no sign of a weapon or anything that can identify her.'

'So was she dumped here or killed here?'

'Almost certainly dumped. And whoever did it covered her with leaves and branches but didn't try very hard to conceal her.'

'Any thoughts on how long she's been here?'

'Well, that's not my area of expertise but I would say a few days and nights at the most. There are residual signs of rigor but not much blistering and skin decay. And be warned, the creatures of the forest have been dining out on her.'

They had to clamber through a patch of wild shrubs to get to the body. It was lying face up and the sight of it drew sharp intakes of breath from Anna and her two colleagues. The woman's skin was pale and bloated and the gaping hole in her throat was filled with foam, blood, maggots and flies.

Her eyes were closed but her lips were parted to reveal teeth that were smeared with dirt and dust. There were small bite and scratch marks on her breasts, stomach and thighs, and about a dozen ants had made themselves at home in her pubic thatch.

'I've seen enough,' Sweeny said suddenly as she put her hand over her mouth and hurriedly retreated to the trail.

Anna shook her head. 'Can't really blame her for that. This is pretty bad.'

'Worst I've seen in a long time,' Walker said. 'The poor kid was in the prime of her life. It's a fucking shame.'

Anna was still staring down at the body while trying to imagine what the woman had looked like before her life was cut short in such a brutal fashion.

She was slim with small breasts and quite tall at about five ten or eleven. Her hair was fair and shoulder-length. It framed a narrow face with high cheekbones and a sharply pointed nose.

'First thing we did was remove the stuff that had been placed on top of her,' the forensics officer said. 'We want to take some more pictures and examine the ground around her before we turn her over and put up the tent. And I'm sure the pathologist will want to be present when we do that.'

Anna asked Walker to take some pictures on his phone while she took out her pad and made various notes, including a list of questions she wanted answers to.

Who was the victim? Had she been reported missing? Why was she dumped here on Barnes Common? Was she stripped to remove traces of DNA? How did the killer get her to this spot? Was it in a car or van? If so where had the vehicle been parked?

Anna looked around, soaking up the scene, and wondered how many people frequented this part of the common. The track snaked deeper into the wood. She would have to find out where it led and if there were any homes close by.

'I've got enough photos,' Walker said. 'Shall we leave these guys to it and go and talk to the woman who found the body?'

Walker removed his white suit but Anna left hers on as they hurried back along the trail.

Sweeny was waiting for them next to the gate. She had also taken off the forensic suit and the navy blue blouse that clung to her plump frame was stained with sweat.

'Are you all right?' Anna asked her.

'I am now,' she said, looking embarrassed. 'Sorry about that, ma'am. The sight of that poor girl just turned my stomach suddenly.'

'Don't worry about it,' Anna said. 'It happens to us all at some point. I'm afraid you'll have to get used to sights like that working with us.'

The woman who had discovered the body had been moved across the road and was sitting on a wooden bench situated next to the cemetery entrance. Her dog, a black and white Jack Russell, lay on the ground in front of her.

Joyce Connor was in her fifties with greying hair and soft features. Her face was gaunt and colourless, and her lips trembled as she spoke.

'We don't often come this way,' she said. 'We usually stick to the fields nearer my home on the other side of the wood. But I fancied a change and the sun was strong so I opted for the shade of the trees.

'Sammy here was off his lead and he did what he always does and went nosing around in the bushes. When he started barking I went to see what he'd come across and that was when I saw the hand poking out from under the leaves.'

She explained that this part of the common attracted few dog walkers and other visitors.

'It's always so quiet here,' she said. Then, in answer to a question from Walker, she confirmed that she had not approached the body or picked up anything from the ground around it.

'I just grabbed Sammy and put his lead back on,' she said. 'Then I hurried away from there and called the police.'

Anna told her a patrol car would take her home where she would be asked to make a brief statement.

Anna then took Walker and Sweeny to one side and gave them instructions. She wanted Walker to arrange for a search team to descend on the wood first thing in the morning.

'There's no point doing it now since there are only a few hours of daylight left,' she said.

She then told Sweeny to start working up a file containing information on the common and the land surrounding it.

'You can download maps and images from Google,' she said. 'Let's locate all the homes in the area along with access routes to this stretch of the common. And find out who's responsible for managing it.'

Anna looked at her watch and was surprised to see that it was already six-fifteen. Tom would soon be setting off from his flat to pick her up. She decided it was time to call him to break the news that she wouldn't be going out to celebrate her birthday after all.

Tom was naturally disappointed but he knew it couldn't be helped.

'I'll ring and cancel the reservation,' he said. 'Hopefully we can go another time.'

'I probably won't be home until very late,' Anna said. 'Or I might even end up working through the night.'

'I'll come over to your place anyway,' he said, and she heard the disappointment in his voice. 'At least that way when you eventually turn up I can give you your birthday present.'

After hanging up, Anna felt a frisson of guilt for not being more appreciative of Tom's attempt to make her birthday special. And there was no question that she would rather be spending the next few hours in a cosy restaurant than at the scene of a grisly murder.

CHAPTER FOUR

Anna was back up at the wood when the on-call pathologist arrived. She was pleased to see that it was Gayle Western. The pair had been friends for some years and had a lot in common. They were both divorced and wedded to their jobs. They were also the same height at just over five and a half feet, and they each had long dark hair that was usually pinned up.

Anna was actually a year younger than Gayle but she looked at least five years older thanks to the stress that had left its mark as lines around her eyes and mouth.

'I see I'm the last to arrive as usual,' Gayle said, a little breathless from dashing to the scene. 'You can blame the traffic. I had to come from Mitcham and the roads are virtually gridlocked.'

Gayle had already donned her white suit and was carrying a small black case in each hand.

'You and I have got to stop only meeting like this,' Anna said. 'Do you realise that it's been four months since we last had a drink together?'

Gayle grinned. 'And do you realise that we have this same conversation every time we turn up at the scene of a crime?'

It was Anna's turn to smile. 'Well, after this one is sorted we should make a point of arranging something.'

'Most definitely. I'm keen to catch up on all your news, and I know there's an awful lot of it. In the last couple of weeks it seems you've become the most high-profile copper in the Met.'

'You always were prone to exaggeration, Gayle.'

'Not this time, my friend. You were all over the media during the kidnap case, and I've read that article in the *Evening Standard* about your ex-husband. Wow. What happened to him must have shaken you to the core.'

Anna nodded. 'You can say that again. But you'll have to wait for me to fill you in on the gory details. Right now there's a young lady over there who needs your full attention.'

Gayle got straight down to business. She walked over to the body, placed her cases on the ground, and then looked at what lay before her with a studied expression. After about thirty seconds she knelt down to examine the body and the area around it.

Anna looked on from a distance, knowing that Gayle did not like to be distracted during the initial assessment. As with all good forensic pathologists she was methodical in her approach and would never express an opinion or answer a question until she was good and ready.

Eventually, Gayle spoke without looking up.

'Well, the level of decomposition and other factors relating to the state of the body suggest to me that this poor lass has been dead for three or four days. And there's little doubt in my mind that the cause of death was a stab wound to the left side of the throat. It looks as though the blade probably severed a carotid artery and penetrated the trachea. I'll know for sure when I carry out the post-mortem. Death would have been fairly quick and there would have been a lot of blood.'

'It's now Friday so we're talking Tuesday or Wednesday,' Anna said.

Gayle nodded. 'My guess would be Tuesday or Tuesday night. It's rained only once this week and that was on Wednesday morning. There are streaks on her flesh where it washed away the detritus that had accumulated. The body was clearly dumped here and that would have happened a short time after she was killed, probably a matter of hours. I reckon she was stripped to remove all trace evidence. And it's likely she was wrapped in a blanket or plastic sheeting while being transported here.'

A cold chill crept over Anna's shoulders and down her neck. As always she found it a struggle to remain emotionally detached from the distressing sight that she was being forced to bear witness to.

'Is there any evidence of defence wounds?' she asked.

'None that I can see,' Gayle said. 'But I'll know for sure after she's cleaned up.'

'What about signs of sexual assault?'

'Nothing that's obvious. There's definitely no bruising on her inner thighs which is usually a tell-tale sign.'

As Anna made notes, Gayle asked a forensics officer to help her turn the body over. As they did so Anna saw that the flattened undergrowth beneath it was swarming with insects.

'She's got a tattoo,' Gayle said, and Anna had to step forward and lean over to see it.

The tattoo was at the top of her back between her shoulder blades. It was a simple three-word design in sinuous Gothic script.

BELIEVE IN YOURSELF

'Hopefully that will help you to identify her,' Gayle said.

Anna took a photo of the tattoo with her phone. She then attached it to a text that she sent back to headquarters.

Gayle drew her attention to the fact that the dead woman was wearing a silver ring on the middle finger of her left hand.

'That looks like an expensive piece of bling to me,' she said as Anna photographed it. 'You'll notice also that her nails are painted and her teeth are in good shape. She seems well nourished and there are no needle marks on her arms. So I don't think she was a homeless person or a druggy.'

Anna looked up as a plane roared overhead, probably on its way to Heathrow airport. She also noticed that the light was fading from the sky. At the same time forensics officers were preparing for nightfall by setting up portable lamps.

Anna knew that the search for clues, even in this small section of the wood, was going to be long and laborious. The person or persons who had left the victim here would have taken care to clear their tracks. And any evidence that had been left behind had probably been contaminated or destroyed by the weather and wildlife.

There was no point her hanging around so she decided to leave the scene to the experts. Gayle told her she would arrange for the body to be removed and said she'd phone if she discovered anything significant.

'I'll give the post-mortem priority,' Gayle added. 'That means I should have her on the table by late tomorrow morning.'

'Terrific,' Anna said. 'I'll try to make a point of being there.'

Back at the roadside, Walker informed her that he'd arranged for the road to be closed at either end for the rest of the night. And Sweeny told her that she'd found out the common was owned by the Dean and Chapter of St Paul's Cathedral.

'It's managed by the London Borough of Richmond-upon-Thames,' she said. 'An official is on his way here to open the gate so we can move vehicles onto the field.'

Anna looked out across the common, knowing that it wouldn't be long before the sun vanished below the horizon. But it was still warm and she could feel a tear of sweat trickling down her back.

She was about to fill Walker and Sweeny in on what Gayle had told her when her phone rang. She looked at the screen. It was DC Fellows, calling from headquarters with some unexpected news.

'We've got a probable ID on the victim, ma'am,' he said. 'And I guarantee you're not going to like it.'

CHAPTER FIVE

For the second time in as many days Sophie Cameron had the uncomfortable feeling that she was being watched.

She'd felt it yesterday when she strolled from her flat to the mini-mart on the corner. By the time she got there the familiar tingling sensation in her neck had spread through her body.

Now, as she walked briskly along Shoreditch High Street, she felt it again. But just as before it didn't appear as though she had seized the attention of any of her fellow pedestrians.

She kept stopping to look back along the street and across the road. There were quite a few dubious-looking characters, both men and women, but none of them seemed interested in her.

That didn't mean she was imagining it, though. She knew from bitter experience that her instincts were sometimes spot on, especially when it came to *Him*.

He had managed to track her down twice before, so had

he done it again? Had he somehow located her in a city of nearly nine million people?

The only person who knew that she was living and working in this part of East London was Lisa. And there was no way her best friend would ever tell anyone. Besides, even Lisa didn't know her address or where exactly she worked. And whenever they met for a drink, which was about once a month, Lisa always took care to make sure she was never followed.

Sophie stopped again to look behind her, but it was so sudden that a large woman clutching a carrier bag bumped into her.

'I'm so sorry,' Sophie said. 'I didn't mean . . .'

'You should be more careful,' the woman snapped. 'In case you haven't noticed you're not the only person on the pavement.'

The woman pushed past her and hurried on ahead, one of hundreds of people on the High Street who were anxious to get wherever they were going.

It was the tail-end of the evening rush hour so the main artery through Shoreditch was at its busiest. As Sophie scanned the unfamiliar faces of those who swept past her, she was forced to concede that even if she was being watched or followed, she probably wouldn't be able to spot her stalker.

She just had to hope that it was indeed all in her mind, an unfounded bout of paranoia fuelled yet again by the fear that she hadn't seen the last of the demon from her past.

She needed a distraction so she fumbled in her handbag for her phone and earplugs. Then she started listening to her favourite Ed Sheeran tracks as she set off again. It was still only six-forty-five so at least she wasn't going to be late.

The dental clinic was around the next corner. On Thursday evenings she did the cleaning after the place closed for business. It was one of several private jobs she did to supplement the income from the company that employed her on a part-time basis. The clinic paid her £30 to clean the floors, polish all the surfaces and wipe the insides of the windows. It was easy money and came in handy.

The clinic had already been closed for half an hour by the time Sophie got there. But as usual Claudia Myers, the young manager, was only just preparing to leave.

'Hi there, Miss Cameron,' she said with her usual bright smile. 'How are you today?'

'I'm fine, thank you, Claudia.'

At twenty-three, Claudia was half Sophie's age but twice her size. The girl blamed her obesity on the fact that she had type 2 diabetes. But if it bothered her she never showed it and she always struck Sophie as one of the happiest people she had ever come across.

'Are you sure you're OK?' Claudia asked, a frown tugging her eyebrows together. 'You look flustered.'

Sophie shrugged. 'That's because it's still pretty warm out there and I've been walking fast.'

Actually the truth is I've got myself in a state because I think someone has been following me.

'Well, you'll be glad to know that we finished earlier than usual today,' Claudia said. 'So I've done quite a bit of tidying up myself. I even managed to go round with the hoover so you only need to mop the floors.'

'You shouldn't have,' Sophie said. 'That's what you pay me for.'

'I know, but I had to hang around because I'm meeting a friend in the pub across the road. It gave me something to do. And speaking of pay, I've left your money in the usual place.'

Claudia picked up her shoulder bag and headed for the door. But before stepping outside, she turned back to Sophie and said, 'By the way, how is that girl of yours? You told me last week that she wasn't very well.'

'Oh, she's absolutely fine,' Sophie said. 'It was just a tummy bug and it only lasted a few days. I've left her at home watching one of the latest teen movies.'

'Well, be sure to give her my regards.'

'I will.'

After Claudia had gone, Sophie set to work. She went to the utility cupboard and took out what she needed. It wasn't a big clinic. There were two treatment rooms, a small office, a unisex toilet, a waiting room and a carpeted reception area.

It took Sophie an hour to get through it and she finished up back in reception where she sat on the leather sofa to drink a glass of water from the cooler.

A bunch of magazines and a copy of the *Evening Standard* were spread haphazardly across the coffee table in front of her. It looked untidy so Sophie put the magazines in a neat pile and checked the date on the newspaper. It was a day old so she picked it up to put in the bin with the other rubbish she'd collected.

But as she did so the paper fell open at a page dominated by three large photographs of a man, a woman and a toddler in a high chair. It was the photo of the man that jumped out at her.

'Oh, dear God, it can't be,' Sophie gasped out loud.

But a moment later, after checking the caption beneath the photo, the cold reality of what she was looking at caused a wave of panic to wash over her. And even before she began to read the words on the page, she knew that her life was about to implode yet again.

CHAPTER SIX

Over an hour had passed since DC Fellows had called Anna to tell her they had a probable ID on the victim. Since then the team had gathered more information and they were now ninety-nine per cent sure they knew who she was.

There would have to be a formal identification process, of course, but Anna was already working on the basis that the body on the common was that of twenty-three-year-old Holly Blake.

It was good news in the sense that it gave the investigation a jump start. But the bad news was that her identity alone was going to ramp up the pressure on the team from the word go.

'The media will be all over it just like they were with the nursery investigation,' Anna told her detectives after racing back to headquarters. 'So brace yourselves. And let's just hope it will be an easy one to solve.'

Anna had returned to Wandsworth in the pool car with DI Walker, leaving DC Sweeny to look after things at the common. She had wanted to put everyone in the picture and assign tasks as quickly as possible, and preferably before the press got wind of what was going on.

The wheels of the investigation had already been put in motion. A whiteboard had been set up and on it was pinned a photograph of the victim downloaded from her Facebook account, plus images of her body in the undergrowth taken from Walker's phone. In addition there was a map of the common showing roads that went around it and through it.

As Anna stepped up to the board, the room fell silent, save for the ringing of a couple of phones. The nine detectives who were present were poised to take notes and ask questions.

Anna tapped a finger against the photo of the woman. In it she was smiling at the camera, white teeth glistening, a sparkle in her bright blue eyes.

'This is Holly Blake,' she said. 'A freelance model aged twenty-three. She was reported missing by her mother yesterday because she hadn't been seen or heard from since Tuesday. She bears a striking resemblance to the young woman found naked on Barnes Common earlier this evening. But that's not all.'

Anna moved away from the whiteboard to a large TV monitor mounted on a stand. She nodded at DC Fellows, who took it as his cue to bring the screen to life remotely from his desktop computer.

The image that appeared was of Holly Blake's Facebook profile and there was a montage of photographs showing her in various outfits and poses. She was quite beautiful, Anna noted, and it looked as though she had been brimming with life and confidence.

Anna pointed to one particular photo which showed Holly

standing on a beach in a bikini. She was glancing back over her shoulder while poking her tongue out at the camera. The photo suddenly filled the screen and Anna drew everyone's attention to the tattoo between her shoulders.

'The young woman on the common has an identical tattoo in exactly the same place,' she said. The picture was replaced by another one showing Holly cupping her bare breasts in her hands. Anna indicated the silver ring on the middle finger of her left hand. 'She also has a silver ring exactly like this one and on the same finger. I therefore have no doubt in my mind that it's Holly Blake whose murder we'll be investigating.'

Anna turned back to her audience and took a long breath before continuing.

'DI Walker and I will go see her parents straight after this briefing. They live in Pimlico. While we're doing that I want DS Prescott and DC Niven to check out Holly's flat. We have an address in Camden.

'I'll come to what we know about Holly and her family in a moment. And it'll be pretty obvious to all of you why this is no run-of-the-mill case. But first let me put you in the picture regarding the scene up at the common.'

Anna explained how dog walker Joyce Connor had stumbled across the body in the undergrowth. She pinpointed the location on the map and described the surrounding area.

'The pathologist believes she was murdered elsewhere and left on the common shortly afterwards,' she said. 'The cause of death is almost certainly a single stab wound to the throat. She was stripped naked before her body was dumped and the killer or killers did not spend a lot of time trying to conceal her.

'It's believed she's been dead for several days and it's likely she was killed on Tuesday or Tuesday night. Nothing has so far been found at the scene to identify her. No phone. No clothes. No bag. At first light a search team will descend on the area but I'm not expecting them to turn up much vital evidence, if any. We believe the vehicle that carried her there parked next to the gate. But the ground around it has been trampled on so it's unlikely we'll get any clues from it.'

As Anna spoke an image of the body resurfaced in her mind and it sent a chill down her spine. It was such a tragedy that a girl who obviously had so much going for her should end her life in such horrendous circumstances.

'The obvious questions are these,' Anna said. 'Who killed her and why? When and where was the murder carried out? Why was the body dumped in that particular place? Was it because the killer was in a hurry or simply didn't worry about it being discovered? And why was she stripped, since there seems to be no evidence as yet that she was sexually assaulted?'

At this point Anna handed over to Walker, who was standing off to one side with a notebook in his hand.

'I've already drawn up a list of checks that need to be carried out right away,' he said. 'So I'm afraid you will all be working late into the night.' He looked down at his notes as he ran a hand across his bald head. 'We need to pull Holly's phone records and get the techies to go through her social media history. We know she's been busy on Facebook for years. So check out Twitter, Instagram and the others.

'There's plenty of information online about her, including the fact that she's on the books of a London-based modelling agency. From what I've seen it doesn't appear that she was a hugely successful model. But she's done jobs for fashion magazines, clothing catalogues and swimwear companies. Let's also check all CCTV cameras around the common. Presumably her body was driven to the spot sometime on Tuesday or maybe early on Wednesday morning.'

Walker then handed back to Anna, who signalled for DC Fellows to change the image on the TV monitor. Holly's photo was replaced by a picture of a woman who looked like an older version of her. She had the same oval face, full lips and well-defined jawline.

'This is Holly's mother,' Anna said. 'As I'm sure you all know her name is Rebecca Blake, and she's the reason that we're going to be under pressure like never before. And that pressure won't just come from the media. It will also come from the top brass in the Met and from the Home Office. At this stage we have no idea why Holly Blake was murdered. But we can't rule out the possibility that it had something to do with her mother.'

CHAPTER SEVEN

Having read the article in the *Evening Standard*, Sophie was struggling to keep her emotions in check. The words had proved as shocking as the three photographs that covered half the page.

She continued to sit there in the clinic's reception, her breath stalled as the blood pounded in her ears.

She didn't want to believe the evidence of her own eyes, but she had no choice. The facts, as laid out, spoke for themselves. They revealed a story that was both sensational and tragic. A story that revolved around a London police officer named Anna Tate.

The woman's photograph was the largest of the three that had been published to help illustrate the article. Sophie squinted at what she considered to be a plain, unremarkable face. Tate had sharp features and dark hair down to her shoulders. She was in her early forties, according to the paper, but looked older.

Sophie let out her breath and returned her attention to the

beginning of the article. She re-read it because her mind had struggled to take it all in the first time.

But as soon as she started her anxiety grew, and a hard knot formed in her stomach.

A MOTHER'S TEN YEAR NIGHTMARE

An Evening Standard two-part exclusive

DCI Anna Tate is the detective in charge of the Major Investigation Team based in South London.

She made headlines two weeks ago when she led the hunt for the kidnappers of nine children from a nursery school in Rotherhithe.

During the investigation it came to light that ten years ago her own two-year-old daughter Chloe was abducted and is still missing.

Thanks to an extraordinary twist of fate the kidnapping case has led to a dramatic development in the search for Chloe – but it has also raised fresh fears over the girl's safety.

Anna has told her story to the Standard because she believes that the more people who know about it the more chance there is that she'll one day be reunited with her daughter, who is now twelve.

Sophie's throat tightened suddenly and for a few seconds she had to fight to get the air into her lungs.

The words on the page became blurred so she closed her eyes and willed herself to stay calm despite the panic that had seized her chest.

She was briefly tempted to stop reading and to throw the

paper in the bin. But she knew that wasn't an option. She had exposed herself to a cold, hard truth and there was no way she could run from it.

She snapped her eyes open and forced herself to take each breath slowly and carefully as she continued to read.

Detective Anna Tate's nightmare began one day in July 2009, six months after she divorced her husband, Matthew Dobson, because of his adultery. He'd been trying to persuade her to take him back but she'd refused. As a result he decided to seek revenge.

He regularly looked after their daughter as part of a joint custody arrangement. But on that day he failed to take Chloe home when he was supposed to. Instead he disappeared with her and sent Anna a text message which read:

You won't let us be a family again because I made a stupid mistake. So I'm starting my life afresh with my lovely daughter. Don't bother trying to find us because you never will. You have yourself to blame, Anna. You should have known that I wouldn't let you have a happy life if I couldn't be a part of it . . . M

Anna discovered that he had packed in his job, sold his car and moved out of his flat. As Anna's police colleagues launched a hunt for Dobson and his daughter, it was feared he had taken her abroad.

Horrific

Anna heard nothing for ten years, but she didn't give up searching for Chloe. She ran various social media campaigns which included a dedicated FindChloe Facebook page and website. And she hired a private investigator to try to find them.

Then, just over two weeks ago, came the horrific abductions of the children from the Peabody Nursery School. Anna appeared on the television news and among the millions of people who saw her was a man named Paul Russell. He was compelled to contact her and his message was:

If you can find the time to come and see me I can tell you what I know about your daughter and her father. And I can apologise for the part I played in what happened ten years ago.

Anna went to see Paul Russell in a London hospice where he has since died of cancer. But in what amounts to a deathbed confession he revealed to Anna that he used to be a master forger who provided fake documents to criminals, illegal immigrants and anyone else who was willing to pay him.

Passports

Anna's ex-husband was one of his customers. Matthew Dobson wanted fake passports for himself and his daughter. Russell produced them for him in the names of James and Alice Miller.

This was a significant development as far as Anna was concerned, but another staggering revelation was to follow. Russell told her that Dobson had contacted him three years ago asking for more fake documents because he and Chloe were returning to the UK from whichever country they had been living in.

Anna passed on this information to her private investigator who went on to find out that James Miller (aka Matthew Dobson) did indeed come back to the UK three years ago. However, shortly after setting up home in Southampton he was murdered.

Anna went to see the detective who led the murder investigation. She had lots of questions for him but the most important was: 'Now you need to tell me what's happened to my baby. Where is Chloe?'

Find out what DCI Anna Tate was told in tomorrow's Evening Standard.

By the time Sophie had finished reading the article her eyes were brimming with tears and her mind was dull with shock. She also felt dizzy, nauseous, as though she were about to pass out.

To stop that happening she made herself stand up and walk unsteadily across reception to the toilet. Once inside she leaned over the sink and splashed cold water on her face. The feeling of nausea receded but her head continued to spin as a wave of despair washed over her.

She got another shock when she saw herself in the mirror. She was deathly white and the fearful expression in her eyes was evidence of the sense of dread that now consumed her.

She had only read the first instalment of the Anna Tate story. On the way back to the flat she intended to pick up today's edition of the *Evening Standard*. And she knew with a high degree of certainty that it would contain more devastating details about the considerable threat she now faced.

CHAPTER EIGHT

Anna received two calls in quick succession minutes after she'd finished briefing the team.

The first she answered as she and Walker were exiting the building on their way to break the news of Holly's death to her parents. It was DCS Nash. He wanted to tell her that he had spoken to Police Commissioner Gary Trimble, the Met's supreme leader.

'He'll be calling you himself for an update,' Nash said. 'So be prepared. He wants to impress on you how sensitive this case is going to be.'

'Well, he won't be telling me anything I don't already know, sir,' Anna said.

'Obviously, but just so you know, he asked me if I was sure that you're the right person for the job.'

'Really? Why was that?'

A moment's hesitation, then: 'He mentioned those new developments in respect of your daughter. He's read what's appeared in the *Evening Standard* and he's aware that Channel

Four are looking to do a documentary. Whilst he has every sympathy for you he's concerned that it will prove to be a distraction.'

'Well, it won't be,' Anna said.

'Which is exactly what I told him. I said you had my full support. So don't let me down.'

'I won't, sir.'

Anna had just closed the passenger door of the pool car when her phone rang again. Before she answered it she clicked on her seat belt and told Walker to start driving.

'Good evening, Commissioner,' she said. 'Detective Chief Superintendent Nash told me to expect a call.'

Trimble had been in the job for a year and this was only the second time that Anna had spoken to him. She had a lot of respect for the man because he had risen to such dizzy heights by the relatively tender age of forty-five.

'First I need to know if you're certain that the body that's been found on Barnes Common is that of Holly Blake,' Trimble said without preamble.

'There's little doubt, I'm afraid,' Anna told him. 'We've downloaded a bunch of pictures of Holly from the internet. There's a definite match and in one of them you can see a tattoo on her back. The victim has the same tattoo in the same position.'

'Has her mother been informed?'

'I'm on my way to do that now, Commissioner.'

'Well, rather you than me, detective,' Trimble said. 'Rebecca and I go back a long way from her time on the force. So I know she's going to be absolutely devastated. She doted on her daughter.'

'How well do you know Mrs Blake, sir?' Anna asked.

'We were colleagues, but we never got together outside work,' Trimble said. 'Since she left the Met our paths have crossed several times at various functions. The last time was earlier this year when I shared a table with Rebecca and her husband Theo at an awards dinner.'

'Theo Blake's a lawyer, isn't he?'

'He's a senior partner in a firm of solicitors. I take it you know that he was Holly's stepfather. He married Rebecca four years ago after she divorced her first husband.'

'I wasn't aware of that,' Anna said. 'There's a lot I need to find out about everyone in Holly's life.'

'Well, bear in mind that as a former Assistant Commissioner in the Met, Rebecca Blake has a lot of friends on the force. She was popular among her colleagues and I've no doubt they'll all want to help with the investigation.'

'I met her myself once,' Anna said. 'It was shortly after my daughter was abducted. She offered to help in any way she could.'

'She's a very generous and caring person,' Trimble said. 'That's why she's doing so well as a politician. But this tragedy is bound to have a serious impact on her life and that includes her bid to become the Mayor of London.'

The involvement of any politician in a major investigation always created problems – from the amount of publicity they generated to the pressure they sought to apply when they felt threatened.

But Rebecca Blake wasn't just any politician. She already had the ear of the Prime Minister and was set to be a high-flyer in political circles.

At present she held the influential post of Leader of the Conservative-controlled Westminster Council. It was a position she took up after retiring from the police. In addition she was now the Tory Party's chosen candidate in the forthcoming election for the role of London's Mayor.

The main thrust of her campaign had been a commitment to substantially reduce crime in the capital, something the current incumbent had failed to achieve after almost four years in office.

'I'll make a point of contacting Rebecca myself tomorrow,' Trimble said. 'It might reassure her to know that I'm taking a personal interest.'

'Of course, sir,' Anna said. 'But before you go there's something I need to mention.'

'What is it?'

'Well, it's early days and so we don't know why Holly was murdered. The motive might become evident very quickly, but if it doesn't then I think we should explore the possibility that it was committed by someone who has a grudge against the mother. I'm sure that like the rest of us on the force Mrs Blake made enemies along the way and it could be that one of them wants to see her suffer. Or maybe the aim is to stop her becoming London's Mayor because of her crusade against crime.'

'It's a plausible theory, DCI Tate,' Trimble said. 'And I'm sure it's one that will fuel the inevitable media frenzy. But it's a line of enquiry that I want us to play down unless we come across some solid evidence to support it.'

'Understood, sir.'

'Meanwhile I'll expect you to provide me with regular updates via DCS Nash. And it goes without saying that you'll have all the manpower and resources you need to crack this case. Just don't lose sight of the fact that every move you make will be scrutinised, and not just by me. I know you were under considerable pressure during the nursery kidnap investigation, but this will be a different kind of pressure and on some levels it will be even more intense.'

'So what's the word from on high?' Walker asked after Anna came off the phone to the Commissioner.

'He warned me to tread carefully, keep him in the loop and expect a lot of pressure,' she said.

'Well, that was to be expected given who the victim's mother is.'

'Yeah, I suppose.'

'So why do I get the impression that you're mightily pissed off, guv?'

Anna heaved a sigh. 'He had the bloody cheek to ask Nash if I was the right person to head up the investigation. If the boss hadn't assured him that I was then I'd probably be on my way home now.'

Walker frowned. 'I don't understand. Does Trimble actually think the case is too sensitive for you to handle?'

'It's not that. Nash said he raised the issue of Chloe and he's worried that I'll take my eye off the ball because of all the new stuff. He's read the *Evening Standard* piece and has been told that I've been approached by C4.'

'C4?'

'Channel Four,' Anna said. 'They want to do a true crime programme on me.'

'Bloody hell, guv. That's a huge deal. Why haven't you mentioned it?'

'I only found out myself just before we left the office to go to the common. I pushed it to the back of my mind for obvious reasons.'

They stopped at traffic lights and Walker turned to face her.

'Then in all fairness, you can't blame the Commissioner for being a teensy bit concerned,' he said. 'I've told you before that there are times when even I don't know how the hell you manage to stay focused on the job.'

Anna gave him a sharp look, so he quickly added, 'And before you go off on one, guv, just remember that we've had this conversation several times so you know that I have a point. You also know that I trust you to do a good job on every case *despite* the fact that you have more on your plate than anyone deserves.'

His words took the wind out of her sails, so instead of snapping at him, she said, 'You're the only person I know who would dare say that to me, Max. And the only person who'd get away with it.'

'Well, I like to think that's because we're friends as well as colleagues,' he said. 'And friends say it like it is whilst remaining loyal to each other.'

Anna shook her head and smiled. 'You do have a way with words, Max. I'll grant you that. And I bet your wife finds it so bloody annoying.'

He laughed. 'She sure does, but she puts up with it because she knows I'm always right.'

'You smug bastard.'

The pair enjoyed a good working relationship, and Anna knew that Walker would always have her back. For instance, two years ago she received an anonymous tip that a man matching her ex-husband's description had been spotted in a Paris suburb. It was during a big murder investigation and she knew her superiors would not have let her take time off to check it out. So she confided in Walker and he told her to go there and then covered for her. They stayed in touch by phone and she returned to London forty-eight hours later after it turned out the man in question wasn't Matthew after all.

Walker was one of the few people who had encouraged her never to give up searching for her daughter. Most were of the opinion that it had become a pointless obsession and that she needed to get on with her life and accept that she would never see Chloe again.

Walker understood how she felt, mainly because he had two young daughters of his own. She couldn't help feeling jealous of him, though, and of her other colleagues in MIT who were mothers and fathers. Whenever they talked about their kids it reinforced the extent of her loss.

Walker was more sensitive to her feelings than the rest of them. He said to her once, 'I can feel your pain, ma'am. I really don't know how I'd cope if I was in your position. I'm not sure I'd even have the strength to carry on.'

Anna carried on because for her giving up was not an option. However, there had been times over the past ten years when she'd almost convinced herself that she was wasting her time.

In the months after Matthew abducted Chloe it was easy to believe that they'd be found or that Matthew would accept that he was in the wrong and bring her back from wherever he'd taken her.

At that time everyone was rooting for the heartbroken mother and the story was attracting a lot of publicity. Thousands of people reacted to her social media campaigns and appeals, and there was good reason to hope that she would be reunited with Chloe before her daughter's third birthday. But interest in the story eventually waned and the abduction became old news.

In a little while Chloe would be thirteen and still Anna had no idea where she was. All she did know for certain was that she was no longer with her father because he was murdered three years ago in a park in Southampton.

CHAPTER NINE

Rebecca Blake and her husband lived in Pimlico, a small, upscale residential area of London bordered by Westminster and Belgravia. Scores of politicians had homes there because the quiet streets were within walking distance of the Houses of Parliament. The three-storey property owned by Rebecca and Theo Blake was in a cobbled mews close to St George's Square.

It was approaching nine p.m. when Anna and Walker arrived in the pool car and parked in front of the blue-painted garage. The lights were on inside so Anna thought it likely that the couple were at home.

As she climbed out of the car her stomach churned at the thought of what they were about to do. No matter how many times she had delivered the devastating news of a person's death it had never got any easier. And it was made worse this time because she had met the woman whose life she was about to ruin.

It was Theo Blake who answered the door. Anna recognised

him at once from the photos she'd seen on the web. He was a tall, rakishly handsome man who looked to be in his mid-fifties. Grey stubble bristled on his head and chin, and his corduroy trousers and black cardigan gave him the rumpled appearance of an academic.

Anna had already taken her ID from her pocket and she held it up for him to see.

'Hello, Mr Blake,' she said. 'I'm Detective Chief Inspector Anna Tate and this is my colleague, Detective Inspector Max Walker. We need to talk to you and your wife. Is Mrs Blake in right now?'

Theo cocked his head to one side and frowned. 'Is this about Holly? Has she turned up?'

'It would be best if we spoke to you inside and together,' Anna said. 'So please may we come in?'

The man's face clouded with confusion.

'This sounds ominous,' he said. 'Can't you just tell me what . . .'

'Who is it, dear? Is there a problem?'

He snapped his head towards the voice, which belonged to his wife. She had stepped into the hallway behind him while tying up the belt of a long silk bathrobe.

When she saw them she froze, and her eyes grew wide.

'What's going on?' she said.

Her husband started to speak, but Anna beat him to it.

'We're police officers, Mrs Blake, and we need to have a word with you and your husband. It's about your daughter. My name is Anna Tate and I'm a DCI with the Major Investigation Team. And this is DI Walker.'

Anna didn't wait to be invited in and she had no intention of breaking the news to them at the door. As she stepped over the threshold, she gently grasped Theo's arm and nudged him along the hallway while Walker closed the front door behind them.

'Can I suggest that we go into the living room,' she said.

Rebecca's mouth fell open and Anna could see the panic in her eyes.

'What's happened?' the woman said, her lips trembling. 'Do you know where Holly is? Please tell me she's all right.'

'I'll tell you everything I know, Mrs Blake, but I really think you need to sit down first.'

Theo hurried forward and put his arm around his wife's shoulders, easing her back into the room she had emerged from.

'Stay calm, Becs, and don't jump to conclusions,' he told her.

Anna felt a wave of heat roll up her chest as she followed them into the living room, which was large and airy with stylish grey furniture and patio doors that gave access to a neat walled garden.

She waited for them to sit side by side on the leather sofa before sitting opposite them on a matching armchair. Walker stood off to one side with his hands behind his back.

It was almost ten years since Anna's brief meeting with Scotland Yard's former Assistant Commissioner. She'd seen her many times since then on the television promoting various causes as well as her own political career. It had always struck Anna how little the woman had seemed to age. But now, seen close up without make-up, Rebecca Blake looked all of her fifty-three years.

She was a thin woman with a small oval face and dark hair that was tied back. Her nose was pointed and delicate with slightly flared nostrils. As her teal-blue eyes shifted between the two detectives, she pressed her lips together, which etched deep lines around her mouth.

Anna cleared her throat and was still searching for the right words when Rebecca said, 'I've seen you before, haven't I? You were the lead on the nursery kidnapping case. And it was your daughter who . . .' Her voice trailed off and she drew a sharp breath. 'Oh, my God, we met once. I remember.'

'We did indeed,' Anna said.

Rebecca swallowed hard and took another deep breath. 'You've got bad news for us, haven't you? So what is it, detective?'

Anna leaned forward, resting her elbows on her knees. The look on Rebecca's face froze the blood in her veins.

'A young woman's body has been found,' she said. 'And there's convincing evidence to indicate that it's Holly.'

A choking sound rushed out of Rebecca and she started to shake her head.

'No, that's not possible,' she screamed. 'It must be a mistake. It has to be.'

'We don't think it's a mistake,' Anna said. 'The description fits Holly and the dead woman has the same tattoo in the same place on her back. We will, of course, need one or both of you to carry out a formal identification. I'm so very sorry.'

Rebecca's whole body convulsed and she let out an anguished cry. Her husband enveloped her in his arms and scrunched up his face as he fought back his own tears.

Anna looked on helplessly, aware that there was nothing she could say or do to ease their pain and suffering. She knew from her own bitter experience that elements of the big bad world can turn up at your door when you least expect it, shattering your life and redirecting your future towards an emotional abyss.

She threw a glance over her shoulder at Walker and saw that he had picked up a framed photograph from the sideboard. It was one of several on display and they were all of Holly.

'How sure are you that it's our daughter?' Theo said suddenly, his voice a hollow rasp.

Anna turned back to them. 'I'm positive. If I wasn't I'd be offering you a crumb of hope. But that wouldn't be fair in the circumstances.'

She took out her phone, pulled up the photo she'd taken of the ring on the dead woman's finger.

'Do you recognise this?' she said, showing it to both of them.

Rebecca flinched and nodded. 'It's Holly's. I'm sure of it because I bought it for her myself on her twenty-first birthday. Oh, Jesus, when can we see her?'

'Tomorrow morning, Mrs Blake. I'll make the arrangements.'

'So why can't we see her now?' Theo asked.

'It's too early, I'm afraid. The body was discovered only a few hours ago and it may still be in situ.'

'And where is that?'

'Barnes Common in South West London,' Anna said.

Sobs had continued to rack his wife's body while this exchange was taking place. Now she straightened herself, wiped at her eyes with her sleeve, and said, 'Since you're here, Detective Chief Inspector, I'm assuming that foul play is suspected.'

Anna nodded. 'That's right, Mrs Blake. We've launched a murder investigation.'

Rebecca squeezed her eyes shut for a couple of seconds and when she opened them again, she said, 'I want the details and I don't want you to hold anything back from us.'

Anna's stomach tightened and her mouth dried up.

'The victim suffered a stab wound to the throat,' she said. 'She was naked and her body had been covered with ferns and branches. However, we're not sure at this stage if she was sexually assaulted, but it doesn't appear so. She was discovered by a woman walking her dog. The pathologist believes she was killed several days ago, perhaps on Tuesday evening, and left on the common soon afterwards. We found out that you'd reported your daughter missing. So we downloaded Holly's photos from Facebook and realised that her description was a match for the victim.'

Rebecca bit into her bottom lip and her husband started patting the back of her hand.

'I therefore need to ask you some questions,' Anna said. 'I know it's going to be difficult for you to answer them but please try to.'

Rebecca gave a slow nod and tears slid down her cheeks. 'I know the routine, Detective Tate. And I fully appreciate that it has to be done.'

She pushed her shoulders back and tried to compose herself. It seemed to Anna that she suddenly looked smaller, as though she'd been crushed by the weight of shock and grief.

'So let's get this over with,' Rebecca said.

Anna nodded. 'I'll start with the most obvious questions. Do either of you have any idea who might have done this, assuming it wasn't a random attack by a person or persons unknown to Holly? Has she upset anyone recently or is there someone you know who has a grudge against her?'

Rebecca clenched her jaw and pursed her lips. When she spoke her voice cracked with emotion.

'There's only one person I know who would want to take my daughter's life,' she said. 'I can give you his name and I can tell you where you can find him. And I'm convinced that he's the bastard who either killed her or got someone to do it for him.'

CHAPTER TEN

Sophie had picked up a copy of the *Evening Standard* after leaving the dental clinic. And she'd been so anxious to read it that she'd considered popping into a café or pub rather than wait until she got home. But the feeling that she was being watched had returned as soon as she'd hit the High Street, so she'd decided to get back to the flat as quickly as she could.

From the moment she stepped through her front door she was battered by a perfect storm of panic and paranoia. She was even grappling with the chilling thought that if she was indeed being stalked then it might have something to do with the revelations in the paper. If so, then perhaps it was already too late to prevent her world from falling apart.

Alice had still been up, of course, so Sophie had made every effort to pretend that nothing was wrong.

'Has the film finished, sweetheart?' she'd asked as she'd walked into the living room with a fake smile on her face.

Alice had jumped up from the sofa, her tablet in one hand, a bag of crisps in the other.

'Ages ago,' she'd said. 'And it was really good. I'm going to watch it again tomorrow.'

'Now why doesn't that surprise me?'

Alice had crossed the room and Sophie had wrapped her in her arms.

'And thank you for looking after the flat while I was at work,' she'd said. 'I take it nobody rang the bell.'

'No one ever does, Mum. You know that. And even if someone did, I would never answer it. You know that as well.'

'Of course I do. And that's why I trust you.'

Alice was a mature twelve-year-old and Sophie was glad of it because it made things so much easier. She rarely answered back or threw a tantrum, and she had such a pleasant, sensitive nature that it was hard to ever be cross with her.

That didn't mean that she was a goody-two-shoes, though. She often demonstrated to Sophie that she had a mind of her own and a stubborn streak that she'd no doubt inherited from her late father.

'It's time for bed now, sweetheart,' Sophie had told her. 'Finish your crisps, clean your teeth and get yourself ready.'

'Remember I'm going to Ruth's house tomorrow.'

'I haven't forgotten. I told Ruth's mum that I would drop you off between ten and eleven.'

Alice was in bed and asleep before eight o'clock and by nine-thirty Sophie was half way through her second bottle of wine. Getting drunk was her way of dealing with the despair that now engulfed her. The alcohol dulled her senses and took the edge off the pain that she'd inflicted on herself by reading the second instalment of the Anna Tate story in the *Evening Standard*. She felt the sting of tears in her eyes as she tried through a boozy haze to process what she had learned along with the wretched implications.

She was sitting at the kitchen table in the downdraught of the ceiling fan. In front of her she'd spread out the centre pages of that day's *Standard*. There were more photographs, and every time Sophie looked at them her heart lurched in her chest.

Detective Anna Tate featured in two of them. One showed her speaking at a press conference during the nursery kidnap case two weeks ago. In the other – taken ten years ago – she was holding her two-year-old daughter in her arms while smiling broadly at the camera. The caption beneath it read: *Anna and Chloe just weeks before her ex-husband Matthew Dobson abducted the child and fled abroad with her.*

Next to it was what the paper described as an age progression photo of Chloe. Beneath it were the words: *This is a computer-generated impression of what Chloe might look like now at the age of twelve.*

The image had taken Sophie's breath away when she'd first laid eyes on it. And even now it was causing a riot of emotions to run through her.

'I just can't believe this is happening,' she said aloud to herself before losing control for the second time that evening. She buried her face in her hands as the tears flowed. Her body shook, and bile burned furiously at the back of her throat.

It was at least a minute before she managed to stop crying. She wiped her eyes and poured herself another glass of wine. She told herself it'd be the last before she sloped off to bed, where she would no doubt lie awake trying to come to terms with the revelation that her life had been filled with so many lies.

As she drank, her eyes were drawn back to the newspaper and she found herself re-reading the second part of the Anna Tate story. And once again the words stirred up bitter memories that sadly had not been subdued by the passage of time.

A MOTHER'S TEN YEAR NIGHTMARE

Part two of this Evening Standard exclusive

DCI Anna Tate is currently one of the most high-profile detectives in the Metropolitan Police. She was in the headlines recently as the officer in charge of the hunt for the gang who kidnapped nine children from a South London nursery school and murdered one of their teachers.

Yesterday we explained why that case was so close to her heart. Her own daughter Chloe was abducted ten years ago by her ex-husband and she hasn't seen either of them since.

But Anna has never given up searching for Chloe, who was two when she was taken.

Sophie skimmed over the next few paragraphs which repeated the information contained in part one – how during the nursery investigation Anna discovered that Matthew had obtained fake passports in the names of James and Alice Miller before disappearing, and how she learned that Matthew had actually returned to the UK with his daughter three years ago but weeks later was murdered in a park close to where they'd set up home in Southampton.

Today's article picked the story up where the first instalment ended – with Anna meeting the detective who investigated Matthew's murder and asking him: *'So where is my baby? Where's Chloe?'*

The answer Anna was given came as another devastating blow.

'We simply don't know,' the detective informed her. 'The child disappeared along with the woman who had been living with her and her father.'

It transpired that Anna's ex-husband and daughter had been sharing a rented house with a mystery woman for three weeks. But on the night Matthew was murdered the woman was seen leaving the house with Chloe and several suitcases. They drove away from Southampton in a car that Matthew had hired in the name of James Miller. The car was later found abandoned in London.

Mystery

The murder of Matthew Dobson (aka James Miller) is as intriguing as the mystery surrounding the sudden disappearance of the woman he had described to their landlord as his partner.

He was stabbed to death one evening while walking through a park in Southampton city centre. It was dark and there were no witnesses, but there were signs he'd been involved in a struggle.

'Police found a mobile phone in his pocket and it seems he made one last call before he died,' Anna told the Standard. 'The call was to a number that was still transmitting a signal

later that night. That was how the police found out where he'd been living.'

But when officers later called at the house they found it had been cleared of all personal possessions except for the unregistered phone that Matthew had called. And there was no way of knowing who it belonged to. The log only showed calls to and from Matthew's own phone.

Buried

The murder investigation is still open three years on but the police have no idea why he was stabbed or by whom. It's now believed that Matthew probably called the woman to tell her to flee the house with his daughter.

Before leaving Southampton, Anna learned that her ex-husband had been buried in a city cemetery, so she visited his grave.

His headstone, paid for by the council, carried the simple inscription:

Here lies James Miller. May he rest in peace.

The real name of the man in the grave is now known to be Matthew Dobson. But to Anna Tate's immense frustration his secrets died with him. She's left with questions that she's desperate to know the answers to.

Who killed her ex-husband and why?

Was his death linked in any way to his return to the UK?

Why did he return from wherever he'd been living for seven years?

Why did he settle in Southampton of all places?

How long had he been with the mystery woman?

And where did she take Chloe?

Nightmare

'The fact that the woman left the house in such a hurry after Matthew was killed suggests to me that she was scared,' Anna said. 'But the police don't know who she was running from.'

Anna has told her story in the hope that someone somewhere has information that might bring her ten year nightmare to an end.

'I live in hope,' the detective said. 'And I'll search for my daughter until I find her, no matter how long that takes.'

Sophie's mind was ranging in all directions as she finished reading the article, and more tears were welling up in her eyes.

It was too much for her to take in, too much to get her head around with a bottle and a half of wine sloshing around inside her.

She pushed her chair back and stood up, which made her feel dizzy.

She drained her glass, but as she placed it on the table her legs gave way beneath her. She collapsed onto the floor like a bag of cement and passed out.

CHAPTER ELEVEN

'The name of the man who murdered my daughter is Nathan Wolf,' Rebecca told Anna. 'You must have heard of him.'

'But you can't be sure he did it, Becs,' her husband chipped in before Anna could respond. 'You shouldn't accuse the man without proof.'

Rebecca shook her head. 'I was a police officer long enough to be certain that I'm right. Wolf knew that Holly was about to destroy him. He was desperate to stop her. And the only way he could do it was to kill her or arrange for someone to do it on his behalf.'

A deep frown scored Anna's forehead as she listened to Rebecca's extraordinary claim.

'These are strong allegations, Mrs Blake, and I need to know why you're making them,' Anna said. 'But I also want to be sure who you're talking about. I know of only one individual named Nathan Wolf and he happens to be a Member of Parliament.'

'He also happens to be the bastard who you need to go and arrest,' Rebecca said.

Anna stared at her in disbelief and behind her Walker whistled through his teeth.

'I'm deadly serious,' Rebecca insisted, her voice punctuated by sobs. 'And when we tell you what we know I'm sure you'll come to the same conclusion.'

Anna shivered with anticipation as she fished out her notebook and pen.

'I'm listening, Mrs Blake,' she said. 'So please tell me everything.'

But at that point the woman succumbed to another blast of emotion and broke down in a paroxysm of tears.

Anna could do nothing other than wait for her to regain her composure. Her husband wrapped her in his arms again and this time rested his chin against the top of her head, his eyes closed.

Their distress brought a lump to Anna's throat, and she struggled to keep her expression neutral. At the same time the fact that the finger of blame was being pointed at yet another politician was sending a tremor of anxiety through her.

An MP no less, and a prominent one at that. Nathan Wolf was considered a rising star in the Tory Party, and was even being tipped as a future government minister. Was it really conceivable that he had murdered Holly Blake?

Anna didn't want to believe it because if it was true then this case was going to be elevated from sensitive to sensational. And that would bring with it a whole bunch of problems.

*

It took several minutes for Rebecca to pull herself together, during which Walker fetched her a glass of water from the kitchen. Her husband got her to sip at it while he held it to her mouth and gently massaged her back.

'Is there someone you would like us to contact?' Anna asked. 'Perhaps a relative or friend.'

'My wife's sister Freya needs to know,' Theo said. 'They're close and she'll want to be here.'

'Then let me have her number and I'll phone her for you.'

Rebecca pushed the glass away from her face. 'That can wait until after I've told you about Nathan Wolf,' she said. 'I'm sorry I lost it just then. I'm all right now so bear with me.'

'Of course, Mrs Blake,' Anna said. 'I quite understand. Take your time.'

Rebecca breathed in deep through her nostrils as she took a moment to gather her thoughts. Her face was flushed and her eyes shone with unshed tears. When she finally spoke her voice was much sharper, stronger.

'The last time we saw Holly was on Tuesday evening,' she said. 'She arrived here unexpectedly because she wanted to tell us something. She was anxious and tearful, and the news she imparted came as a massive shock to us.'

Rebecca paused as her breath faltered. She blinked away the tears and swallowed hard before continuing.

'She told us that she was selling her story to a Sunday newspaper and she felt it only fair to forewarn us because of the explosive nature of what would be in it.'

Anna and Walker shared a glance, and Anna was pretty sure they were thinking the same thing – that this case was becoming more interesting by the minute.

'All I know about your daughter is that she was single and had a career in modelling,' Anna said. 'I'm not aware of anything in her life that would be likely to cause a stir.'

'And neither were we until she 'fessed up,' Rebecca replied. 'That's why I was so taken aback. And so furious with her because by revealing her shameful secret to the world she was going to make life unbearable for all of us.'

'So what exactly was Holly planning to disclose in the newspaper?' Anna asked.

'She was going to make it known that she had been Nathan Wolf's secret mistress for over a year. That he paid the rent on her flat in Camden after he persuaded her to move into it. And that he gave her spending money so that he could have her on tap for regular sex sessions.'

Rebecca paused, wiped her eyes and wet her lips. Anna wasn't sure that she had it in her to continue, but after a couple of seconds she did.

'It started while he was married to his wife, who died of a stroke ten months ago,' she said. 'And we had no bloody idea. We thought she was earning good money from modelling, which was how she could afford the flat and the lavish lifestyle. But we were wrong. That pervert was supplementing her income so he could have his way with her.'

'But it must have been a consensual arrangement,' Walker pointed out.

Rebecca shot him a look. 'That's not the point. Wolf was married and Holly is – was – over twenty years younger than him. She also had issues that made her vulnerable. That man seduced her and she succumbed to his charms. As if that wasn't bad enough she even went and fell in love with him.'

Rebecca heaved a breath and closed her eyes. Anna could tell that she was on the brink of losing it again. Theo sensed it too and picked up the thread.

'Wolf apparently strung her along after his wife died,' he said. 'He assured her that after a suitable period of mourning they would be able to move their relationship onto a different footing and make it known that they were a couple. But then last week he dumped her and revealed that he had fallen for another woman he wanted to be with. He told Holly she would have to move out of the flat and he offered to pay her a sum of money to go quietly.'

'But I take it she decided not to accept it,' Anna said.

Theo nodded. 'She was heartbroken and felt that he'd betrayed her. She told him she was going to ruin him and that's what she set out to do. She approached the *Sunday Mirror* and they jumped at the chance to run her story after she whetted their appetite with some sordid details which she refused to reveal to us.

'The paper agreed a fee and arrangements were being made to set up a proper interview. It was due to take place this week. That's why she came here. She wanted us to know before the shit hit the fan.'

'And did you try to talk her out of it?' Anna asked.

It was Rebecca who answered. 'Damn right we did. But she wouldn't listen. As always it was hard to get through to her when she'd decided to do something, even if she knew that her actions would probably end in tears.'

'Are you alluding to the issues that you just mentioned?' Anna asked.

Rebecca sniffed back tears. 'My daughter never found it easy to cope with life, detective. As a teenager she suffered from depression and went through a phase where she self-harmed. She was also terribly insecure and was never happy with the way she looked. It didn't help that she was addicted to social media and took every criticism personally.'

'So how did you try to persuade her not to go public with her story?'

'I told her it would serve no useful purpose and that she should be grateful that Nathan Wolf would no longer be a part of her life. But she was adamant that she wanted to get her own back on him. She wanted revenge.'

'And then what?'

'It turned into a big row and I got so worked up that I said she had been a fool to let him treat her like a whore. That was when she screamed at me and stormed out of the house. It was the last I saw of her.'

'And what time was that?' Anna asked.

'About nine.'

'Was she driving a car?'

'She doesn't – didn't – own one. She had a Fiat but sold it a few months ago because it never got used. I assumed she either walked until she got a cab or headed for the tube station, which isn't far from here.'

'Do you know where she went?'

'I thought she'd go straight home, but she didn't.'

'How can you be sure?'

'Because after I tried to ring her and realised she'd turned her phone off, Theo offered to go to her flat in the hope he could persuade her to come back so that we could talk some more.'

Anna looked at Theo, who responded with a shake of his head. 'I went by taxi because our car was at the garage having some repairs done. I got there about an hour after she left here. I rang the bell several times but there was no answer. And there were no lights on inside. I waited around for about fifteen minutes but she didn't turn up.'

'Couldn't you have let yourself in?'

Another shake of the head. 'Holly wouldn't let us have a key. We asked a few times but she refused, and now we know why.'

'So what did you do then, Mr Blake?' Anna said.

'I came straight home.'

Rebecca snapped her head towards him.

'But not straight away,' she said. 'You rang to say you were going to the pub. You didn't get in until after midnight. I was already in bed having taken a sleeping tablet. You woke me.'

He nodded. 'Oh, that's right. Sorry. I went for a drink. My head was all over the place by then.'

Anna was at once suspicious. She felt there was something unconvincing about what he'd said. Something not quite right. But she didn't think that now was the time to put him on the spot so she made a mental note to follow it up when she had him on his own.

Instead she turned back to Rebecca. 'Do you know Nathan Wolf personally, Mrs Blake?'

'I do, but not very well,' Rebecca said. 'We've met a few times and I'm afraid it was me who introduced him to Holly when she accompanied me to a fundraising event that he attended. That's something I'll never forgive myself for.'

'And did she tell you how and when exactly she started a relationship with him?'

'All she told us was that it began over a year ago. At the time she was sharing a flat in Eltham with her then boyfriend,

Ross. But she was intending to break up with him and that was probably why she let Nathan Wolf into her life. They saw each other for a little while before he took her to see the flat.'

'We'll need to contact this Ross,' Anna said. 'Do you know his surname and his contact details?'

'His second name is Moore. I don't know his number but the flat he shared with Holly was 12 Primrose Court, Manor Road, Eltham. I've no idea if he still lives there.'

'Do you know if she and Ross stayed in touch after she broke up with him and moved out?'

'I know that he pestered her to get back with him and as a result she changed her phone number,' Rebecca said. 'He kept ringing her and he even turned up at her flat a couple of times.'

'Did she put in a formal complaint?'

'Not to my knowledge. She regarded him as irritating but harmless.'

While Anna scribbled some notes on her pad, Walker picked up the questioning.

'You told us you were angry with Holly because by selling her story she was going to make life intolerable for everyone else,' he said. 'What did you mean by that?'

'Isn't it obvious?' she responded sharply. 'She would have made herself look foolish and spiteful, and she would have involved us in a sordid scandal. It would have impacted on Theo's career and ruined my chances of becoming this city's Mayor. I told her all this and she accused me of being selfish.'

'Did you try to contact her again after that night?' Walker asked.

'Of course. I kept trying to phone, but it was switched off.

I sent her emails and messaged her on Facebook asking her to call me. I rang her friends and her modelling agency but nobody knew where she was. That was when I got my secretary to call round the hospitals to see if she had been involved in an accident. Then yesterday morning I phoned Nathan Wolf but he claimed that he hadn't heard from her since Sunday. I let him know that Holly had told us everything and said he should be ashamed of himself.'

'And what was his response?'

'I didn't give him a chance to respond. The sound of his voice made me see red and I slammed the phone down. I made one final call to the editor of the *Sunday Mirror* and after he told me that he too had been trying to contact Holly because she hadn't turned up for the interview I went into a panic and called the police.'

'So why didn't you get in touch with us sooner?' Walker asked.

'Up until then I'd convinced myself that she was avoiding everyone because she was in a strop. She's always been headstrong and volatile, and it wasn't the first time she'd cut off contact with us following an argument.'

'What about her biological father?' Anna asked, looking up from her notes. 'He'll need to be informed.'

'He died three years ago in Australia,' Rebecca said. 'That's where he moved to after our divorce. Holly went there to attend the funeral.'

Anna had more questions, but she didn't get to ask them because suddenly it all got too much for Rebecca. Her face folded in on itself and she started to cry out as though in pain.

'I can't believe this is happening,' she wailed. 'I should

have been there for her. My baby should be here with me. Not . . .'

Rebecca leaped to her feet, covered her mouth with her hand, and rushed into the kitchen. A moment later Anna heard her retching into the sink.

'I have to insist that you call a halt to this now,' Theo said. 'My wife is struggling. She needs time to take it in. We both do. Holly was everything to us.'

'I appreciate that, Mr Blake,' Anna said. 'You've both had a tremendous shock and despite that you've been really helpful and we're grateful.'

'So what happens next?' he asked, getting to his feet.

Anna stood up too. 'You've given us information that we'll follow up. But we will need to come back and ask you some more questions, especially about what Holly told you. In the meantime I'll arrange for a Family Liaison Officer to get in touch. He or she will keep you informed of progress and answer your questions in relation to the investigation.'

Anna fished a business card from her pocket and passed it to him.

'My mobile number is on the back,' she said. 'Don't hesitate to call me at any time. And I must advise you both not to contact Mr Wolf however tempting that becomes. I'll be interviewing him shortly.'

Rebecca re-entered the room at that point and sat back down on the sofa while attempting to stem her tears with a crumpled tissue. Anna's heart went out to her and she repeated her condolences.

'Your husband has my number,' she added. 'And I'll be in touch as soon as I have more news.'

Rebecca looked at Anna through red, swollen eyes and gave a slow nod.

'I know how it works, detective,' she said. 'Just sort it so that I can see my daughter as soon as possible. And don't underestimate Nathan Wolf. He's a ruthlessly ambitious bastard and he'll do whatever it takes to save himself. That includes enlisting the help of friends in high places.'

'I promise you that if he is the person responsible then he will be made to pay,' Anna said as Theo ushered them out of the room.

At the front door he told them he would call Rebecca's sister Freya and get her to come over.

Before stepping outside, Anna asked Theo for Holly's mobile number. Then she said, 'Just for the record, Mr Blake, where did you go for a drink after you went to Holly's place and discovered she wasn't there?'

Shock registered in his eyes. 'Surely you're not suggesting that I had anything to do with what's happened?'

'Absolutely not. But it's essential that we eliminate those close to Holly from our enquiries at the outset. I'm sure you can understand that. I know that your wife will appreciate that it's something we have to do.'

He blew air out of his mouth through pursed lips. 'Very well. I went to the King's Head in Chappell Road, between here and Holly's flat. I stayed there about an hour, then came home. That's why I didn't get back until after midnight.'

'Thank you, Mr Blake,' Anna said. 'We'll be on our way now and let me say once again how sorry I am for your loss.'

When they were back in the car, Anna took out her phone and told Walker that she needed to alert DCS Nash to the latest developments. But the phone rang just as she was about to tap in his number.

Caller ID showed it was DS Prescott who had been tasked, along with DC Niven, to check out Holly's Camden flat.

'I'm listening, Doug,' she said. 'What have you got for me?'

'One of Miss Blake's neighbours is also her landlord,' he said. 'He let us into her flat and I really think you need to come and see what we've found, ma'am.'

CHAPTER TWELVE

Anna read out Holly's address from her notes and told Walker to drive straight there.

'This is likely to be an all-nighter,' she said. 'Do you need to let your wife know?'

'I sent her a text before we left the office,' he answered. 'It was obvious to me then that I wouldn't get to see my bed tonight.'

She passed on what DS Prescott had told her, then called DCS Nash, who answered on the first ring.

'How did it go with Rebecca Blake?' he asked her.

Anna told him how Holly's mother had reacted, and how she had gone on to put Nathan Wolf, MP in the frame.

Nash's reaction was predictable. 'Jesus Christ, Anna. This is going from bad to worse.'

'My thoughts exactly, sir,' she said.

'And do you think it could actually be true?'

'It's too early to say. We need to check with the newspaper that was about to dish the dirt on him. And then we'll go and confront the man with the allegations. Have you got any thoughts on how it should be handled?'

'Just don't approach him until I get back to you,' he said. 'I'll have to talk to the Commissioner, make sure he's in the picture before the news breaks.'

'Well, our next step is Holly Blake's flat in Camden,' Anna said. 'The team have already come up with something interesting there apparently. But I don't want to wait too long before we confront Wolf. If he is our man then he's already had too much time to cover his tracks. And just because he's a politician he shouldn't be treated differently to any other suspect.'

'I'm with you on that, but whether you like it or not Nathan Wolf is not just any other suspect. Once his name is out there it will trigger a media storm the like of which we haven't seen in years. And the wave of panic will roll all the way up to the Prime Minister's office.'

Having made his point, Nash hung up, leaving Anna to wonder just how tricky and frustrating things were going to get in the days ahead.

Walker could tell that she was uptight and it amused him.

'This really is the stuff of nightmares, guv,' he said, a slight grin playing on his lips. 'Victim's a beautiful model. Her mum's a top Tory councillor and potential Mayor of London. And the prime suspect is a bloody MP. It doesn't get more complicated than that.'

She looked at him. Shook her head.

'And it plays right into your warped sense of humour doesn't it, Max?'

He shrugged. 'You've either got to laugh or cry, guv. I mean, we'll either come out of it smelling of roses or else all our careers will be cut short if we fuck up.'

'That's why I like having you as my right-hand man, Max,' she said. 'Knowing you're there at my side instils me with confidence.'

'Seriously, though,' he said. 'This is a real fuckfest. But if I'm honest there's no place I would rather be right now than working this case. I can't wait to see what else it throws up.'

'You won't be surprised that I don't share your enthusiasm, Max. I'm the one in the firing line. And even before we get started the Commissioner has seen fit to call my competence into question.'

'Nothing new there then,' Max said.

Not for the first time Anna wanted to slap him. Instead, she said, 'So what does your gut tell you, Max?'

He thought about it and replied, 'It's clear that if Holly was doing a kiss-and-tell job on Nathan Wolf then he had a motive for wanting her silenced. But it strikes me that we also need to pay attention to the ex-boyfriend as well as the stepdad. Theo Blake would have made us believe that he went straight home after going to Holly's flat. We only know he didn't thanks to his wife. What we don't know is if he told her the truth about going for a drink.'

That was one of the action points she phoned through to the office. She wanted someone to call the King's Head to check if they had any security footage from that evening. She also asked for files to be produced on Holly Blake, her mother and stepdad, and Nathan Wolf.

'And run the name Ross Moore through the system to see if it throws anything up,' she said. 'He's Holly's ex-boyfriend and we think he lives at Primrose Court in Manor Road,

Eltham. We need to trace him. Have everything ready for a full team briefing at seven in the morning. If I decide to bring the time forward I'll let you know.'

Anna then used her phone to go online in search of information on Nathan Wolf. Wikipedia listed the salient facts next to a head-and-shoulders photo.

Nathan Daniel Wolf, aged 45, is a British politician of the Conservative party, serving as Member of Parliament for the Central Somerset constituency.

Anna squinted at his picture. There was no denying that he was good-looking. He had chiselled features and a square jaw, with a full head of dark, wavy hair.

A number of facts were listed beneath the photo and Anna read them out for Walker's benefit.

'Wolf was born to a single mother,' she said. 'Educated at Eton. Ran a successful financial services company before becoming a politician six years ago. He and his first wife were divorced in 2005. He married Shelley Montague four years later but she died of a stroke. Currently single. No children. Resides in Kensington, London and Bridgewater, Somerset.'

'No mention of him having a pretty young mistress on the go then,' Walker said.

Anna shook her head. 'But it'll be all over social media as soon as it becomes public knowledge, which it surely will even though Holly is dead.'

'And then Mr Wolf will join the ranks of those senior politicians whose secret sex lives were exposed by the very women they were shagging.'

'That will be the least of his worries if we find out that he killed Holly to save his own neck,' Anna said.

Camden, North London: one of the capital's most popular areas, famed for its lively market and thriving nightlife.

Stanhope Street was centrally located close to Regent's Park, lined with a wide range of apartment buildings. Holly Blake's flat was on the ground floor of a five-storey block that looked about ten years old.

Anna could see why it would appeal to Nathan Wolf if he was indeed paying the rent. It was discreet, nondescript, somewhere he'd be able to nip in and out of without drawing too much attention to himself. What's more it was only about five miles from his home in Kensington and three miles from the Houses of Parliament.

A patrol car was parked on the road in front of the block, behind an Audi A4 that Anna recognised as one of the team's unmarked pool cars.

DS Prescott was waiting at the entrance smoking a cigarette. The smell of burning tobacco made Anna crave a nicotine fix, but she knew she had to resist for the time being.

Prescott dropped what remained of his fag onto the ground and let the smoke jet from his nostrils.

'I didn't expect you to get here so quickly, ma'am,' he said.

'We weren't that far away,' she responded. 'Who's inside?'

'DS Niven and a PC. I've called up forensics, who should be here soon. And the landlord, a Mr Jason Lattimer, is up in his flat on the first floor waiting for you to talk to him. You'll want to hear what he has to say.'

'So show us what you've got then.'

Anna and Walker snapped on latex gloves and followed

Prescott into the building. There was a small, spotless entrance hall with a lift, stairs and corridors to the left and right. A uniformed officer was standing outside the first front door on the left, Holly's flat.

'We got lucky because the landlord happened to arrive just as we did so he let us in,' Prescott said. 'He told us this is one of several flats he owns and rents out. Holly Blake moved in just over twelve months ago.'

DC Niven was waiting inside to give them a tour of the flat. It was decorated in whites, creams and pastel colours. There was a mix of wooden floors and carpets. The furniture looked fairly new and expensive, and Anna was struck by how tidy it was. There was nothing to suggest it had been the scene of a crime, although she knew that the forensics officers might well come across something that was invisible to the naked eye.

In the living room, Niven pointed to a sideboard below a wall-mounted TV. On top of it rested an iPad and a laptop.

'The techies are working on getting into them now,' he said.

The surfaces were adorned with framed photos of Holly. In some she was fully clothed and in others she was wearing bikinis or underwear. They had all clearly been taken by a professional photographer and had probably graced the pages of fashion magazines at some point.

The small kitchen gleamed with brushed aluminium and the contents of the fridge included no fewer than four bottles of champagne.

'It's a two-bedroom flat and this is the one Holly obviously slept in,' Niven said as he pushed open a door and they followed him in.

The room contained a double bed with a purple duvet, a large dressing table and a fitted wardrobe across one wall that was filled with designer labels and shoes.

'Check this out,' Niven said, as he took out one of the many hangers. 'A pair of men's trousers. There are also a couple of shirts. And in the bottom drawer socks and pants and a soap bag with shaving gear in it. According to the landlord, Holly had a regular male visitor, a guy who he says is a lot older than her. But before you talk to him there's something you have to see.'

He led them along the corridor to the second bedroom.

As he waved Anna inside, he said, 'Needless to say this is not what we expected to find.'

And it certainly wasn't what Anna had expected to see. Her stomach muscles contracted and the hairs on her neck stood up. It was left to Walker to put into words what she was thinking.

'I don't fucking believe it,' he said. 'I thought we'd already had enough surprises for one day.'

CHAPTER THIRTEEN

When Sophie woke up she was shocked to find that she was lying on the kitchen floor. It was several seconds before she realised that she must have passed out.

Then it came back to her. The bottle and a half of wine. The shocking revelations in the newspaper about Detective Anna Tate. The knowledge that she might soon lose the only good thing in her life – her daughter.

And the fear that someone had been watching her as she walked to and from the dental clinic.

Her head was pounding and there was a foul taste in her mouth. She hauled herself into a sitting position and planted her back against the wall. Thank God Alice hadn't got out of bed and found her like this, she thought.

The digital display on the oven told her it was eleven o'clock, which meant she had been unconscious for less than an hour. But that had been time enough for the past to resurface in a familiar dream that took her back to where it all began ten years ago.

Those images, so frighteningly vivid, returned now as she closed her eyes in the hope that it would ease the pain that raged behind them. It was like she was actually there watching herself re-enact the encounter that was to change her life and eventually lead her to this flat in Shoreditch.

Ten years ago

He enters the restaurant with the child in a pushchair. He has fair hair and a handsome face, and is dressed in a tight blue T-shirt and jeans.

The little girl, who looks about two, is wearing a pretty red dress and matching sun hat. She's fast asleep with her head back and her mouth open.

The sight of her is a painful reminder to Sophie that she isn't able to have a child of her own because she's infertile thanks to fucked-up ovaries.

The man decides to sit at a table close to the big window that looks out on the shaded patio. He's the first customer of the day and as she approaches him with the breakfast menu she can't help wondering where his wife or girlfriend is.

'Buenos dias,' she says. 'Or should I say good morning?'

The man beams at her, white teeth gleaming.

'You've guessed that I'm English,' he says. 'And I'm guessing that you are too despite the perfect Spanish accent.'

'I am indeed,' she tells him and places the menu on the table. 'Are you here for breakfast or just a drink?'

'I'd like a bacon sandwich and a large Americano coffee with milk and sugar,' he says.

She gestures towards the child. 'And what about that sweet little lady? Would she like something?'

He laughs. 'That sweet little lady is really the devil in disguise. She kept me up most of the night, which is why she's out to the world now.'

For some reason she feels emboldened to ask him if the child's mother is with them.

'Her mother died a while ago,' he tells her, the smile vanishing. 'She contracted a rare form of blood cancer. That's why we've moved to Spain. I want us to start a new life here.'

'I did that four years ago,' she says. 'I got fed up with the crowds and depressing weather in London.'

'We're from London too,' he says. 'We've been here just over three weeks. I'm renting an apartment close to the marina while I look around for a business to invest in.'

'What kind of business?'

'Not sure yet, but I've always wanted to run a bar ever since I spent some time here in Spain as a teenager. Of course, it needs to be something that will allow me to be a proper father at the same time.'

'That sounds exciting.' She holds out her hand. 'By the way, my name is Sophie and I'm the head waitress here at The Clover.'

He takes her hand and the smile is back.

'And I'm James. James Miller. This is my daughter. Her name's Alice. She's two and she means the world to me.'

Sophie opened her eyes and wondered briefly what would have happened if they hadn't lied to each other that morning. Would they have hit it off like they did and stayed together for the next seven years? Or would James have eaten his bacon sandwich and walked out of her life?

He'd almost certainly be alive now if he had done so. And

she would probably still be in Spain, having never experienced true love or the sheer joy of motherhood.

Sophie sat on the kitchen floor for almost five minutes as dark thoughts trampled through her mind.

At the same time the pain in her head was getting worse, insistent, and it seemed like the silent walls of the flat were closing in on her.

She had to force herself to resist the weakness that was taking her over. But it required an enormous effort.

As she clambered to her feet her head spun and the floor seemed to shift beneath her. She had to hold onto the worktop until she regained her equilibrium.

Then, squeezing the memory of ten years ago to one side, she staggered across the kitchen, grabbed a glass and filled it with water from the tap. She downed it in one go, filled the glass again, and carried it unsteadily towards the bedroom.

On the way she paused to look at her reflection in the hall mirror and it made her cringe. Her eyes were glassy, her face sweaty, her shoulder-length black hair a total mess.

She wanted desperately to talk to someone, to unburden herself. But who could she trust? Her parents were dead and she hadn't spoken to her sister for well over a year. She had also lost touch with her uncles and aunts.

There was Lisa, of course. But Sophie wasn't sure she wanted her to know what she'd found out. Since her friend lived and worked outside London it was likely she hadn't read the Anna Tate story in the *Standard*. If she had then surely she would have called by now.

She couldn't resist looking in on Alice on the way to

her own room. Thankfully she was still asleep, one arm dangling over the edge of the bed. Sophie leaned over and gave her a gentle kiss on the forehead.

It was Alice who gave meaning to Sophie's life. Alice who had helped her to bury the past and embrace the future.

She loved that wonderful, beautiful girl as if she were her own. And she knew that Alice loved her back. As far as Alice was concerned Sophie was her mother now. Her biological mum wasn't even a distant memory. She existed only in a couple of photographs that James had kept.

It was Sophie who had helped to potty-train her. Sophie who had taken care of her while James worked in the bar he opened. Sophie who had looked after her since they'd been forced to flee from Spain to Southampton three years ago. And Sophie who had had to break the news to her that her father had died.

And that was why it was such a shock to discover now that all along Alice's real name was Chloe. That her mother was still alive. And that James had lied to her about being a widower.

It felt to Sophie as though her heart had been ripped out of her chest. The urge to drink herself into oblivion was strong. But the urge to hold onto the life she had was much stronger.

And for that she needed to stay sober, focused and determined.

CHAPTER FOURTEEN

There were various ways to describe the second bedroom in Holly Blake's flat. But Anna felt that Walker put his finger right on it when he said, 'It's like a poor relation of The Red Room in *Fifty Shades of Grey*.'

He was referring to the movie about a billionaire who's into S and M and has an elaborate pleasure dungeon he calls The Red Room of Pain in his luxury apartment. Holly Blake's DIY version was on a much smaller scale, but it clearly served the same purpose.

The room, which was only slightly smaller than the one Holly had slept in, was equipped with all kinds of kinky sex paraphernalia. Some of the items were hanging from hooks on the walls and others were neatly laid out on shelving units.

There were ankle and wrist restraints, canes, rolls of bondage tape, chains, handcuffs, lengths of rope and a variety of sex toys.

A single bed had pride of place in the centre of the room

and there was a flat-screen TV fixed to the wall above it. Leather straps were attached to the bed frame at both ends, and on a small table next to it was a DVD player. Anna's eyes were drawn to a contraption that she had never seen before. It stood about three feet off the floor and had four steel legs and padded rests to support a person's body and limbs.

'What the hell is that thing?' she asked.

Walker shook his head. 'It looks like some weird piece of exercise equipment.'

'It's known as a fuck bench,' Niven said. 'It allows those who like to play rough to position each other so that they can gain full access for penetration and stimulation.'

Anna and Walker stared at him and saw the blood rush to his face.

'Well, it's a new one on me,' Anna said.

'Don't jump to the wrong conclusion,' Niven responded quickly, holding up his hands, palms out. 'I'm not a fetish freak and I'm not into BDSM. I just happen to have heard about it, that's all.'

Walker raised his brow and tutted. 'You shouldn't be ashamed of what turns you on, mate,' he said, a smile tugging at the corners of his mouth. 'I read somewhere that one in five couples is into painful sex. And it's no longer taboo to talk about it. So relax, Tom. We're not judging.'

'Oh, for fuck's sake, I wish I hadn't opened my gob,' Niven said, and Walker responded with a chuckle.

'Stop winding him up, Max,' Anna said. 'This is serious. I'm assuming that when Holly told her mum that she was going to reveal a bunch of sordid secrets this is what she meant. I can see the headlines now – "Top Tory MP and his spanking sessions".'

'Looks to me as though spanking would have been one of the least painful activities they got up to in here,' Walker said.

Anna stepped further into the room to look around. There were no cupboards, drawers or wardrobes, and nothing filled the space under the bed. So everything was on display, and the more Anna looked the more she found.

There were bottles of massage oil, several pairs of rubber gloves, a roll of plastic cling-film, a bright red latex catsuit, no fewer than five vibrators, a blindfold and a scary-looking mouth ball gag.

'It's enough to make your eyes water and your skin prickle,' Walker said.

One of the shelf units was filled with books, magazines and DVDs. The titles sent a shudder along Anna's spine. *Mistress of Torment, How to be Kinky, Erotic Fantasies, Diary of a Submissive, Bound to Cum, Domination and Submission, Hogtied.*

'I'm reminded of the time I went into an Ann Summers store in search of a birthday gift for the wife,' Walker said.

'And did you buy anything?' Niven asked him.

Walker rolled his eyes. 'You don't really expect me to answer that question in front of the boss, do you?'

Anna decided they had seen enough of the playroom and that the contents were becoming a distraction. She was also concerned about contaminating forensic evidence.

Turning back towards the door, she said, 'This room is off limits until the SOCOs get here. And it's time to dispense with the inappropriate repartee, guys. OK?'

Back in the living room, Anna told Prescott and Niven about Nathan Wolf and said he was no doubt the regular visitor the landlord had mentioned.

'So it means he has to be a suspect in Holly's murder,' she added.

'It seems he's not the only one,' Prescott said.

Anna frowned. 'What do you mean?'

'Well, according to the landlord her ex-boyfriend, a bloke named Ross, came here last week and started a row with her. She accused him of stalking her and was very upset. The landlord also thinks he saw him hanging around outside on Tuesday night.'

CHAPTER FIFTEEN

Jason Lattimer was a short, overweight individual in his late fifties. He described himself as the son of an immigrant couple from Barbados.

He had the same dark skin as Anna's partner Tom, who had lived on another Caribbean island, Antigua, before moving to the UK with his family at the age of five.

Lattimer had been told only that Holly Blake was missing and her parents were becoming increasingly worried, hence the need to gain access to her flat.

Anna and Walker spoke to him in his sparsely furnished living room while detectives Prescott and Niven went knocking on the other flats in the block. The first few questions to the landlord were aimed at eliciting information about the man himself, partly to determine whether he should be treated as a suspect.

But it took Anna less than a minute to weigh him up and rule him out, although they would still subject him to the usual checks.

Lattimer told them that he owned a total of five properties in and around Camden and that he had inherited them from his parents. Holly's flat had been let unfurnished and was on a rolling lease.

'She viewed the flat with an older man who's been a frequent visitor this past year,' Lattimer said, his voice quiet, nervous. 'All the furniture was delivered before she moved in and she's been an ideal tenant. In fact I've come to regard her as a friend. She's such a pleasant girl and the rent's always paid on time.'

'Have you been inside the flat?' Anna asked.

'A couple of times, but not recently. I only ever went into the lounge and kitchen and I was very impressed with the way it had been decorated.'

'Is the rent paid by direct debit?'

He nodded. 'Fifteen hundred pounds a month transferred directly from her bank account into mine.'

'What do you know about the man who helped her set up home here?'

He shrugged. 'Nothing at all except that he usually arrives and leaves by taxi and that he rarely stays overnight. He's in his forties, I reckon, and I've always suspected that he's some kind of sugar daddy.'

'Why is that?'

'Well, the age difference for one thing, and the fact that he doesn't live with her. She described him once as her boyfriend and let slip that he had paid for all the furniture.'

'Have you spoken to him much?'

He shook his head. 'The longest conversation I had with him was when they viewed the flat, and that was over a year ago. He's quite posh and polite, but he also comes across as very shy. He always wears dark glasses and sometimes a baseball cap pulled low over his forehead. It's as though he doesn't like people seeing his face, which is another reason I figured he was more a benefactor than a boyfriend.'

'Do you know his name?'

'Not his full name. Holly refers to him as Nate, which I'm certain is short for Nathan.'

Anna fished her phone from her pocket and opened up a photo she'd saved of Nathan Wolf.

'Is this Nate?' she said.

Lattimer leaned forward and picked up a pair of glasses from the coffee table between them. He slipped them on, looked at the picture and nodded without hesitation.

'That's him.' He then tilted his head to one side, furrows texturing his forehead. 'Do you think something bad has happened to Holly, detective? Is that why you're asking all these questions?'

'Her family are concerned about her, Mr Lattimer, and so are we. When was the last time you saw her?'

He chewed on the inside of his cheek for a few beats as he thought about it.

'That would have been on Tuesday,' he said. 'I saw her come and go a couple of times during the day because I was out front doing stuff to the car.'

'Did you speak to her?'

'Only to say hello and ask her if she was going on a modelling assignment. She told me she was on a day off but had things to do.'

'And at what time did you last see her?'

'Well, that was actually much later in the evening,' he said. 'I was having a smoke on my balcony about half ten when I saw her crossing the road. I didn't notice if she'd been dropped off so she might have been. She came into the building but then about fifteen minutes later she came out again and walked off down the street.'

'Did that not strike you as odd?'

'Not at all. People around here are in and out at all hours. It's a lively part of town, especially at night.'

Anna jotted down what he'd told her in her notebook and then asked him if the man named Nate had also turned up on Tuesday at any time.

'If he did I didn't see him,' Lattimer said. 'But then I was out during the early part of the evening myself.'

Anna made another note and said, 'That's really helpful, Mr Lattimer. Now I'd like you to tell us about the incident involving Holly's ex-boyfriend. I believe you witnessed an altercation.'

He nodded. 'It was early last week. I was in the kitchen when I heard shouting outside. From the window I could see Holly and she was screaming at him to leave her alone. She was clearly distressed so I hurried down to make sure she was all right.'

'And what happened?'

'Well, by the time I got there the bloke was sobbing like a bloody baby and begging her to take him back. But Holly was accusing him of being a stalker and threatening to call the police. I thought she was going to hit him so I stepped between them and told him in no uncertain terms to fuck off. When he refused to move I gave him a shove and told Holly to go inside. That was when he finally got the message and walked away.'

'And then what?'

'That was it. He buggered off and I escorted Holly to her flat. I offered to go in and make her a cup of tea because she was in a right old state and had started to cry. But she insisted she was OK and wanted to be left alone. I'd never seen her so angry or upset.'

'How did you know the guy was her ex-boyfriend?'

'Because he's been here a couple of times before. The last time I saw him was four or five months ago when they were having words outside. She told me later that his name was Ross and that he couldn't get over the fact that she'd dumped him.'

'I see. And you mentioned to the other detectives that you think he was hanging around outside on Tuesday.'

'That's right. It was while I was on the balcony. There was a figure standing across the road next to the big tree. I only noticed him because he lit up a cigarette and I glimpsed his face. I'm eighty per cent sure it was him, the ex. He must have spotted me watching because he suddenly moved off and disappeared around the corner.'

'And what time was this?'

'About half an hour before Holly arrived home.'

Anna wound up the interview by explaining that a forensics team would soon be examining Holly's flat, and it would therefore remain out of bounds.

'Are you holding something back from me, officer?' he said, but she dodged the question and asked him if he could provide them with the locations of CCTV cameras in the vicinity. He did so, and also confirmed what she had already noted, that the block itself did not have its own internal or external security cameras.

Back downstairs, Prescott and Niven had finished

speaking to most of the neighbours. They had all acknowledged that they knew Holly but only as someone they'd met from time to time when entering and leaving the building.

However, there was one exception, the woman who lived on the opposite side of the corridor to Holly's flat.

'Her name is Pamela Steele,' DS Prescott said. 'And she claims she witnessed Holly being threatened on Friday of last week.'

'I've seen the same bloke coming and going many times,' Pamela Steele said when Anna asked her to repeat what she'd told DS Prescott. 'But that was the first time I'd heard the pair of them arguing. It was during the afternoon so there was no one else around.'

Pamela was a thirtysomething shift worker at a nearby Royal Mail sorting office. She had been on first-name terms with Holly and had a clear recollection of what had happened last Friday.

'It started out as a heated conversation and got louder the longer it went on,' she said. 'I was getting ready to go to work and their raised voices were carried through the walls, which are pretty thin.'

'Could you make out what they were arguing about?' Anna asked.

Pamela shook her head. 'Not until it spilled over into the corridor. Before then it was a bit muffled. Holly was making the most noise and out of curiosity I looked through the peephole and saw them standing in her doorway. She was yelling at him to go and he was telling her to calm down and grow up.'

'You told Detective Prescott that you heard him threaten her.'

'That was after she pushed him out the door. I saw him jab a finger at her and tell her that he wouldn't let her get away with it and that if she didn't take the money, then she'd regret it. They were his exact words. I know because it was quite shocking.'

'And how did Holly respond?'

'She slammed the door in his face and he walked off.'

'Did you speak to her about it afterwards?'

'Of course not. It was none of my business, and besides, I went to work shortly after and I haven't seen her since.'

Anna took out her phone and showed her a photo of Nathan Wolf.

'Could you confirm that this is the man in question?' she said.

Pamela nodded. 'That's him. Holly calls him Nate and he's here quite often, but I never see them go out together.'

Anna told her they would need to speak to her again and took down the woman's contact details before leaving the flat.

The forensics team arrived as the four detectives were conferring outside the block and Anna quickly put them in the picture.

'It's possible a crime was committed in the flat in question,' she said. 'Start off in the second bedroom and work out from there.'

She instructed Prescott to stick with them and provide them with all the information they needed.

'Bag up all Holly's personal stuff, including bank statements and other paperwork,' she said. 'And separate out the men's things. We need to run print and DNA checks on every item.'

She then told Niven to enlist the help of a couple of

uniforms and go in search of CCTV and private security cameras in the area.

'Make a note and relay the details back to the office so we can start bringing in the footage as soon as possible,' she said.

Anna then called the office herself and it was DC Forbes who answered. She gave her a list of instructions, which included finding out if they had managed to track down Ross Moore.

'And make contact with the editor of the *Sunday Mirror*,' she said. 'Give him my number and tell him to call me because I need to speak to him as a matter of urgency. You can say it's about Holly Blake.'

Anna then signalled for Walker to follow her back to the car.

'Where to now, guv?' he asked her.

'It's time we spoke to Nathan Wolf,' she said.

'But don't you need to clear that with Nash?'

'I'll do that on the way to Kensington.'

Nash had been waiting anxiously for Anna to call.

'I've spoken to the Commissioner,' he said. 'He's given the green light to question Wolf. But I had a job persuading him not to refer it straight up to the Home Secretary before you've done so. I made it clear that it would be a sure way of delaying the whole process.'

'Thank you, sir,' Anna said. 'We're on our way to his London pad now. And you need to be aware that the evidence, although circumstantial, is stacking up against him.'

She told Nash about the argument between Wolf and Holly and the threat he made.

'That's pretty incriminating,' he said.

'But that's not all, sir. It seems the honourable Member of Parliament and his young model mistress have been using and abusing each other for quite a while.'

As she described the kinky playroom in the flat she heard Nash catch his breath and tried to imagine the look on his face.

'The landlord also gave credence to the accusations that Nathan Wolf has been acting as a kind of sugar daddy to Holly,' Anna said. 'The MP viewed the flat with her and helped her move in. He even paid for all the furniture. And he's been a regular visitor the whole time she's lived there.'

Anna then pointed out that Holly's ex-boyfriend, Ross Moore, was also in the frame as a suspect.

'He's been stalking her for ages,' she said. 'And the landlord is convinced he saw the guy lurking in the street in front of the block on Tuesday night. We're doing a sweep of all the CCTV cameras in the immediate area.'

'Well, you're clearly on top of it,' Nash said. 'But update me straight after you've talked to Wolf, however late. And I advise you not to go in with all guns blazing, or make an arrest without irrefutable proof that he's your man.'

'I won't, sir.'

Walker suggested they make a pit stop at an all-night café, which Anna was up for because she was gasping for a hot drink and her stomach was growling ferociously.

They each got a takeaway coffee and packaged sandwich and consumed them in the car while parked up somewhere in Paddington.

They were half way through it when Anna's phone rang. The caller turned out to be the editor of the *Sunday Mirror*, Ralph Fleming.

'I've been asked to call you about Holly Blake,' he said.

'Thank you, Mr Fleming,' Anna said. 'I really appreciate it.'

'It's no trouble. I happen to be working late in the office anyway.'

'Well, I'd like you to confirm something for me if that's OK.'

'Fire away.'

'Holly's mother Rebecca has informed us that her daughter approached your paper with a view to selling her story. A story that involves a prominent Member of Parliament.'

'That is correct, detective. In fact we're very keen on publishing. We had a brief meeting with her last week. Terms were agreed and the wheels were put in motion. But Miss Blake then suddenly dropped out of sight.'

'Is it true that she claimed to have been having a long-running affair with Nathan Wolf, the MP for Central Somerset?'

A pause, then: 'What are you not telling me, detective? I'm beginning to suspect that either something has happened to Holly or the powers that be have been mobilised in order to protect Nathan Wolf's reputation.'

'I can't go into the details at this stage, Mr Fleming,' Anna said. 'I just need you to confirm what Rebecca Blake has told us.'

'Well, yes, that is true. We were going to approach the MP after we'd carried out the proper interview so that we knew exactly what to ask him.'

'And can you tell me if you still intend to carry the story?'

'Almost certainly. Why wouldn't we? It's a belter. We've yet to do the full interview, of course, but we do have a short tape recording of Holly which includes some allegations. Unless she retracts them I see no reason to bury the story. And I trust that you won't try to pressure me into doing so.'

'Not at all, Mr Fleming. I can see why you're so excited about it. For any Sunday newspaper it would be—'

'Can I please stop you there, detective?' he said, interrupting. 'What's been puzzling me is why this business is of interest to the Major Investigation Team that's based south of the river. Well, now I think I know. You see, we're aware that the body of a young woman has been found on Barnes Common. She's yet to be formally identified, but I would love you to tell me that I'm wrong to make the connection between the dead girl and Holly Blake.'

Anna saw no point in lying since the story had broken much sooner than expected. By morning every paper and broadcast news operation would be following it up.

'I really wish I could tell you that you're wrong to make the connection, Mr Fleming,' she said. 'But I'm afraid I can't.'

'Jesus.'

'I will, of course, require you to send me a copy of the recording you just mentioned of Holly.'

CHAPTER SIXTEEN

Nathan Wolf's home was a two-storey end-of-terrace property not far from the Olympia Exhibition Centre in Kensington. It was small but impressive, with a red-brick façade and a driveway on one side on which was parked a gleaming white Range Rover.

'How much do you reckon this place is worth, guv?' Walker said as they pulled up outside.

'I don't suppose you would get much change from three or four million,' Anna replied. 'But I could be way out. I lost track of property prices in London a long time ago.'

It was approaching midnight, but it appeared they were in luck because lights were showing through the windows both upstairs and down.

Anna didn't know what to expect from the MP and she began to wish she'd collected some more information on him. She didn't know, for instance, if he lived alone or with the woman he'd dumped Holly for.

There was a video bell in the centre of the door and about

thirty seconds after Anna rang it a man's voice asked her to identify herself.

She held up her warrant card. 'I'm Detective Chief Inspector Anna Tate and I'm with the Major Investigation Team. My colleague here is Detective Inspector Max Walker. If you are Mr Nathan Wolf then we need to speak to you, sir. It's about Holly Blake.'

'I assume you're referring to Rebecca Blake's daughter.'

'That's correct, and I should make clear that we know you've been in a relationship with her and she threatened to sell her story to a tabloid newspaper.'

There was a long pause before he responded.

'I haven't seen her for days and she's been refusing to take my calls,' he said. 'I have no idea where she is or what she's playing at.'

'Well, if you'll let us in, Mr Wolf, I can tell you. There's been a serious development that you should know about.'

When the door was opened, Anna was surprised to see that despite the hour Wolf was smartly dressed in trousers, shirt and tie. He was even wearing shoes.

'I've only just arrived home from a late night in the office,' he said, as though he felt the need to explain. 'The new session of Parliament begins next week and there's a lot of preparatory work to do.'

He gestured for them to come in, then walked ahead of them along a wide corridor with magnolia walls and dark, polished floorboards.

His destination was a large living room that was furnished in contemporary style with two white leather sofas, a huge glass coffee table and a drinks cabinet full of bottles of wine and spirits.

Wolf sat on one of the sofas without inviting them to be seated so Anna and Walker perched themselves on the sofa facing him.

'Is there anyone else in the house at the moment?' Anna asked him.

'No, there isn't,' he said, his tone brusque. 'I live alone at present. But what has that got to do with anything, detective? Given how late it is, could you please state your business? Because I have an early start in the morning and want to go to bed.'

It occurred to Anna that Wolf wasn't so good-looking in the flesh. His face was broad, his features pugnacious, and there were lines around his eyes that didn't show up in the online photos she'd seen. His hair was also lighter in colour, and there was a dusting of grey at the temples.

'I'd like to begin by asking you when you last saw Miss Blake,' Anna said.

He crossed one leg over the other and rolled out his bottom lip. He looked confident, bordering on arrogant.

'It was Friday of last week if you must know,' he replied.

'Was that here or at the flat?'

'The flat. She's never been here.'

'And am I correct in saying that you pay the rent on her flat and also supplement her income as a model?'

His eyes flared along with his nostrils.

'With respect, Detective Tate, that is none of your bloody business. And if you're here because the bitch has made some wild accusation against me then you had better spell it out so that I can pass it on to my lawyer. You're obviously aware that she's out to destroy my reputation.'

'It's more serious than that, Mr Wolf. And as I've already

mentioned we do know about her plan to embarrass you through a Sunday newspaper. Understandably you were upset and angry when you found out, which is presumably why you saw fit to threaten her during an argument you had with her in her flat on Friday.'

'What's this?'

'Holly's neighbour witnessed the row and heard you tell her that if she didn't take the money you were offering then she would regret it.'

A nuance of uncertainty flickered behind his eyes and he poked a finger under his shirt collar, which suddenly appeared to be too tight for him.

'It wasn't a serious bloody threat,' he insisted. 'So if you're here to tell me that what I said constitutes a crime then you must be barking mad. I was just angry after she dropped her bombshell and then refused to talk to me about it. My reaction was perfectly normal in the circumstances.'

He uncrossed his legs and stood up suddenly, then thrust his jaw in Anna's direction.

'Surely the police have more important things to do than follow up a spurious complaint from a girl who refuses to accept that a relationship she was in is over.'

The arrogance in his tone angered Anna, but she didn't allow it to rise to the surface. Instead, she said, 'I suggest you sit back down, Mr Wolf, because what I'm about to tell you will come as a shock.'

Or perhaps not, if you're the person who killed her, she thought.

His eyes shifted between Anna and Walker before he slowly lowered himself back onto the sofa.

‘Thank you,’ Anna said, and then focused on his body language for any signs of guilt.

As he locked his gaze on her she was reminded of what Rebecca Blake had said about him.

. . . don’t underestimate Nathan Wolf. He’s a ruthlessly ambitious bastard and he’ll do whatever it takes to save himself.

From the look in his eyes, Anna got the impression that Rebecca was spot on. The man projected an almost palpable air of conceit and brutishness, qualities that had probably helped steer him towards a career in politics.

‘A young woman’s naked body has been found on Barnes Common in South West London,’ she said. ‘A formal identification has yet to take place but we’re certain it’s that of Holly Blake. She’d been brutally murdered before being dumped in undergrowth. Her parents have been informed and it was her mother who suggested that we come and speak to you. The question that she and others will soon be asking is whether you killed Holly because it was the only way to stop her revealing the secrets of your affair.’

Wolf’s eyes bulged and the tendons stood out on his neck. He opened his mouth, but then closed it again without speaking.

Anna couldn’t tell if he was genuinely shocked or putting on an act. After all, he’d had plenty of time to prepare for this moment. He might even have practised in front of a mirror if he was indeed guilty of Holly’s murder.

‘So the reason that Holly has not responded to your calls is because she’s been lying dead in a wood across the river,’ Anna said.

Wolf started shaking his head, and his voice, when it came out, was weak and strained.

'My Lord, that's terrible. Surely it can't be true. Not Holly. She's so . . . so . . .'

The words appeared to get stuck in his throat and his face creased up.

'Would you like us to get you something?' Anna asked him. 'A glass of water perhaps?'

He sucked in a loud breath and leaned forward, clutching his hands together against his stomach.

'Just tell me how she died and when,' he said.

'She was last seen by her parents and her landlord on Tuesday evening. And so far the evidence points to her being killed on that same night. But we don't know the precise time as yet.'

'And how . . .?'

'I can't reveal details about that,' Anna said. 'The pathologist still needs to ascertain the cause of death.'

'Was she raped?'

'We will hopefully know that after the post-mortem.'

Wolf closed his eyes and it looked to Anna as though he was going to break down in tears. But after a moment he opened them again and took another deep breath that made his body tremble.

'I didn't do it,' he said, his voice even but weak. 'And I resent the fact that you're insinuating that I did. I was furious with Holly because of what she intended to do to me. But I am not a violent man and there is no way I could physically hurt anyone, let alone a person I'm fond of.'

'Did you love Holly?' Walker asked him, and the question seemed to throw Wolf. It was several seconds before he responded.

'In my own way I suppose I did,' he said. 'We had a great

deal of fun together. I know what I did was morally questionable, but many men have had secret affairs with much younger women.'

'So do you admit to being Holly's sugar daddy for over a year?' Walker asked him.

Wolf screwed his face up in disgust. 'That's a horrible phrase and it's not how either of us saw the relationship. When we met she was about to leave her boyfriend and was very unhappy. She was also struggling to make an impact in the modelling world. I have a friend in the business. He runs an agency and I said I would help out by putting her in touch with him. They took her on and she was grateful. One thing led to another and we started going out.'

'And who initiated the S and M stuff?' Walker said. 'Was it you or her?'

'Are you fucking serious?'

Walker nodded. 'Of course I am. We've just come from Holly's flat. We saw the torture chamber and it made us wonder if you might have got carried away during a punishment session and she died as a result.'

He stared daggers at Walker. 'This is ridiculous. I can't believe I'm actually a suspect.'

'Well, can you account for your movements last Tuesday evening?' Anna said.

Wolf leaped to his feet for the second time, anger contorting his features. He pointed over their heads towards the door.

'I want you to leave my home,' he yelled. 'I'm not prepared to say another word without my lawyer being present. And you can be assured that I will be taking this up with your superiors. How dare you accuse me of murder just because I had a heated exchange with Holly?'

'There's no need to lose your temper, Mr Wolf,' Anna said. 'We haven't accused you of killing Holly. But given the circumstances we have to regard you as a suspect.'

'That's nonsense. I know of at least two people you should be questioning rather than wasting your time with me.'

'So who are they?' Anna asked him.

'The ex-boyfriend is one of them,' he said. 'He started stalking Holly again recently. She showed me some of the texts he'd sent her. It's no wonder she was scared of him.'

'We know about the ex, Mr Wolf, and we'll be talking to him shortly. So who is the other person?'

'Her stepfather, Theo Blake. Holly hated him. That's one of the reasons she moved out of their house three years ago. She claimed he tried it on with her behind her mother's back.'

Anna's brow shot up at what she saw as another bolt from the blue. Theo Blake had already aroused her suspicions because he hadn't gone straight home after going to Holly's flat following the row with her mother.

CHAPTER SEVENTEEN

Anna managed to persuade Wolf to sit back down by threatening to arrest him if he refused to cooperate.

'The first forty-eight hours are crucial to every murder investigation, Mr Wolf,' she said. 'We therefore need to gather as much information as we can as quickly as we can, even if it means causing some upset. So just bear with us and think of poor Holly. If you are innocent, as you say, then you have nothing to worry about.'

'The fact that I had nothing to do with what happened to Holly won't stop the media from crucifying me,' he said. 'She opened the floodgates to my private life when she approached the *Sunday Mirror*. I dread to think what she told them, and now there's no way I can get her to take it back. My career is on the line and it will be a miracle if my girlfriend doesn't end things.'

The angry look on his face morphed into a blank, shell-shocked expression. There was no sign of grief there, only concern about how Holly's death would impact on his own life.

Anna had already taken an instant dislike to the man. He was clearly a cheating scumbag who was devoid of integrity. But the jury was still out on whether he was also a murderer.

'The sooner you answer our questions the sooner we will be on our way, Mr Wolf,' she said. 'If you insist on having a lawyer present then it will have to be at the station. But this is not a formal interview. We're just trying to establish the facts and find out as much as we can about Holly Blake.'

He sat back and loosened his tie, then rubbed at his eyes with his knuckles.

'It really is in your own interest to be open and honest with us,' Anna said. 'I need you to tell us about your relationship with Holly and explain where you were on Tuesday evening. I'm also keen to hear about the situation between Holly and her stepdad. Plus, I want you to tell me the name of the new woman in your life.'

He sighed heavily. 'It's Jennifer Rothwell. She's an accountant and lives in Clapham.'

'How long have you been a couple?'

'Just six months. I told her that we shouldn't go public with it because I felt it was too soon after my wife's death.'

'But I'm guessing you didn't want it to get out that you were continuing to see Holly.'

He nodded, his eyes downcast. 'It wasn't supposed to turn out the way it did. Holly appeared on the scene at a time when my wife and I were going through a bad patch, partly because our marriage was unfulfilling sexually.'

He paused there and shifted position on the sofa. It appeared to Anna that he wasn't going to elaborate so she said, 'I'm afraid you need to be more explicit, Mr Wolf.'

He nodded again, his expression grave. 'Very well. I'll be

open with you because I don't believe I have anything to be ashamed of.' Another pause. 'It had started going wrong a few years earlier when I developed an interest in unconventional sex. Shelley found it distasteful so it became an issue even though she did her best to indulge me. But then I met Holly at a fundraising event and we hit it off immediately. She was desperate to end things with her boyfriend so I suggested she move into a flat that I would pay the rent on. And before you ask, she did know about my sexual preferences. To my delight it didn't put her off. In fact it was like a real-life *Fifty Shades of Grey*.

'The whole S and M scene was new to her but she went along with it because it turned her on and made me happy. Most of the time I was the submissive and because of her being a model we had to be careful not to leave cuts and bruises on her body.'

'Was it your idea to create the playroom in her flat?'

'Yes, but she was up for it and I paid for everything.'

'So your relationship consisted of you visiting the flat regularly and the pair of you got your kicks by laying into each other.'

'You make it sound as though we were doing something illegal, Detective Tate,' he said. 'Millions of people are into S and M. And the arrangement we had worked well for both of us while it lasted. But then my wife died suddenly of a stroke. At the same time I realised that Holly had fallen in love with me. I did not feel the same way about her, but I didn't want what we had to come to an end. So I let it continue.'

'But then you met Jennifer.'

'She was appointed as my personal accountant by the company that handles my affairs. Unlike Holly she's only two years younger than I am and I was smitten with her from the start. We started going out, and on the third date I steered the conversation around to intimate matters and got a pleasant surprise when I discovered that she was also into rough sex. It convinced me that we were destined to be together. After that I decided it was time to end it with Holly.

'So early last week I went to the flat and told her. I offered her money to go quietly and she got really upset. She couldn't accept that I'd fallen in love with someone else and begged me to stay with her. When I left there she was in bits and all I could do was to tell her that I was sorry. Two days later, on the Thursday, she phoned me to say she was selling her story to a newspaper. I was gobsmacked because I hadn't expected that reaction and I realise now that perhaps I should have.'

'So tell us what happened next,' Anna said.

He shrugged. 'I went to see her again on the Friday to try to talk her out of what she was going to do. But she insisted she wanted to hurt me. We had words and it ended when she shoved me out of the flat. That was when I told her she'd regret it if she didn't take the money I'd offered. But it wasn't a real threat. They were just words spoken in the heat of the moment.'

'And after that what happened?'

'Nothing much. I spent the weekend in my constituency because I had some business to attend to there. I kept trying to reach Holly but without success. She was obviously turning her mobile off and on.'

'So where did you stay in Somerset?'

'I have a house there.'

'And were you alone?'

'No. Jennifer came with me. But she returned by train on

Tuesday morning while I spent the day in my constituency office.'

'So what time did you return to London?' Anna asked.

'I left Bridgewater at nine. Traffic was heavy all the way back along the M4 and it took me over three hours.'

'And you didn't drive over to Holly's flat before going home?'

He shook his head. 'I was tired and I didn't see the point. So I decided to try to make contact with her on Wednesday morning. But she wouldn't answer her phone. Then yesterday her mother rang me to ask if I knew where Holly was. Before hanging up she said that Holly had told her everything.'

'Now tell us more about Holly's relationship with her stepdad,' Walker said.

Wolf licked his dry lips. 'It was strained from the moment she was introduced to him by her mother. That was because Holly held him responsible for her parents' break-up. Rebecca had a short affair with him behind her husband's back. It's what led to the divorce.'

'And she told you he came on to her,' Walker said.

'It happened just after her twentieth birthday. She said she felt uncomfortable around him, but then one night they were alone in the house and he put his arms around her and kissed her on the neck. She went berserk and gave him a piece of her mind. She told her mum but Rebecca believed him when he said she'd got it wrong and that it was merely an affectionate father-daughter gesture.'

'And did it happen again?' Walker asked.

'I don't think so, but after that she did her best to avoid him and it wasn't long before she moved out.'

'Is that when she moved in with Ross Moore, the ex-boyfriend?' This from Anna.

'No. She shared a flat with another girl for about a year before she met him.'

'And how long were they together?'

'Fourteen months or so.'

Anna was satisfied that they'd got a significant amount of information out of Wolf, far more than she'd expected. But despite his denial he was, as far as she was concerned, still very much in the frame for Holly's murder. His alibi was hardly watertight and they had irrefutable evidence that he'd made a threat against her.

But Anna suspected that he would be less cooperative with what came next.

And she was right.

He wasn't prepared to let them search the house without a warrant. He refused to provide a DNA swab, and he declined to let them examine his car and his phones.

'I've said all I'm going to say,' he told them. 'I know my rights and I won't be intimidated by threats to arrest me. From now on any contact with me will be through my lawyer.'

The two detectives stood up and Anna dropped one of her cards on the coffee table.

'Before we go, Mr Wolf, I need you to provide me with contact details for your lawyer and your girlfriend,' she said. 'And I have to advise you that we will be checking out your alibi and seeking a court order that will give us access to your phones and online history.'

'And let me advise you, Detective Tate, that if you try to bolster your case by leaking sensitive information to the media about me then I will bring you down. The Home Secretary is a close personal friend and I won't hesitate to call in a favour.'

Anna stared down at him. 'You're quite the one for making threats, aren't you, sir?' she said.

'It's not a threat, detective. It's a promise.'

CHAPTER EIGHTEEN

'So what did you make of the honourable Member of Parliament?' Anna asked as they headed back to the car.

'He's a hard man to like, for sure,' Walker said. 'As well as being a sleazeball of the highest order.'

'But do you think he killed his sugar lady before driving her to the common?'

'I wouldn't put it past him, guv. He had a lot to lose. Or I should say he has a lot to lose because the genie's out of the bottle with respect to his sordid personal life and he can't put it back in.'

'We need to let the SOCOs loose on both his homes and his car,' Anna said. 'And that means obtaining a warrant.'

'Hopefully that will just be a formality.'

'You can never bank on that in high-profile cases involving politicians. Strings get pulled and obstacles get put in the way of the investigation. I've seen it happen a number of times.'

When they reached the car, Walker opened the door and

slipped behind the wheel. But Anna paused to look around, her eyes seeking out CCTV cameras. It surprised her that there weren't any obvious ones in the street, given how upmarket it was.

'We'll get uniform down here,' she said as she climbed into the passenger seat. 'I'm sure that some of the houses must have security cameras. We need to check the comings and goings of Wolf's car.'

She looked at her watch. It was one-thirty a.m. already, a difficult time of the night to make much progress.

'I feel I need to freshen up,' she said. 'We've got a tough day ahead of us and we ought to recharge our batteries. So can you drop me at home, Max, so I can shower and change? I won't bother going to bed because I know I won't sleep. You can either pick me up after a couple of hours or I'll make my own way to the office.'

'I might as well pick you up,' he said. 'My place is only a mile or so from your house and like you I don't see the point in trying to get any shuteye.'

Anna then called headquarters and got through to DC Forbes, who was working the night shift. She told her to scan for CCTV cameras within a half-mile radius of Nathan Wolf's home.

'And we need a court order to get access to Wolf's phones and a warrant to search his homes,' she said. 'Make it clear that he's our prime suspect in the murder of Holly Blake, and the evidence against him includes a threat he made against her.'

'I've got a couple of updates for you, ma'am,' Forbes said. 'First, Holly's ex-boyfriend no longer lives at the address you gave us. We're still trying to find out where he moved to.'

'Noted. What else is there?'

'I've just received a call from DC Sweeny at Barnes Common. Holly's body has been removed and the search team will arrive at dawn. Forensics have called it a night and they've found nothing significant.'

'OK, we'll be back in a couple of hours,' Anna said. 'Call me if there are any developments.'

Next she rang Nash and told him what Wolf had said.

'But I'm not convinced he's innocent, sir. We need to put him through the ringer. I've asked the team to chase up a warrant and court order.'

'I'll do what I can to make sure nothing holds up the process. Meanwhile Media Liaison are already taking calls from the press and the TV stations about the body. And there must have been a leak somewhere along the line because they're asking us to confirm that it's Holly Blake.'

'So now we can expect the pressure to really build,' Anna said.

'We can indeed,' Nash responded.

CHAPTER NINETEEN

The sound of a gunshot rang out just as Anna let herself into the house. But instead of being alarmed she just smiled.

'He's done it again,' she mumbled to herself as she closed the front door behind her.

A few moments later she saw that she was right. Tom was fast asleep on the sofa and the light from the TV flickered across his face.

More shots rang out and on the screen Anna saw Bruce Willis firing a round of bullets at a bunch of bad men. It was an old movie and one that Tom had seen a couple of times already.

He was an action movie fanatic but when he sat up late watching them by himself, either here or at his own flat, he invariably dropped off. His job as a social worker was pretty demanding, and he got up early most mornings so that he could spend an hour in the gym before going to work. It meant he was tired for much of the time. And he failed to appreciate that at forty-seven enough sleep was as important as enough exercise.

Not that Anna was complaining about the effort he put into keeping in shape. Just looking at him lying there now in nothing but a pair of jockey shorts, she realised how lucky she was. Tom Bannerman had a body that was lean, beautiful and black. And for her that was the icing on the cake. He was thoughtful and gentle and had helped her to overcome the depression that she had lived with for so long after Matthew abducted Chloe.

He was nothing like the man she had met and fallen in love with fifteen years ago. Her ex-husband had been selfish, controlling and short-tempered, traits she had chosen to overlook back then. He had also had an inflated opinion of himself, and had frequently reminded her that his own career as a financial adviser brought in far more money than her job as a copper.

She discovered too late that the marriage didn't mean as much to him as it did to her. It was his five-month affair with a work colleague that caused the break-up, but Anna strongly suspected that he'd been unfaithful with more than one woman.

She'd met Tom at the gym a year and a half ago. Like her he was divorced, and he had a nineteen-year-old daughter who lived with her mother while attending university in Portsmouth.

The big issue between them was whether Tom should give up his rented flat and move in with her. He wanted to but she was happy with the existing arrangement. It meant she was able to dedicate much of her free time and evenings to searching for Chloe without feeling she was being unfair to Tom. She did accept, however, that it was probably time she got over her fear of commitment and invited him to move in. The last thing she wanted was for Tom to get fed up waiting and end the relationship. That would be devastating.

She debated whether to wake him and decided to wait until after she had showered and changed. It was unlikely he would wake up before then since he looked to be in a deep sleep.

She went upstairs and stripped off her clothes. While waiting for the shower to heat up she checked herself in the mirror. Not bad for a forty-three-year-old, she thought to herself. She was only slightly overweight, and the hour-glass figure was still clearly defined. But she did acknowledge that it was time to return to the gym to tone up her muscles.

After showering, she dried her hair and pulled on black trousers. Then she tucked a blue blouse into them and applied a little make-up.

Before going back downstairs she popped into the study, which used to be Chloe's bedroom. The cot and baby stuff had been replaced by a desk, chair and computer. But the walls were covered with photos of Chloe taken during the first two years of her life before Matthew took her away.

Even now, after all this time, she found it hard to believe that he could have done it to her. Before their divorce she had believed they would grow old together. But after his affair and his lies came to light she knew that she could never trust him again. When she refused to have him back he decided to inflict on her the most unbearable pain, and for that she would never forgive him.

Entering the study always brought a lump to Anna's throat, but it was here that she had spent much of her leisure time during the past ten years. Night after night she had searched the web and monitored the social media sites she had set up in the hope of finding clues to her daughter's whereabouts. But it had been soul-destroying because she had got nowhere despite all her appeals and the scores of leads she'd followed up.

It had almost reached the point where she was forced to accept that she would never see Chloe again. But then everything changed when she received the message from Paul Russell, the ex-forger who was in a hospice dying of cancer.

If you can find the time to come and see me I can tell you what I know about your daughter and her father. And I can apologise for the part I played in what happened ten years ago.

Thanks to him Anna went on to find out that Matthew had died three years ago after returning to the UK. And thanks to him her story was back in the spotlight – first the two-part feature in the *Evening Standard*, and next a true crime documentary on Channel Four.

Anna was once again full of hope that soon she and her beloved daughter would be reunited after a decade apart.

She was about to sit at her computer to check her emails when she heard her name being called. It seemed that Tom had woken up and she suspected it was down to her showering and stomping about in the bedroom.

He was standing at the bottom of the stairs, a confused look on his face.

'You gave me a fright,' he said. 'I thought for a second that someone had broken in while I was sleeping.'

She walked down and straight into his arms.

'I decided not to wake you until after I'd showered and changed,' she said. 'You were out to the world.'

They kissed and she smelt the beer on his breath.

'I didn't think you were coming home,' he said.

'Neither did I, but I won't be staying. I just needed to freshen up. Max is picking me up shortly.'

'It sounds like another big case,' Tom said.

She rolled her eyes. 'You're not kidding. You can either go straight up to bed or I can give you a brief summary over coffee.'

He yawned. 'Coffee it is. But before you tell me something that's bound to give me nightmares I've got a surprise for you.'

The surprise was on the kitchen table and it was wrapped in colourful paper.

'Happy birthday, sweetheart,' Tom said, stifling another yawn. 'I'm so sorry we didn't manage to go out and celebrate.'

She unwrapped it while he put the kettle on. It was a short-break gift voucher from Debenhams entitling them to two nights at a choice of luxury hotels across the country.

'I had a hard time deciding what to get you,' he said. 'Then I remembered you saying that it was about time we had a weekend away.'

'It's lovely,' Anna said. 'I can't wait to look at all the different hotels.'

He picked up an envelope from the worktop and handed it to her. Inside was a birthday card with the words: *To the woman I love.*

During the last few hours Anna had completely forgotten that it was her birthday and she felt the emotion rise up inside her. Tom gave her a cuddle and then poured the coffees.

While they drank she told him about the body on the common and how it had led them to Nathan Wolf, MP. Although Tom was keen to hear the grim details he could barely keep his eyes open.

'I think you need to go to bed,' Anna said. 'I'll fill you in tonight, by which time I'll know a lot more.'

'I apologise, hon,' he said. 'I had a rough day at the office and then made the mistake of stretching out on the sofa.'

She walked up the stairs with him, waited for him to empty his bladder and then pulled the duvet up over him when he was lying down.

'Love you,' he said, his eyes half closed.

'Love you too,' Anna said as she kissed his forehead and slipped out of the room.

She wasn't expecting Walker to turn up for another half hour so she returned to the study. She checked her Facebook and Twitter pages and the FindChloe website. Nothing new had come in, which was disappointing. Then she opened up her personal Hotmail account and noticed that she had received two messages earlier in the evening.

The first was from a guy named Eric Ramsay at Channel Four.

Just want to touch base with you, Detective Tate. I was delighted to hear that you're happy for us to produce a programme on your search for your daughter. I'll be in touch soon and we can set up a meeting.

The second message was from Anthony Liddle, the *Evening Standard* journalist who had interviewed her.

I'm pleased to inform you that the second instalment of the feature that appeared tonight generated some responses. Two people have phoned the special number we put in the paper to say that the age progression image of Chloe that we published reminds them of someone they know or have seen. As you requested I passed on the details to the private investigator who is working on your behalf. FYI it's believed that one lives in Lewisham and the other in Shoreditch. If we hear from anyone else I will let you know.

Suddenly Anna's heart felt fit to burst. Could it really be that one of these people had seen Chloe?

She told herself not to build her hopes up. It seemed far too good to be true. They could have made a genuine mistake or they could be pranksters.

She looked up at the photo on the wall above the desk. The age progression picture that had been computer-generated by a forensic artist. It was supposed to show what Chloe probably looked like now at the age of twelve.

Anna had no idea if it was a true likeness, but she wanted to believe so. And she was glad that Chloe's baby features had been retained – the dimpled chin, button nose, bright blue eyes.

Anna felt the prickle of tears so she stood up, switched off the light and went back downstairs.

As always it was hard not to be distracted by every twist and turn in the search for Chloe. But she knew she had to resist because once again she needed to give her all to the job.

CHAPTER TWENTY

Sophie was having another dream in which she saw herself as she was a decade ago. She was still pretty and vivacious then despite the hell that she'd been through. It was no doubt why James Miller had been attracted to her in the first place.

She'd had the same dream before. It was one of the good ones. A vivid snapshot of those glorious times the three of them spent together on Spain's Costa Calida.

James and Alice and Sophie. A family unit in all but name.

They were on the beach, soaking up the morning sun. It was a month after they had first laid eyes on each other and Sophie already knew that she was in love with both of them. James was so warm and kind and generous, and when she was with him it was like a light was shining on her world.

He didn't pry into her past like she feared he would. He believed the story she told him that she had moved to Spain after divorcing her husband in order to start over.

It was too late by then to tell him the truth. Too risky. She was terrified that, if he knew, it would scare him away.

After a picnic lunch on the beach, James said he wanted to go and view a bar along the coast that was available to rent.

'I made an appointment with the owner of the lease,' he told her. 'But there's no need for all of us to go, and it seems a shame to spoil Alice's fun.'

'Then go by yourself and I'll stay here and take care of her,' Sophie said. 'She'll be fine, and I promise not to lose her.'

His face lit up. 'Are you sure you're OK with that?'

'Of course. It will be my pleasure. She's a little darling and no trouble at all.'

Alice was ignoring them both as she ran around on the sand in her full-body swim suit and sun hat.

James picked up his daughter to give her a kiss and she shrieked in protest. Then he bent down and planted a kiss on Sophie's mouth.

'I won't be long and later I'll treat us all to a nice dinner,' he said.

It was the first time James had left her alone with Alice and the fact that he entrusted her with his most precious possession meant so much. And what a wonderful experience it was. Her first taste of what it would be like to be a mother.

Alice clearly enjoyed it too. She was well behaved, funny, excited. For almost two hours the pair of them played on the sand and bonded. And that was when Sophie realised that at last her luck had changed and that she had a bright future to look forward to after all.

When she woke up her heart was beating rapidly and her face was coated in sweat.

The images from the dream faded the moment she opened her eyes, but they left a warm feeling inside her.

She had replayed that day on the beach a thousand times in her mind because it was the first significant milestone in her relationship with James.

Seven weeks later she moved in with him and three months after that she gave up her job at the restaurant so she could take care of Alice while he got his new bar off the ground.

They were great times, full of joy and laughter, and the best sex she had ever had. And they lasted for seven wonderful years before the past eventually caught up with her and wreaked havoc.

She blamed herself for what happened, and for the fact that James was so brutally murdered when they returned to the UK.

The guilt was something she had struggled to live with, and it had been compounded by her unwavering belief that he'd been a good, honest man, a man with no faults and no secrets, a man who had been forced to make a new life for himself after the tragic death of his wife.

She'd been drawn in by his charm and charisma, and the way he had made her feel so very special. He'd been an easy man to fall in love with, and she had fallen hook, line and sinker.

But now she knew that he had been living a lie. What he had done to his wife was both despicable and unforgivable. Sophie couldn't begin to imagine the pain he had inflicted on her.

If she'd found out the truth during the seven years they were together she would have left him, reported him, told him in no uncertain terms that he deserved to be locked up.

He would have known all along that Anna Tate had continued to search for her daughter. He had probably monitored her online efforts, the appeals, the news stories, the interviews she would have given to the papers.

Sophie wondered if she should have guessed that he wasn't the man she thought he was.

There were clues, after all. The fact that he never wanted to talk about his 'late' wife Anna because he found it too upsetting. The fact that in the few photographs of her with their baby she always had her face turned away from the camera. And those photos of her by herself were taken from a distance so her features were ill-defined.

But Sophie couldn't bring herself to hate James for making her part of his callous deception, for the simple reason that she had lied to him as well.

All the while they were together she had hidden her own wretched secret. It was why she had persuaded him that they didn't need to get married after he proposed to her two years into their relationship.

'Well, if you change your mind and decide you want to tie the knot then just say the word,' he'd told her.

But as much as she wanted to be his wife back then, she'd known that it could never happen so long as she stayed married to someone else.

She was glad it was Saturday and she didn't have to go to work. She was planning to spend the day alone while Alice went to her friend's house. Then on Sunday they were going shopping for a new backpack and winter coat for Alice, ready for the start of the autumn term next week.

The digital clock on the bedside table informed her that

it was only seven a.m. She thought about staying in bed for a while but decided not to as she knew there was no way she was going to fall back to sleep. Too many thoughts and fears were crowding her mind, and there were things she wanted to do.

It wasn't until she pulled back the duvet and sat up that she realised she had slept in her clothes. But at least she didn't have a headache, which was a big relief. However, she was still weighed down by dread and felt emotionally bereft.

She opened the bedroom curtain and looked out on a moody grey day. Dark clouds were amassed above the city and it looked like it might rain for the first time in over a week. Their rented flat was just off a main road and the sound of traffic was loud and constant.

She had a quick shower, ate a bowl of cornflakes in her dressing gown, and then gulped down a mug of black coffee that was so hot it scalded her throat.

She remained seated at the kitchen table and re-read both parts of the Anna Tate story in the *Evening Standard*. It was an act of self-harm but she wasn't able to resist. She just couldn't reconcile the words and pictures with the dream she'd had and with the fragments of memories that were constantly slipping in and out of her mind.

There were references to dates and events that she wanted to find out more about, so she flipped open her laptop and began searching online.

She typed in Anna Tate's name and sure enough, up popped news stories spanning the last ten years. Each headline made Sophie's heart jump.

Husband of London detective abducts their baby

Distraught mother appeals for husband to bring back their daughter

Girl, two, victim of parental abduction

Heartbroken mum steps up search for her stolen child

Police officer sets up Facebook page in desperate bid to find missing daughter

Sophie checked out the FindChloe Facebook page. It had thousands of followers and there were a dozen or so photos of baby Chloe and her father, including an age progression image of each of them. It alarmed Sophie that they were both so accurate.

She then came across various stories relating to Tate's exploits as a police officer. Sophie now remembered that she had seen her on the TV news just a couple of weeks ago after those nine children were kidnapped from a London nursery school.

Detective Tate had fronted a press conference and given several interviews and . . .

A flash of memory took Sophie's breath away suddenly. She pictured herself and Alice on the sofa in the living room. They were idly watching an early evening news bulletin on the BBC when the nursery story grabbed their attention. During it Detective Tate appeared before the cameras and made an emotional appeal to the kidnappers to free the children.

It had prompted Alice to say, 'That's so horrible, Mummy.

I do hope that lady finds them and that they haven't been hurt.'

The flashback made Sophie feel sick. Alice had actually laid eyes on her real mother. The shock of it rammed home to her the awful dilemma she now faced.

Did she bring an end to Anna Tate's ten-year-long nightmare and accept that it would mean losing Alice?

Or did she seek to preserve the life they had and the love they shared by taking steps to avoid being found out?

It was a decision she didn't want to make, but knew she would have to.

CHAPTER TWENTY-ONE

It was a full house for the seven o'clock briefing. There were detectives, civilian support staff, cyber technicians, forensics officers and a couple of reps from the Media Liaison Department whose job it would be to construct a strategy for dealing with the press and TV news operations.

The discovery of a woman's body on Barnes Common dominated online news outlets and had made it onto the front pages of the morning papers.

Now that Holly's name was known the story had really taken off and was dominating the breakfast TV shows, even though she hadn't been formally identified. It was no surprise to Anna, though. Holly was a pretty young model who happened to be the only daughter of Rebecca Blake, distinguished London politician and a former senior officer in the Met Police.

Anna knew that it was only a matter of time before Nathan Wolf, MP, was drawn into it. So far the editor of the *Sunday Mirror* had kept that bombshell connection close to his chest.

Anna had already been in the office for a couple of hours. She was dog-tired but pretty sure that she'd be feeling a whole lot worse if she hadn't popped home for a shower and change of clothes.

She had spent the time preparing for the briefing by typing up summaries of the interviews they had conducted with Rebecca and Theo Blake and Nathan Wolf. She'd also pulled together her notes on what Holly's landlord had told them about Ross Moore.

Anna had kicked off the meeting by reminding everyone how sensitive this case was and issuing a stark warning that she wouldn't tolerate leaks.

'I don't want any of you talking to the media unless you've cleared it with me or the press office,' she said. 'If you're tempted to, then just pause to think through the consequences. If I found out then you'd be looking for other jobs.'

She announced that a search team had moved onto Barnes Common at first light. At the same time officers were pulling in CCTV footage from roads close to the common, plus various other locations including Holly's flat and Nathan Wolf's house.

'At the moment both her ex-boyfriend Ross Moore and Nathan Wolf are in the frame. But Holly's stepfather Theo Blake is also at this early stage a person of interest to us for two reasons. He went looking for Holly after she stormed out of their house and claims he didn't find her so went to the pub. And Wolf alleges that Holly hated Theo because he once tried it on with her.

'It means we already have three potential suspects, although Wolf is at the top of the list given that Holly had set out to destroy him. And we know he threatened her because the neighbour heard him and he's admitted it. However, Ross Moore has to be close second since the landlord thinks he saw him loitering outside Holly's building on Tuesday evening. I gather we're still trying to find out his current address.'

Anna was standing between two whiteboards. One contained photographs of Holly and the crime scene. On the other were photos of Nathan Wolf and a large map with black markers indicating Barnes Common, Holly's flat in Camden, her mother's home in Pimlico and Wolf's house in Kensington.

Anna ran through what they'd learned about Holly's movements from her parents and landlord. She then referred to the briefing note she had circulated on the interview with Wolf.

'Wolf claims he spent Tuesday in Somerset and then drove back to London in the evening, arriving home about midnight,' she said. 'It means he doesn't really have a foolproof alibi, assuming Holly was killed that evening. So we need to trawl as many CCTV and ANPR cameras as we can. He reckons traffic was heavy on the M4 so start there.'

Anna invited the team to provide her with updates. First up was one of the techies from the cyber unit who said they had managed to gain access to the laptop and tablet found in Holly's flat. They had started to sift through the documents and history, along with her social media accounts.

DS Prescott said he was going through the personal belongings taken from the flat. Bank statements confirmed that she'd been receiving a monthly payment from Nathan Wolf of £2500 – enough to cover the rent and leave her with a thousand pounds to spend on other things.

'Her income from modelling wasn't regular,' Prescott said. 'Without Wolf's money she would have struggled to get by. She had no savings, but expensive taste in clothes and champagne.'

'No wonder she was prepared to let him rough her up,' someone said.

But Walker shook his head. 'I got the impression that for most of the time it was the other way round. He likes to be the submissive and enjoys being spanked and poked and humiliated. And you can bet that's what Holly was going to say to the *Mirror*.'

Anna told the team that a post-mortem would be performed on the body later in the morning.

'The pathologist will get to work after her mother has formally identified her,' she said. 'I've just made the arrangement with the FLO who's with Rebecca Blake. Max and I will be going to her house after this to ask a few more questions and then we'll take her and her husband to the mortuary.'

Anna paused the meeting to take a call from the Commissioner, who had decided to bypass DCS Nash.

'I thought you ought to know that the Home Secretary has been on the blower to me,' he said. 'Nathan Wolf woke him by phone in the early hours.'

'I suspected he might, sir,' Anna said. 'He told me they were pals.'

'Well, I'll be surprised if that friendship lasts beyond today. Wolf confessed to his affair with Holly Blake and tried to play it down. However, he told the Home Sec to expect some nasty stuff to come out in the papers. But he emphatically denied killing her.'

'Well, that's hardly a surprise, sir.'

'DCS Nash told me about the threat he made and about the kinky stuff you found in the girl's flat. Do you think he's guilty?'

'There's a good chance he is, sir, but we haven't got enough to bring charges. We're still checking his alibi. He had a strong motive, though. Holly had made it clear that she wanted to ruin him because he'd ended their relationship.'

'I think she might have succeeded in that respect,' the Commissioner said. 'The Government, and by extension his party, will want to distance themselves from this. And the Opposition will try to turn it into a full-blown scandal, which, from what I already know, won't be difficult.'

'Did he say anything else to the Home Secretary?' Anna asked.

'He did make a point of saying that he's going to lodge a formal complaint against you. He claims you turned up at his house to break the news about Holly and then proceeded to accuse him of murder. When he told you he had nothing to do with it you threatened to take him into custody. He described your actions as aggressive and unprofessional.'

'I can assure you that we didn't—'

'Save it, Detective Tate. I don't for a second believe that there's any substance to his allegations. He's just trying to salvage some dignity whilst putting building blocks in place for his defence.'

'I've applied for a warrant to search his homes here and in Somerset,' Anna said. 'Will there be a problem with that?'

'There shouldn't be in view of the salacious revelations about his private life. I'll see if I can fast-track it.'

'Thank you, sir.'

'Meanwhile, keep me informed. And be circumspect about

what you release to the media. I don't want Rebecca Blake to suffer any more than she is.'

Anna resumed the briefing, which lasted for another thirty minutes. She was about to wrap it up when she was told that the editor of the *Sunday Mirror* had sent over the audio recording of part of the initial conversation the paper had with Holly Blake.

The recording arrived on a flash drive that Anna plugged into one of the computers, and the whole team gathered round to listen to it.

In a note that came with it the *Sunday Mirror* editor explained that they hadn't recorded the whole conversation, only a short Q and A session that was forwarded to the paper's lawyers in order to alert them to what was to come.

The person asking the questions identified himself as feature writer Dan Resnick, and he began by asking Holly to provide her full name and address for the tape.

She spoke in a low, clear voice that made her words sound as though they had been rehearsed.

Resnick: 'Thank you, Holly. Now can you briefly explain why you are here today?'

Holly: 'I have a story to tell about the MP Nathan Wolf and I want you to publish it.'

Resnick: 'What is your relationship to Mr Wolf?'

Holly: 'We've been having sex on a regular basis for the past year or so and it began when his wife was alive. It took place at my flat, which he pays for.'

Resnick: 'Is it conventional sex that you have?'

Holly: 'No. He prefers S and M and he likes to be slapped and beaten. He also enjoys hurting me and has even gone to the trouble of creating a torture chamber in my flat.'

Resnick: 'Can you prove that you're not making this up?'

Holly: 'Of course. I can provide documents and text messages. And I have photographs of the torture room.'

Resnick: 'So why are you doing this, Holly? You must know it will embarrass Mr Wolf and impact on his career as a politician.'

Holly: 'Because the bastard led me to believe that he loved me. I know now that he just used me and has entered into a relationship with another woman who knows nothing about me. He offered me money to go quietly, which shows what a scumbag he is.'

Resnick: 'Thank you, Holly. We will now make arrangements to do a full interview and carry this forward.'

CHAPTER TWENTY-TWO

The vultures had already started to gather outside Rebecca Blake's mews house in Pimlico. There were five photographers, three reporters and a TV news crew from the BBC.

Anna was pleased to see two uniformed officers standing either side of the front door. But their presence was unlikely to stop the hacks and snappers from making a nuisance of themselves.

Anna and Walker pushed through the media scrum, ignoring the questions that were thrown at them. They flashed their IDs at the uniforms and rang the bell.

A man Anna didn't recognise answered the door. He was forty-odd with cropped, iron-grey hair and a muscular frame beneath a checked shirt that was tucked into his trousers.

After Anna introduced herself, he told her his name was Robert Gregory.

'I'm Rebecca's brother-in-law,' he said. 'My wife Freya and I came over last night. This is so shocking. I can't believe it's happened. Have you arrested that bastard Nathan Wolf?'

'We have spoken to him, Mr Gregory, but right now we'd like to come in and speak to Rebecca and her husband. And as you probably know we've made arrangements to take them to the mortuary for a formal identification.'

'They're both smoking in the back garden with Freya and the Family Liaison Officer,' he said, stepping aside. 'Rebecca is in a terrible state. She's told us what Holly said about Wolf. He's obviously the one who did it to her.'

'Well, that's still to be determined, sir,' Anna said. 'But please be assured we're doing all we can to find out exactly what happened.'

Before he could respond, Anna walked past him and strode along the hall to the living room. From there she saw the group gathered outside on the patio.

Rebecca and Theo were sitting on a rattan sofa and another woman she assumed was Freya Gregory was sitting opposite them on a matching chair. She was short and plump with straight blonde hair. She was wearing jeans and a tight yellow top, and she bore little resemblance to her sister. She'd clearly been crying and dark shadows hung beneath her eyes.

Standing to one side of them was the familiar figure of Sue Bond, the FLO, whom Anna knew quite well. She appeared to be the only one not smoking.

Robert crossed the room, pulled open the patio door, and said, 'Detective Tate and her colleague have arrived.'

The three smokers stood up, outed their fags in an ashtray on the table and stepped inside.

Officer Bond followed them and Anna acknowledged her with a nod, pleased that someone with so much experience had been assigned to the couple.

Rebecca looked dreadful. She wasn't wearing any make-up, and the skin around her eyes was red and puffy. She clutched a hanky in one hand and held onto her husband's arm with the other.

As the couple sat down, Officer Bond gestured towards the blonde woman who remained standing and explained to Anna that Freya was Rebecca's sister.

'Hello, Mrs Gregory,' Anna said. 'I'm sorry we're having to meet in these circumstances.'

'I was Holly's only aunt,' Freya said, her voice low and quivering. 'I loved that girl and I can't imagine never seeing her again. None of us can.'

Her husband put his arm around her but kept his eyes on Anna.

'What I don't understand is why that bastard Nathan Wolf hasn't been arrested yet,' he said. 'What the hell are you lot waiting for? The man's obviously guilty.'

'It's not as simple as that, Mr Gregory,' she replied. 'As I explained to you outside we have spoken to him but he strenuously denies killing your niece. He's provided us with an alibi and we're in the process of checking it out. It's one of several lines of enquiry.'

He was about to say something else but Rebecca got there first.

'I want you to tell us what he said to you, Detective Tate. And don't you dare feed me the line that it's something you can't discuss because the investigation is ongoing.'

Anna sat down in a chair, took out her notebook and rested it on her knee.

'It's only fair to warn you that what you are about to hear will in no way ease your suffering,' she said. 'But you need to hear it because certain things will appear in the papers in the days ahead that will make for uncomfortable reading.'

'Just get on with it,' Theo said. 'Nothing could be worse than what's already happened to our daughter.'

Anna began by telling them what they had discovered in Holly's flat, including a description of the S and M playroom. They all reacted with total shock, and Theo said that Holly hadn't mentioned any of that when she'd spoken to them about her relationship with Wolf.

'Your daughter told the *Sunday Mirror* about it,' Anna said. 'They have her on tape making it clear that she was determined not to hold anything back.'

Theo shook his head. 'I can't imagine Holly doing that stuff. Wolf must have forced her into it. There can be no other explanation.'

Rebecca just stared into the middle distance, as though in a trance, while the tears boiled over in her sister's eyes.

Anna went on to say that Wolf had also been trying to contact Holly, but she stopped short of revealing the heated conversation between the pair that was overheard by the neighbour.

'He claims he was in his Somerset constituency during the day on Tuesday,' Anna said. 'In the evening he drove back home.'

'So how do you know he didn't drop in on Holly or meet her somewhere?' Robert shouted.

'We're looking into it, Mr Gregory. What we do know for certain is that after Holly left here she did indeed go home, but it took her an hour and a half to get there and she arrived about ten-thirty.'

'Well, that explains why I missed her,' Theo said. 'I got to her flat at ten and left at quarter past.'

Anna nodded, but she still wasn't entirely convinced he was telling the truth.

'Her landlord saw her go out again just before eleven,' she said. 'He told us he watched her walk off along the street. She was alone but he didn't know where she was going.'

Again, Anna decided it was best not to disclose the fact that the landlord thought he'd spotted the ex-boyfriend in the street earlier in the evening.

'So how do you know she didn't go straight to Wolf's house?' Robert said. 'Or that she didn't get into his car where he killed her?'

'We'll be exploring every possible scenario,' Anna said. 'And we'll be talking to everyone who had links with Holly. That includes her friends, colleagues in the modelling world and, of course, her ex-boyfriend.'

'But that's a waste of time,' Robert said. 'Nobody else would have had a motive for killing Holly. Wolf is the only one who felt threatened by her.'

'Robert's right,' Theo said. 'Nathan Wolf only cares about one person and that's himself. Holly was going to expose him for what he is – a no good, cheating pervert.'

Anna made a show of looking at her watch and said as delicately as she could that it was time to leave for the mortuary.

Rebecca responded by getting quickly to her feet and pushing her hair away from her face.

'I'm ready,' she said, her voice strong. 'Take me to see my baby. I need to tell her for the last time how much I love her.'

CHAPTER TWENTY-THREE

Walker left the house first in order to bring the pool car up close to the front door. Anna didn't want Rebecca and Theo to run the gauntlet of reporters and photographers.

She managed to get them into the car in under ten seconds, but that was time enough for some stupid and insensitive questions to be hurled at them.

'What's your reaction to your daughter's death, Mrs Blake?'

'Will this make you more determined to become London's Mayor so that you can crack down on crime in the capital?'

'When did you last see Holly, Mr Blake?'

'Is it true that your daughter approached a Sunday newspaper about selling her story?'

Both Rebecca and Theo kept their heads down until they were in the back seat and the car was moving away from the crowd.

Sue Bond followed in her own car. The plan was for her to take the couple home afterwards where Rebecca's sister and brother-in-law would be waiting for them.

Anna's intention was to make the most of the short journey to the mortuary. There were two subjects she had chosen not to broach back at the house. Now, turning in her seat to face Rebecca, she raised the first one.

'Assuming that Nathan Wolf is telling the truth then we have to consider the possibility that Holly was targeted by someone who has a grudge against you, Mrs Blake,' she said. 'You're an outspoken politician and a former high-ranking police officer. I'm sure there are people out there who don't want you to become the Mayor of London, in part because of your commitment to get tough on crime.'

Anna was braced for an angry rebuke which didn't come. Instead, Rebecca looked at her and said, 'I suppose that is possible in the highly unlikely event that Wolf is innocent.'

'Have you yourself received any threats recently either directly or through social media?' Anna asked.

'Like all public figures I get my share of generic online threats and abuse,' Rebecca said. 'Some of it is vicious and sickening, and some downright childish. Holly was also targeted by jealous trolls on a regular basis, but unlike me she found it more difficult to ignore them. Sometimes she lost her temper and got into an online spat. At other times it would bring on a bout of depression.'

'We're examining all her online accounts,' Anna said. 'But

it would be helpful if we could also take a look at yours, Mrs Blake.'

Rebecca nodded. 'My secretary takes care of all that. I'll give you her number. She's been instructed to keep a file of all messages, tweets and posts that are abusive and hostile.'

'Thank you so much,' Anna said. Then she craned her neck further so she could see Theo. 'There's one other issue I'd like to raise quickly. It concerns something else that Nathan Wolf said during the course of our interview.'

She paused to consider how best to frame the question. Then: 'He claimed that you and Holly had a problem that dated back several years, Mr Blake. Is that true?'

Theo's jaw muscles flexed and a flicker of irritation crossed his face.

'It wasn't a problem,' he said. 'She blamed me for the break-up of Rebecca's marriage and the fact that her father moved to Australia. That's not an untypical reaction in a situation such as ours.'

'Holly told Wolf there was more to it than that. He said Holly hated you because you once tried it on with her.'

It was Rebecca who responded this time, her face suffused with anger.

'Stop it right there, Detective Tate. I will not have you insinuating that my husband is somehow implicated in his own daughter's murder.'

'But I'm not—'

'Yes, you are,' Rebecca snapped. 'So do not insult my intelligence by pretending you aren't. As an ex-police officer I can appreciate that you have to ask difficult questions. But as the grieving mother of the victim I feel obliged to put you straight before you cause more upset with this particular line of enquiry.'

She paused to take a breath and grab her husband's hand.

'Holly found it hard to forgive both of us for the affair we had,' she went on. 'And it got worse after her father moved to Australia following the divorce and killed himself with an overdose of sleeping pills. Theo took the brunt of her anger and once when he tried to give her an innocent kiss she deliberately chose to misread it and make a stupid accusation. For a while my relationship with her was really stressed, but gradually she got over it and after she moved out things got much better between us.

'It's no doubt true that she did hate us both at one time, but that changed in recent years. Holly was fully supportive of my efforts to become London's Mayor. She's been helping me campaign and only a few months ago she told me that she was happier than she had ever been.

'But I didn't know that her happiness was based on the delusional belief that what she had with Nathan Wolf was real and that they had a future together. In truth the bastard was playing her along and she . . . she . . .'

Rebecca lost it then and fresh tears filled her eyes.

Theo pulled her into his chest and fixed Anna with a hard stare.

'Are you happy now?' he seethed, his voice a low growl.

Anna cursed herself for misjudging the moment. She turned back to the front and did not speak again until they reached the mortuary.

When the sheet was pulled back by the pathologist's assistant, it took Rebecca only seconds to confirm that it was her daughter.

The grief engulfed her with such force that she screamed like a banshee and dropped to her knees on the floor, her face in her hands.

She refused to move for over a minute, telling her husband that she wanted to remain at Holly's side.

Eventually he persuaded her to get up and escorted her out of the room to where Anna was waiting, having witnessed their ordeal through the window.

'I realise how hard that was for you,' Anna said. 'Please allow me to once again offer my condolences.'

'All we want from you is justice, detective,' Rebecca said as tears spilled from her eyes. 'Make Nathan Wolf pay for killing my daughter and destroying all of our lives. If you're not able to do that then I'll get the Commissioner to replace you with someone who is.'

Rebecca's words echoed in Anna's mind as the couple left the building accompanied by Officer Bond.

'Don't let it get to you, guv,' Walker said. 'That was grief talking.'

'I know that, Max,' she said. 'And I'm sure I'd be saying something similar if I were in that poor woman's shoes.'

Anna decided to stay at the mortuary while pathologist Gayle Western carried out the post-mortem.

'You go back to the office,' she told Walker. 'I'll follow on as soon as we've got some preliminary results. And set things up for a mid-day briefing. Find out if we've managed to trace the ex-boyfriend and if the search teams have found anything on the common. And I want to know if Holly's laptop and phone have yielded anything of interest.'

'Do you want me to leave the car for you?' Walker asked.

'I'm not a safe driver when I've had no sleep so I'll get a taxi from here.'

Anna nodded. 'Good idea. I shouldn't be long.' She glanced at her watch. 'Gayle works fast and she's starting straight away. It'll probably only take her a couple of hours.'

There was nothing more stomach-churning than witnessing an autopsy and Anna tried to avoid them whenever possible. But she was desperate to know if Holly Blake's body was going to offer any clues to who killed her. She had seen so many cases where investigative theories were debunked by a tiny mark on the victim's flesh or a DNA trace beneath the fingernails.

She donned a gown and smeared some Vick's VapoRub under her nose even though it was seldom enough to stop the smell from making her want to throw up.

She stood back from the dissection table and took notes as Gayle provided a running commentary.

'I've already determined that there are no defence wounds on her arms and legs,' Gayle said. 'And there's nothing but dirt under her nails. The only external wound is the one to her throat and I'm certain that is what killed her.'

Anna looked away as Holly's torso was sliced down the middle and clamps were fitted so that her organs remained exposed. During the next thirty minutes Gayle carefully removed pieces of Holly's insides.

'On the face of it all her organs appear to be in working order,' she said. 'She was well nourished and in her stomach there are the contents of a light meal.'

Gayle confirmed her earlier assumption regarding time of death.

'The knife used on her has a serrated edge and is probably between six and ten inches long. It's the type you'll find in virtually every kitchen in the country. It pierced the trachea and internal carotid artery and there would have been extreme blood loss,' she said. 'But there wasn't much blood at the scene, which tells us that she wasn't murdered there.'

Anna was disappointed because there was nothing new or unexpected in what she was being told.

'I'll get the results of the toxicology tests to you as quickly as possible,' Gayle said. 'But don't expect it to contain anything startling. Meanwhile I think it's safe to assume that Holly Blake's killer did not leave any clues on her body that might lead to him or her being easily identified. There are no marks to indicate rape or sexual assault and no trace of semen inside her.'

Anna thanked Gayle and walked out of the autopsy suite feeling despondent. She removed the gown and went outside on the forecourt to have a smoke. While there her phone rang.

'It's me, guv,' Walker said when she answered. 'A report has just come in that I think you'll want to respond to yourself.'

'What is it?'

'Nathan Wolf has been attacked in his home. It was his girlfriend who phoned the three nines.'

'Shit. Is he seriously hurt?'

'I don't know yet. Uniform have only just arrived at the house.'

'So what about the attacker? Do we know who did it?'

'We sure do. It was none other than Holly's angry uncle, Robert Gregory.'

CHAPTER TWENTY-FOUR

Sophie woke Alice at eight with a cup of tea and a bowl of cereal.

'Get that down you and then go and have a shower,' she told her. 'I'll make your bed and take you to Ruth's house.'

Alice's friend Ruth lived less than a mile away and they often spent time in each other's homes.

On the way there Sophie continued to act as though nothing was wrong. She bought Alice some sweets and told her she would pick her up at about four, a time that had been agreed with Ruth's mum.

When she returned to the flat she found it hard to relax and even harder to concentrate.

She wanted to pull her thoughts together and work out a response to the threat she now faced. But her mind was all over the place and it was making her head ache again.

She decided to tidy up Alice's room, which had a view of the small communal garden at the rear of the three-storey block.

Pictures of pop stars were plastered across the walls,

including Taylor Swift, Ariana Grande, Justin Bieber and Selena Gomez. Alice loved her music and was always saying that when she grew up she wanted to be a singer or musician. In one corner of the room stood the kids' karaoke microphone on its adjustable stand that Sophie had bought her last Christmas. On one of the shelves sat the electric keyboard that had given Alice so much joy this past year.

After making the bed, Sophie couldn't resist opening the drawer where Alice kept all her personal bits. These included her father's reading glasses, his 'fake' passport, his favourite mug with the Chelsea Football Club emblem on it, and the DVD with the compilation of video clips from their time in Spain.

There was also the photo album that was Alice's pride and joy.

Sophie took it out and sat on the bed to look through it, something she hadn't done in quite a while.

The first few pages contained photos from before Alice and her dad arrived in Spain, but only two of them featured her real mother, who Alice had believed had died.

There were lots of pictures after that because Sophie had made a point of capturing as many precious moments as she possibly could. And she had gone to the trouble of printing them off just in case the digital versions ever got lost.

It was a journey down memory lane for Sophie, and every turn of the page caused her heart to leap.

There was Alice paddling in the sea at two, surrounded by unopened presents on her third birthday, sitting on her father's shoulders during a walk along the beach, pulling a face at the camera while standing outside the bar James opened in Puerto de Mazarron.

Sophie felt her heart go into meltdown as the images took her back to the events that had shaped Alice's young life. The Christmas when Santa brought her a bike, her first day at the English-speaking school, the time spent in hospital after having her appendix removed.

One of Sophie's favourite photos showed Alice sitting on the floor with her face smeared with chocolate. It was special because it was then that she referred to Sophie as 'Mummy' for the first time. James heard it too and that was when he asked her if she would be his daughter's adoptive mother. She told him it would make her the happiest woman in the world.

But now Sophie couldn't help feeling sorry for Detective Anna Tate. The woman had missed so much because of what James did to her.

But it wasn't my fault, she told herself. *I had no idea that the man whose child I helped bring up had lied to me.*

Many more precious memories were recorded in the album, but only up to three years ago, when they left Spain and fled to England.

Sophie's vision blurred as she studied the last photo on the last page. It showed a nine-year-old Alice eating an ice-cream with the marina in the background. It was taken just minutes before Sophie realised that the pair of them were being followed.

As Sophie studied the photo, her mind spiralled back to that day. The day her idyllic life came to an abrupt end.

Three years ago

Sophie has just picked Alice up from school and they're walking to James's bar.

For the past six and a half years they've been living in the apartment above it and they've all really enjoyed it. But the building and those around it will soon be pulled down to make way for a new seafront development. So this evening they're going to discuss where to go next and James has already got his eye on a bar up the coast in Alicante where he's confident they can make a real success of things.

It's hot and humid and Alice is having to devour the ice-cream as quickly as she can before it melts. But some of it has already dropped onto her blouse and it's such a funny sight that Sophie can't resist taking a picture.

Alice responds by rolling her eyes.

'I've told you before, Mum. Only take nice pictures.'

Sophie laughs and hands her a hanky to wipe herself.

'Come on, sweetheart,' she says. 'Let's get a move on. I'm gasping for a drink.'

For no particular reason she looks back along the promenade – and that's when she sees him. He's about fifty yards away and he's wearing a loose vest top and jeans. And he's looking right at her.

At first she thinks she's mistaken because she had long ago convinced herself that she would never see him again.

But then he grins and she knows that it's him.

Against huge odds he's managed to keep the promise he made the last time she saw him.

'You can run and hide, bitch, but wherever you go I'll find you eventually. And so help me, I'm going to make you suffer big time for what you did.'

The flashback was cut short by the strident ringtone of Sophie's mobile. And it came as a relief because she was in no mood to relive what else happened that day – the day her world fell apart and the truth came out.

'Hello,' she said into her phone without checking who was calling.

'It's me, Sophie, Lisa.'

Her first thought was that her friend had read the two features in the *Evening Standard* and that was why she was ringing.

Lisa had never met James or Alice, but Sophie had told her all about them. Lisa was the only person from her past life in London she had stayed in touch with while in Spain, and that was only by phone and email.

It was Lisa whom Sophie had called on for help three years ago when she found herself alone with Alice in a city that she was no longer familiar with.

'Are you there, Soph?' Lisa was saying. 'Can you hear me?'

'Oh, yes, sorry,' Sophie responded. 'I was trying to do two things at once.'

'That's OK. How are you?'

'I'm fine, thanks. It must be a couple of weeks since we last had a chat. What about you?'

Lisa hesitated, and Sophie heard her draw breath.

'Is everything all right?' Sophie asked.

Here it comes, she thought. She's seen the Anna Tate story and she wants to know what I'm going to do about it.

'I went to a funeral two days ago,' Lisa said, and Sophie was thrown. 'Do you remember Jonas Peel from the old days?'

'Of course. Didn't he marry Janet Brookmyre?'

'That's right. Well, it was Janet who invited me to Jonas's funeral, along with a few other people we used to knock around with.'

'I can't believe Jonas is dead,' Sophie said. 'He must have been in his early forties, like us.'

'He was. He died within weeks of being diagnosed with a brain tumour.'

'That's awful.'

'I know. It was really sad. But, look, one of the other guests at the funeral was Michael Taylor. Do you recall him?'

'How could I forget? He was Bruno's best mate.'

'Exactly. Well, he asked me if I was still in touch with you and I said I hadn't heard from you in years. He then told me that was just as well because Bruno was still looking for you, and was still going back and forth between Spain and the UK.'

Sophie felt a shiver skitter down her spine.

'Do you think he believed you?'

'I'm not sure.'

'Why not?'

'Well, after the service there was a wake in a nearby pub. I went along and so did Taylor, and he didn't stop talking about you and saying that Bruno was never going to forgive you for what you did to him.'

'And did he mention what happened three years ago in Southampton?'

'No, he didn't, and I'm guessing he probably doesn't know about that. I certainly didn't tell him.'

'I don't understand why you haven't told me about this before now if the funeral was two days ago,' Sophie said.

'I couldn't. Someone stole my phone from my bag while I was at the wake. I got a bit tipsy there so I didn't realise until the following morning.'

'So have you got a new phone now?'

'I've just been to pick one up, but that's not important. The thing is, I'm sure it must have been Taylor who pinched the old one. My bag was between us on the bench in the pub for part of the time we were talking and like an idiot I left it there while I went to the loo.'

'So why not go to the police?'

'There's no point. I can't prove it and anyway it's not the phone I'm worried about. It's the fact that your number is on my contacts list along with your name. And I can't help thinking that Taylor took it to find out if I'd told him the truth about you.'

'Fucking hell, Lisa.'

'I know, it's the pits, Soph.'

'You're not bloody kidding. I need to change my number.'

'But don't you see? It might already be too late. If Taylor passed it on to his old pal Bruno then there's a chance he got someone to trace your mobile signal for him. In which case he might well know where you are.'

Sophie thought back to the day before when she sensed she was being followed.

'I'm really sorry, Soph,' Lisa said. 'I know I might be scaring you for no good reason. Someone else could have swiped the phone. But I thought you should know, just in case . . .'

Sophie had heard enough. She severed the connection and sat there with her eyes closed as the blood drained from her face.

CHAPTER TWENTY-FIVE

Just before Anna arrived at Nathan Wolf's house, Walker phoned her with an update. The MP had been punched twice in the face, apparently, but wasn't seriously hurt.

'Robert Gregory scarpered before uniform got there,' Walker said. 'An alert has gone out for him and I've requested that when he's collared he's brought straight to Wandsworth so that we can grill him.'

'Good thinking, Max.'

'And just so you know, guv, the Yard's Protection Command has sent a two-man unit to the house. And their boss had a spat over the phone with Nash because he said they should have been informed that an MP was a suspect in a murder investigation.'

'I don't see what it's got to do with them.'

'Well, they reckon it increased the threat level against him and, although it pains me to say it, they've been proved right.'

Anna conceded the point and asked Walker if there

was any news on the search warrant for Wolf's house and whether they were able to seize his car.

'It's all just been signed off,' Walker said. 'But Nash doesn't want us to move on it until he's heard back from the Commissioner, who's locked in a meeting with the Home Secretary. I assume they're discussing damage limitation.'

The clouds over London had thickened by the time Anna got to Wolf's house and the air felt close and moist. A marked patrol car was parked outside on the road and directly behind it was a black BMW with two men inside. Anna found a space against the kerb about twenty yards further on. As she walked back along the pavement she wasn't surprised when one of the men got out of the BMW. He introduced himself as Paul Childs, an officer with the Protection Command. He was a tall man in a suit, with a flat, square face and a neck like a tree trunk.

He showed her his ID and said, 'You must be DCI Tate. We were told to expect you.'

They shook hands and Anna asked him what was going on.

'Uniform are inside taking a statement from Wolf and his girlfriend,' he said. 'But he basically told us to clear off because he doesn't feel threatened. We're waiting here for further instructions.'

'Is he OK?'

'He's got a black eye and a sore nose but it's not stopping him from acting like an arrogant tosser.'

Anna smiled. 'I take it you know he's one of the suspects in the murder of the girl found on Barnes Common yesterday evening.'

'We do now. I'm surprised this place isn't crawling with press people.'

'That's because it's not public knowledge yet. But it soon will be.'

'Well, good luck, detective,' Childs said. 'Sounds to me like the kind of case where you'll need bucket loads of it.'

A uniformed officer answered the front door when Anna rang the bell. She showed her ID and he told her they were just wrapping up.

'Mr Wolf is in the living room with his partner,' the officer said.

The couple were sitting apart on different sofas and the other uniformed officer was standing between them, notebook in hand. When Wolf saw Anna, he let out a heavy sigh. 'Well, if it isn't Detective Tate. Does this mean I can expect a visit from just about every division in the Met?'

Anna chose to ignore the sarcasm. 'I came as soon as I heard. How are you, Mr Wolf?'

'How do you think? I've been attacked in my own home and accused of being a murderer.'

His voice trembled as he spoke, and phlegm rattled in the back of his throat.

Anna had to admit that he did look a shadow of his former self. His face was sallow and unshaven, and there was a large dark bruise beneath his left eye.

She turned her attention to his girlfriend, who sat with her hands clasped together on her lap. Her eyes were heavy and red from where she had obviously been crying. Despite that, she was still a striking-looking woman, Anna thought, smartly dressed in a grey suit and blouse and with locks of vibrant red hair.

'You must be Jennifer Rothwell,' Anna said.

She looked at Anna through narrowed eyes and nodded.

'It was me who called the police. The door was open when I arrived and I saw that man attacking Nathan.'

Anna turned back to Wolf. 'So what happened exactly?'

He shook his head. 'I've just been through it all with these officers. And with those other two who just left.'

'And you're sure it was Rebecca Blake's brother-in-law Robert Gregory who attacked you?'

'Well, that's who he told me he was when he turned up on the doorstep. He said he wanted to talk to me about Holly and that if I didn't let him in he would knock on every door in the street and tell whoever answered what I had done to her.'

'So why did you let him in?' Anna said.

'Like a fool I thought I'd be able to persuade him to go away, but the first thing he did was punch me in the face. Then he pushed me into the kitchen and hit me again. He kept yelling at me to admit I'd killed Holly. I told him I had nothing to do with it and he called me a liar.'

'So was it a coincidence that Miss Rothwell turned up when she did?'

'I'd earlier asked her to come over so that I could tell her what was happening. The door had been left open so she came right in. That's when Gregory stormed out, but not before warning me that if the police didn't put me away he'd be back. Jennifer called you lot straight away.'

Anna asked Wolf if he intended to press charges.

'Damn right I do. That man was like a crazed animal. He just wouldn't listen to me when I said I didn't kill his niece. So I want him punished.'

Anna asked the officers if they had got all they needed. When they said they had she told them they could go.

When they'd left the room, Wolf said, 'So why aren't you going with them, Detective Tate? I've already told you I'm not going to answer any more questions in relation to Holly Blake without my lawyer being present. And you ought to know that I've told the Commissioner how you treated me last night and I've also made an official complaint.'

'I am aware of that, Mr Wolf,' Anna said. 'But I thought that since Miss Rothwell is here I might as well speak to her now rather than later.'

He shook his head again. 'Well, I don't think that's appropriate in view of what's just happened. She still—'

'It's all right, Nathan,' Jennifer said. 'I can speak for myself and I would rather get this over with.'

Anna went and sat next to her on the sofa, while Wolf stood up and left the room, clearly angry with everyone but himself.

'My first question is, do you know why Robert Gregory came here today, Miss Rothwell?' Anna asked.

She held Anna's gaze. 'Yes, I do. Nathan hasn't had time to tell me everything. But I do know he's been having an affair with a young woman who was murdered. You think he did it because he ended their relationship and she was going to sell her story to a Sunday tabloid.

'But for what it's worth I believe him when he says he didn't do it. I realise now that he's a lying, cheating bastard, but I know he's not a murderer. And for your information I haven't yet decided whether to stick by him.'

Anna at once warmed to Jennifer Rothwell. Even though she'd been rattled to the core she was putting on a brave face. She seemed a decent, pragmatic woman who was far too good for the likes of this shameless politician.

'I feel I should point out that we haven't actually accused Mr Wolf of killing Holly Blake,' Anna said. 'But he's been questioned for obvious reasons and will be questioned again.'

'I don't see how he can argue with that in the circumstances. After all, he's got himself into this mess.'

'Mr Wolf has told us that you spent the weekend with him in Devon and you came back by train on Tuesday morning. Is that correct, Miss Rothwell?'

'It is. I was in the office by eleven.'

'And did you hear from Mr Wolf again that day?'

'We talked on the phone just before he left Bridgewater to drive back to London. That must have been about nine.'

'And how did you yourself spend that evening, Miss Rothwell?'

The muscles around her eyes tightened.

'So am I a suspect as well now?'

'Not at all, but it's a question I have to ask because of your relationship with Mr Wolf.'

Jennifer shrugged. 'After I got in I unpacked, showered and went straight to bed. I didn't go out again until the following morning when I went to work.'

Anna closed her notebook. 'I think that's all for now, Miss Rothwell. I appreciate your cooperation.'

Jennifer clenched her eyes shut then started to sob. At that moment Wolf came back into the room.

'Nice work, detective,' he snarled. 'I heard what you said to her and it's fucking out of order. Jennifer didn't know that Holly even existed until just now. So she shouldn't have to provide a bloody alibi.'

'Calm down, Mr Wolf,' Anna said. 'You really need to get

a handle on that temper of yours. If you're not careful it will get you into trouble.'

He glowered at her. 'Are you trying to be funny?'

Anna shook her head. 'Not at all. Just making a point.'

'Well, that's not your job, is it? Your job is to find out who killed Holly, so I suggest you leave us alone and go and do it.'

Anna decided not to wind him up still further by telling him that she would soon be back with a warrant to search the house.

Instead she said a polite farewell to Jennifer and showed herself out. When she got back to the pool car she phoned Walker, who had an update for her.

'The full story is now out there, guv,' he said. 'The press office is receiving calls from reporters asking if it's true that Conservative MP Nathan Wolf is a suspect in the Holly Blake murder investigation.'

CHAPTER TWENTY-SIX

Anna was feeling flushed and light-headed when she got back to headquarters. She needed a blast of caffeine and something to stop her stomach from rumbling like a cement mixer. The ground-floor vending machine offered a large black coffee and a cheese and pickle sandwich, which she began digging into whilst climbing the stairs.

The office was throbbing with activity, and much of it was concentrated around the three TV monitors on the walls. What had the attention of her team was a BBC lunch-time news report on the Holly Blake murder. Anna watched as a male reporter in a suit did a piece to camera from near where the body was found on Barnes Common. Behind him officers were searching the undergrowth under a depressingly grey sky.

'The body has now been positively identified as that of twenty-three-year-old model Holly Blake,' he was saying. 'She was stabbed in the throat and according to an unconfirmed report she was naked when a woman walking her dog discovered the body. Police are working on the theory that the murder took place on Tuesday at a different location and her body was then left here on the common.'

A photo of Holly appeared in which she was standing next to her mother outside the Houses of Parliament in London. The reporter's commentary continued over it.

'Holly was the daughter of well-known politician Rebecca Blake, who is the leader of Westminster Council and the Conservative candidate in the forthcoming London Mayoral elections.'

Another shot change to a video clip of Rebecca and Theo leaving their house this morning to go to the mortuary.

'Mrs Blake and her husband Theo, a prominent lawyer, are said to be devastated. They apparently hadn't seen their daughter for several days and had not been able to contact her.'

The reporter referred to Rebecca's career in the Metropolitan Police and how she rose through the ranks to become an Assistant Commissioner before retiring to enter the political arena. There were photos of her in uniform and one of her shaking hands with the then Prime Minister.

'There is a tragic irony in what has happened to Mrs Blake's daughter,' the reporter said. 'In her bid to become Mayor she has promised that if elected she would launch a major crackdown on crime in the capital, in particular knife crime, which she's described as an insidious epidemic.'

The emphasis switched back to Holly, and he talked over a series of modelling photos of her, most of them taken from her Facebook page. There were a couple of sound bites from people who knew her, including the boss of her modelling agency. They all described her as a fun-loving young woman who was popular, ambitious and genuine.

The report ended with a video clip of the outside of Holly's block of flats in Camden. Wreaths and bunches of flowers had been laid on the grass to one side of the entrance.

Before signing off, the reporter said, 'The murder enquiry is being conducted by the Major Investigation Team based in Wandsworth, South London, and the officer in charge is Detective Chief Inspector Anna Tate. Just weeks ago she led the hunt for the gang who kidnapped nine children from a nursery school in Rotherhithe, which is just eleven miles from Barnes Common.'

The reporter handed back to the studio where a female presenter announced that in the last few minutes there had been a major development in the case.

'Reports are coming in that Nathan Wolf, the Member of Parliament for Central Somerset, has been questioned in connection with Holly Blake's murder,' she said. 'Police have yet to confirm whether or not this is true. Mr Wolf, who has a home in Kensington, is a widower and has been a Conservative MP for six years. There's been widespread speculation in recent months that he's being lined up for a ministerial position in the Government, and it's known that he's very highly thought of by the Prime Minister. We'll bring you more details as and when they come in.'

Detective Chief Superintendent Nash was back from his conference in Newcastle and determined, as usual, to impose his authority on the proceedings.

After he'd received an update from Anna in her office, he called everyone together for a briefing.

He stood between the whiteboards, a tall, bulky man

with a short grey beard that matched the colour of his thin, receding hair.

He began by announcing that Ross Moore had been traced to a flat in Stepney, something that Anna had only just learned herself.

'I understand that officers arrived at his place minutes ago and he's being brought in for questioning,' Nash said.

Nash then invited DC Sweeny to tell the team what was known about Ross Moore.

'He's aged twenty-four and currently works as a shelf stacker and general dogsbody in a local retail warehouse,' she said. 'According to his neighbours he moved into the flat in Stepney nine months ago. I put in a call to his employers, who say he's a good worker but he's been on annual leave this past week so hasn't been in. He has a criminal record. Seven years ago he was working in a mobile phone shop when he assaulted his boss during an argument over his timekeeping. He was fined and given community service. Two years later he was done for possession of drugs and received a suspended sentence.'

'So it's not a great surprise that Holly Blake had the good sense to dump him,' Anna said. 'As soon as he arrives in the building have him put in an interview room and alert the duty solicitor.'

Nash then announced that the go-ahead had been given to seize Nathan Wolf's car and to search his properties in London and Somerset.

'A forensics team is ready to move in and we'll be liaising with Devon police, who will check out the house in Bridgewater.'

Before handing over to Anna, Nash referred to the news report they had just watched on the TV.

'It should be obvious to you all by now that we are about to find ourselves at the centre of a febrile media circus,' he said. 'The involvement of a Member of Parliament propels this story into the stratosphere. And that's before all the details of Wolf's somewhat sleazy relationship with Holly Blake are out there.

'It's therefore essential that we play everything by the book and don't make any mistakes. All aspects of this investigation will be under the media microscope. And the vultures won't show any mercy when it comes to the victim and her family. Her mother's life will be subjected to intense scrutiny, including the years she spent with the Met.'

Nash went on to say that a press conference was being scheduled for Sunday morning, and would be held at New Scotland Yard.

That was something Anna wasn't looking forward to. It was bound to turn into a raucous feeding frenzy. But she knew it had to be done.

When Nash stood to one side, Anna took his place between the whiteboards.

'Right then, everyone,' she said. 'There's a lot to get through and I'll start with the attack on Nathan Wolf, whose house I've just come from.'

Anna ran through the MP's description of what had happened and said she was confident that it wouldn't be long before Robert Gregory was picked up.

'Holly's uncle was obviously wound up by her mother, who is convinced that Wolf killed her daughter,' she said. 'Gregory's aim in going to the house appears to have been to get Wolf to confess. And who knows what would have happened if Wolf's fiancée hadn't turned up when she did.'

Anna told the team what Jennifer Rothwell had said and how Wolf had got into a strop.

'I'm beginning to suspect that the man has anger management issues,' she said. 'It was the second time I'd seen him lose it. So it's something we all need to bear in mind. It could be his aggression turns to violence when enough buttons are pushed. If he confronted Holly again on Tuesday night it's possible her refusal to back down sparked a colossal temper tantrum and he took it too far.'

Anna then turned to her notes to summarise the preliminary findings of the post-mortem. After that she listened to the various updates from her team. The latest from the cyber unit was that they were still sifting through Holly's online history, her phone records and the hard drive on her computer.

'She was very active on social media,' one of the technicians said. 'Inevitably she attracted some trolls who were critical of her looks and her views on things such as make-up and clothes. But we haven't come across any remarks that could be deemed actual threats.

'She sent and received thousands of texts and emails this past year. We've got her cloud storage so we've accessed everything that's been deleted. There are scores of text messages between her and Nathan Wolf, and most relate to what a great time they each had the night before. The messages she received from Ross Moore are more interesting, though. He kept pleading with her to take him back, and in several of them he threatened to kill himself if she didn't.

'The last message she got from him was on Sunday, two days before she died, begging her to meet him so they could talk. But she messaged back, warning him to stay away from her.'

The technician finished off by saying they were about to go through Rebecca Blake's online history to see if there was any evidence to suggest that Holly was killed by someone with a grudge against her mother.

DS Prescott then provided an update on the trawl of CCTV cameras.

'We've picked up Wolf's car close to his house just before one on Wednesday morning,' he said. 'There are no cameras in his actual road, which is a bit of a blind spot, but he does appear to be heading home. We've also caught sight of Holly on a security camera outside a shop close to where she lived.'

Both clips of CCTV footage were then shown on the monitors. The shot of Wolf's car was so clear you could read the number plate without having to zoom in. But the shot of Holly was grainy, and she was walking away from the camera. She was wearing jeans and a light-coloured T-shirt and carrying a bag over her shoulder.

'It's definitely her,' Prescott said. 'I went back to her flats to show it to her landlord and he confirmed it. We'll have more footage to look through this afternoon.'

'What about the King's Head pub?' Anna asked. 'We need to know if Theo Blake did go there after he failed to find Holly.'

Prescott shook his head. 'Turns out the cameras have been out of order for a couple of weeks. The proprietor says he's waiting for the security system to be repaired. But there is a camera on a building across the road apparently. Uniform are now in the process of getting access to it. If it goes back as far as Tuesday then we might see Theo Blake entering and leaving the pub.'

'Well, let me know as soon as you hear about that,' Anna

said. 'Meanwhile have we found out what Holly's movements were that day?'

DC Niven spoke up. 'We know she was out for much of it, but we don't know where she went before going to visit her parents. We've spoken to people at her modelling agency and some of the friends listed in her contacts, but none of them saw her or heard from her on that day. It could be she went shopping or met someone who's not on our radar yet.'

Anna finished by passing back to Nash who gave another short pep talk. As the team drifted back to their desks she was told that Ross Moore was now in the building.

'We'll talk to him before we go to Wolf's house,' she told Walker. 'Find out if a forensics team is already en route and if so tell them to wait for us outside. I just need to make a quick call.'

Anna went into her office, took out her mobile, and speed-dialled the man who was eating up her savings.

His name was Jack Keen and he was an ex-copper who had retired from the force twelve years ago. Since then he'd made a living as a private investigator. Anna had employed his services on and off for nine years in her search for Chloe. It was Keen who found out that Matthew had been murdered after returning to the UK three years ago in the guise of James Miller.

'What took you so long to call?' he said.

'I've been busy,' she answered.

'So I heard. That's why I didn't ring you. I thought I would just get on with the job.'

'I had a text from Anthony Liddle at the *Standard*,' Anna said. 'He told me he'd sent you the details of two people who rang the paper in response to Chloe's age progression picture.'

'He did indeed. I've already contacted them. One is a guy in Lewisham, but he turned out to be a prankster. He said he phoned the paper as a bet with one of his mates.'

'What about the other one?'

'It's a woman and what she told me sounds more promising. Her kid goes to a school in Bethnal Green. She says the age progression picture bears a striking resemblance to a young girl she's seen while waiting outside the school gates. And her son, who's eleven, thinks her name is Alice.'

Anna felt her breath burn in her chest.

'So what are you doing about it, Jack?' she asked.

'The kids don't return from their summer hols until next week,' he said. 'But I've left a message with the headmistress to ring me. I've also emailed her the picture and asked her if the face and name are familiar to her.'

'What school is it?'

'Oakfield Community.'

'Well, if the head's not forthcoming for whatever reason let me know and I'll call her myself.'

'Will do.'

She then told Keen that the Channel Four documentary team were going to produce a programme on the search for Chloe.

'That's more like it,' he said. 'It'll get national exposure, which is what we need.'

When she came off the phone, Anna picked up the copy of the previous day's *Evening Standard* that was lying on her desk. It was folded open at the page that featured the age progression photo of Chloe. As always it caused her heart to miss a beat.

'I really do hope that's what you look like now, my darling,'

she said under her breath. *'Because if so there's every chance that I'm getting closer to you.'*

She kissed the photo and dropped the paper back on the desk before emotion could overwhelm her.

CHAPTER TWENTY-SEVEN

A nervous-looking Ross Moore was waiting in interview room one. He was sitting at the table next to the duty solicitor, his fingers curled around a Styrofoam cup. He was a tall, thin man, his face the same shade of grey as the shirt he was wearing. He had dark blond hair, just long enough to cover the tops of his ears.

Anna introduced herself and Walker as they took their seats. She started the recorder and when the formalities were out of the way, she said, 'I trust it's been made clear to you that you haven't been arrested, Mr Moore. You agreed to come here and be interviewed as part of the investigation into the murder of Holly Blake.'

'They told me I'm a suspect.'

'And does that surprise you, given the fact that you've been stalking her for months? You even turned up at her flat not long ago and got into an argument with her because she wanted you to leave her alone. The landlord stepped in and told you to leave.'

He shook his head. 'I loved Holly more than anything and I would never have hurt her.'

'But she thought differently, didn't she? You pestered her so much that she made it known to others that she was scared of you.'

'I just wanted her to know that I was desperate to win her back.'

'So you decided that the way to do it was to stalk her, beg her to meet you, and even threaten to kill yourself. It must surely have upset her.'

'That only happened once when I was on a real downer,' he said. 'I apologised afterwards and acknowledged that it was over the top.'

Blood was creeping into his cheeks now and tears glistened in his eyes.

'I understand that you and Holly were together for just over a year,' she said. 'Is that correct?'

'It was fourteen months, one week and two days.'

'And how long did you share the flat in Eltham?'

'Ten months. And we were good together. We talked about marriage and kids and buying our own place one day.'

'So what went wrong?' Anna asked. 'Why did she walk out on you?'

He lifted his chin and fixed his eyes on the ceiling, as though concentrating on a problem he couldn't solve.

After a beat, he said, 'She dumped me for no reason. She became distant, kept finding fault with what I did and said. And she started accusing me of being possessive and controlling. But I wasn't. It was all in her head. At one point I said that maybe we should have a break from one another. I suggested that she go back to live with her parents until she got her head together. But she refused to entertain that idea, mainly because of her stepdad.'

'Did she have a problem with Theo Blake?' Anna asked.

'Yes, she did. Soon after we met, she told me he used to ogle her and then once he kissed her when she wasn't expecting it. It creeped her out. They had a falling out over it and she didn't like to be around him after that.'

So Holly had relayed the same story to Nathan Wolf and Ross Moore. Did that mean it was true? Anna wondered.

'Tell me how she ended it then,' Anna said.

He shrugged. 'She met this other bloke and he must have turned her against me because I came home one day and she was gone. It took me a while to find out she'd moved to Camden.'

'And what do you know about this other man who appeared on the scene?' Walker asked.

Moore dropped his eyes and a rush of anger was evident in his expression.

'I know now that he's an MP and that he turned her into a fucking slut.'

'So you didn't know who he was before this weekend?'

'I'd only seen him a few times when he turned up at her flat while I was outside, but he was always careful to obscure his face with a hat or a scarf. I wondered if he was married because of the obvious age difference. I didn't recognise him as a well-known politician, if that's what you mean.'

'Did you ever approach him?'

'No. I was tempted to once or twice, but I thought it best to stay out of it in the hope that Holly would see sense and leave him, then come back to me.'

'Have you read what she told the newspaper?'

He took a deep breath. 'It's made me feel sick. I didn't know she was doing all that kinky shit. When she was with me we never got into any of that stuff. I don't think we even talked about it. Our sex life was normal. And good.'

'So how do you feel now that you know what she was doing this past year?'

'I feel crushed,' he said, his voice laden with emotion. 'It was bad enough when I heard she was the woman whose body was found on the common. Knowing she's dead has made me realise that I don't want to go on living.'

He was trembling now and tears were spilling from his eyes.

'Holly was murdered on Tuesday night,' Anna said. 'It happened at some time after ten-forty-five. We know that because she was seen leaving her flat then. So can you tell us where you were at that time?'

He sucked on his bottom lip and wiped tears from his cheeks with his sleeve.

'I was at home,' he said. 'I've been on leave so I've made the most of it by going to bed early.'

'Are there any witnesses who can corroborate that?'

He shook his head. 'I live by myself, so no, there aren't any. You'll just have to take my word for it.'

'Well, it's not as easy as that, Mr Moore, because you were reportedly seen outside Holly's block on Tuesday evening between ten-thirty and eleven.'

'Well, whoever says they saw me there is mistaken.'

'It was the landlord. The same man who confronted you that other time. He says you were standing across the street smoking a cigarette.'

'Then he's either lying or he imagined it. I wasn't there so you can't prove that I was.'

'What car do you drive?' Anna said.

'That's the thing,' he replied. 'I don't have a car. So how the fuck was I supposed to have taken Holly all the way across London to Barnes Common?'

It was a fair question, and one that Anna didn't yet have the answer to.

The duty solicitor stepped in there, pointing out that they had no grounds to hold his client because there was no solid evidence linking him to the murder. Anna knew he was right, but that didn't mean that Moore wasn't still a suspect.

'We intend to make further enquiries, Mr Moore,' she said. 'We will most definitely want to talk to you again.'

'Well, you know where to find me,' he said.

CHAPTER TWENTY-EIGHT

Sophie now had another reason to be scared. Her friend Lisa had raised the possibility that the demon from her past had tracked her down. Was that why she had sensed that she was being watched yesterday as she walked along Shoreditch High Street?

Lisa's theory that her phone was stolen by Michael Taylor so that he could see if she'd been in touch with Sophie sounded all too credible.

'If Taylor passed it on to his old pal Bruno then there's a chance he got someone to trace your mobile signal for him.'

It was a terrifying thought and one that Sophie could not ignore because Bruno had managed to find her twice before. The first time was ten years ago in Spain. And the second time was three years ago in Southampton.

The problem was he had friends, contacts and influence, and he had always managed to get whatever it was he wanted by using charm, threats, intimidation or bribery.

The biggest mistake Sophie ever made was to get involved

with him. But back in 2005 she was twenty-eight and keen to settle down and start a family. And Bruno Perez seemed like a real catch. He was handsome, charismatic and built like a well-toned athlete. The fact that he was half Spanish with a sexy accent added to his appeal. They met at a New Year's Eve party in Camberwell, South London, close to where Sophie was living and working as a catering assistant at the time.

Lisa was there along with the rest of their group of single friends, including Michael Taylor. It was Taylor who brought Bruno along. The pair were members of the same snooker club, where they'd become drinking buddies.

Bruno's cheesy chat-up line made her smile, which was a good start.

'Since you are the most beautiful woman in the room I assume you must be Spanish,' he said as he sidled up to her while she was sipping her first G and T of the night. 'And I'm guessing that your name is Isabella or Valentina or Maria.'

'It's Sophie,' she told him. 'And I'm a native Londoner, born and bred this side of the Thames.'

He raised his bushy brow. 'Well, I admit I am surprised since you have such smooth black hair and dark, broody eyes. And you clearly ooze panache. In fact you remind me of that lovely actress Penélope Cruz.'

Sophie wasn't flattered because she didn't believe a word of it. But nevertheless he had her hooked, and over the course of the evening he reeled her in. At midnight they kissed and at three in the morning they went back to his flat where they made love.

Romance quickly blossomed and in the weeks that followed she found out that he was the same age as her, had been born in Marbella on Spain's Costa Del Sol, where his family still lived, and was employed as the manager of two large warehouses in South London.

What she didn't find out until much later was that he dabbled in drugs, his boss – who was also his dad – was a crook, and he had a violent disposition.

By then she was already married to him, having ignored the advice of her widowed mother, who was still alive back then.

'You've only been together for five months,' her mother said to her just before the wedding, which took place in Marbella. 'It's too soon. And I know he's not right for you. There's something about that man I don't trust – or like.'

They moved to Spain shortly after the wedding. She didn't need much persuading to up sticks after she'd had a taste of the laid-back lifestyle and year-round sunshine.

To begin with she was so blinded by love and infatuation that she didn't see him for what he was – a complete and utter control freak.

The first time he made her feel uncomfortable was six weeks into the marriage. By then she was bored with doing nothing all day and told him that it was time she started looking for work.

'You don't need to,' he said. 'I earn enough money to provide for us. A wife's job is to stay in shape and look after the house.'

'Is that a joke?' she said.

He arched his brow at her. 'You should know by now that I don't tell jokes.'

'But you can't be serious, Bruno. We're not living in the nineteen thirties. If I want to work then I bloody well will.'

'But I wouldn't be happy with that,' he replied. 'None of

the other wives in my family go to work. For them taking care of the home and raising a family is a full-time job.'

'We don't have a family, though. It's just you and me.'

'But we're trying for a baby, aren't we? So soon we'll have kids and you won't have any time for yourself. So make the most of it while you can.'

She didn't push it. She did as she was told, without realising that she had taken the first step towards a life of subjugation.

It took her a while to accept that she was in an abusive relationship. At first it was subtle. He would ask her where she'd been, unjustly accuse her of flirting with other men, put her down in front of his family and friends. It made her feel confused, off balance, like she was walking on eggshells all the time.

And it gradually got worse. He started checking her phone to see who she'd been talking to, and refused to be clear about why he was always so flush with cash, seeing as he was supposedly working as a salesman in his father's wholesale business.

Every so often he threw her a bone to keep her happy, a compliment, a nice gift, a special treat – as though it would erase his bad behaviour.

And then, after trying for so long to have a child, they learned that she couldn't have children. It was a blow to both of them, but Bruno was furious as well as gutted.

A week after the diagnosis he laid a hand on her for the first time. It happened after he came home drunk one lunchtime and said he wanted to have sex. When she said she wasn't in the mood he called her a sterile bitch and shoved her hard against a wall.

She should have walked out then but she didn't and the next morning he was full of contrition. And that was the usual pattern of his behaviour as he became increasingly aggressive.

Sophie's life was intolerable, but she learned how to pretend to her friends that she was happy while at the same time hiding the bruises from them. She felt suffocated by him, and every day he would do something that would eat away at her self-respect. There were the guilt trips, the degrading tirades, the unpleasant tone of voice, the refusal to communicate.

He was possessive, manipulative, bullying. But Sophie didn't leave him because she was scared of what he would do to her if she did.

It did not stop him from threatening to dump her, though. He told her that he would be off like a shot if the right woman came along who could give him babies.

The nightmare lasted for almost three years before something happened that presented Sophie with an opportunity to escape.

Bruno came in late one night while she was watching television and told her that she had to provide him with an alibi. She noticed bloodstains on his shirt and chinos and the worried look on his face.

'I'm expecting the police to come here and when they do I want you to tell them that I've been with you all evening and that I didn't go out,' he said.

'What have you done?'

'I got into a fight and someone got hurt. That's all you need to know. Just do as I say and everything will be all right.'

The cops came the next day, by which time she had heard on the radio that a man had been stabbed outside his house in one of the Marbella urbanisations. And her husband matched the description of the attacker.

After they took him away a detective came to interview her.

'Your husband has told us that he spent the entire evening with you,' he said. 'Is that true, Mrs Perez?'

Sophie saw her chance and went for it.

'No, it isn't,' she said. 'He came in late with blood on his shirt and trousers. He told me he'd been involved in a fight.'

'What did he do with his clothes?'

'He burned them in the back garden.'

Bruno was charged with the attempted murder of a known drug dealer and at his trial it emerged that he himself was part of a rival drugs gang, which explained where all his ready cash came from. Sophie gave evidence at the trial after police moved her to a safe house. It was her testimony that sealed the case for the prosecution and Bruno was sentenced to a minimum of seven years in prison.

She agreed to his request to visit him just once because she wanted to tell him that she was going to file for divorce. But he told her that if she did that he would arrange for someone to visit London and kill her mother.

'And that will be just the start,' he said. 'If you go on to settle down with another man, or, God forbid, get married, then I'll arrange for other people you know and love to be murdered as well. And don't think I won't be able to because I'm stuck in here. My family hate you just as much as I do for what you've done, and they'll be only too pleased to carry out my wishes.'

Then he issued his final threat – he was going to find her when he got out of prison and make her suffer for betraying him.

'You're getting what you deserve, Bruno,' she told him. 'Not only for stabbing that man, but also for what you've done to me.'

That same day she flew back to the UK to visit her mother. She told her about Bruno's threat, and persuaded her mother to move to a new flat.

But Sophie feared that wherever her mother moved, Bruno would find her if he was determined enough. So she decided not to seek a divorce, at least for the foreseeable future. She just couldn't risk any harm coming to her mother, her sister and any of her friends.

She stayed with her mother for a couple of months but couldn't settle and came to another momentous decision, which was to move back to Spain.

'I fell in love with the country,' she said when she broke the news to her mother. 'London no longer feels like home to me.'

And so she returned there with her mother's blessing. She rented a flat in a town five hundred miles from Marbella and got a job in a restaurant there.

Two months later James Miller walked into the restaurant with Alice, and a new chapter in her life began.

CHAPTER TWENTY-NINE

Anna felt a flare of excitement sweep through her as they headed across the river to Nathan Wolf's home in Kensington.

Things were developing at breakneck speed, and not just with the investigation. Jack Keen clearly thought he was onto something with the lead he was following up in Shoreditch. But Anna knew that she had to remain cautious. Too often in their search for Chloe her hopes had been raised only to be dashed again.

At least right now she had something to occupy her mind while Jack earned his money.

The interview with Ross Moore had been interesting. He had failed to convince them that he wasn't Holly's killer, but right now there wasn't enough evidence against him to hold him in custody. They needed to be sure that it was him the landlord had seen outside Holly's flats. They also needed to confirm that he didn't own a car or at least have access to one.

Before leaving the station, Anna had instructed the team to carry out various checks and to seek a warrant to search Moore's flat.

Now her thoughts turned to Holly Blake. The victim. A girl who seemingly had the world at her feet. Young, attractive and popular, by all accounts. But also someone who'd had mental health issues in the past.

It seemed she'd also had questionable taste in men. A guy twice her age who used her for his sexual gratification, and a drug user with two convictions to his credit. And both men had become hostile towards her. Ross Moore because she had walked out on him, and Nathan Wolf because she was threatening to destroy his reputation and relationship with another woman.

As yet there was no firm evidence against either of them, so Anna and her team could not rule out the possibility that poor Holly had fallen victim to a stranger. Or perhaps to someone else she had upset.

Crucial questions remained.

Why did it take her so long to get to her flat after leaving her mother's house?

Why did she then leave the flat after only about fifteen minutes, and where did she go from there?

And was Theo Blake telling the truth when he claimed he went to her flat but didn't see her?

Hopefully they would pick her up on more CCTV, but it wasn't something they could bank on. A popular misconception – encouraged by TV detective dramas – was that virtually every street in the capital was covered by surveillance cameras. But that was far from the truth. Despite there being over half a million cameras, thousands were turned off at any given time, some by cash-strapped councils. Plus, there were countless blind spots, which was hardly surprising given that Greater London spanned six hundred square miles and had a population of almost nine million.

The scene outside Nathan Wolf's house sucked the breath out of Anna's lungs. A crowd of about fifty reporters and photographers packed the pavements on both sides of the road. There were also several TV crews and satellite trucks.

Walker parked up between a patrol car and a forensics van that had beaten them to the location. Crime scene investigators in white suits sat inside waiting for the cue to enter the property.

As soon as Anna and Walker stepped out of the car reporters clustered around them, waving microphones and recorders and shouting their questions.

'Has Nathan Wolf been arrested?'

'What is the MP's connection with Holly Blake?'

'Can you confirm that the two were lovers?'

'Is Mr Wolf your only suspect?'

As Anna shouldered her way through the crowd, she signalled to the CSIs to exit their van and follow her.

Two uniforms stood either side of the gate preventing the media mob from entering the front garden. They'd arrived earlier after Wolf had called the police to say his home was under siege. Anna showed the officers her ID and was waved through. She marched straight up the path armed with the search warrant and the front door swung open before she had a chance to ring the bell.

A rattled-looking Nathan Wolf stood there, his face strained and anxious.

'Is this your doing?' he yelled, as he pointed an accusing finger at Anna. 'Did you stir things up so that this lot would come here and harass me?'

Anna ignored the question and held up the piece of paper she was holding.

'I have a warrant to search your house, Mr Wolf. We've also been given permission to take your car away for forensic examination. You are quite within your rights to remain on the premises while we conduct the search.'

He looked fit to explode. 'This is fucking outrageous. I've told you that I did not kill Holly. And you won't find anything in this house to prove that I'm lying.'

'Then you've got nothing to worry about, have you?' Anna said.

'Are you being serious? Look at that lot out there. My reputation is in ruins and I've no doubt that the court of public opinion has already found me guilty.'

Anna had some sympathy with him there, but she had no intention of telling him.

'So how do you want to play it, sir?' she said. 'Are you going to invite us in or are you going to cause an unnecessary scene in front of all those cameras?'

He stood there for several seconds, rocking backwards and forwards on the balls of his feet, then said, 'I don't really have a choice, do I?'

Anna shook her head. 'I'm afraid not. By the way, is Miss Rothwell still here?'

'No, she isn't,' he replied, his voice a harsh whisper. 'She left a couple of hours ago and truth be told I don't know if I'll ever see her again.'

CHAPTER THIRTY

Anna gestured for Walker to enter Wolf's house ahead of her. It had already been decided that he would remain at the MP's side during the search. Anna held back to brief the SOCOs on what to look for.

'It's possible that this is where Holly Blake died,' she said. 'We know she was stabbed in the throat and the weapon used was a long blade with a serrated edge. So we're looking for a knife, blood, contaminated clothing and anything that might suggest Holly could have been killed here.'

As the SOCOs went about their work, Anna put on latex gloves and walked around the house, noting that Nathan Wolf was seated outside on a patio chair smoking a cigarette while Walker stood behind him.

The rooms were smart without being extravagant. There were three bedrooms, two with en-suite bathrooms, a separate dining room and a large modern kitchen.

Scattered about the house were photographs of Wolf's wife Shelley, who had died of a stroke months after he began his affair with Holly. She was an attractive woman, Anna noticed, with a soft, open face and short fair hair.

There were no pictures of Holly, but there were several of his latest girlfriend – or soon to be ex-girlfriend – Jennifer Rothwell. In one the pair were at a table in a restaurant raising wine glasses to the camera and smiling broadly.

The search team came across some women's clothes in one of the wardrobes and Wolf confirmed that they belonged to Jennifer, who had often stayed overnight.

That was one of the reasons he had never invited Holly to spend time in his house. Another was that he didn't want to take the chance that they'd be seen together and their relationship would be exposed. After all, Holly had been no more than his bit on the side, whereas Jennifer was the woman he loved and wanted to marry.

Anna ventured into the back garden several times to ask Wolf questions and each time she saw that he was becoming more anxious and agitated. When she said they needed the key to open a cupboard in the main bedroom he reacted furiously by saying that he was going to sue the police for what they were doing to him.

After reluctantly telling her where to find the key, he stood up and stormed across the garden, where he had to walk around forensics officers who were looking for freshly turned earth in the lawn and flower beds.

It became apparent, as soon as it was opened, why the cupboard in question had been locked. Inside was an array of BDSM gear, including a whip, some restraints, a slave collar, blindfolds and several items that looked like medical equipment from a hospital.

Anna remembered Wolf telling her that Jennifer was

also into S and M sex. What was stored in the cupboard did not compare with the stuff in Holly's playroom, but it had no doubt provided the couple with hours of painful pleasure.

Elsewhere in the house officers were going through Wolf's wardrobes, drawers and filing cabinets in his ground-floor study. They were spraying Luminol, the chemical used to detect trace amounts of blood that are invisible to the human eye and can remain on surfaces even after they've been cleaned, on the kitchen floor, sinks and shower trays. But after an hour Anna was beginning to think that they weren't going to find any physical evidence that would link Wolf to Holly's murder.

Some items would of course be taken away to be examined in the lab, including a couple of kitchen knives, clothing and a few pairs of shoes.

Before his Range Rover was taken away, Anna was told that nothing incriminating had been found in it, but it was clear the vehicle had recently been cleaned both inside and out.

Then, just as she was about to halt the search, she was summoned into the hall by an officer who said he had something to show her. The object he'd found had been placed in an evidence bag, which he handed over to her. As she examined it a damp shiver rippled down her spine.

'So this wasn't a waste of time, after all,' she said.

Seconds later she stepped back out onto the patio. Wolf had returned to his seat, where he was smoking another cigarette while staring up at the sky. His body tensed when she held the evidence bag in front of his face.

'Can you please explain why this was in the pocket of

one of your jackets that's hanging up in the hallway?' she asked him.

His brow creased and he shook his head. 'I don't understand. What is it?'

'It's a driving licence, Mr Wolf. Or to be precise it's Holly Blake's driving licence, and I'm guessing that those dark specks on it are blood. Holly's blood.'

Wolf tried to snatch the bag from her but she pulled it back.

'You must have planted it there,' he shouted. 'I've never seen it before.'

He shot to his feet, his whole body shaking, eyes protruding from their sockets.

'You've got to believe me. I had nothing to do . . .'

Suddenly he clutched at his chest and scrunched his face up as though in pain. Then he started struggling to breathe, and Anna heard Walker say that it looked as though he was having a panic attack.

A moment later Wolf doubled over and vomited on the paving stones in front of Anna.

'Get him some water,' she called out, and then spent the next five minutes trying to calm him down while hoping that it was indeed a panic attack and not something more serious.

When he'd finally stopped shaking and his eyes had refocused she told him she was arresting him in connection with the murder of Holly Blake.

'You do not have to say anything,' she said. 'But it may harm your defence if you do not mention when questioned something you later rely on in court. Anything you do say may be given in evidence.'

'I want to call my lawyer,' he said.

Anna nodded. 'I'll let you do that on the way to the station. But is there anything you would like to get off your chest before we go?'

He thought for a moment and said, 'No comment.'

CHAPTER THIRTY-ONE

'My client is in no fit state to be interviewed this evening. That should be strikingly obvious to you, Detective Tate.'

So said Nathan Wolf's lawyer, a sharp-suited man named Gavin Peake who turned up at headquarters soon after Anna arrived back with the MP.

'I actually agree with you, Mr Peake,' she said. 'It's why I've arranged for him to see the on-call doctor. Mr Wolf is clearly in a state of high anxiety. We believe he had a panic attack which has left him confused and somewhat disoriented.'

'So can I assume that after he's seen the doctor he can return home?' Peake said. 'He will of course undertake to report back here tomorrow so he can be interviewed then.'

'You know that won't be possible,' Anna said. 'Your client is suspected of murdering the young woman he was having an affair with. He will have to remain in custody until we're able to question him, and I'm hoping that will be first thing in the morning. It'll give you plenty of time to talk to him.'

'Well, if that's your position I would like to know what

evidence you have against Mr Wolf other than the fact that he was in a relationship with the victim.'

Anna pursed her lips. 'For one thing he threatened Holly when he went to her flat. He told her she would regret it if she sold the story of their time together to the *Sunday Mirror*. Then, less than an hour ago, during the search of his house, we found Holly Blake's driving licence in the pocket of one of his coats. There are specks of what appear to be blood on it so it's been sent for forensic analysis.'

The lawyer's face twisted into a frown and Anna could almost see the questions swirling around inside his head.

She herself had no problem with delaying the interview. It gave the SOCOs time to come up with further evidence from the search of Wolf's home in Kensington. At the same time Devon police had just gained access to his property in Somerset and his Land Rover would shortly be subjected to a thorough examination by experts. Plus, she was hoping that by morning she would know if the stains on Holly's driving licence were actually her blood.

Among the questions for Wolf would be: did he mean to keep the licence or did he forget that he put it into his pocket after he stripped her and dumped her body on the common?

Anna and the lawyer had been speaking in her glorified pigeonhole of an office while his client was being processed through the custody suite. But at this stage there was only so much they could say to each other so she was glad when the call came that Wolf was ready to see his brief.

Before leaving the office, Peake told Anna that he had applied for an injunction to stop the *Sunday Mirror* from publishing the story about Holly and Wolf.

'It's the last thing he needs,' Peake said. 'And I believe it will be grossly unfair to him and to Holly's family.'

But Anna didn't think he had a hope in hell of stopping publication, not unless Wolf was charged with her murder before the paper went to press tonight, and that wasn't going to happen.

From her window she could see the media pack down below, gathered on the steps in front of the building.

Anna had used the back entrance to bring Wolf in, but he'd been filmed and photographed getting into their car outside his house. Anna knew from checking her phone that those images of a member of the British Parliament being arrested had already set social media sites such as Twitter and Facebook on fire. It was big news and it fed into the public's insatiable appetite for political scandals and crimes involving public figures, especially politicians.

Wolf wasn't the only person associated with the case who was currently in the building waiting for Anna to talk to them.

Robert Gregory had been brought in an hour ago after being arrested at Rebecca Blake's house in Pimlico.

He had already admitted that he had punched Nathan Wolf and had been told that he was going to be charged with common assault. And he'd said to the officer who'd collared him that he did it because the man had murdered his niece.

Anna knew that because of the extenuating circumstances, and the fact that Wolf wasn't seriously hurt, he would likely receive just a fine. But she was in no mood to reassure him of that when she entered the soft interview suite. He had already been questioned by another detective and had made a statement, but Anna wanted to talk to him off the record before he was formally charged and granted bail.

'What you did to Nathan Wolf was stupid and reckless, Mr Gregory,' she said when she was seated opposite him.

He nodded. 'Maybe so, but I couldn't help myself. And don't bother telling me that he might not have killed her. We're all convinced that he did and from what I hear so are you. And even if he didn't he still deserves to suffer for making my niece his sex slave. And we all know that's exactly what she was to him.'

'That's all beside the point, Mr Gregory. You can't take the law into your own hands.'

'You're just repeating what the other detective told me,' he said. 'I know what I did was wrong in the eyes of the law, but I'm only sorry I didn't land a few more punches before that woman turned up.'

'Is that why you stopped hitting him, because of the woman?'

'Of course. I had no idea who she was but I could see that she was shocked and upset so I walked out. It was that bastard I wanted to hurt. Nobody else.'

'How did your sister-in-law react when you told her what you'd done?'

'She thanked me. And so did Theo. They were in a real state when they got back from the mortuary and they were glad I'd done it.'

'I take it you were close to your niece, Mr Gregory,' she said.

'We all were. She was a sweet girl and would frequently come over to see Freya and me. You see, we were never able to have children so my wife treated her like her own daughter rather than a niece. Holly would often tell her things she wouldn't tell her parents.'

'Such as?'

His nostrils flared as tears gathered in his eyes.

'When she went to university her plan was to become a teacher. But then she decided she wanted to be a model and it was Freya she sounded out before she dared mention it to her mum. My wife, who's a teacher herself, told her she should follow her heart and that's what she did. And she didn't regret it. And it was Freya who told her that she should dump Ross Moore. He was a crap boyfriend and he made Holly unhappy, but she kept hoping he would change.'

'What was his problem?'

'He wasn't good enough for her. He was lazy, dependent and possessive. A right scumbag.'

'But Holly never confided in your wife about her relationship with Nathan Wolf?'

He shook his head. 'That's why it came as such a shock when Rebecca told us the day after Holly broke the news to her and Theo. It's hard to believe it was going on for so long and none of us knew.'

'Why is that if you're such a close-knit family?'

He used his knuckle to wipe a tear that had escaped from his left eye.

'I suppose because we were all wrapped up in our own lives,' he said. 'Holly was all over the place on modelling assignments. Rebecca was busy with her political career and campaign to become Mayor. Theo spent most of his time in court. And Freya and I had our jobs. We got together, of course, but not as often as we should have.'

'Where do you work, Mr Gregory?'

'I'm a partner in an estate agent's based south of the Thames in Mortlake. I've been in the property business for fifteen years.'

Anna paused while Robert dabbed at his watery eyes with a hanky. Then she asked him how he and Freya got on with Rebecca's husband. His reaction was not unexpected.

'We get on fine with him,' he said testily. 'He's a great bloke and was a good stepdad to Holly. As you heard from Rebecca, it took time for Holly to accept him, but she did eventually. It's bloody obvious that Wolf is lying when he says that she told him she hated Theo. It's a way of diverting attention away from himself. And you'd be mad to fall for it.'

'So you don't believe that Theo tried it on with her?'

'She either imagined it or she . . .' He stopped himself and shook his head.

'She what, Mr Gregory?'

He sighed. 'I was going to say that she might well have made it up. At the time she was unhappy and angry so it's something I've always suspected, but never mentioned to Rebecca.'

'Have you asked Holly about it?'

'Freya did once, but naturally Holly denied it. I was never convinced, though, because back then she was always slagging Theo off, and urging her mum to dump him. Things got out of hand one Christmas when the family got together and Holly had a pop at Theo. He reacted angrily and told her she was a liar. It was the first time I'd seen him fly off on one and they ended up having a fierce argument before she left in tears. After that things calmed down, though it was always obvious she held a grudge. But I wouldn't go so far as to say she hated him.'

By now he was struggling to keep the emotion out of his voice, and Anna sensed that he was on the verge of either breaking down or losing his temper. She didn't want that to happen so she pushed her chair back and stood up.

'There's something you might as well know because you'll find out as soon as you leave this building,' she said. 'We've arrested Nathan Wolf and he'll be formally questioned in due course. We're also in the process of searching his homes and examining his alibi for when we believe Holly was murdered. If he did kill your niece then I can assure you that we will find out.'

He glared at her as fresh tears made tracks down his face.

'And I can assure you, detective, that if he fools you into believing him then he'll have me to answer to. Next time I get my hands on that pervert he won't be walking away with a couple of bruises on his face.'

Back in the office, Anna called DCS Nash with an update. He was at the Yard meeting the Commissioner and other senior Met officers.

He had already been told by phone about Wolf's arrest and had been given the salient details. In turn he had alerted the Media Liaison Department and the Home Office.

When Anna got through to him she was put on speaker so that all those with him could hear what she had to say.

Relief flooded through her when the Commissioner himself told her that she had made the right call in arresting Wolf. She explained why she wouldn't be formally interviewing him until the morning and warned them to expect the hysteria around the story to grow after the *Sunday Mirror* hit the streets.

'I've been told they're running TV promotions this evening and the reporter and editor who spoke to Holly are being lined up to give interviews,' Anna said.

'The paper has approached the PM and Conservative Central Office for quotes,' the Commissioner told her. 'And we understand that Holly had sent them a photograph of the room in her flat where all the action took place. It just shows how determined she was to stitch Wolf up.'

'Hell hath no fury like a woman scorned,' Anna said.

'Never a truer word spoken,' the Commissioner replied.

While Anna had been busy with Wolf's lawyer and Robert Gregory, DI Walker had started briefing the team. He'd filled them in on the interview with Ross Moore and the search of Wolf's house, including the discovery of Holly's driving licence. He had also explained why the MP wasn't going to be interviewed until Sunday morning.

When Anna joined them he was telling everyone that the next twenty-four hours were going to be full on.

'We'll know if the forensics teams have found anything else important at Wolf's two homes,' he said. 'We'll also have the results back on what look like specks of blood on the driving licence, and we should know if there's any forensic evidence in the MP's Range Rover. If Wolf did kill Holly then it's likely he would have taken her to Barnes Common in his boot.

'And speaking of the common, the search there has now been called off. Nothing of interest was found but the area where the body was discovered remains sealed off.'

Anna listened as Walker said that the SOCOs had found no evidence to indicate that Holly was murdered at any of the three properties being searched – her flat, her ex-boyfriend's flat and Wolf's Kensington home.

'The only blood that's turned up so far appears to be on the victim's driving licence,' he said. 'It means we still don't know the location of the crime scene and that inevitably makes our job much more difficult.'

On the CCTV front many hours of footage had still to be viewed and they hadn't yet been able to chart the movements of Holly, Wolf, Moore and Theo Blake on the night of the murder.

The briefing ended after Anna told them about her chat with Robert Gregory and reminded them that the *Sunday Mirror* would be publishing Holly's kiss-and-tell story the next morning.

'It's time for those of us who've been on duty all day and most of last night to go home and get some sleep,' she said. 'We need to be firing on all cylinders when we come in tomorrow. And don't forget I'll be attending a press conference first thing at the Yard. So I would like you lot to—'

She was suddenly interrupted by DC Sweeny, who held up her mobile phone and said, 'I need to stop you there, guv. There's been another development. Ross Moore has just been rushed to hospital. It seems he went straight home from here and tried to kill himself.'

CHAPTER THIRTY-TWO

Anxiety clawed at Sophie's chest as she walked along Shoreditch High Street on her way to pick Alice up.

It was early evening and some of the shops had already closed even though there were still plenty of people about.

The feeling that she was being watched had returned with a vengeance. She found herself looking around to see if the man who had wrecked her life had managed to find her again and was aiming to cause her more harm.

She didn't see him among the scores of pedestrians who crowded the pavements on either side of the street. But that didn't mean he wasn't nearby, waiting to pounce, waiting to remind her that he hadn't forgotten what she did to him.

She pictured Bruno Perez in her mind with unwelcome clarity. Not as he was when they married fourteen years ago, but as he was when he crashed back into her life following his release from prison. His kind, handsome face had become hard and brutish, his thick black hair had all but disappeared, his wide green eyes were like tiny windows through which she could see into his dark, malevolent soul. And it wasn't just his face that had suffered in the seven years he'd been behind bars. He'd gained weight and had an ugly scar below his left eye.

If he appeared now she knew she would recognise him instantly, just as she had that day three years ago when she'd spotted him following her after she'd picked Alice up from school.

Her breath caught in her throat as the memory snapped into place. She remembered how desperation had crashed over her like a wave, how she had grabbed Alice by the hand and told her she had to hurry up . . .

Three years ago

'But what's wrong, Mum? Why are you acting funny?'

'Please just do as you're told, sweetheart. We need to find your dad.'

If she had her mobile she would phone the police, but she left it in the bar with her handbag, not thinking she would need it.

Thankfully it will only take about five minutes to get to the bar where James will be waiting. But every time she looks back over her shoulder she sees that Bruno is still there and closing the gap between them.

Lisa had told her over the phone a month ago that he'd been let out of prison having served his full sentence. Her friend had been given the news by a mutual acquaintance in the UK. The Spanish police hadn't informed Sophie because they had no idea where she was. Sophie had hoped and prayed that he wouldn't come looking for her, and that if he did decide to he would never trace her to Puerto de Mazarron.

But she should have known that he would use all the resources at his disposal to seek her out and make her pay for refusing to provide him with that false alibi. The promise he made is never far from her thoughts.

'You can run and hide, bitch, but wherever you go I'll find you eventually. And so help me, I'm going to make you suffer big time for what you did.'

Myriad questions are tearing through her mind as they approach the bar.

What is she going to tell James?

Will there be enough time to summon the police?

Will Bruno really try to hurt her in a public place?

How the hell did he track her down?

The door to the bar is open and she pushes Alice through ahead of her. The place is empty except for an elderly couple in the booth by the window.

And James.

He's clearing glasses from one of the tables, and when he sees her panicked expression he flinches.

'You need to phone the police,' she yells at him. 'And don't ask me why. Just do it.'

But there's no time because Bruno enters the bar at that moment. His smile has turned into an ugly smirk and it causes Sophie's heart to take a leap.

'Stay away from me,' she shouts at him. 'You shouldn't be here.'

He stops just inside the door and looks around to see who else is in the bar. His eyes rest on James, who's frozen to the spot, a glass in each hand.

'You must be the bloke she's shacked up with,' Bruno says, his voice as rough as sandpaper.

A flash of anger crosses James's face.

'Who the fuck are you?' he demands to know.

Bruno ignores him and turns to Alice, who's cowering next to Sophie.

'There's no need to be afraid, little girl,' he says. 'I've just dropped by to say hi to your mum. I take it she is your mum.'

James puts the glasses he's been holding down on the table and strides across the room towards Bruno.

Sophie doesn't want Alice to bear witness to whatever is going to happen next so she quickly ushers her through the door next to the bar that leads to the flat.

'Go upstairs and wait in your bedroom,' she tells her.

'But I don't want to,' Alice wails.

'I'm not asking you, Alice. I'm telling you. Now go.'

She closes the door behind her and spins round just as James is squaring up to Bruno, who stands about four inches taller than him.

'I asked you a question,' James is saying. 'Who are you and what are you doing here?'

Bruno remains calm and the smirk reverts to a smile.

'I heard Sophie was living here so I decided to pay her a visit to tell her that I'm a free man at last,' he says. 'It's only fair that she knows, bearing in mind that she's still my wife.'

It takes James a couple of seconds to find his voice.

'You've either made a big mistake, mate, or else you're trying to wind me up. Sophie isn't married and we've been together for almost seven years.'

'Well, there's a coincidence. It was seven years ago that I went to prison.' Bruno points a finger at Sophie. 'And all

because that woman wanted to get rid of me so that she could do a runner.'

James swings round towards Sophie, his face contorted by alarm and confusion.

'Tell him it's not true, for Christ's sake.'

But she can't speak, and as she stands there she feels an ache swell in her chest.

'It took my family a long time to track her down,' Bruno says. 'They had to call in a lot of favours from their police contacts. When they told me she was living here and playing happy families it made me wonder if she'd told you about her past.'

Sophie suddenly snaps out of herself and rushes forward, shaking her head.

'What is it you want?' she screams at him. 'You have no right to come here.'

James puts an arm out to stop her closing in on Bruno and she grabs hold of it.

Bruno's grin widens. 'I'm not breaking any laws. But seeing as I'm clearly not welcome I'll be off. You'll be seeing me again, though. I have every intention of keeping the promise I made to you seven years ago. And I've decided not to get it over with quickly. I want it to be a long, slow process because it's all I've been thinking about for the past seven years. And a word of advice. If you try to involve the police then your man and your little girl will be put at risk.'

With that, he turns around and walks slowly out of the bar.

As Sophie watches him, her knees start to shake and bile rushes into her throat. Suddenly she can't breathe, and it feels as though the air is being sucked out of the room.

After a few seconds she shifts her gaze from the door and looks at James, who is clearly struggling to make sense of what just happened.

'I've got two questions for you,' he says after a beat. 'Was that man telling the truth? And is he a serious threat to all of us?'

She knows the game is up and that it's time to tell the truth. 'The answer is yes to both questions. We are still married and he is extremely dangerous. He went to prison for stabbing a man.' She clears her throat and adds, 'Now I've got a question for you, James. Do you think you can find it in your heart to forgive me?'

As he stares at her, his eyes grow sad. When he speaks it's as though there's gravel in his throat.

'That all depends on why you've lied to me all this time.'

Before Sophie can tell James her story they have to politely ask the two elderly customers to leave so that they can close the bar.

Then they spend a while reassuring Alice that everything is all right. She's upset and tearful, but they manage to convince her that the man who followed them into the bar is a drunk and they won't see him again.

They tell her to stay in her bedroom while they talk about their plans to move to a new home in Alicante, something she's already been made aware of and fully accepts.

James then listens to Sophie's story in silence. She tells him about the verbal and physical abuse she suffered while she was with Bruno, and why she decided to seize the opportunity to free herself from his clutches by refusing to give him an alibi.

And then she explains why she didn't seek a divorce after he went to prison.

'He threatened to kill my mother if I did,' she tells him. 'And he warned me that if I got into another relationship or remarried then other people close to me would be murdered.'

'But your mother died of a heart attack a year ago. We went back for the funeral.'

'That's right. But I like to think she lived as long as she did because I took his threat seriously.'

She then explains how she chose to reclaim her maiden name of Cameron and make a new life for herself in another part of Spain, a country she had grown to love.

Much to her surprise and relief, James does not criticise or condemn her for keeping her past a secret. Instead he sympathises with her plight, and it makes her realise why she loves him so much.

For hours that night they discuss what they should do. James is reluctant to inform the police because he thinks it unlikely that Bruno will be locked up again and even if he is, he could get others to do his dirty work.

They both agree that if they stay put they won't be safe, but a move up the coast to Alicante no longer seems so appealing.

'It's not far enough away,' James says. 'That nutter would still pose a serious threat to us. For Alice's sake we need to put more distance between us and him.'

It's James who proposes in the early hours of the following morning that they should move back to England.

'It won't take us long to pack,' he says. 'We just take what we need and tell the landlord he can have everything else. He wants us out anyway so it won't be a problem.'

'But what will we do when we get there?' Sophie asks him.

'Let me worry about that. We've got enough cash in the bank to get us started. As soon as we're there we can open a new account and transfer it. We'll start over and make sure that sick bastard is never able to find us.'

They don't sleep at all that night and spend the next day packing and making arrangements for the move. James also makes calls to people he knows in the UK who can provide him with some fake documents. She hears him telling a man named Paul that he wants a birth certificate for a child and a driving licence for himself. But Paul says he's retired and so James has to ring someone else.

Sophie is confused and so James explains that they need the paperwork to settle down quickly back in England. He also tells her that the birth certificate he's asking for will have her name on it as Alice's mother.

'I'm having the original certificate doctored,' he says. 'That way it'll still be registered but it's highly unlikely that anyone will ever go to the trouble of checking the original names. It'll allow you to take custody of her if anything ever happens to me. You can use it to get her in a school for one thing. Is that OK with you?'

'Of course it is,' she says.

'And hopefully it will only be short term because now your secret is out we can try to find a way to sort your psycho husband out so that he no longer poses a threat to your family and friends. Then we can get married at last.'

They decide not to fly so that they don't leave a trail for Bruno to follow. Instead, they plan to drive up through France, dump the car at or near one of the ports, and then cross the Channel.

He tells the landlord they have to leave in a hurry but doesn't tell him why or where they're going.

They both spend time explaining to Alice that they've changed their minds about moving to Alicante and are going on a long adventure to England instead. She's excited about the idea because she's only ever been to England once, and that was when they went to Sophie's mother's funeral. For that trip James had had to get her passport updated so they didn't have that to worry about.

The bar stays closed all day and the doors and windows remain locked in case Bruno turns up again. But he doesn't, and when they set off they're convinced that they aren't being followed.

Sophie was determined not to let Alice see what a state she had got herself into. But it wasn't easy pretending that nothing was wrong.

Her heart was in overdrive and her mind was struggling to shut out more painful memories. Plus, she couldn't shed the cloak of despair that had wrapped itself tightly around her.

She kept expecting Bruno to step out in front of her from a doorway, and it got to the point where she wished that Lisa hadn't told her that she believed Michael Taylor had stolen her phone while they were at the pub wake.

It was wild speculation on her friend's part to suggest that he might have used it to locate Sophie so that he could tell his pal Bruno. But even so it added to the weight of unease that was bearing down on Sophie's shoulders.

She put on a brave face when she picked Alice up from her friend's terraced house just off the High Street. Alice was so full of it on the walk home that she didn't notice that Sophie wasn't really listening because she was too busy looking around to see if they were being followed.

'Ruth's dad took us to that place that does all the coloured ice-creams,' Alice said. 'Then we went to the park because they had a fair on.'

'So you had a good time,' Sophie said.

'I did. Ruth is one of my best friends. She said I can sleep over there next week. Would that be all right?'

'Of course it will. I like Ruth too. She's a nice girl.'

'Did you know that her mum is pregnant again? Ruth says that she wants it to be a boy so that she can have a baby brother.'

'No, I wasn't aware of that,' Sophie said. 'Her mum didn't mention it, and she doesn't look pregnant.'

'That's because she only found out on Friday and she's not fat yet.'

Sophie felt that familiar sting of jealousy. If only she herself had been able to have children. It was so unfair. Still, she couldn't allow herself to be too downhearted because at least she had Alice.

Sophie took Alice into a newsagents on the High Street and treated her to some sweets and a couple of magazines.

When they arrived at the flat, Sophie told her they were going to share a pizza for their tea. While she took it out of the freezer, Alice went into the living room to switch on the television.

For Sophie it was times like this that made life worth living. Just the two of them together. Finding comfort in each other's company. Not needing anyone else. This flat had been their home for three years and they both enjoyed living here. It was a good size, in a great location and, most importantly, it was affordable.

The last thing Sophie wanted to do was move away and have to look for a new home, a new job, a new school for Alice. But she'd be forced to do so if Bruno had succeeded in tracing her, or Anna Tate got wind of their whereabouts as a result of all the exposure her story had received.

The threats were coming from two different directions, and although they seemed entirely credible, there was a good chance they'd recede if she held her nerve and stayed put.

But why take that chance when there was nothing to hold her here in Shoreditch except a reluctance to start all over again somewhere else?

She had already answered in her mind the question of whether she should call Anna Tate up voluntarily and end the woman's suffering. She simply couldn't do it. She loved Alice too much to let her go, and it wouldn't be fair on the child to expose her to such a horrible truth. It would shatter every memory she had of her father and force her to accept that a woman she believed had died years ago would become the dominant force in her life.

Sophie reasoned with herself that it would be different if Alice remembered her real mother, but of course she didn't because her father abducted her at the age of two.

Having put the pizza in the oven, Sophie poured herself a glass of wine and a fizzy drink for Alice and walked into the living room. The TV was on but Alice wasn't paying attention to it because she was already absorbed in a game on her tablet. It was just as well because it was tuned to a news bulletin and they were reporting on the fact that a Member of Parliament had been arrested in connection with the murder of a young woman whose body was dumped on a common in South West London.

Sophie sat down and put Alice's drink on the table next to her, then took a sip of wine. She was about to check her phone for new messages and emails when the news reporter's voice snared her attention.

'This was the moment when Nathan Wolf, the MP for Central Somerset, was arrested and escorted from his Kensington home by Detective Chief Inspector Anna Tate, who is leading the investigation into the murder of model Holly Blake,' he said.

Sophie felt her stomach clench into a hard ball as she watched the woman she had just been thinking about emerge from the front door of the two-storey house clutching the arm of a man in a suit. She looked surprisingly composed as they were both jostled by a crowd of reporters and camera operators. Within seconds Tate managed to hustle him into a car that sped away from the scene followed by several other cars.

Sophie's interest was aroused, and she would have viewed the rest of the report if Alice hadn't looked up and said, 'Do we have to watch the news? You promised me I could watch the Harry Potter film and it's about to start.'

Sophie was actually glad of the interruption. She didn't like the thought of Alice seeing her real mother on the TV even though she had no idea who she was.

After switching to the channel that was about to show the Harry Potter film, Sophie sat back, drank some more wine and returned her attention to her phone. She hadn't had any text messages, which came as no surprise, but she had received an email with an attachment in the last hour.

She opened the email and what she read caused the air to drain from her lungs.

She didn't bother to open the attachment because there was no need. Instead, she closed her eyes and listened to the sound of her heart pounding as a dark sense of foreboding crept over her.

CHAPTER THIRTY-THREE

Anna got home just after eight. Her eyes were heavy with tiredness and her mind felt like it was being overloaded. She needed a stiff drink, something to eat and a hot bath, and not necessarily in that order.

She'd called ahead to let Tom know that she was on her way, and he managed to get there before her, having spent most of the day at his own flat. He was used to nipping between both homes, and he never made a secret of the fact that it annoyed the hell out of him. It was one of the reasons he was so keen to move in with her.

Sooner or later she would let him, of course. But first she would have to accept that it was time to give up the degree of independence that she valued so much. After all, Tom was a ray of sunshine in her life and she was lucky to have him.

'I take it you've had a tough day,' he said, as he handed her a vodka and tonic in a glass half-filled with ice cubes. 'I saw you on the news arresting that MP. I assume you've found out that he did kill the girl.'

She told him they'd found Holly's driving licence in Wolf's pocket and it appeared to be stained with blood. She shouldn't have revealed the information, of course, but as always she trusted Tom to keep it to himself.

'We'll get to formally question him in the morning,' she said. 'And by then it's possible we'll have unearthed more incriminating evidence against him.'

She then told him about Ross Moore.

'Just before I left the office we were informed that Holly's ex-boyfriend had tried to top himself,' she said. 'He apparently went home after we had him in for an interview and overdosed on pills and booze. The only reason he isn't dead is because a neighbour called at his flat to ask him if he had heard about Holly's murder. When he failed to answer the door the woman looked through the window and saw him lying on the floor. He was alive but unconscious and the paramedics took him to the Royal London Hospital.'

'So does that suggest to you that he's your murderer?'

Anna shrugged. 'Possibly. Could be he tried to end it because he couldn't live with the guilt, or because he knew we would eventually collar him for it.'

Tom offered to make the dinner while she had a bath.

'I brought a couple of frozen cottage pies with me,' he said. 'Would that be OK?'

'Perfect.'

She gave him a kiss and went upstairs where she ran the bath and stripped off her clothes.

Every muscle in her body was tense, her shoulders rigid, so it felt like heaven when she finally slid beneath the water. She closed her eyes and breathed in the heady aroma of lavender bath essence.

It's time to relax, she told herself. But that was easier said than done.

Forcing herself not to think about the case opened a door in her mind through which rushed a couple of poignant memories. She recalled the first time she put Chloe in this very bath. Her daughter splashed, giggled, peed and cried when Anna lifted her out and handed her to Matthew for him to dry her.

Then it was Chloe's second birthday and Anna's mum arrived with a giant Peppa Pig that was to become a permanent fixture in Chloe's cot. It was now in one of the boxes in the loft, along with the rest of Chloe's toys and clothes. Two years of memories and memorabilia, neatly packed away in the hope that one day she would be able to show her daughter that she'd kept them.

But by now Chloe would have built up a decade's worth of memories of her own, and Anna wouldn't be in any of them. Her father would be, and so would the unidentified woman who had been living with Matthew and Chloe in the rented house in Southampton.

Anna had no idea how long the woman, whoever she was, had been a part of their lives, but she suspected it was a long time before they turned up in the South Coast city.

She wondered yet again if Matthew had known the woman before he abducted their daughter. Was she someone else he'd been having an affair with? Someone the bastard had charmed into his bed with his good looks and unflinching self-confidence? And did he take Chloe straight to her so that she could assume the role of her mother? Or did he meet her weeks, months or years later?

And where was the bitch now? Did she take Chloe abroad

after she fled Southampton the night Matthew was murdered? Back to where they'd been before?

There was another scenario that in many ways was even more disturbing – that the woman had abandoned Chloe because she didn't want to be responsible for her.

Whatever the truth, Anna was sure that the woman must have been aware all along that James Miller was really Matthew Dobson and that his daughter's name was Chloe and not Alice. Which made her complicit in what the bastard had done. An accessory to his crime. As morally corrupt as he was.

Someone Anna hated with every fibre of her being even though they had never met.

Anna eventually snapped out of the thoughts she'd been losing herself in and climbed out of the bath. When she was towel-dry, she slipped into her robe and went downstairs. It was perfect timing because Tom was ready to serve up dinner.

They tucked in while sitting next to each other on the sofa, and after a while of trading small talk Anna began to relax. But it only lasted until they finished eating and she turned on the TV news while Tom went to refill their glasses with wine. Within seconds she was wrenched back into work mode and she knew that for the rest of the evening she wouldn't be able to switch off.

Holly's murder and Nathan Wolf's arrest dominated the news agenda. There was wall-to-wall coverage, and the most used clip was the one in which Anna led the MP out of his house to the waiting police car. She cringed at the sight of herself, the tousled hair, the dirty looks she gave reporters, the fact that she always appeared ill at ease.

It brought to mind something her late father once told her. He was a copper himself before he was so badly beaten by drug dealers that he was forced to resign from the force as a result of his injuries.

'It got to the stage, Anna, where I wouldn't watch the news if I knew I was going to be on it,' he said during one of the heart-to-hearts they had while he was in a hospice dying of cancer. 'It just served to make me feel bad about myself, which in turn made me avoid the cameras, and that sometimes hindered an investigation.'

Thankfully Anna was less troubled about how she came across on screen, and she had long ago accepted that it didn't pay to be camera shy, especially on the high-profile cases.

And they did not come much more high-profile than this one. The story was like manna from heaven for the news outlets. The victim was a young, attractive model and daughter of an ex-police chief who was hoping to be London Mayor. The suspect under arrest was a Member of Parliament who'd been having an affair with the model, despite her being half his age.

And there were two other suspects in the mix – the ex-boyfriend and the stepdad.

As if that wasn't enough, another explosive development beefed up the story even further as the evening progressed. This was the exclusive Holly Blake interview in the *Sunday Mirror*, which every other news organisation picked up after the early edition of the paper was rolled out. Anna read the online edition on her phone.

In it Holly laid bare the nature of her relationship with Nathan Wolf. The paper pointed out that they didn't get a chance to do a full interview with her, but she told them enough at a preliminary meeting to fill the front and two inside pages. Anna suspected that they had made up a few of the quotes, or at least exaggerated some of what she'd told them.

The headline read: *'I was MP's secret sugarbabe,' revealed Holly Blake in an exclusive interview before she was murdered.*

There were photographs of Holly and Nathan, although they weren't seen together in any of them. There were also two photos of the playroom in her flat, taken by Holly and given to the paper.

'Nathan chose and paid for everything in the room,' she told the *Sunday Mirror*. *'And we've been enjoying ourselves there two and sometimes three times a week for more than a year. He preferred being the submissive partner during our sex sessions and would like me to spank him and use the restraints to cause him excruciating pain.'*

Holly also disclosed how she fell in love with Wolf and believed him when he promised that they would eventually get married.

'But I realise now that he didn't love me and that he was lying all along,' she said. *'He was just using me for sex, and when he told me he was going to marry someone else it broke my heart.'*

The paper's editor, Ralph Fleming, was quoted as saying, *'Holly came to us because she wanted the world to know that the man who was supposed to be a respectable and honourable Member of Parliament was nothing of the sort. She was going to tell us more about Mr Wolf and their time together but she didn't get the chance to give us a full interview.'*

Further down the page the report included the line: *'We*

now know that Holly told Mr Wolf that she was going public with her story just days before she was stabbed to death.'

They were sailing close to the wind with that, Anna thought, because the clear insinuation was that he had killed her.

The paper also devoted space to the investigation itself and to the fact that the police were planning to question Holly's ex-boyfriend. There were sidebars that focused on Nathan Wolf's career and Rebecca Blake's bid to become London Mayor, which the paper said would most likely be put on hold. And there was a collection of quotes from various people, including politicians from all the main parties, who were calling on Wolf to step down as an MP.

One of them reportedly said, *'If it's true that this man has been leading a sordid double life then he should think seriously about his position. He's brought disgrace on himself, his party and those people in his constituency who voted for him at the last election.'*

As Anna watched and listened to what amounted to a brutal hatchet job, she couldn't help thinking that even though Holly Blake was no longer alive, she had succeeded in doing what she had set out to do: to get her own back on the man who betrayed her.

CHAPTER THIRTY-FOUR

Anna had a restless night. She was jolted awake several times by dreams about Chloe that brought tears to her eyes.

In one of them she was transported back to the day her daughter walked for the first time, in the garden. Chloe managed to stay on her feet for about five yards before falling on her face. But she didn't cry. She just giggled, and carried on giggling even when she tumbled sideways onto a flower bed and cut her knee on a thorny bush.

In another dream Chloe was older, eighteen months or so, and she and Matthew had taken her to a local leisure centre for her first swimming lesson. She was wearing armbands and goggles, and she took to the water like a fish. She splashed about for almost an hour and cried when it was time to get her out. Anna promised her that they would go again, but it never happened because soon afterwards Matthew's affair came to light, followed by the break-up and divorce. And then the bastard took their daughter away and broke Anna's heart.

*

She finally got out of bed at seven. Tom had downed quite a few drinks the previous evening so she left him there nursing a mild hangover.

Her first task on Sunday morning was to front the press conference at New Scotland Yard alongside DCS Nash and Simon Thackery, head of media relations. It kicked off at nine and was attended by journalists, photographers and camera crews from around the world. Anna recognised several reporters from the American networks and European news channels.

The story had continued to gather momentum overnight with the revelations in the *Sunday Mirror*. Now everyone involved in the case was being chased for interviews by desperate journalists, including Holly's family, Jennifer Rothwell and anyone who was acquainted with Ross Moore.

This was the first time the hacks had been given the chance to put the police on the spot and get on-the-record answers to their questions. Much to Anna's surprise it turned out to be a fairly orderly event, unlike some of the big press conferences she had fronted. Most of the questions that were thrown at them they'd been primed to expect.

Why was Nathan Wolf arrested?

Has he been charged with Holly's murder?

Is he denying the claims attributed to Holly Blake in the Sunday Mirror*?*

Can you confirm rumours that Rebecca Blake will now withdraw from the Mayoral race?

Was Mr Wolf badly hurt when he was attacked in his home yesterday?

Is it true that another suspect is in hospital after trying to kill himself?

Nash answered most of the questions, but that was normal since he relished the sound of his own voice.

'Mr Wolf is being questioned about Holly's murder because we know he was in a relationship with her,' he said. 'However, I must stress that he has not been charged at this time or even formally interviewed. His properties have been subjected to a search as you all know and so has Holly's flat in Camden. I am not at liberty to disclose what, if anything, was found that is relevant to our enquiries.'

He went on to reiterate what he had said earlier, that Holly's body had been left on Barnes Common but she hadn't been killed there. He then handed over to Anna, who explained that her team were still trying to establish a timeline for Holly on the day she died.

'We'd like to hear from anyone who was on or near Barnes Common on Tuesday evening or early on Wednesday morning,' she said. 'We believe the person who placed Holly's body there would have done so when it was quiet. So it's possible someone was seen acting suspiciously in the area around the old cemetery, or perhaps a car was noticed parked in a spot not usually frequented by vehicles.

'We're also keen to know where Holly spent most of that day. She had no official modelling assignments and the people who work with her have no knowledge of her movements. The last recorded sighting of her was at ten-forty-five that evening when she left her flat on foot. She was never seen alive again. We want to know where she went and who she met.'

Nash wound up by reading out a statement from Holly's mother. 'We're still trying to come to terms with what has happened to our precious daughter. We can't believe she's gone and we find it hard to accept that somebody took her life. My husband and I, and other family members, are shocked and grief-stricken. So I appeal to you all to respect our privacy. In time I'm sure I'll feel strong enough to face the media, but right now we all just need to be left alone.'

After the press conference, Anna went straight back to Wandsworth, where DI Walker had been holding the fort.

Her next task was to interview Nathan Wolf, but first she needed to get a handle on what progress the team had been making. She asked Walker to start the briefing so he took up position at the front of the room between the whiteboards.

'Firstly I can report that forensics have confirmed that it *is* Holly's blood on her driving licence,' he said. 'The licence also contains prints and DNA, but only hers. There was nothing on the knives taken from Wolf's house except his prints but he's had a lot of time to get rid of any trace evidence.'

'What about his Range Rover?' Anna asked.

'Sweet fuck all,' Walker said. 'But the officers who examined it say that without a doubt it was cleaned both inside and out at some point in the last few days. The boot is spotless, apparently. It's been tidied up and vacuumed, so if a body was carried in it then no clues have been left behind.'

Walker went on to say that Devon police had found nothing of interest in Wolf's Bridgewater home.

'Same outcome in respect of the clothes we took. There's no blood on the jacket that contained the licence, but we do know that he wore that particular jacket while he was in his constituency on Tuesday and possibly when he drove home.'

'How do we know that?' Anna said.

'A local newspaper carried a picture of him that was taken when he opened a new community centre that afternoon. It's a distinctive beige jacket with a badge pinned to the lapel and he had it on then.'

Anna asked if the SOCOs had turned up anything more at Holly's flat.

DC Niven answered that one. 'Nothing that points to it being the scene of a crime. And I'm afraid the same goes for the ex-boyfriend's flat. We obtained a warrant to search it. The techies found plenty of photographs of Holly that had been uploaded from his phone to his computer hard drive, including some of her out walking that in all probability she didn't know he took.'

'So what's the latest from the hospital?' Anna said. 'When can we get to question him?'

'We should know within the next half an hour,' Niven said. 'The doctor is about to do his rounds and I'm expecting a call straight after.'

Anna then asked DS Prescott for a progress report on the CCTV trawl.

He began by saying they'd had no further luck tracing Wolf's Range Rover on the journey he took from Somerset to London.

'We still only have the one shot when the vehicle was

captured on camera close to his home just after midnight,' Prescott said. 'The problem is he's being vague about the roads he used after he arrived back in the capital. He says he was forced to deviate from his usual route because of road works and heavy traffic. As you know he insists he went nowhere near Barnes Common and so far his Range Rover hasn't turned up on any of the cameras in that area.'

'And do I take it we're still seeking footage of Holly after she left her flat?' Anna said.

Prescott nodded. 'We've got tons of it to go through and it's time-consuming. For all we know she hopped in a taxi or got a lift to wherever it was she was going.'

Anna knew that if that was the case then it was going to make the task of tracking her movements much more difficult, if not impossible.

'We have had one interesting result, though,' Prescott said. 'But it relates to Holly's stepdad, Theo Blake.'

'Oh?'

He checked his notes. 'If you recall, he told you that after Holly left their house in Pimlico following the row with her mother, he went looking for her.'

'He claimed he went to her flat and got no answer there,' Anna said. 'Then instead of returning straight home he went for a drink at the King's Head pub in Chappell Road. He reckons he stayed for about an hour before walking back to his house, which is why he didn't arrive there until almost midnight.'

'That's right. When we checked the pub the proprietor told us the security cameras weren't working. But there's a shop across the road from the pub with an external camera and the footage gathered is kept for nine days.'

'So what does it show?'

'That's the thing, guv. It confirms that he did go there on Tuesday just like he said. He arrived by taxi and left on foot.'

'So he told us the truth then?'

'Well, not quite. You see, he claimed he stayed in the pub for about an hour. But he lied. It was more like two minutes. And when he came back out he was no longer alone.'

CHAPTER THIRTY-FIVE

It was eleven a.m. and Sophie was on her third cup of coffee. She felt dreadful. Her eyes were sagging with exhaustion and she was struggling to think straight.

She had gone to bed the previous evening at a quarter to twelve, two hours after Alice. But she'd hardly slept, and had lain awake fretting over the contents of the email she'd received.

It was from Mrs Holland, the headmistress of Oakfield Community School in Bethnal Green, where Alice was a pupil. Attached to it was the age progression photo of Detective Anna Tate's daughter Chloe that Sophie had already seen in the *Evening Standard*.

Hi Miss Cameron

I've been approached by a private investigator named Jack Keen. He's working on behalf of a Metropolitan police detective named Anna Tate.

You might have seen a newspaper story relating to her twelve-year-old daughter who has been missing for ten years.

As part of her efforts to find the girl, Miss Tate commissioned someone to produce an age progression photo of her which Mr Keen sent to me and which I've attached.

Apparently someone contacted the newspaper in question to say that a young girl resembling the child in the photo, and who is named Alice, goes to Oakfield Community School.

Mr Keen is now asking me to confirm that this is so.

As you may or may not know we have three girls here whose first name is Alice. And they're all aged either twelve or thirteen.

However, you'll note that your own daughter does look quite similar to the artist's impression, which I'm sure is simply a bizarre coincidence.

I haven't yet responded to Mr Keen because I'm reluctant to provide him with personal details about you and your daughter without your permission. But having thought it through I believe that given the nature of the enquiry it would be best if you contacted him directly yourself. You can then explain that despite the similarity between your daughter and the girl in the photo, they are not one and the same.

Mr Keen's email address and phone numbers are below, and if you want to chat to me about this matter then don't hesitate to call.

Sophie's reply had been short and to the point.

No problem, Mrs Holland. I'll get in touch with Mr Keen asap and tell him he's quite welcome to come and visit my Alice so that he can see for himself that she's not the girl he's looking for.

Sophie was well aware that all she had done was buy herself a little time. She had no intention of contacting the investigator, but when he didn't hear from her he was bound to call Mrs Holland again, or maybe even turn up unannounced at the school to see if he could spot Alice himself.

Sophie knew that she was now in an impossible position. Fate had conspired against her and she'd been driven to despair by a series of events over which she'd had no control.

It began a couple of weeks ago when Anna Tate discovered that her missing husband Matthew and daughter Chloe had been living under false identities for the past decade. There could be no denying that it was a fascinating human interest story, and so it was picked up by the *Evening Standard*.

As part of the coverage the paper had carried the age progression image of Chloe. And that had reminded one or more of its readers of a young girl who attended Oakfield School.

It was shocking bad luck for Sophie and now she was paralysed by indecision. An inner voice was telling her to take flight before it was too late. That private investigator was closing in and he wouldn't just leave her alone if she refused to speak to him. Anna Tate wouldn't let him do that. The woman was probably paying him a fortune to find her daughter. And as a police officer she could count on her colleagues to lend her support.

But Sophie knew that running away from everything would be hellishly difficult. She had a day or two at the most.

And in that time she had to construct a plausible story to tell Alice, then pack up their things, decide where to go and work out how to get there.

It would be a nightmare and there was no guarantee she could pull it off. All it would take was one mistake and it could go terribly wrong. Just like it did three years ago when they fled Spain because Bruno had found out where she was living.

The memory of what happened back then crept into her mind again now and caused her saliva glands to dry up and her guts to twist involuntarily.

Three years ago

The drive up through Spain and France is long and uneventful. They make one overnight stop in Bordeaux.

While there James books seats on the Eurostar from Calais. When they arrive the next day they abandon the car in a street close to the port, leaving the windows open and the key in the ignition. Chances are it won't be long before it's stolen.

Soon they're on a train passing under the English Channel en route to London.

'We'll be OK,' James tells Sophie. 'I promise I will look after you and keep you safe from that monster.'

Alice is fast asleep on the seat facing them, her mouth wide open.

'I'm really sorry it's come to this,' Sophie says. 'I should have been honest with you from the start. I was just so afraid that you wouldn't stay with me.'

'It was the wrong call, but we all make them. There are things I've done that I bitterly regret. But it's not always

easy to change direction once you've embarked on a particular course of action.'

'I really don't deserve you,' she says as she snuggles up to him. 'My life changed for the better that day you walked into the restaurant with Alice. And I've loved every moment of every day since then. You both mean so much to me.'

Once they reach their destination they check into a bed and breakfast close to St Pancras Station and stay for three days and nights. While there James goes off to get the fake driving licence and birth certificate from someone who has promised to produce them within forty-eight hours. Sophie had no idea they could be so easily obtained.

They spend hours making arrangements about where to go next. The decision on where to set up home for at least the first six months is left to James. He decides on Southampton because he knows the city well having gone to university there.

When they get there they lease a furnished house with two bedrooms from a local estate agents and move in, hoping against hope that Bruno Perez will never find them.

But he does – and after only three weeks.

They're caught completely off guard. It's early evening and already dark outside. Sophie is in the kitchen preparing dinner for when James gets home. Alice is sitting at the table playing on her tablet.

The poor child still isn't settled, and who can blame her? She knows that despite what they've told her all is not well. Fear and anxiety followed them from Spain and it's proving difficult to move beyond it.

Alice can sense their unease and is confused by it. She keeps asking questions that they try not to answer. Are we going to stay here? When will I have to go to school? Why won't you let me go out by myself? Why is Daddy so miserable these days?

Sophie knows that on the face of it they must seem like a normal family – cosy, comfortable, content in their own little world. But that couldn't be further from the truth.

Sophie is already missing her adopted country and still can't believe what's happened. Both she and James are still in a state of flux. The drama they were swept up in has taken a heavy toll. Their nerves are frayed and uncertainty over what the future holds is a constant worry.

What savings they have left – mainly from the money James inherited after his mother died – will soon run out, so one of them will need to get a job. They also have to decide how long to stay in Southampton, and whether to enrol Alice in one of the local schools.

On the plus side they all like the little terraced house within walking distance of the city centre, and they've hired a brand new Fiat for a couple of months to get around in. Sophie is also relieved that James isn't blaming her for their predicament. He says he's forgiven her for lying about her past and insists that as long as the three of them are together they'll be able to weather any storm.

She's expecting him back any minute. He walked into the city centre via the park to pick up a parcel. It's been sent from Spain by their former landlord and arrived late this afternoon at the courier company's office off the High Street.

The parcel contains a few treasured items – including Sophie's only photo of her late father – that they accidentally left behind when they hurried away from their flat above the bar.

The landlord was kind enough to get the stuff together after

James rang him and then said he was happy to bear the cost of sending the parcel to the UK.

It's just after six-thirty when James calls her on her new mobile phone. They both got rid of the old ones so they couldn't be used to trace them.

'It's me,' he says, but she knows that because he's the only person who has her number.

She starts to ask him when he'll be home but he talks over her.

'We've got a problem, Sophie. The bastard has found us.'

A blast of ice whips through every vein in Sophie's body.

'What do you mean?' she says.

'I mean Bruno is here in Southampton. I just spotted him and I think he's been following me since I left the courier company's office. It could be that the landlord told him I'd be picking the parcel up today.'

'Oh no. Are you sure it's him?'

'Positive.'

'So where are you?'

'I'm crossing the park. I just lost sight of him, but I know he's close by so I daren't come straight back to the house because I'll lead him to you.'

'Then what will you do?'

'I'm not sure.'

'Please don't confront him, James. He's a dangerous psycho.'

'That's why he needs to be stopped. We can't keep running from him.'

'No, James. Stay away from him. For all our sakes.'

He ignores her plea. 'You need to leave the house right away in case he knows where we live.'

'But we can't just—'

'Do it, Soph, and do it now. He might have others with him and I don't want you and Alice there if someone turns up at the door.'

'Then I'll call the police. Get them to come here.'

'You can't do that,' he says.

'Why not?'

'I've got no time to explain, Soph. Just trust that I know what I'm doing. You need to get out. Cram all our stuff into the cases and leave. I don't want to have to worry about you.'

'But where will we go?'

'Drive out of town and find a hotel or a B and B to check into for the night. I'll call you as soon as I can.'

'Why can't I just meet you somewhere now?'

'It's too risky. I have to be sure I've lost him first.'

'But are you certain we need to do this?'

'We haven't got a choice. He's come all this way for a reason. He wants to hurt you, Sophie. And there's a chance he'll hurt Alice as well.'

'But you have to promise me that you won't approach him.'

'OK, I promise. But you need to promise me that whatever happens you'll look after Alice. Don't let anyone take her from you. You're her mother now, Sophie, and you're all she's got.'

'Oh, Christ, James. You're making it sound like I'll never see you again.'

'Don't be daft. Of course . . .'

He stops speaking suddenly and she hears him catch his breath. 'I have to go,' he says. 'I can see him again and I think he's seen me. Please get out of the house now, Sophie. I love you.'

He ends the call before she can tell him that she loves him too. Fear clutches at her stomach as she screams for Alice to come down the stairs.

In a blind panic she follows James's instructions while praying that he keeps his promise not to approach her estranged husband.

It only takes her thirty minutes to pack up the car because they have relatively few possessions.

After locking the house, Sophie heads straight for the M3, which is less than a mile away, and they drive north for twenty minutes to the turn-off for Winchester. By the time they get there Alice is in tears in the back seat, demanding to know why her father isn't with them. Sophie tells her he's got some business to attend to but it fails to placate her.

It takes Sophie forty minutes to find a small hotel that has vacancies and she manages to calm Alice down enough so that they can check in.

But once inside the room, Alice starts crying again and Sophie comes to realise that the only way to ease the girl's growing alarm is to get her dad on the phone.

But that's when she realises that she doesn't have her mobile. She tells Alice to wait in the room while she goes outside to see if she's dropped it in the car. But it's not there and it's not in any of the cases either.

It dawns on her then that she must have left it behind in her rush to get away. And that's a big problem. It's her only way of contacting James since she still hasn't memorised the number of his new phone.

It means she'll have to return to the house even though it might not be safe to do so.

*

Since that fateful night three years ago Sophie has deeply regretted doing what James told her to do. She should have gone straight to the park to look for him or called the police.

She now knows why he was reluctant to alert the cops. He'd been afraid that it would have uncovered Alice's true identity and led to his own arrest for parental abduction.

She recalls now how she drove back towards the house with poor Alice half asleep in the back. But to get there she had to drive alongside the park and her attention was drawn to the flashing blue light of an ambulance just beyond the low perimeter fence. She pulled over to the kerb. Gut instinct told her that it had something to do with James. Alice had fallen asleep in the car so she left it parked with the doors locked and went to check it out.

A small crowd had gathered just off the path. They were watching as two paramedics attended to a figure lying on the grass. Sophie was swamped by a rush of intense dread as she approached them, but even before she was close enough to see the face of the person on the ground she knew it was James.

She had to stifle a scream when she saw the blood on that familiar white shirt and she froze when she heard one of the paramedics tell his colleague that the man had been stabbed twice and was dead.

Sophie was about to throw herself on the ground next to James's body but stopped herself when her mind seized on an image of Alice in the Fiat. It made her realise that she couldn't let anyone know that she was the dead man's partner. If she did she risked having Alice taken away from her. And she couldn't let that happen.

Her best bet was to disappear so that no one, not even the police, knew how to find her.

'You're her mother now, Sophie, and you're all she's got.'

So with James's words ringing in her ears, Sophie did what proved to be the most difficult thing she had ever done. She turned around and walked slowly away from the scene of what was obviously a brutal murder.

And from the only man she had ever truly loved.

CHAPTER THIRTY-SIX

Anna decided to keep Nathan Wolf and his lawyer waiting in the interview room. Before going downstairs she wanted to view the CCTV footage that proved Holly's stepdad hadn't been entirely candid with them.

'The camera is in an elevated position across the road from the King's Head pub,' DS Prescott said as he played the short sequence through the TV monitors in the office. 'Fortunately it's a well-lit street and the quality of the video is high-end.'

It began with a black taxi pulling up in front of the pub. A passenger got out and was still standing on the pavement when the cab drove off.

'That's definitely Theo Blake,' Walker said.

They watched him put what looked like cash back into his wallet before he turned and entered the pub.

'Keep an eye on the time code,' Prescott said. Two minutes later Blake came out of the pub with a woman who was holding onto his arm.

It wasn't his stepdaughter or his wife. But they did look

like a couple who were planning to have a good time. The woman had dark shoulder-length hair and was wearing a light-coloured blouse over tight jeans. Anna couldn't see her face clearly because they were too far away.

'Can you get a screen grab and blow it up?' Anna asked Prescott.

'I've already done that, ma'am,' he said.

He waited until the pair walked out of shot along the pavement and then brought up a freeze frame that had been magnified. The woman's features were slightly blurred, but Anna could tell that she was probably in her mid-thirties or early forties. She was slim and about five foot five tall, and she was carrying a small shoulder bag.

'Methinks that Holly's stepdad is playing away from home,' Walker quipped. 'That's probably why he offered to go after her that night following the bust-up with her mum. It gave him a chance to pop out for a quickie.'

It was certainly a turn-up for the books, and Anna felt immensely sorry for his wife.

She turned to face the room and said, 'I don't want Rebecca Blake to know about this. We keep it to ourselves. She has enough on her plate as it is. I intend to drop in on the family later on today so I'll take Theo to one side and get him to explain himself.'

'Maybe there's an innocent explanation,' someone said. 'Or perhaps he and his wife have an open marriage.'

'Extremely unlikely on both counts,' Anna said. 'It seems obvious to me that he's been caught bang to rights.'

She told Prescott to send the clip to her mobile phone and then to go to the pub.

'Ask the proprietor and bar staff if they know who she is

and where she lives,' she said. 'I'm assuming he arranged to meet her there but I want to know where they went. So check every other CCTV camera around there. I also want to know if that woman is connected in any way to Holly or Nathan Wolf.'

The interview room was small and sparse with dull green walls and a hard, grey floor. It was equipped with state-of-the art recording equipment and a large two-way mirror.

Anna took DC Sweeny in with her because she wanted Walker to write up a briefing note for Nash and the Commissioner.

Wolf was sitting next to his lawyer, Gavin Peake. On the table in front of them was a copy of the *Sunday Mirror*, which Anna guessed Peake had brought in to show his client. The MP looked rough after his night in the cell. His face was taut and pallid, and dark shadows hung beneath his eyes.

'It's about time you graced us with your presence,' the lawyer said after they took seats opposite and Anna placed a folder on the table. 'We've been waiting here for over half an hour.'

'Well, I'm sorry about that,' Anna said, her voice laced with sarcasm. 'But we're pretty busy trying to solve a vicious murder.'

'That may be so, Detective Chief Inspector, but I would like to remind you that the custody clock is ticking and my client has already been here for fourteen long hours.'

'And that means we can hold him for another ten hours without charge,' Anna said. 'At which point we can apply to have it extended.'

'I'm well aware of the rules,' Peake said.

Wolf banged a fist on the table. 'Look, can we just get on with it? The sooner I've answered your bloody questions the sooner I can get out of here.' He gestured at the newspaper. 'I need to tell my side of this story before I lose everything. That bitch has made it sound as though she was forced into doing what she did and that's not the case.'

His eyes flashed furiously and his nostrils twitched. Peake put a hand on his arm in an effort to calm him down.

'Before we continue I'd like to know how you're feeling this morning, Mr Wolf,' Anna said. 'As you know this interview was delayed as a result of your panic attack.'

'It wasn't a panic attack,' he said. 'I just got over-anxious. It was the shock. I couldn't believe what was going on and I still can't.'

'But you're OK now?'

'Of course I'm not. But I'm able to do this, so can you please stop wasting time?'

Anna moved quickly on with the formalities by switching on the recorder and announcing who was in the room and why they were there.

'Let's begin with you telling us how long you were in a relationship with Holly Blake,' she said.

'But I've already told you that,' Wolf responded.

'Then tell us again.'

He rubbed at the stubble on his chin. 'We'd been seeing each other for just over a year.'

'And what was the nature of that relationship?'

'We liked each other and got on well. It was fun while it lasted.'

'So why didn't you move in together or allow yourselves to be seen in public?'

His hands balled into fists on the table. 'Surely that's obvious. When it started I was married. Then after my wife died I thought it best to keep it quiet at least for a time. But you know all this.'

'And can you confirm for the record that you paid the rent on Holly's flat and for all the S and M equipment that's installed there?'

'Yes, I can. And she was entirely happy with the arrangement.'

'But she wasn't happy when you told her that you were ending the affair because you were in love with someone else.'

He sighed. 'I honestly didn't expect her to react the way she did. I had no idea that she thought we'd be spending the rest of our lives together. I always assumed we would eventually go our separate ways.'

'So what was your reaction when she told you that she was going to sell her story to a newspaper?'

'I pleaded with her not to do it. I offered her money and tried to convince her that although we'd had a lot of fun together it was better for her that it was over. She could move on, marry someone her own age, have kids.'

'But she didn't see it that way,' Anna said. 'And that's when you resorted to threatening her.'

'What my client said during that argument hardly constitutes a serious threat,' said Peake.

'I beg to differ,' Anna said. She opened the folder in front of her and took out a sheet of paper. 'Let me remind you. Mr Wolf said, and I quote: "Take the money I've offered and move on or I swear you'll regret it."'

Wolf's eyes stretched wide and he shook his head.

'It was an off-the-cuff remark. I didn't mean it literally.'

Anna reached into the folder again and pulled out a transparent evidence bag.

'For the benefit of the tape I'm showing the suspect item twelve, a driving licence in the name of Holly Blake. Do you recognise this, Mr Wolf?'

'Of course I do.'

Anna slid it across the table between Wolf and his lawyer.

'Forensics have confirmed that those marks on it are specks of Holly's blood. That suggests to me that it was in her possession when she was stabbed. The forensic report says the licence could have been contaminated with a spray of blood during the act itself or when her clothes were removed, assuming she wasn't naked when she was murdered. But to be honest we're not sure how it happened. Perhaps you can tell us.'

'I wouldn't know because I wasn't there,' Wolf said.

'Then can you explain why it was in your jacket pocket?'

'I've already told you I don't know.'

'So you're claiming that someone must have put it there.'

'Well, I can't think of any other explanation.'

Anna picked up the evidence bag and slipped it back into the folder. While she did this, DC Sweeny asked her first question.

'When was the last time you wore that particular jacket, Mr Wolf?'

He looked at her, his brow furrowed.

'I can't remember.'

'Really?'

'I've got lots of jackets and suits. I don't keep a note of what I wear and when.'

'Well, I can tell you that you wore it on Tuesday,' Sweeny said.

It was Anna's cue to take a newspaper cutting from the folder, which she placed before Wolf.

'That picture was taken for a local rag in your constituency shortly before you drove back to London,' Sweeny said.

Wolf glanced at the cutting and shrugged a single shoulder.

'So what if I wore it that day? I'd forgotten. But now I think about it I'm sure I wore it to the office on Wednesday too. It doesn't prove anything.'

'My client is right,' Peake said, leaning forward and directing his words at Anna. 'This so-called evidence is at best circumstantial. You know that Miss Blake was murdered, but you don't know where it happened so you can't place Mr Wolf at the scene of the crime. I'm assuming that his Range Rover was not picked up on roads near to where the body was found otherwise you would have mentioned it. The so-called threat he made is not as sinister as you're suggesting, considering what she was planning to do.

'You also have to concede that the driving licence might well have been planted in my client's pocket on Wednesday or at any point since then. And as for the blood, well, you can't be certain that it wasn't put there by the killer as part of a crude attempt to frame him.'

'I think you would have trouble convincing a jury of that,' Anna said.

'Well, I can't really see this ending up in court,' Peake said. 'Not unless there's incriminating evidence that we're not being made aware of. Did you find anything else apart from the licence in the house in Kensington, for instance? Or at his property in Somerset? And what about his Range Rover? Did that contain traces of Holly Blake?'

'I was going to come on to the vehicle next,' Anna said,

turning to Wolf. 'The technicians say it's been cleaned thoroughly both inside and out during the past week. Did you do that yourself or did you take it to a car wash?'

'I did it myself on the driveway,' he replied. 'I always do it myself.'

'And when did you do it?'

'On Wednesday morning. I didn't have to go to the office until after lunch so I cleaned the car because it was in a mess.'

'But you have to admit that sounds suspicious, Mr Wolf,' Anna said. 'In fact as far as I'm concerned it feeds into the perceived narrative of events.'

'I don't see how,' Wolf said.

Anna rested her elbows on the table. 'Then let me explain. Holly reacted badly when you told her that you were dumping her for another woman. She threatened to expose your relationship with her, along with all the sordid details. So you threatened her. Then when you returned from Somerset you somehow found out where she was going after she left her flat. You confronted her, killed her, then dumped her body on Barnes Common. But first you stripped her and took her possessions so as not to leave any trace of yourself. In doing so you slipped up and forgot about the licence you'd placed in your pocket. The next morning you took the extra precaution of cleaning your Range Rover to get rid of any evidence that Holly might have left behind.'

Wolf just sat there with his mouth open, but his lawyer shook his head and grinned.

'You have got to be kidding, Detective Tate. That account of what might have happened is so full of holes that the Crown Prosecution Service would throw it right back at you. You'll need much more before you can even consider charging my client with Holly Blake's murder. And I'm sure you know it.'

'I think the lawyer's right, guv,' Sweeny said when they stepped out of the interview room. 'We'll need more evidence to be certain of securing a conviction.'

'Do you reckon he did it, Megan?' Anna asked her.

'I don't think there's any doubt. He had motive and opportunity. He told her she'd regret what she was going to do. And for me the clincher is the licence. I don't for a minute believe it was planted. It could be that after he killed her he was in a real state mentally. Maybe he put her purse in his pocket and the licence fell out. Or perhaps she slipped it in there herself while she was alive.'

Neither of those scenarios seemed even remotely plausible to Anna. Killers often made stupid mistakes in the heat of the moment, and that was how many of them ended up getting caught. But another thing killers often did was to keep mementoes of their victims, including personal belongings such as jewellery, spectacles, watches and underwear.

Anna also knew of at least two cases where murderers had kept their victims' driving licences. She even recalled one of them saying during his trial that he did it because he regretted committing the crime and it was his way of keeping his victim close. So Anna couldn't help wondering if that was why Wolf hadn't thrown Holly's licence away, along with her handbag, mobile phone and purse. Did he keep it intentionally and then forget that he'd put it into his pocket? It was one of far too many unanswered questions that were playing on her mind.

She informed the Custody Sergeant that Wolf was to be taken back to his cell after his lawyer had finished speaking to him. She wasn't prepared to charge him or let him go just yet even if she came under pressure to do so.

The rest of the team were eager to know how the interview had gone so she called them together to relay the relevant details.

But just as she started to speak, DS Prescott came bounding into the office, his face flushed with excitement.

'We've just found some more CCTV footage,' he announced for all to hear as he waved what looked like a USB flash drive above his head. 'And believe me this clip is a real eye-opener.'

Anna felt her pulse rate spike, thinking what they had come up with would strengthen the case against Nathan Wolf.

But when she viewed it she realised it did no such thing. Instead it turned out to be a dynamite piece of evidence that put one of their other suspects firmly in the frame.

CHAPTER THIRTY-SEVEN

Sophie let Alice lie in while she showered and dressed. She wished now that she hadn't promised to take her shopping. It was the last thing she felt like doing with her mind in such disarray.

She was also nervous about leaving the flat because she continued to believe that someone had been stalking her over the past couple of days. If she was right then whoever it was might well be preparing to confront her, and God only knew what the outcome of that would be.

Was it Bruno who was out there, biding his time while waiting for the right moment to pounce? Or was it someone she didn't know? Detective Anna Tate's private investigator, perhaps? Or even the person who had contacted the *Evening Standard* to say that a child resembling the Chloe Tate age progression image was a pupil at Oakfield School?

Sophie was cold with panic even though the heat from the shower had made her skin go red. She knew she had to come up with a plan but she was struggling to get her head around it.

From her bedroom window she looked out on a dull, wet day. The rain she'd heard pounding the city overnight had stopped, but the sky was still bruised and threatening. It made her think of Spain and how the sun shone for most of the year. She missed the bright, warm days that had filled her with a glorious sense of wellbeing.

From time to time during the past three years she had actually thought about moving back there. But having finally settled in London she hadn't been able to work up enough energy to do so. She had no regrets about rushing up to the capital the day after James was murdered in Southampton. Out of desperation she sought help from her friend Lisa, who was living alone in Dulwich back then and was only too willing to allow Sophie and Alice to move in with her for a couple of weeks.

It was a hard, distressing time during which Sophie had to cope with her own grief and explain to Alice that she would never see her father again. She chose not to lie, but didn't tell the whole truth. She said James told her they had to leave the house in Southampton because they could no longer afford to live there. He was due to meet them that night but he was attacked and killed by an unknown assailant in the park.

The child was naturally heartbroken and inconsolable, but she believed what Sophie told her because she was only nine years old.

While staying with Lisa, Sophie monitored the news reports about the murder of James Miller in Southampton and learned that the cops had no suspects. They were also looking for the unnamed woman and child who had been living with him.

Lisa tried to persuade her to go to the police, but she said no for two reasons. Firstly, it would have been a waste of time because Bruno would have made sure he couldn't be implicated in James's murder. No doubt he'd have secured himself a cast-iron alibi. And secondly she didn't feel that she could trust the police enough to risk making herself known to them. It was an open secret that Bruno and his dodgy pals – men like Michael Taylor – had contacts in the Met who were not averse to providing them with information in return for hard cash.

Sophie left Alice with Lisa while she pretended to go and talk to the police and then to attend James's funeral. It was all part of creating a story that Alice wouldn't be able to pull apart when she was older.

Sophie and Alice moved out of Lisa's flat after two and a half weeks. It was just too risky to stay there given that her friend was still in touch with the group who hung around with Bruno. As a precaution she didn't tell Lisa where she was moving to, but she promised to continue their friendship.

A month later Sophie made enquiries and discovered that James Miller had been given a pauper's funeral by Southampton Council. She found out where his grave was and took Alice to see it in the hope that it would help them both find closure, as well as add credibility to the story Sophie had constructed. It was an emotional pilgrimage, and Sophie took a photograph of the headstone with the inscription:

Here lies James Miller. May he rest in peace.

Sophie turned from the window and tried to blink away the memories so that she could focus on her current problem.

She went into the kitchen and put the kettle on to make herself another coffee, but just as it started to boil Alice appeared in the doorway in her pyjamas. She was crying and her face was awash with tears.

'What on earth is the matter, sweetheart?' Sophie said as she rushed across the room to her.

'I had a horrible dream,' Alice said. 'It made me wake up.'

Sophie hunkered down and put her arms around her.

'Oh, baby, don't cry. What was so terrible about the dream?'

Alice struggled to get the words out. 'Y–you went away and left me like Dad did and a policeman came to tell me that you'd died as well and I was all by myself.'

Sophie's own eyes filled with tears. This wasn't the first time that Alice had dreamed of being abandoned, but in view of what had happened in her short life it was hardly a surprise.

It made it that much harder for Sophie to tell her that she was going to be uprooted yet again. If only there was some other way to keep her safe, to keep them both safe.

'Dreams don't always come true, do they?' Alice said.

Sophie pressed out a smile. 'Only the nice ones, sweetheart. The nasty ones don't. That's a fact. So you need to remember that. I'm not going to leave you and I'm not going to die. OK?'

Alice nodded. 'OK.'

Sophie stood up and ruffled her hair. 'Now what would you like for breakfast?'

Alice sniffed back a sob. 'Cornflakes and tea, please.'

'Then I'll sort it while you dry your eyes and sit at the table. You can watch the television if you want.'

Sophie was pouring milk over the cornflakes when

the small TV was switched on behind her. The first thing she heard was a catchy jingle, followed by a familiar holiday company commercial.

She stiffened suddenly and listened to the sales pitch from a well-spoken female presenter. And by the time the thirty-second commercial was over, Sophie had the answer to her prayer.

She whirled around to face Alice. 'I've got a surprise for you,' she said. 'I was going to tell you later but you might as well know now.'

'What is it?'

'You and I are going on holiday. I've had a really good month at work and it means we can afford to go abroad for a couple of weeks.'

Alice looked shocked. 'Really? But what about school? We're supposed to be going back on Tuesday.'

'That's all sorted,' she lied. 'I've spoken to Mrs Holland. She's given permission because I told her that it's an early birthday present for you.'

'That's great, Mum. Where are we going?'

'Well, I'm going to surprise you, and you won't know until we get to the airport.'

'Wow. Do you mean it? When are we going?'

'Hopefully tomorrow. We're not just shopping for clothes this afternoon but we are going down the High Street. While I go and sort out a late holiday bargain you can go to that trendy hairdresser's your mates are always on about and get your hair done. And I'm going to let you choose what to do with it. If you want it short for a change then so be it. And I know you've been keen for ages to have it dyed blonde, so go for it. How does that sound?'

Alice clapped her hands together, her face full of childish excitement.

'It sounds fab,' she said.

Sophie was also excited at the sudden prospect of jetting off somewhere as early as tomorrow. It would solve the problem of how to respond to the threats they were facing.

And it would give her time to come up with a longer-term plan that could include never coming back to London.

CHAPTER THIRTY-EIGHT

Anna and Walker arrived at the Royal London Hospital just after mid-day. They were armed with the CCTV footage that DS Prescott had described as dynamite.

And he was right. What it represented was a significant development in the investigation. Ross Moore had some serious explaining to do.

'Remind me what we know about him,' Anna said to Walker as they were going up in the lift to where Moore was recovering in a private room.

Walker took out his notebook, slipped on his glasses.

'He's twenty-four and works at a retail warehouse near to where he lives in Stepney,' he said. 'He's got two previous convictions. One for assaulting his boss during an argument seven years ago and another for possession of drugs. That was two years ago. He was in a relationship with Holly and they lived together in Eltham before she dumped him.

'After that he started stalking her and bombarding her with text messages, including at least one in which he threatened to kill himself if she didn't take him back. He denied being outside her flat on Tuesday night, but we now have evidence that proves he lied to us.'

Before leaving the office they'd received word from Moore's consultant that he was in a fit state to be questioned. They had also been told that since he'd been admitted he hadn't had any visitors. He was apparently the only child of a single mother who had died five years ago and he had no brothers or sisters.

'He's got to be a serious contender,' Walker said.

Anna nodded. 'As is the not so honourable MP, Nathan Wolf. We've got two suspects from different ends of the social spectrum and Holly had upset each of them. Wolf realised he had a lot to lose after she threatened to publish her story, and Moore wasn't prepared to let her go even though she didn't want to be with him. Both are viable motives for murder.'

They were expected by the medical team, and before they were shown to Moore's room one of the doctors gave them a brief summary of his condition.

'He's very lucky. When he was found he was in a coma, due to a cocktail of sleeping pills, antidepressant tablets and too much alcohol. It all amounted to a potentially lethal dose, but he was saved by the trauma team who brought him round and regulated his breathing. Fortunately he didn't suffer any brain damage or organ failure, and I'm glad to say he should make a complete recovery and will be discharged at the latest tomorrow morning, although I'm not sure he's happy about that.'

'Is that because it was a genuine suicide attempt and not an accident?' Anna asked.

'That's what he's told us, but he's refused to say what made him do it. I'm assuming that you're here to talk to him about that.'

A uniformed officer was standing outside Moore's room to make sure he didn't do a runner or receive any unwelcome guests.

Holly's ex was sitting up in bed when the two detectives entered. He'd been told they were coming so he wasn't surprised to see them. It occurred to Anna that he didn't look like someone who'd had a close shave with death. His face was alabaster pale and unshaven, the skin damp with a sweaty sheen, but his chocolate brown eyes were clear and alert.

'So how are you feeling, Mr Moore?' Anna asked him.

'Like shit,' he said.

'So why did you do it?'

'Why do you think? The love of my life is dead. Murdered. The last thing I want to do is carry on.'

Anna stepped closer to the bed, shook her head.

'I reckon it's more likely that you did it because you can't live with the guilt,' she said.

'What do you mean?'

'Well, while we were waiting for you to wake up, your flat was searched. We now know that you made a habit of following Holly around. We've seen all the messages on your laptop and phone, as well as the photos you took without her knowing. You're an obsessive stalker, Mr Moore, and you're a liar to boot.'

'I haven't lied to you.'

'But you told us you didn't go to Holly's flat on Tuesday night. You said you were in bed at the time she was murdered.'

'And that's the truth.'

'No, it isn't,' Anna said.

She took out her phone, swiped the screen, brought up the clip of CCTV footage that Prescott had sent to her. She held it up for Moore to see and pressed play.

'This is from a camera close to Holly's flat,' she said, and Moore's mouth dropped open as he stared at the little screen. 'It was recorded at ten-fifty on Tuesday evening and captured Holly as she walked along Drummond Street five minutes after leaving her flat. Now watch as suddenly a white Nissan Micra drives up and pulls into the kerb just ahead of her. The front door is thrown open and out pops the driver.' Anna paused the video with her finger. 'As you can see, Mr Moore, that driver is you. And before you try to convince us that it's a case of mistaken identity you should know that we've already established that the car is registered to a Mr Paul Mason, whom you're acquainted with because he happens to be your next-door neighbour. Detective Inspector Walker here spoke to him by phone about an hour ago and he told him he let you borrow the vehicle while he's away for two weeks in Italy on holiday.'

Moore said nothing so Anna pressed play again and the video resumed.

The clip showed Moore stepping in front of Holly, blocking her path. Words were exchanged and then she stabbed an angry finger against his chest before pushing him to one side and striding along the pavement and out of shot.

Moore then got into the car and drove off in the same direction.

'We now know that you lied to us when we last spoke to you,' Anna said. 'So perhaps you can save us a lot of time and effort now by telling us what happened that night. Did you drag her or coax her into the car further along Drummond Street and then take her somewhere to kill her before dumping her body on the common? And is that why you wanted to die? You just couldn't live with what you had done to the woman you loved?'

Anna put her phone back in her pocket and Moore turned to face her. His eyes were wet and solemn, his breathing suddenly loud and laboured.

'You've got this all wrong,' he said. 'I tried to end it because I can't bear the thought of never seeing her again. It's as simple as that. I'm not a murderer.'

'But why should we believe you?' Anna told him. 'You told us you stayed at home on that night.'

'It was a mistake. I didn't want you to know that I went to Camden because I knew you'd just assume I'd killed her. And I didn't.'

'So why did you go there?'

He shrugged. 'I was at home watching the telly and dreading the thought of going to bed because I knew I wouldn't be able to sleep. As usual I was pining after Holly and kept thinking about how much better my life was when we were together. I decided that since I had Paul's car I might as well make use of it. So I drove to Camden. I had to park up the road from Holly's block and walk to it.

'I waited across the street having a smoke while trying to pluck up the courage to go and see if she was in. But then I spotted her landlord sitting on his balcony. He was looking right at me. We knew each other because I'd had a run-in with him before. When I realised he'd noticed me too I walked back to the car and sat inside it for a half hour or so smoking another fag.

'I was about to drive off when I saw Holly hurrying past me on the other side of the road. I couldn't believe it. By the time I'd got the engine started she'd turned into Drummond Street and that's where I caught up with her. I asked her where she was going and she told me to mind my own business. Then I asked her to go for a drink with me, and that's when she poked me in the chest and walked around me.'

He shut his eyes then and clamped his lips together, as though he had run out of words. Anna prodded him to continue.

'We know you got back in the car and went after her,' she said. 'So tell us what happened next.'

He opened his eyes, heaved a breath. 'I was going to give it one more try but I didn't get the chance. A little further along Drummond Street I saw her flag down a passing black cab. I was curious to know where she was going so like an idiot I tried to follow her. But being London it proved impossible. The taxi turned into Hampstead Road, but there was a ton of traffic even at that time and black cabs were everywhere. So I soon lost it and drove home instead.'

Anna didn't know whether to believe him or not. But she did know she would need more than the CCTV footage to charge him with Holly's murder.

'We can't take what you've told us at face value,' she said. 'We need to check out your version of events. For your information, officers will by now have impounded Mr Mason's car from outside your flat and it'll be subjected to a thorough forensic examination. We will also be rounding up more CCTV footage to try to determine if the vehicle was in the area of Barnes Common on Tuesday. While these procedures are being carried out you'll have to remain in our custody.

Officers will be standing outside this door until you're discharged tomorrow and we'll review the situation then. Is there anything else you would like to tell us or ask us before we go, Mr Moore?'

He pushed his head back against the pillow and said, 'Just that I'm sorry I'm still alive. Next time I'll make sure that no busybody can come along and fuck things up.'

CHAPTER THIRTY-NINE

Anna suggested grabbing a light lunch in the hospital cafeteria so they could eat and discuss their next move. The place was packed, but they managed to find a table for two, which Anna saved while Walker went to get coffees and sandwiches.

When she checked her phone, she saw she had two messages. The first was a text from Tom, reminding her that he was spending the day with his daughter Grace in Portsmouth and that he would be staying at his own flat tonight, but would call later.

They rarely shared a bed on Sunday nights because he needed time on his own to prepare his workload for the week ahead. That was another reason she was hesitant about him moving in. He often worked from home, but her house wasn't big enough to allocate him his own office. So it would mean sharing with her in what used to be Chloe's bedroom.

And she wasn't keen – not just because the room was small and already cluttered with her own books and files, many related to the search for her daughter. It was also where she sat for hours at a time when she was alone in the house, thinking about Chloe and talking to the photos of her that were plastered over the walls.

It was their room. Hers and Chloe's. Mother and daughter. She just wasn't sure how she would feel if Tom put his own stamp on it.

The second message was from the guy at Channel Four, asking if she had time to meet him at some point next week to discuss the proposed documentary.

She was just as anxious as he was to get the ball rolling on that, but she replied that it might not be possible because she was tied up with the Holly Blake murder investigation. She said that she would have to get back to him.

'They've run out of bacon so I got you a cheese sandwich,' Walker said, when he returned to the table. 'Hope that's all right.'

'As long as there's pickle in it,' she said.

He grinned. 'There is.'

As they started tucking in, Anna said, 'A couple of hours ago my money was on Nathan Wolf. I thought we'd delivered a knock-out blow with the blood-spattered driving licence. But now I'm not so sure. Ross Moore just didn't convince me that he was telling the truth.'

'What are the chances of tracing the black cab he says Holly got into?' Walker asked.

Anna shook her head. 'We'll put out an appeal and gather up as much CCTV as we can in Drummond Street and Hampstead Road, but this was five nights ago, and there are nearly twenty thousand black taxis operating in London.'

'Let's assume for a minute that he's not lying, guv. If she

did go off in one then it could be that she got the driver to take her to her final destination, the place where she was murdered.'

'And that gives rise to another disturbing possibility,' Anna said. 'What if it was the cabbie who killed her? It might be we've been wrong to focus virtually all our attention on people she knew.'

'I don't think we're wrong, guv. We homed in on Wolf and Moore for good reason. There's a whole host of compelling factors that make them both prime suspects. In the case of the MP we have at least one piece of physical evidence, Holly's driving licence. And we only have his word that he went straight home when he returned to London from Somerset.

'So it's conceivable that Holly did agree to meet him, but at a neutral location, and that was where she was going when she left her flat. I mean, it's hard to believe she went out that late in the evening if she didn't have somewhere to go.'

According to her landlord, Holly arrived home at about ten-thirty after visiting her parents in Pimlico. It had to be assumed that she was pretty upset after the argument with her mum. So what prompted her to leave the flat again fifteen minutes later? Her phone records had been analysed and she hadn't made or received any calls during that time.

Was it possible that she had simply decided to go for a stroll to clear her head and by sheer coincidence her ex-boyfriend happened to be lurking outside at the time? Or had she decided to pay someone a surprise visit and travel there by taxi?

'Unless and until we can prove that Moore is lying about the black taxi then we need to treat it as a major new line of enquiry,' Walker said.

Anna knew he was right. Attacks by taxi drivers in London had increased in recent years. They usually took place late at night and the victims were invariably young women.

Anna was reminded of the case of John Worboys, the so-called Black Cab Rapist, who was convicted and jailed for attacking twelve of his female passengers, but there were claims he'd raped many more.

The pathologist was convinced that Holly hadn't been sexually assaulted, but perhaps her killer had been motivated by some other uncontrollable urge.

'We'd better get the team working on it,' Anna said, then took a bite out of her sandwich before making the call.

It was DC Niven who answered at MIT headquarters. She told him to put her on speaker and gather the rest of the team together so that they could hear what she had to say.

She began by summarising the interview with Ross Moore. 'He claims that Holly got into a taxi in Drummond Street just before eleven,' she said. 'This would have been a matter of seconds after he was caught on CCTV stopping her next to the Micra. We need to find out if that particular street camera and any others in the area captured the taxi as well.'

'I wouldn't bank on it, ma'am,' Niven said. 'We've had some more footage in from there but the Micra doesn't appear. It's partly down to the fact that some of the cameras aren't operating, for various reasons.'

'Well, expand the search,' Anna said. 'And at the same time get the press office to put out an appeal aimed at black cab drivers. There's always the outside chance that we'll strike lucky and that particular driver, if he or she exists, will see it.'

She wanted to know if the Micra had been impounded and was told it had. But the forensics crew had only just started working on it.

'Has DS Prescott got an update for me on the mystery woman who was seen leaving the King's Head pub with Theo Blake?' Anna asked.

'Indeed I have,' Prescott said. 'I just got back from there. The woman's name is Charlene Hamilton and she works behind the bar in the pub. She isn't working today, but the proprietor, a Mr Ted Somerville, said she's been open with them about seeing a married man for the past few months. They know his name is Theo but they don't know who his wife is, presumably because Charlene didn't want that getting out.

'Theo apparently popped into the pub a few times when Charlene's shifts were about to end. The last time was on Tuesday night. Anyway, the woman lives a couple of streets away from the pub, but when we called there she wasn't in. DC Flynn has stayed outside her place in the car in case she turns up. I've been given a mobile number for Charlene, but she hasn't picked up yet. I'll keep trying.'

'OK, keep across that and let me know when you've spoken to her. Meanwhile, we'll be leaving the hospital soon and I want to have a full case review when we get back. On the way we'll pop along to Pimlico to see how Rebecca Blake is doing. I want to ask her some more questions, including if she can shed any light on Holly's driving licence.'

'Before you go, ma'am, I've got something for you.'

Anna recognised the voice as belonging to DC Sweeny.

'So what is it, Megan?' she said.

'Well, I've been going through Holly's mobile phone

records and I've spotted something that contradicts what we've been told.'

'Go on.'

'Correct me if I'm wrong, but the family insisted they knew nothing about Holly's relationship with Nathan Wolf before she turned up at her mother's house and told them.'

'You're not wrong,' Anna said. 'Robert Gregory told me that Holly had never let on about it.'

'Well, it seems that she did,' Sweeny said. 'I've come across a text exchange between Holly and her aunt Freya. Holly asks Freya not to tell her mother that she's involved with Nathan Wolf.'

'When was this?'

'Nine months ago.'

'Then forward the messages to me straight away,' Anna said. 'Or better still paste them onto a single document and send that as an attachment. Then find out if Freya and her husband are still at Rebecca's house. If not they might be at home so let me have the address. I need to pay them a visit.'

CHAPTER FORTY

Freya Gregory had stayed at her sister's house until late on Friday night, according to the Family Liaison Officer. She and her husband Robert had then returned home, shortly after he was released on police bail following the attack on Nathan Wolf.

The couple lived in a detached house overlooking Hurlingham Park, Fulham. It was a smart, two-storey property with its own driveway and a front-facing balcony.

Anna hadn't called ahead to check that they were in so she was glad to see two cars parked on the driveway – a Toyota Hybrid and a Vauxhall Corsa.

Freya's face registered a mixture of shock and relief when she answered the door to them.

'I thought you might be yet another reporter,' she said. 'Two have called here already today wanting to speak to Robert about what he did to the MP. I told them to go away.'

'Is your husband in?' Anna asked.

'He is, but he told me that the police had finished with him for now.'

'This is not to do with the assault, Mrs Gregory. We're here to talk to both of you.'

'Is it about Holly's murder? Has Wolf finally admitted that he did it?'

'We'd like to come in and discuss it with you if that's all right.'

Freya gave Anna a long, questioning look before motioning for them to come inside. And in those few moments the detective saw in the woman's face the strain of the last few days. Her eyes were heavily bloodshot, and the shadows around them had become bigger and darker since they had last met at Rebecca's house.

She had clearly been hit hard by her niece's murder, but Anna wondered if she was also feeling a weight of guilt on her shoulders for not having told her sister about Holly's secret affair with Wolf. If she had then perhaps Rebecca might have persuaded Holly to end it ages ago and the girl wouldn't now be lying dead in the mortuary.

They followed Freya into a spacious kitchen/diner where her husband was flipping through a selection of Sunday papers spread out on the breakfast bar.

He was so shocked to see them that his voice shuddered when he said, 'What's going on? Why are you here?'

'Don't panic, Mr Gregory,' Anna said. 'We just want a chat with you and your wife. I'm going to update you on where we are with the case and then ask you a few questions about Holly that will hopefully help us with the investigation.'

Anna chose to delay getting to the point of the visit so that she could find out a bit more about the couple first.

They moved into the living room and sat around a large rectangular glass coffee table.

The couple held hands and listened intently as Anna told them how the investigation was going.

'Nathan Wolf is still in custody pending further enquiries,' she said. 'And I'm sure it won't come as a huge surprise that he continues to deny killing Holly.'

'But of course he bloody well did it,' Robert said, and Anna could hear the impatience in his voice. 'I can't believe he didn't make a mistake somewhere along the line. Have you searched his car and his house for clues?'

'You know we have, Mr Gregory, and you also know that I'm not at liberty to go into details about what, if anything, we found.'

She had already decided not to mention the driving licence. That was something she intended to ask Holly's mother about.

'We've also interviewed Holly's ex-boyfriend, Ross Moore,' Anna went on. 'He insists he's not the killer.'

'Is it true that he tried to kill himself?' Freya asked.

Anna was surprised she knew. 'What makes you say that?'

'I heard it on the radio that he was rushed to hospital after a suspected overdose.'

'I see. Well, I can't discuss his condition with you or the circumstances surrounding his hospitalisation, as I'm sure you can appreciate.'

'I'll take that as confirmation that he did try to top himself then,' Freya said. 'But do you know that he threatened to do it before when Holly refused to take him back?'

'We are aware of that, yes,' Anna said. 'Your husband told me earlier that you encouraged Holly to end the relationship with him.'

'I did. He was out of her league and he knew it. He hated the fact that other men found her attractive. It made him jealous and possessive. And he was always smoking cannabis and we were worried that he'd get Holly hooked on it.'

'Did your sister share your opinion of him?'

'Not really, but only because it was me that Holly poured her heart out to. Rebecca didn't take that much of an interest in Holly's life. She's always been totally absorbed in her own career, first as a police officer, then a politician. And since she decided to run for London Mayor everything else has taken a back seat. Unfortunately now that Holly is gone Rebecca bitterly regrets it. She told me yesterday that she's consumed with guilt for not having been a better mother. She even confessed to resenting me for being there for Holly when she wasn't. That really hurt.'

The woman was shaking with emotion now, so Robert put an arm around her shoulders.

'I told you earlier that since we don't have kids of our own Freya was like a second mother to Holly,' he said. 'We always thought it was something that Rebecca was happy with.'

Anna leaned forward, elbows on knees, and seized the opportunity that had presented itself.

'I'd like to remind you of something else you told me earlier, Mr Gregory,' she said. 'I asked you if Holly had ever confided in your wife about her relationship with Wolf. You said she hadn't and that the first you heard about it was when Rebecca told you, which was the day after Holly let her parents know that she was going to sell her story to the *Sunday Mirror*.'

Robert cocked his head to one side and frowned. 'So what has that got to do with anything?'

'Well, we've since discovered that it isn't true.' Anna fished out her phone as she switched her attention back to Freya. 'On here I have an exchange of text messages between Holly and yourself, Mrs Gregory. Your niece starts it by referring to a conversation between the pair of you in which she'd apparently revealed that she was falling in love with Nathan Wolf. She pleaded with you not to tell her mother. You responded by promising to keep her secret.'

Freya's face paled. 'How did you . . .?'

'We got access to Holly's phone records,' Anna said. 'That exchange took place nine months ago.'

Her husband started to speak, but she held up a hand to stop him.

'I'm solely to blame,' she said. 'Robert wanted to tell you but I wouldn't let him. If my sister finds out that I was aware all this time of Holly's affair she'll never forgive me.'

'So have you known about it from the start?' Anna asked.

'No. She told me after they'd been seeing each other for several months. She swore me to secrecy and I kept hoping it would fizzle out. But it didn't, and the longer it went on the more I came to realise that I'd made a mistake in not letting Rebecca know.'

'Was Holly frank with you about the nature of the affair?' This from Walker, who had been the one taking notes.

Freya shook her head. 'She told me nothing about the sex stuff. Only that Wolf was paying her rent and would often turn up unexpectedly. That was the excuse she gave for not inviting me or any of the family to the flat after the first few weeks. But I now suspect that it was really because she didn't want anyone to see what was going on there.'

Walker then asked Robert when he learned about the affair.

'About six months ago,' he said. 'I wasn't happy about

keeping schtum, but I was given no choice. And I'm really sorry that we didn't tell you. I hope you can understand why.'

'It will destroy my relationship with my sister if it comes out now,' Freya said. 'She'll hold me responsible for Holly's death and with good reason. If Rebecca had known about the affair she would have done her best to break it up and Wolf wouldn't have gone on to kill her.'

'We still can't be sure that he did,' Anna said.

'You might have your doubts, detective, but we don't.' Freya could no longer hold back the tears and they ran down her face as she spoke in a voice that was frail and tremulous. 'That man ruined our lives and we need each other to get through this. That's why I'm begging you not to reveal what you know to my sister. It would break her heart and serve only to compound her suffering.'

'I don't intend to tell her,' Anna said. 'But I really can't promise that it won't come out during the course of the investigation.'

CHAPTER FORTY-ONE

'I was put in that same awkward position once myself,' Walker said when they were back in the car and heading towards Pimlico. 'I was out drinking with my brother one night when he let slip that he was having an affair. He made me promise on pain of death not to tell my wife or his. Keeping his secret for months was a nightmare, so I can sympathise with Freya Gregory.'

'Did your brother get rumbled?' Anna asked.

'Eventually he did, and his wife divorced him. When my wife asked me if I'd known he was being unfaithful I lied and said I hadn't. I felt ashamed of myself but it saved a lot of aggro.'

Anna knew what he meant, but it wasn't Freya she felt sorry for. It was her sister, Rebecca. The poor woman's only daughter had been murdered. Dealing with that was going to be painful enough. But there was now every chance that she would soon be reeling from two more devastating blows – her husband's infidelity and her sister's long-held secret.

Anna swore to herself that she would do all she could to stop Rebecca from finding out about either, at least during the course of the investigation. But she knew it wouldn't be easy, especially since she had no control over how events were going to unfold.

'It's funny how the secrets and lies within a family start to unravel when there's a crisis or a tragedy,' Walker said. 'Since Holly Blake's body was found we've learned that she was having an affair with an MP, that her father is cheating on her mother, and that her aunt turned a blind eye to a situation that resulted in her embarking on a course of action that might well have led to her death.'

'That's true enough,' Anna said. 'And I'm wondering now what other secrets are waiting to be unearthed, and if they're in any way relevant to Holly's murder.'

'Well, one way to find out is to have a closer look at all the family,' Walker said. 'And that includes her parents.'

'But you don't seriously believe that they could have had anything to do with it?'

Walker took his eyes off the road to look at her. 'I really think we need to consider every possibility, guv. For instance, what if Holly found out that her stepdad was playing away? Maybe she confronted him, and threatened to tell Rebecca. He might have flipped and taken extreme action to stop her blabbing. I know it sounds far-fetched, but most domestic murders are anger-related and not premeditated.'

Anna reached for her phone. 'You've got a point, Max. I'll get the team to do some digging. They can start by accessing the phone records and digital footprints of every member of the family.'

She called the office and this time it was DS Prescott who

answered. She told him what she wanted done. He then told her that he had an update on Charlene Hamilton, the barmaid Theo Blake had been seeing.

'She arrived home a short while ago and DC Flynn managed to have a word with her,' he said. 'She confirmed what we already know – that they've been having an affair behind his wife's back. She also said that she wasn't expecting to see him on Tuesday night. He phoned her just before ten and asked her if he could come over. He then turned up at the pub and they went back to her place.

'But he was in a foul mood apparently and told her about the bombshell his stepdaughter had dropped. He then said he wouldn't be able to see her for a while because of all the publicity Holly's kiss-and-tell story would generate. She wasn't happy and they had words. He then left in a huff.'

'And what time was that?' Anna asked.

'According to Charlene it was about eleven.'

'But by his own admission he didn't arrive back home until after midnight. And when he got there his wife was in bed so for all we know it might have been much later.'

'I suppose so, ma'am,' Prescott said.

Anna hung up the phone and told Walker what Charlene Hamilton had said.

'So there's quite a gap between when he left his mistress and when he finally got home,' Walker responded.

Anna nodded. 'And we need to ask him where he went and what he did during that time.'

The media pack was still hounding Holly Blake's parents, despite the appeal for them to let the couple grieve in peace.

The crowd of reporters, photographers and television crew

members now numbered about thirty. A couple of uniformed officers were preventing them from entering the mews so they were gathered on either side of the main road, where they could see who entered and left the house.

Sue Bond, the FLO, was waiting at the front door to greet Anna and Walker. Once they were inside, she told them that Rebecca and Theo were still in a state of shock.

'They're both finding it really hard to cope,' she said, her voice low so the couple wouldn't hear. 'They've stopped answering the phones and they've withdrawn into themselves. I've tried to persuade them to let me arrange for a doctor or a bereavement counsellor to visit, but they're not interested.'

The couple were sitting on the sofa in the living room. The television was on and tuned to one of the rolling news channels, but neither of them seemed to be paying much attention to it.

Rebecca was in a dressing gown with her hair gathered up and pinned. She had no make-up on and her face was swollen with crying. The sight of her caused Anna to catch her breath, and a surge of sorrow rose within her.

Theo was wearing jeans and a black shirt that wasn't tucked in. His face was firm, stoic, and when he saw the detectives he sat up straight and said, 'We were told to expect you earlier than this.'

'We had to make a stop on the way,' Anna told him. 'But we're here now and if you don't mind we'd like to bring you up to speed with the investigation and ask you a few questions.'

As Anna talked them through what had been happening she maintained a gentle, benevolent tone. They both leaned forward and hung onto her every word, but neither of them spoke. She explained that Nathan Wolf and Ross Moore were continuing to be questioned and told them that officers were sifting through hours of CCTV footage.

'We still don't know where your daughter was going when she left her flat,' she said. 'So can you possibly shed any light on it? Ross Moore is claiming that he saw her get into a taxi, but we haven't yet established if it's true.'

'Well, isn't that a question you should be asking Nathan Wolf?' Rebecca said. 'He either arranged to meet her somewhere or she went out to one of her usual late night haunts and he followed her, then at some point managed to get her into his car.'

'What do you mean by late night haunts, Mrs Blake?' Anna asked.

'I mean the West End clubs she used to frequent. Holly suffered badly from insomnia. It was a big problem with her as a teenager and the doctors said it was a symptom of her depression. Quite often when she couldn't sleep she would go clubbing. The fact that she didn't have a nine-to-five job meant that she rarely had to worry about getting up early.'

'Do you know which clubs she frequented?' Anna said.

'She gave me a few names over the years but I can't remember them. And she didn't like to talk about what she was getting up to because she knew I would disapprove.'

Anna and Walker exchanged a glance. This was a nugget of information about the victim's lifestyle that they hadn't been offered before now. It made the possibility that she'd been abducted and murdered by a stranger – perhaps a black cab driver – all the more credible.

While Anna was turning this thought over in her mind,

Walker told the couple that one of Holly's personal possessions had turned up.

'It's her driving licence,' he said. 'I can't tell you where it was found, but I can tell you that it had traces of her blood on it.'

Rebecca gasped and put a hand over her mouth.

'Do you happen to know where Holly kept her licence?' Walker asked. 'Was it in her bag, her purse, or did she keep it somewhere else?'

Rebecca looked at Theo, and Anna studied his reaction, but it told her nothing. He seemed as genuinely shocked and confused as she was.

'As far as we know she kept everything in her purse,' he said. 'Credit cards, store cards, cash. And she still hired cars from time to time so I'm sure she would have carried her licence with her.'

Rebecca stiffened suddenly and gave Anna a hard look.

'I want you to tell me where you found it,' she said. 'Was it in her flat or in someone's car?'

'You know I'm not able to say.'

'Oh, for heaven's sake, Detective Tate. Holly was my daughter, and I want to help you catch her killer.'

'You need to leave that to us, Mrs Blake. I can assure you that we are doing everything we can.'

'Leave it out, please. I used the same spiel myself on countless occasions during my time on the force. You can bend the rules when it suits you and if you won't this time for me then I'll go over your head.'

'I would value your input under any other circumstances, Mrs Blake,' Anna said. 'But as the mother of the victim there is no way I can involve you. It wouldn't be right, and it certainly wouldn't make things any easier for you and your husband.'

Rebecca opened her mouth to speak, but then closed it again. At the same time the fighting spirit that had briefly flickered in her eyes was blinked away and her face crumpled.

'I'm really sorry,' she sobbed. 'I should know better. It's just so frustrating not being able to do anything.'

'That's understandable,' Anna said, and she could almost feel the woman's pain.

Rebecca got to her feet, tightened the belt of her dressing gown. 'Look, I need to go outside and have a cigarette. If you have more questions you can ask my husband.'

As Rebecca walked out of the room, Anna signalled for Sue Bond to go with her.

'My wife is really struggling,' Theo said as he shoved a hand through his hair.

'I can see that,' Anna said, while taking Rebecca's place next to him on the sofa. 'But I'm glad she's left us alone because I think it best that she doesn't hear what I'm about to ask you.'

Theo drew his eyebrows together and deep lines appeared on his forehead.

'I'm listening,' he said, his voice low but firm. 'Ask away.'

Anna cleared her throat and said, 'Will you please tell me where you really went on the night your stepdaughter was killed, Mr Blake?'

'I've told you already. I got a taxi to her flat and because she wasn't in I came back but stopped off at a pub on the way.'

'So far so good, Mr Blake. But you didn't stay in the pub, did you? You simply went there to meet Miss Charlene

Hamilton, your mistress. Then together you walked to her place, and you only stayed for a short time before leaving there. So I want to know where you went then.'

Theo's jaw dropped and his eyes suddenly widened. He looked from Anna to Walker and back again.

Then he slumped against the back of the sofa and said, 'Shit. I was hoping you wouldn't find out.'

CHAPTER FORTY-TWO

Before Theo began his confession, he repositioned himself so that he could see his wife through the patio windows. She was standing in the garden, a plume of smoke rising above her head.

'You should know that I'm deeply ashamed of myself, especially in view of what's happened,' he said. 'I can't really explain why I decided to cheat on Rebecca. It just happened, and I can only think that it was because when it started I was in a bad place.'

'Can you explain what you mean by that?' Anna asked him.

He wiped perspiration from his forehead. 'At the time my wife and I were going through a difficult patch. Her job and the hours she was devoting to the Mayoral campaign meant that we were seeing very little of each other. I began to imagine what life would be like if she won the election and it scared me.

'I raised my concerns with her once, but she dismissed

them out of hand. I started to hope that she would give up on it or lose so that our marriage could return to how it was before she got it into her head that she wanted to be in charge of London.'

He paused, glanced nervously into the garden and then sighed.

'I met Charlene at the end of a particularly bad week on the home front,' he went on. 'Her mother was a client of mine and on that day we'd won a court case on her behalf. The family invited me out for drinks at the Savoy in London and Charlene was there. After downing a few glasses of wine we began to flirt with one another. At the end of the evening she gave me her phone number and told me to call her if I fancied taking her out. I had no intention of doing so, but three days later I had a row with Rebecca and I was so pissed off that I rang Charlene. We met up, had a great time, and it carried on from there. I'd go to her place and sometimes to the King's Head to meet her.'

'And that's what you did on Tuesday night,' Anna said.

He nodded. 'Correct. When I'd established that Holly wasn't in or refusing to answer her door I was in no mood to go straight home, so I went to see Charlene. But I couldn't relax. I told her about Holly and that we needed to cool it for a while. She got cross with me and I just couldn't face a full-blown argument so I walked out.'

'And where did you go?'

'I strolled around aimlessly for a while, then hailed a taxi and came straight home.'

'We'll be checking CCTV again, Mr Blake,' Anna said. 'So for your sake I hope you've told us the truth this time.'

'I have, and I'm sorry I've caused you to waste your time.

But please understand that although I admit to being a bad husband I am not a murderer. I loved Holly and her death has left a huge hole in my heart.'

'But it's true, isn't it, that your feelings for her were not reciprocated? She continued to bear a serious grudge against you for breaking up her parents' marriage.'

'Not at all. Rebecca told you that she eventually came around and—'

'I recall exactly what your wife said, Mr Blake, but that doesn't mean I believe it. I've since been told that it was never a case of domestic bliss in your household. Holly continued to have a problem with you up until the day she died.'

'Are you seriously giving credence to what Nathan Wolf said? She didn't tell him that she hated me. It was a lie.'

'But it wasn't just him she told,' Anna said. 'She also confided in Ross Moore. He heard the same story – that you tried it on with your own stepdaughter.'

'But it's bollocks. I—'

'Please don't tell another lie, Mr Blake. We already know that you haven't been a faithful husband. So if you did act inappropriately towards Holly some years ago – and that was one of the reasons she was uncomfortable with you – then for heaven's sake own up to it. It doesn't appear to be relevant to what's happened and I give you my word that I won't mention it to your wife.'

He began to speak, but stopped short of forming the first word and turned his head again to look at Rebecca through the window.

After a long pause, he said, 'OK, I admit it. I made a terrible mistake in a moment of madness. Holly didn't make it up. We were at home alone one night and sharing a bottle of wine. I got the wrong end of the stick and thought she was up for it. She was mortified and furious when I kissed her and I've regretted it ever since. I had no choice but to deny it because it would have been the end of my marriage.

'Holly never forgave me and I've never forgiven myself. But I swear that despite what she thought of me I grew to love her like she was my own daughter. And I would never have harmed her in any way.'

CHAPTER FORTY-THREE

Sophie had to keep telling herself that she wasn't over-reacting. The threats they faced were real, so she had no choice but to do what she was doing.

Her priority now was to keep Alice safe, and the only sure way to achieve that was to flee.

Again.

She'd spent forty-five minutes in the travel agent's after seeing Alice settled in the hairdresser's close by, where she had her hair cut short and coloured.

Sophie had booked an all-inclusive holiday for the two of them in Spain. She'd chosen a resort hotel in Lloret de Mar on the Costa Brava, more than 450 miles from where they used to live in Puerto de Mazarron.

She'd paid by credit card and the deal included return flights that she knew they might not use.

Now they were on their way back to the flat, after a late lunch in their favourite deli. With Alice's blessing they had put on hold shopping for her new winter coat and backpack.

There were things to do, arrangements to make. They had to be at Heathrow airport by five p.m. tomorrow for a flight that was scheduled to leave at seven. So booking a taxi was on Sophie's list of things to do.

She also intended to email a letter of resignation to the cleaning company she did work for. But she wasn't going to tell them or anyone else where they were going. The reason she was keeping Alice in the dark was because she knew she'd want to tell her friends.

Sophie had to assume that Detective Anna Tate's private investigator would try to find out where they had gone. Or the woman might even do it herself using police resources.

And who could blame her? Sophie found it impossible not to feel some compassion for Alice's birth mother. After ten years searching for her daughter she was closer than she knew to finding her.

But Sophie could not allow guilt or sympathy to cloud her judgement. Alice had a new mother now. Someone who loved her unreservedly. Someone who had been with her since she was two years old. Someone who was prepared to do whatever it took to protect her.

And to keep her.

Sophie was as sure as she could be that nobody followed them back to the flat.

She stopped several times to look around and even left the busy High Street to walk along a near-deserted residential road. Thankfully she didn't see any familiar faces or shadowy figures lurking in doorways.

Even so her body was tight with tension when she finally closed the front door behind them.

She had taken a huge step by booking the trip to Spain and there was no turning back now. She needed to banish any doubts and trust her instincts. Every sinew in her body told her it was the right thing to do, that any other course of action would be grossly irresponsible.

'Shall I start packing?' Alice said, her eyes still sparkling with excitement.

'Of course, sweetheart. I'll come and give you a hand in a bit.'

'But I need to know if we're going somewhere warm or cold so I know what clothes to take.'

Sophie laughed. 'It'll be hot and sunny.'

'Goody.'

Alice was on cloud nine, what with the upcoming holiday and the pixie-style haircut that was all the rage among her school friends. Sophie was surprised how much it suited her round face, and how it made her appear older, which had to be a good thing because she looked less like the Chloe Tate age progression image. The same applied to Alice's passport photo, the one James had updated four years ago, which she now suspected was another forgery. She was eight when that one was taken and it bore little resemblance to how she looked now.

As Alice went into her bedroom, Sophie poured herself a glass of wine in the hope that it would help her to relax. But panic continued to churn in her belly, and she could almost hear the steady thud of her own heart.

It was hard to believe that this time tomorrow they would be at Heathrow waiting to board the plane that would take them to another new life. Just a few days ago she could never have imagined that they would be in this situation. It had taken three years to convince herself that the past was buried and would not come back to haunt her again. But it had, and this time she had more than just her estranged husband to worry about.

Thinking about Bruno Perez prompted her to take out her phone and call Lisa. When her friend answered it sounded like she was outside because there was a lot of background noise.

'Can you speak?' Sophie asked her.

'Yes, I can. I'm in a mall but I can hear you clearly enough.'

'Good, because I want to apologise for putting the phone down on you yesterday.'

'There's no need. I know that what I told you came as a shock. I was actually going to give you a ring tonight with an update.'

'An update on what?'

'Well, it's been driving me crazy wondering if I'm right in thinking that Michael Taylor swiped my old phone. So I made some calls and asked a few discreet questions about him.'

'And?'

'And I discovered something that he didn't let on to me at the wake. He's actually working for Bruno these days.'

'Doing what?'

'He manages a warehouse for him in Peckham. As you know Bruno's family have business interests here and in Spain and they're fronts for shady dealings. Taylor looks after the place while Bruno's abroad.'

'But you still can't be sure that Taylor took your phone to find out if you've been in touch with me.'

'No, I can't, but I did learn from a mutual friend that Bruno flew into London early this morning having spent the past month in Spain. It might well be a coincidence, but what if it's not? What if Taylor did get your number from my phone and passed it on to Bruno and he now knows where you are?'

Sophie felt the breath freeze in her lungs.

'If I was you, Soph, I wouldn't just assume I'm talking bollocks,' Lisa continued. 'I think you should alert the police or go somewhere safe for a while. And switch off your bloody phone because the signal is like a beacon. Get another mobile and a new number and then call me. In the meantime I'll try to keep track of what Bruno and Taylor are up to.'

Sophie closed her eyes as Lisa's words slammed into the side of her head.

'So promise me you'll err on the side of caution,' Lisa said. 'If anything happens to you I know I will never forgive myself because this is my fuck-up.'

Sophie wanted desperately to tell her friend that she had already decided to play safe by leaving the country. But instead she said simply, 'I love you, Lisa. And I don't blame you for anything. I'll ring you when I can.'

Then she ended the call and turned off her phone.

CHAPTER FORTY-FOUR

The team were still going at it full throttle when Anna and Walker returned to HQ. Some of them were into overtime while others were anxiously hoping they'd be able to clock off as soon as their shifts came to an end.

DCS Nash was waiting in Anna's office and wanted to be updated before the case conference. But first he passed on a message from the Met Commissioner.

'He's becoming increasingly impatient with what he regards as a lack of progress,' Nash said. 'The political pressure he's under to bring this case to a close is immense. The Home Secretary is demanding to know why Nathan Wolf is being held in custody while not being charged with Holly Blake's murder. That situation serves to encourage wild speculation in the media and keeps the story on the front pages.'

Anna cast her eyes towards the ceiling. This wasn't unexpected.

'If and when I'm ready to charge him I will, sir,' she said. 'But right now I don't have a strong enough case.'

'Are you sure about that? You have the victim's driving licence with her blood on it, found in his home. You have him on tape threatening her. And you have a clear-cut motive. What more do you need?'

'Wolf claims he doesn't know how the licence got into his jacket pocket,' Anna said. 'And there's a chance he could convince a jury that he's telling the truth and that someone else put it there. As for the threat, well, it could be argued that he was justified in lashing out at her after she told him that she was going to destroy his reputation. We need something more to be sure of a conviction.'

'What about his Range Rover? It seems iffy to me that he gave it a thorough clean just hours or days after the murder.'

'You're right about that, sir. It is bloody iffy. But a forensic examination has been carried out and there's no evidence that a body was ever placed inside it. It's doubtful that he would have cleaned it so thoroughly as to get rid of all trace evidence.'

'But not impossible.'

'For sure, but his defence team will be able to use the uncertainty as ammunition.'

Nash shook his head. 'So what do you intend to do then?'

'I'm going to apply to keep him in custody longer pending further enquiries,' she said. 'I intend to interview him again, and there's still a chance that we'll come up with something on CCTV. But you have to bear in mind that Wolf is not the only suspect in the frame. There's also the ex-boyfriend.'

She told him about the interview with Ross Moore at the hospital.

'He's presented us with two other possible scenarios,' she said. 'Either he's lying and he killed Holly after he got her into his car. And then out of guilt he tried to commit suicide with an overdose. Or he's telling the truth and he saw her get into a taxi, which means she was murdered by somebody else, possibly the cab driver.'

There were enough unanswered questions in the picture Anna had painted to get Nash to change his tune.

'Very well, I accept that it's not as straightforward as it first appeared to be,' he said. 'But that won't stop the powers that be from keeping up the pressure. I've got to prepare an update for the Commissioner that he has to submit to the Home Secretary within the hour. The Home Sec needs it for a seven o'clock meeting with the PM at Downing Street.'

'Well, I suggest you sit in on the case conference,' Anna said. 'I'll be briefing the team and they'll be providing me with whatever information has come in since this morning.'

'Then let's get on with it,' Nash said, as he rose to his feet behind Anna's desk.

It was six p.m. when Anna called the team together. Before she began the briefing she rolled her shoulders in an effort to ease the tension between them.

She began with the confessions that had been extracted from Holly's stepfather and aunt.

'The more we delve into their family the more secrets are being unearthed,' she said. 'And the more complicated this case is becoming.'

She began with Theo's admission that he had once tried it on with his stepdaughter and that was partly why she didn't like him.

'But I can't see how it could have had any bearing on Holly's murder,' she said. 'It happened three years ago and there's no suggestion that Holly had been making an issue of it again.

But let's do some more digging into Blake. Perhaps Holly found out about his affair with Charlene and was threatening to expose it. That might well have given him a motive for killing her.'

Anna then ran through the conversation she'd had with Freya Gregory.

'She admitted that Holly told her about her affair with Nathan Wolf, but she was sworn to secrecy. She now feels partly responsible for what's happened. I've agreed that we won't pass this information on to her sister. And I've given the same undertaking to Theo Blake in regards to his affair. This is purely for Rebecca's sake and not theirs. I'm pretty sure that both secrets will come out eventually but right now I see no point in adding to Rebecca's woes.'

Anna then said she wanted checks carried out on the phone records and digital footprints of the entire family, including Holly's mother and stepfather.

'We need to find out if they're holding anything else back,' she said.

The detectives took it in turns to provide updates. DC Niven explained that the Nissan Micra that Ross Moore had been driving on Tuesday night had also undergone a forensic examination, but nothing linking it to Holly's murder had been found.

'And unlike Nathan Wolf's Range Rover it hadn't been cleaned recently,' Niven said.

It wasn't conclusive proof that Holly had never been in the car – either alive or dead – but it did make it more likely that her ex had told the truth.

DC Sweeny then said that an appeal aimed at black cab drivers would go out later in the evening.

'We're pointing out that it may have been the last journey Holly made,' Sweeny added. 'But it's bound to prompt some difficult questions from the media. It will only take one reporter to ask if the taxi driver is a suspect and others will jump on it. They'll demand to know why we're holding Nathan Wolf in custody if we suspect Holly might have been murdered by a stranger.'

Anna knew that today's developments had raised the tempo of the investigation, but they'd fallen short of providing definitive answers to the outstanding questions. It meant there was still a lot of work to be done. But Anna felt a frisson of unease at the prospect of being forced by pressure from on high to charge Wolf prematurely just to end the media frenzy.

She wasn't as sure as others were of his guilt, despite the threat he made and the discovery of her driving licence.

She kept thinking back to when she and Walker turned up at his house and broke the news about Holly's body being found on the common. The shock on his face had seemed genuine and nothing he had said since then had convinced her he was lying.

But if he didn't kill Holly then who did?

Anna was about to open it up for discussion again when Walker seized her attention by holding aloft his mobile phone.

'I've just taken a call from Sue Bond, the FLO who's with Holly's parents,' he said. 'She wants us to know that Rebecca Blake has decided to stage an impromptu press conference. She's insisting the media are allowed into the mews so that she can speak to them in front of her house. And she's told Sue that she's got something important to announce.'

CHAPTER FORTY-FIVE

The team gathered around the television monitors to see what Rebecca was going to say. The BBC news channel had a satellite truck outside her home so its crew was set up to cover it live. There was a growing sense of anticipation as the cameras focused on her front door while an out-of-shot reporter explained what was happening.

'Mrs Blake hasn't spoken publicly since her daughter's body was found on Barnes Common three days ago,' he said. 'Then in the past hour she announced through her office that she was going to address the media. Just a reminder that Mrs Blake is the Conservative leader of Westminster Council and is currently one of the candidates who will be standing in the forthcoming Mayoral election in London.'

When she appeared she was wearing a sober grey suit and tinted glasses, and her 'loyal' husband had an arm around her shoulders.

The couple stepped onto the paved street where the crowd

of reporters and photographers were bunched together behind two uniformed police officers.

Once in position, Rebecca squared her shoulders and inhaled a long breath before speaking.

'It's not easy for me to stand before you today,' she said, her voice surprisingly clear and strong. 'In fact, after what happened to our daughter, just getting through the day is a struggle. But I need to make an announcement regarding a decision I've made.'

She paused there to fish a tissue from her pocket. She blew her nose with it before continuing.

'I have decided to withdraw my candidacy from the London Mayoral election. It will be impossible for me to focus on the campaign and that would not be fair to those who support me.

'The loss of our daughter is indescribable. Holly was a wonderful, kind, beautiful person and we loved her so much. The manner of her death adds to the pain, as does the revelation about her private life.

'I just want to make clear that Holly was a vulnerable young woman who was taken advantage of by a much older man, a man whom she should never have trusted. I won't be drawn on who I believe murdered our daughter because I don't want to compromise the police investigation. But I will say that I hope the bastard rots in hell.'

The questions came thick and fast.

Did you know about your daughter's relationship with the MP?

Did Holly tell you she was going to sell her story to the Sunday Mirror*?*

Is or was Mr Nathan Wolf a friend of yours?

Do you rule out the possibility of running for Mayor at a later date?

The couple took turns answering, but it quickly became too much for both of them. Rebecca started to sob so Theo hustled her back into the house.

Anna was full of admiration for what Rebecca had done. It couldn't have been easy to face the press like that and to subject herself to what was in effect an unsympathetic grilling.

Nathan Wolf was looking even worse for wear when Anna faced him a second time across the table in the interview room. New lines were etched into his face and there was a vacant expression in his eyes.

His lawyer Gavin Peake sat beside him. No doubt he had briefed him on the media storm that continued to rage on the outside.

Anna explained that she had applied successfully to extend the length of time they were able to hold him in custody without charge.

'We're continuing our enquiries,' she said. 'And until we're satisfied that you've told us the truth you won't be going anywhere, Mr Wolf.'

Peake objected and described the police actions as outrageous, but Anna didn't bother to respond because it was the line taken by most lawyers when they failed to get their clients released.

Unsurprisingly, Wolf stuck to his story that he went

straight home on Tuesday evening after returning from Somerset. And he continued to insist that he had no idea how Holly's blood-spattered driving licence got into his jacket pocket.

'We've established that you wore the coat both on Tuesday in Somerset and on Wednesday to the office,' Anna said. 'Did you leave it unattended at any point?'

He gave a slow nod. 'Probably. It was a warm day and I would have left it over the back of my office chair while I attended meetings.'

'So do you think that someone in the office placed the licence in your pocket while you were away from it?'

'It's possible, I suppose.'

'But extremely unlikely unless one of your colleagues was involved in Holly's murder and decided to frame you.'

Wolf ran a palm over his forehead. 'Why won't you listen to me, detective? I've told you until I'm blue in the face that I don't know what's going on. I did not kill Holly. And I haven't a clue how her driving licence got into my pocket. All I did was end my relationship with her and I really wish to God that I hadn't.'

The interview went downhill from there and Wolf struggled to hold it together as Anna tried to push him into making a confession. His answers became more incoherent and at one point he started to cry.

It was his lawyer who demanded that the session be brought to an end, but Anna was about to do so anyway.

The blood was thundering in her head as she walked out of the interview room and a tightness had settled in her chest.

The first person she encountered in the corridor was

Nash, who had watched the interview through the two-way mirror.

'I don't know what you think, sir,' she said. 'But my gut is telling me that Nathan Wolf did not kill Holly Blake.'

CHAPTER FORTY-SIX

It was dark by the time Anna got home. She was exhausted, her eyes squinting with tiredness, her mind thumping out of control.

Her aim was to get an early night and be up at the crack of dawn to return to the office. Tomorrow she would review every aspect of the case – her notes, the forensic reports, the CCTV logs, photographs of the body on the common, the new batch of phone records. She needed to pull all the threads together in her head and try to make sense of things.

She was one of the few people who didn't believe that Nathan Wolf had killed Holly. She wasn't convinced he had lied to them, and the evidence against him just felt somewhat contrived.

But before she left the office DCS Nash made it clear that he thought there was enough evidence to get a conviction.

'I believe that what I saw in that interview room was a first-class performance,' he said. 'The man knows how to fool people, and I reckon that's because he's had plenty of practice as an experienced politician. Your gut might be telling you otherwise, Anna, but to my mind the evidence is overwhelming.

'Holly set out to destroy him and he reacted by telling her she'd regret it. He doesn't have a foolproof alibi, and he cleaned his car straight after the murder was committed. And to top it all he can't explain how her driving licence got into his pocket.'

Anna was the first to admit that when put like that it sounded pretty convincing. But something wasn't right about it. She could feel it in her blood. It seemed too pat. And she was sure that if he was lying then she would have seen through it during the two face-to-face conversations in his home and the two formal interviews at HQ.

One problem was the lack of a conclusive piece of evidence to rule him out. Without it the pressure would build to charge him with Holly's murder.

The other problem was that she hadn't yet established a credible alternative.

Anna jotted down a few notes on a pad. Then she put a ready meal in the oven and poured herself a large glass of white wine. She took it out onto the patio where she lit up a cigarette and sat on her favourite rattan chair. It was a balmy night and the sky glistened with stars. At any other time she would have settled back and relaxed, but not tonight. She had work to do.

She looked at the notes she'd written and read them out loud to herself.

'As I see it there are five scenarios. First – Nathan Wolf murdered Holly at an unidentified location, then dumped her body on the common in the dead of night or early hours of Wednesday morning. Second – Ross Moore committed the murder after stalking her. Third – she was killed by a stranger, possibly a taxi driver. Fourth – the murder was carried out by someone whose aim was to stop Holly's mother becoming Mayor of London. Fifth – her stepdad killed her, perhaps because she found out about his affair with Charlene Hamilton.'

Anna put a line through number four. She no longer believed that it was a worthwhile line of enquiry even though Rebecca had thrown in the towel on the Mayoral race. Having given it some thought, Anna decided it was time to put it on the back burner.

She also scrawled a line through number one, having made up her mind that unless she could be persuaded otherwise then the MP wasn't the perp.

That left Ross Moore, Theo Blake and an unknown subject – what the police called an unsub. It was not a good position to be in three days after Holly's body was found and five days after she was murdered. There were still far too many questions that remained unanswered.

Where was the crime scene?

If Holly was the victim of a sex predator then why wasn't she raped?

Where was she going when she left her flat so late on the night she was stabbed to death?

Was there more than one killer?

Was she being stalked by someone other than Ross Moore, someone who'd become obsessed with her after following her modelling career?

The ringing of her phone wrenched her out of her thoughts. It was Tom, and it took her a few moments to switch her mind away from the list of questions.

He wanted to know if she was OK, and told her that he'd been following the case during the day.

As much as she was glad he had called she didn't want to be drawn into a protracted conversation. For that reason she didn't open up about the investigation, and instead got him to talk about the visit to his daughter in Portsmouth.

It had gone well, he said. They'd had lunch and Grace had said she was hoping to visit him in London before the start of the new university term.

'I told her that you and I would spend some time with her,' he said. 'If you can get a few days off perhaps we can take her up west, stay in a hotel for a couple of nights, maybe go see a show.'

'I'd like that,' Anna said, and she meant it. She was fond of Grace, a pleasant girl who shared her father's good looks and easy charm.

The small talk continued for a few more minutes until Tom brought it to a close by saying that he had to crack on with some work.

Anna finished her wine before going back inside. By the time she took her dinner from the oven she'd lost her appetite. She picked at it as she returned her thoughts to the investigation, and then continued to wade through the facts and theories while she soaked in a hot bath and prepared herself for bed.

At ten o'clock her phone rang again and this time it was Jack Keen on the line. Her private investigator sounded excited as he told her about a new development in the search for her daughter.

'The *Evening Standard* called me earlier to say that another woman rang the hotline that was included in their article,' he said. 'Her name is Jamila and she works at a hairdressing salon on Shoreditch High Street. I just came off the phone to her and she claims she had a young customer in today who's a dead ringer for Chloe's age progression image. She'd seen it in the paper. What's more the girl told her that her name is Alice and she's twelve years old.'

Anna felt the blood stiffen in her veins.

'Did she go to the salon by herself?' she asked.

'No, her mother dropped her off there. Unfortunately Jamila didn't twig the likeness until after her mum picked her up an hour later, so it didn't occur to her to ask questions.'

'Shit.'

'However, the girl did say that her mum had gone off to book a foreign holiday for the pair of them. So tomorrow I intend to visit the area to check on local travel agents. It's a long shot, I know, but worth pursuing.'

'It sounds promising, but I'll try not to build my hopes up,' Anna said.

'Well, there's one other thing that's worth noting,' Jack said. 'Shoreditch High Street is within walking distance of Oakfield School in Bethnal Green. That's where one of the other sightings was reported. So it's possible the same girl was spotted by two different people.'

'Have you heard back from the school's headmistress yet?'

'No, but I've sent her another email asking if the pupil in question happens to live in Shoreditch. I'll let you know if anything comes of it. So keep your fingers crossed.'

Anna was wide awake suddenly, and her heart was drumming in her chest like cannon fire.

Instead of heading for the bedroom she went into her study, where she sat at her desk surrounded by photos of Chloe.

She hadn't thought about her daughter during much of the day, which was a good thing in that she hadn't been distracted from the investigation. But all the same it made her feel guilty.

Was it really possible that she was actually getting closer to finding Chloe after all this time? If so then she had the age progression image to thank for it. But what if it was inaccurate and looked nothing like her? The forensic artist who'd created it had used a lot of guesswork, after all. He'd focused on Chloe's bone structure, the shape of her eyes, the dimpled chin and button nose. But it wasn't an exact science. Perhaps her features had developed in a different way over the past ten years. Or maybe Matthew had taken steps early on to alter her appearance in some way. He'd been callous enough to take her away from her mother so Anna would not have put it past him to subject her to some form of cosmetic surgery.

Despite those lingering doubts, Anna clung to the slim hope that the image was a true likeness and that Chloe had blossomed into a beautiful girl. If that were the case then maybe fate would be kind to her for once and they would soon be reunited.

That prospect filled her with a different kind of nervous anticipation.

How would Chloe react to me? Would there be an instinctive, instant connection between us? What would I say to the daughter I haven't seen grow up?

More unsettling questions.

More anxious thoughts raging through Anna's mind.

As she stood up and headed for her bed, she could feel an ache swell in her chest, the throb of tears behind her eyes.

And she knew she wasn't going to get much sleep tonight.

CHAPTER FORTY-SEVEN

It was eleven o'clock and Sophie was still up. Thankfully Alice had been in bed for an hour, having crammed as much of her stuff as she could into two suitcases and a shoulder bag.

She had used her own mobile phone to send selfies to three of her friends so they could see her new haircut. And she'd told them she was going away on a surprise holiday so they wouldn't be seeing her for a couple of weeks.

Sophie knew it was going to break Alice's heart when she learned they would not be coming back to London after leaving the all-inclusive resort.

Sophie had now made up her mind that she couldn't risk it. There was too much at stake. Anna Tate's private investigator was breathing down their necks, and there was no knowing when or where he would show up.

And then there was Bruno Perez, the demon from her past. The man who had murdered James and who had vowed to make her suffer for what she had done to him.

His face kept pushing itself into her thoughts, and she

recoiled as the memories of their time together came flooding back.

According to Lisa he had returned to London from Spain. Was that because his employee Michael Taylor had tipped him off after stealing Lisa's phone? The thought of it chilled Sophie to the bone, made her wonder if she should leave the flat tonight and succumb to the panic that was growing inside her.

But of course that was impractical. She had left it too late. She still hadn't packed her own cases or sent the resignation email to the cleaning company. She'd spent the best part of the evening surfing the web, looking up schools, apartments for rent and job vacancies in and around Lloret de Mar. It seemed to her to be the best option to begin with. There was enough money in the bank to cover a six-month lease on an apartment there and she was sure she'd be able to find work in a bar or a restaurant. It wasn't ideal and it was going to be hard. But what choice did she have?

She got up from the kitchen table and crossed to the window for the umpteenth time. There were still people on the street outside, but she didn't spot anyone watching the flat or acting suspiciously.

She inhaled deeply, filling her lungs with a calming breath. She didn't feel tired enough to go to bed. Instead she started checking all the drawers and cupboards, looking for things she didn't want to leave behind. But most of what was in the kitchen belonged to the landlord, and those items she had purchased could easily be replaced in Spain.

It was much the same in the living room. She picked up a few small items, including a framed photo of James and Alice on the beach in Puerto de Mazzaron. It was taken when

Alice was five, at a time when Sophie truly believed that the bad times were behind her.

In her bedroom it was a different matter. That's where she kept her jewellery and paperwork, including their passports, bank statements, the lease on the flat, and the fake birth certificate that had her name on it as Alice's mother.

She didn't have that many clothes, and most of them were old, so she took only her favourite garments from the wardrobe and drawers. One drawer contained the two editions of the *Evening Standard* that featured the Anna Tate story. She'd hidden them under some folded bed linen so that Alice wouldn't see them.

She pulled them out now and carried them into the kitchen in order to throw them away. But as she approached the pedal bin she couldn't resist reading them one last time. As she did so, tears clouded her eyes. Even now the shocking revelations were hard to take in. All the lies. The betrayal. The part she herself had played in the whole sorry saga.

What had happened was a tragedy on so many levels. James was dead. Alice had lost her father. Anna Tate was trapped in a never-ending nightmare. And Sophie would always be looking over her shoulder no matter where she went.

By now salty tears were streaking her cheeks and her blood was pounding in her ears. She got up and returned to her bedroom where she stripped off her clothes and left them on the floor.

It was midnight when she finally slipped beneath the duvet. Its weight provided a small measure of comfort. But it wasn't enough to halt the churn of destructive thoughts that were going to make it hard, if not impossible, for her to fall asleep.

CHAPTER FORTY-EIGHT

Anna had another bad night. She only managed to sleep for a couple of hours and woke up at three a.m. There was no way she was going to drop off again because her mind started to run through all the things she wanted to do. By four a.m. she was showered and dressed and had downed a cup of coffee and two slices of buttered toast.

It was another mild day outside, the air soft, the sky clear. At this time of the morning traffic was light so it was an easy journey to MIT HQ, and she arrived just after four-thirty.

The night shift detectives were not surprised to see her since she had warned them that she would probably be in early. Before getting down to business she picked up the newspapers that were delivered every morning and carried them into her office along with a black coffee from the vending machine.

Every single front page carried the story of Rebecca Blake dropping her bid to become Mayor of London. There were photos of her speaking to the media outside her home and some of her quotes appeared in large, bold type.

Her dramatic statement jostled for position with coverage of the investigation into her daughter's murder and the fact that Nathan Wolf, MP, was still being held in custody.

Prominence was also given to Holly Blake's ex-boyfriend being a suspect while at the same time languishing on suicide watch in hospital.

The appeal aimed at taxi drivers had been issued too late to make it into any but two of the papers, the *Telegraph* being one of them.

Police say that Holly may have travelled in a taxi across London on the night she was murdered.

A witness has come forward to say he believes he saw her get into a black cab in Drummond Street, Camden just before eleven o'clock on Tuesday evening.

Drummond Street is only a short walk from Holly's flat in Stanhope Street.

Detectives want to hear from any taxi drivers who were in that part of the city at the time and gave a lift to anyone matching Holly's description.

The Media Liaison team had done as instructed, which was not to attribute the sighting to Ross Moore. Anna did not expect a significant response. In order to reach most of London's black cab drivers they would have to put far more effort into it. She made a note to mention it at the press conference that had been scheduled for later in the day.

After reading the papers, she got the team to brief her on

any overnight developments. It didn't take long because there hadn't been any.

They *were* able to confirm that Theo Blake had told the truth when he'd said that his car had been in the garage on Tuesday and Wednesday. And they also reported that no new CCTV had come in that included footage of Nathan Wolf and Ross Moore, or the cars they'd been driving.

Anna was disappointed. It was becoming clear that the investigation was losing momentum. They needed a breakthrough, or at least some new leads to follow up.

She started to wade through everything that had been accumulated. The case notes, the interview transcripts, the CCTV logs, the forensic reports, the file on Holly Blake. She was hoping they had missed something that would shed at least a glimmer of light on the circumstances surrounding the young model's death.

She looked again at the photos taken of Holly's body on the common, and was reminded of the ghastly wound that the killer had inflicted on her throat.

'I would give anything to be able to communicate with you, Holly,' Anna whispered, as she stared down at Holly's face. 'I'd ask you where you went on Tuesday night, who took your life and where it happened. Why did they do it and was it someone you knew?'

If only the dead could speak, she thought. It would make her job so much easier.

Anna looked at her watch. It was still only six-fifteen. She asked DC Fellows, who had worked through the night, to check on their two suspects. It didn't take him long to establish that they had both had a rough night and were now awake. Ross Moore's lawyer was demanding to know when his client would be released. Anna said she would talk to him later and Fellows gave her the brief's contact details.

'And who shall I pass these on to, ma'am?' Fellows said, holding up a document wallet. 'They're the phone records for Holly's parents and her aunt and uncle.'

'I'll go through them myself,' Anna said, taking the wallet from him.

She spent the next ten minutes ploughing through Rebecca and Theo's mobile phone records, but nothing stood out as unusual. She was about to start on Freya and Robert's when DI Walker appeared at her office door.

'I gather you've already been in for several hours, guv,' he said. 'I take it you couldn't sleep.'

'Too much to think about,' she said. 'I've been reviewing everything we've got.'

'Have you come across anything we've overlooked?'

'Not as yet.' She glanced at her watch again. 'Would you do me a favour and tee everyone up for a seven o'clock briefing? We need to decide what to do about our two suspects. I'll be out as soon as I've finished here.'

'Would you like another coffee?'

'I'd love one, Max. Thank you.'

Anna's eyes felt dry and gritty as she returned her attention to the call logs. It was a job she would normally have delegated but she was half way through it now so she carried on.

There was nothing to arouse suspicion in the calls and messages to and from Freya and Robert's mobiles. But when Anna examined their landline list there was one call that jumped out at her.

It was made at eleven-fifty-five on Tuesday evening but

only lasted for five seconds and the caller didn't wait for it to be answered.

Anna felt a twist of alarm and was unsure what to make of it. But she *was* sure of one thing – it needed to be followed up asap.

CHAPTER FORTY-NINE

For Sophie it had been a long, unpleasant night. She wasn't sure when she finally fell asleep, but it was well into the early hours.

She was awake again at seven-thirty, and it took a mighty effort to haul herself out of bed and into the kitchen.

She felt drained of energy and emotionally raw, and for a while it was a struggle to force air past the knot in her throat.

She boiled the kettle and made herself a mug of tea. She would drink it and then get showered before waking Alice up.

The day ahead was going to be tough. She was certain of that. She would have to try to keep the anxiety out of her voice, give the impression that she was upbeat because they were going on holiday.

But inside she was an eddying mass of fear and self-doubt, and her brain felt scrambled. She knew she wouldn't be able to relax until their plane touched down in Spain. Once there they'd be out of harm's way and she could focus on the future.

She sat at the table with her tea and switched on the television. The murder of the model Holly Blake was still the main story on the news.

They showed her distraught mother talking to the press and announcing that she was giving up on her attempt to become the Mayor of London.

Then they cut to a photo of the politician who had been arrested in connection with the murder. They said he hadn't yet been charged but Sophie suspected it was only a matter of time.

Her thoughts inevitably turned to the police officer who had collared him, the one who was in charge of the investigation.

Detective Anna Tate.

Sophie was curious to know how she managed to cope with such a high-powered job. The constant pressure. The seriously unsocial hours. Frequently putting her life on the line in a city gripped by an epidemic of violent crime.

And all the while grieving over the loss of her child.

The last ten years must have been so hard on her. Not knowing where her daughter was or even if she was alive. None of the news reports Sophie had read in the papers or online had alluded to Tate's personal life. She wondered if she had remarried and given birth to any more children. Or was she a lonely singleton who spent all her spare time searching for her beloved Chloe?

Sophie decided it was best not to go looking for the answers. The less she knew about the woman the better. Otherwise every new fact she discovered would no doubt feed into the sense of guilt that occupied a corner of her mind.

She shook her head, took a long, deep breath and expelled it. Now was not the time to dwell on something that would make her feel worse than she already did.

She got up from the table to pour herself another mug of tea, but just then the house phone rang. Her first reaction was to ignore it because it was probably a cold caller. But since it was mounted on the wall only an arm's length away she lifted the receiver so the ringing wouldn't wake Alice.

'Hello,' she said.

'Is that Miss Cameron?' A woman's voice.

'It is.'

'I'm sorry to bother you this early. It's Mrs Holland here from Oakfield School. I tried calling your mobile but I couldn't get through on it.'

'It's switched off,' Sophie said.

'I thought as much. It's just that I've received another message from that private investigator I told you about, the one who's helping that police officer to find her missing daughter.'

Sophie felt her chest contract like a fist.

'I told you I was going to get in touch with him,' she said. 'What does he want?'

'He says there's been another sighting of someone who resembles the artist's impression of the missing girl. This time it was yesterday at a hairdressing salon on Shoreditch High Street. It was one of the hairdressers who contacted the newspaper. She said her young customer told her that her name was Alice. So this Mr Keen is now trying to find out if it could be the same girl who was spotted outside the school. He's asking if we have any pupils named Alice living near the High Street.'

'What have you said to him?'

'Nothing. I've not responded because I don't feel it's my place to. It would be different if it was an official police enquiry but it isn't. Of course, if you want me to . . .'

'No, don't worry, Mrs Holland. I'll call him. And for your information my Alice didn't go to a hairdresser yesterday. We spent the day together in the West End.'

'Well, there you have it. Obviously another mistake. I'll leave you to sort it then, Miss Cameron. Is that all right?'

'Of course.'

'That's great. Thank you.'

When Sophie came off the phone every nerve in her body was vibrating. She could not believe that someone else had noticed the likeness. She thought back to when she dropped Alice off at the salon. The hairdresser was a pretty Asian woman in her twenties who introduced herself as Jamila.

'And what is your name, young lady?' she'd asked.

Alice had told her before going on to say that she wanted her hair cut short and dyed blonde.

There had been two other staff members in the salon at the time so any one of them could have called the *Evening Standard*, who in turn must have contacted the investigator.

It reinforced Sophie's belief that she was doing the right thing by leaving London. It was obvious to her now that the net was fast closing on them.

CHAPTER FIFTY

The morning briefing was put back to seven-forty-five so that Anna could make some enquiries in respect of Robert and Freya Gregory's phone records.

The call that was made on their landline at eleven-fifty-five on Tuesday evening had sparked a surge of curiosity. But before presenting it to the team as a potential new lead, she'd had to check it out. And once she'd done that she sensed that she was onto something. Thoughts started to take shape in her head, and she felt a rush of excitement.

'I'm shifting the focus of the investigation,' she announced when she stood before the team. 'I've come across something that raises a lot of questions, and we need to move quickly.'

Her detectives were at once alert. Eyebrows were raised, coffee cups put down, notebooks produced.

Anna held up the Gregorys' phone records and explained what they were.

'On Tuesday just before midnight a 999 call was made

from the Gregory household in Fulham,' she said. 'But the caller didn't wait for it to be answered and hung up after only five seconds. It was therefore recorded as a silent call and an operator rang the number back some minutes later to see if it had been a mistake. The brief conversation that took place was recorded and has been played to me over the phone. You can all listen to it later, but basically the caller identified himself as Robert Gregory and said that his young son had made the call without his knowledge after he woke up and wandered into the living room.

'Mr Gregory apologised profusely and said he would make sure that it never happened again. The operator gave him a polite but stern telling off and that would have been the end of the matter if we hadn't requested the phone records.'

'And as a result of that we now know that Robert Gregory is a liar,' Walker said. 'The couple don't have any children.'

Anna nodded. 'Precisely. So what I want to know is why the call was made and why Holly's uncle lied about it.'

'Could it have been a domestic violence situation?' DC Sweeny said. 'We know Mr Gregory is not averse to using his fists. He demonstrated that when he laid into Nathan Wolf. So maybe his wife picked up the phone and dialled the three nines because he was assaulting her. But he got to it before it was answered.'

Anna shrugged. 'That could well be the case, but somehow I very much doubt it. I don't get the impression that their relationship is an abusive one. Nevertheless we should check to see if there's any kind of history of violence or if the couple have made a habit of calling the emergency service. For me it's the timing of the call that's significant. Eleven-fifty-five on

Tuesday evening. It was around then that Holly Blake was murdered.'

It dawned on everyone then what Anna was getting at, but it was clear from their faces that most of them were surprised.

'So are you saying that you think the uncle and aunt had something to do with it, ma'am?' DS Prescott said.

Anna nodded. 'It just strikes me as too much of a coincidence. We know someone called 999 and we know it wasn't Robert Gregory's son because he doesn't have one. He must have made that up because he was suddenly put on the spot and couldn't think what else to say.'

'So it could have been Holly herself who made the call,' Prescott said.

'That's what we need to find out. I've spent the last half an hour turning this over in my head and it occurs to me that this could be the first piece of the puzzle we've been endeavouring to put together. We haven't been able to figure out where Holly was heading when she left her flat that night. So let's now assume that her ex-boyfriend did see her get into a taxi. Well, it could be that she told the driver to take her to her aunt's house in Fulham. Don't forget we've already been told that Holly often went there. If she did so that night then there's every chance she was there shortly after eleven.

'That would have been fifty-five minutes before the three-nines call, in which case something might have happened during that time that led to her death. And that's not all. Another missing piece of the puzzle that's been worrying me is Holly's driving licence and how it got into Nathan Wolf's pocket. The general assumption is that he put it there after he killed her. But supposing he didn't, and it was planted. We know that he left it on his office chair while he attended meetings, but I don't think any of us believe that one of his colleagues placed it there. However, we've overlooked the fact that Robert Gregory turned up at Wolf's house not long before we searched it and found the licence. Now it could be that he went there not just to give Wolf a hiding, but also to slip the licence into the guy's pocket. It would have been a simple thing to do when he stormed out of the house after Wolf's girlfriend arrived.'

'That makes sense, guv,' Walker said. 'I can't believe that didn't occur to us.'

'But then why would it have?' Anna said. 'We've not regarded Robert Gregory as a suspect. He and his wife are the grieving relatives. Perhaps an alarm should have gone off when his reactions proved more than a little OTT. Or even when we found out that Freya had known all along about Holly's affair with Wolf.'

'So what's our next move, guv?' Walker asked. 'Do we bring them in for questioning?'

'I'd rather go and see them,' Anna said. 'I wouldn't mind having another look at the house. You come with me, Max, and while we do that I want the rest of you to dig up whatever you can on Robert and Freya Gregory. There were two cars on their driveway when we paid them a visit so get the registrations and see if they turn up on CCTV. And put a forensics team on standby. Robert told us that his wife is a teacher so find out which school she works at. He himself is an estate agent with a base in Mortlake. So we should gather some details on that.'

'Did you say Mortlake, guv?' DC Sweeny said.

'That's right. Why?'

'Well, think about it. The drive from Fulham to Mortlake takes you through Barnes. So I reckon it's safe to say that Mr Gregory must be pretty familiar with the layout of the common.'

CHAPTER FIFTY-ONE

Alice came into Sophie's bedroom clutching her phone in one hand and a plastic carrier bag in the other. She had only just woken up and was wearing her pink llama fleece pyjamas.

'I just spoke to Rachel and she wants me to take her things back to her before we go on holiday,' she said.

Sophie looked up from the two suitcases that lay open on her bed.

'What things?'

'I borrowed some of her DVDs and a couple of T-shirts.'

'Well, can't it wait until we're back?'

'She wants them now. And her mum said I can have breakfast with them if I want.'

Rachel was one of Alice's best friends. They went to different schools but attended the same youth centre just off the High Street. She lived in a small block of flats about three hundred yards away and Sophie usually let Alice go there by herself as long as it wasn't dark.

But today was different. It was too risky because for all she knew Bruno was close by, or someone else who was on the lookout for a young girl who resembled Anna Tate's missing daughter Chloe.

'I would rather you didn't go,' she said, and Alice's face fell. 'We've got a lot to do before we leave for the airport.'

'But I'm all packed, Mum. And I'm bored. So please let me go.'

'I said no, Alice. I want you to stay here with me.'

'But that's silly. I'll only be in your way. And I've already told Rachel I can go. She's expecting me. Please let me. Please, please, please.'

Alice continued to beg for another few minutes and against her better judgement Sophie finally gave in. She felt bad that she was taking Alice away from her friends and that she might never see Rachel and Ruth and the others again. And she told herself that she was probably being over-protective anyway and that Alice would be perfectly safe. After all, Rachel's flat was only three hundred yards away along a busy street.

'Very well, you can go,' she said. 'But call me as soon as you get there to let me know you arrived safely. And tell Gloria that you're only allowed to stay for a few hours and I'll come and get you.'

Gloria, Rachel's mother, was housebound following a stroke four years ago that had caused her to lose the use of her left arm and given her a serious limp in her right leg. Her life took another turn for the worse twelve months ago when her husband left her for another woman. Since then Sophie had been cleaning her small council flat once a week for free. The pair got on well, and Gloria was one of the very few people she was going to miss.

'Go and have a shower then,' Sophie said to Alice as she

switched her mobile back on. 'Then put something on that you're not taking with you. And get out what you want to wear on the journey. I'll see if it needs ironing.'

Alice left the house at nine and Sophie got on with the packing.

Through the window she saw that it was another beautiful morning, the sun a blazing orange ball in the sky. It brought a rare smile to her lips because she was reminded of all those wonderful mornings in Puerto de Mazarron, when the beaches beckoned and the sea sparkled invitingly.

She knew it was going to be strange going back to Spain, but it would be easier than seeking refuge elsewhere. She spoke fluent Spanish and she was fond of the country. It almost felt like she was going home.

On the Costa Brava they could start afresh. It was a lively region with a large expat community, and she felt sure that after the initial shock Alice would quickly settle.

As she packed the cases she kept expecting her phone to ring with the call from Alice. But when she was still waiting after fifteen minutes panic set in.

Why was it taking her so long to walk a few hundred yards? she asked herself.

She stopped what she was doing and dialled Alice's mobile. But it was switched off. Her heart was beating furiously as she called Gloria.

'It's Sophie, Gloria,' she said, when the call was answered. 'I hope you're OK.'

'I'm as well as can be expected,' Gloria said. 'I hear you're going on holiday later today.'

'That's right. Can't wait. It's why I'm ringing. I need you to confirm for me that Alice got to your flat OK.'

A moment's hesitation. 'She's not here yet, Soph. Should she be?'

Sophie felt a sudden stab of anxiety.

'She left home fifteen minutes ago with some DVDs that Rachel wanted back. She said she was going to have breakfast with you both.'

'I know the girls spoke on the phone and Rachel invited her over. But she hasn't arrived.'

Words formed in Sophie's throat, but they wouldn't come out. Instead, she just stood there, open-mouthed, as a pit opened up in the bottom of her stomach.

CHAPTER FIFTY-TWO

Anna had chosen not to forewarn Robert and Freya Gregory that she and Walker were going to revisit their home in Fulham. She wanted to surprise them so that they didn't have time to discuss between themselves how they would respond.

'It looks like only one of them is in,' Walker said when they arrived at the house.

Yesterday there had been a Vauxhall Corsa and a Toyota Hybrid parked on the driveway. Now it was just the Corsa.

Anna wondered if Holly Blake's body had been placed in either of the cars and driven to Barnes Common. It was among the many thoughts that had been whirling inside her head since she had spotted the 999 call on the phone log.

And the questions were piling up.

Did Holly come to this house on Tuesday night?

Did someone kill her while she was here?

If so then what could the motive have been?

Why was the call made to the emergency services? And why did Robert pretend that his non-existent son was responsible?

Anna knew there was a risk that she was attaching too much significance to the call, and was now leading the team on a wild-goose chase. But she also knew that there was nothing to lose except a small amount of time.

It was Freya Gregory who answered the door. She was wearing a baggy striped shirt over faded jeans and her blonde hair was tied back in a ponytail. Her plump face was without make-up, and her eyes were lost in the shadows that surrounded them.

She was clearly taken aback to see them. Her body went stiff as she opened her mouth to speak, but no words came out.

'Would it be OK if we came in for another chat with you and your husband, Mrs Gregory?' Anna said. 'Something has come up that we need to discuss.'

Freya swallowed hard and when she found her voice her lower lip trembled.

'Robert has had to go to the office,' she said. 'He'll be gone for a few hours. Can it wait until he gets back?'

'I'm afraid it can't,' Anna said. 'But it's not a problem. I'm sure that you can answer our questions.'

'I'd rather he was here.'

'Then by all means call him and ask him to come home. Or if he's not able to then we can easily arrange for another team of detectives to visit his office and speak to him there. They can be in Mortlake in half an hour or so.'

Clearly flustered, Freya turned and hurried along the hallway.

'Methinks the lady has been on the booze,' Walker commented. 'Did you smell it on her breath?'

Anna nodded as she stepped over the threshold. 'I did. And she doesn't look too steady on her feet either.'

Walker pushed the door shut and they followed Freya into the kitchen. She was already on the phone, standing over by the French windows with her back to them.

While they waited for her to finish the call, Anna glanced around the room. She saw a half-full bottle of vodka on the table and an empty glass next to it. On a shelf above the table she also noticed a framed photo of Freya sitting in a restaurant with Holly and Rebecca. All three were holding up glasses in a toast to the camera.

'That picture was taken on Holly's last birthday,' Freya said, coming off the phone. 'It was the last time all three of us went out together.'

Freya stared at the photo for a couple of seconds, her features taut, her jaw clenched. Then she turned to Anna and said, 'Robert's leaving the office now and will get back here as quickly as he can.'

'That's good,' Anna said. 'In the meantime there's a question I need to ask you, Mrs Gregory.'

Freya stepped forward, pulled a stool out from under the breakfast bar and sat on it.

'Robert told me not to speak to you until he's back,' she said.

'And why is that?' Anna asked her. 'Is he afraid that you'll tell us something that you shouldn't?'

'No, of course not. It's just, well, I can't . . .'

The sentence ran out of steam and Freya shifted her gaze away from Anna. She licked her dry lips and stared longingly at the vodka bottle.

Anna moved across the room so that she stood opposite Freya.

'Can you tell us what happened here on Tuesday evening, Mrs Gregory?' she said.

Freya shook her head. 'Nothing happened, except that we went to bed quite early.'

'Well, a call was made to the emergency services just before midnight. Was it because you or your husband were involved in some kind of accident?'

Freya's eyes flared. She obviously hadn't expected the question.

'No, not at all. It . . . it was a mistake. I thought there was an intruder in the house.'

'Really? So you dialled the three nines?'

'Yes, I did. I panicked. Robert told me I was being silly and there was nobody else in the house so I hung up.'

'Then why did your husband tell the operator when she called back that it was your son who did it?'

'We don't have a son,' she said quickly.

'I know that, Mrs Gregory. So why did your husband lie to the operator?'

She shook her head again. 'He didn't.'

'Well, actually, he did,' Anna said. 'I've listened to the recording of the conversation. It didn't last long, but there's no mistaking what was said.'

Freya was now struggling to contain her emotions. She was sweating and shaking, and it looked as though she was very, very scared. Anna wondered how much vodka the woman had consumed and why she had hit the bottle so early in the day. Was it her way of dealing with grief or was it something else? Whatever the reason, the alcohol was fogging her brain and impairing her judgement.

Anna realised that there was no better time to exploit her vulnerability. So she decided to chance it and go for broke.

'We know that Holly was in this house on the night she was murdered,' she lied. 'We've spoken to the taxi driver who dropped her off outside about an hour before the 999 call was made. We'd now like to know what happened to her.'

Freya stared at Anna, her face white, immobile.

'So tell us what happened, Mrs Gregory,' Anna said. 'Which one of you murdered your niece and why?'

When Freya failed to respond, Anna feared that she had misjudged the moment and might well come to regret what she'd said. But then, suddenly, the woman's face collapsed in on itself and she broke down. Her face fell into her hands and her shoulders heaved with every sob.

It was a full two minutes before she got a grip and started talking.

CHAPTER FIFTY-THREE

Panic was filling Sophie's lungs as she raced along the street towards Gloria's flat. This was the route that Alice would have taken to get there. But there was no sign of her.

Sophie looked in front gardens and doorways on both sides of the road, keeping her eyes peeled for the bag Alice had been carrying. She also checked out the newsagents on the corner, the greasy spoon café and the veterinary surgery. She asked as many people as she could if they had seen a girl matching Alice's description. But nobody had.

Sophie had tried to call Alice straight away after learning that she hadn't turned up at her friend's flat. But her phone remained switched off. Sophie had also called three of Alice's other friends whose numbers she had in her own contacts list. They all lived within walking distance, but none of them had seen or heard from her. She'd been gone for over two hours now and Sophie had no idea where she was.

Gloria and her daughter Rachel lived in a four-storey block set back from the road. By the time Sophie got there her stomach was tied in knots and a scream was building in her throat.

This had never happened before and she was sure that if Alice had changed her mind about going to see Rachel then she would have let her know. She certainly wouldn't have just wandered off. Alice was too considerate, too sensible, and she'd had it drummed into her that the streets of London were not safe for a young girl by herself.

Sophie was therefore convinced that something must have happened to her. Was she lying injured somewhere, having been attacked by a mugger who had taken her phone? Or had she been snatched by Bruno himself, or one of his accomplices? It was a ghastly thought and she cursed herself for having given in to Alice by allowing her to go out by herself despite the risk.

It was a stupid, reckless thing to have done.

So was it time to call the police? If she did then they would want to know everything about Alice and the truth would inevitably come out. But there was no other option open to her. She couldn't search for Alice by herself. At least the police would be able to check the CCTV cameras she'd seen along the street and hopefully at least one of them would help to determine what had happened.

Sophie walked around Gloria's block. She checked the car park and bin cupboards at the rear, and then the stairs and lifts.

She then went to Gloria's flat just to satisfy herself that Alice wasn't there.

Rachel answered the door to her. 'She's still not here, Miss Cameron,' she said. 'I keep calling her phone but there's no answer.'

Sophie hurried past her into the kitchen where Gloria was sitting at the table with a mug of tea or coffee in front of her.

'I'm sure there's nothing to worry about,' Gloria said. 'You know what kids are like. She probably met up with one of her other mates and decided to go off somewhere like the park to have some fun.'

'But she has a bag with Rachel's things in it,' Sophie said. 'She was bringing them here.'

'Then if you think that something bad might have happened to her you should inform the police,' Gloria said.

A breathless Sophie replied, 'I know and I will as soon as I get back home. If she does turn up then please call me straight away.'

Sophie rushed out of the flat and back down the stairs. She retraced her steps along the street, but there was still no sign of Alice.

She stopped more people, showed them a photo of Alice she had on her phone, but she had to explain that her hair was shorter now, and blonde. However, those she spoke to just frowned and shook their heads.

When she stepped back into her own flat, she called out to Alice, but she was met with an ominous silence. She dropped onto a chair in the kitchen and felt the paralysis of fear taking over. Tortured thoughts tore through her mind and she found herself struggling to breathe.

A voice was telling her it was time to call the police, and she was about to do so when her phone rang. A wave of relief swept over her as she swiped the screen and Alice's name came up. She pressed the green icon and said, 'Oh, thank God it's you. Where are you, sweetheart?'

There was no immediate response.

'Will you talk to me, Alice? I'm worried.'

The silence on the line stretched for another two seconds before she heard a voice that was all too familiar.

But it didn't belong to Alice.

'There's no need to worry, Sophie. The girl is perfectly all right, at least for now.'

Sophie's heart stopped beating and she found she couldn't speak.

'I appreciate that it must be quite a shock to hear from your husband after all this time,' he said. 'I would have been in touch sooner, but after you left Southampton I gave up searching for a while to concentrate on other things.'

Sophie managed to swallow the lump in her throat and force words out.

'What have you done with Alice, Bruno?' she said.

'First tell me if you've called the police.'

'Not yet. I was about to.'

'Then don't. If you do you will never see your precious Alice again. Do you understand?'

'Of course. And I won't. I promise. Just don't hurt her. Please.'

'She'll be OK as long as you do as I tell you.'

'What is it you want, Bruno?'

'I should have thought that was obvious. I want to see you.'

CHAPTER FIFTY-FOUR

When Freya started talking, the first thing she said was, 'I need another drink.'

She got down from the stool at the breakfast bar and walked over to the table. She poured a shot of vodka into the empty glass and swallowed it in one go.

Anna didn't try to stop her. It was obvious that the drink, along with the lie she'd swallowed about a taxi driver telling them he had dropped Holly off at their house, had weakened the woman's resolve and breached her defences. She was ready to offload whatever guilty secret she'd been struggling to live with.

While they waited for her to speak, Walker took out his phone and switched on the recorder. It was questionable as to whether what she was going to say could be used as evidence, given the state she was in, but nonetheless it'd be useful to have it on tape.

Freya sat down at the table and stared into the empty glass. Anna knew they were lucky to have caught her off guard like this. But that was sometimes how it worked. A break came out of nowhere and changed the entire dynamic of an investigation.

Freya's speech was slurred when she started talking again, and her eyes were liquid.

'I loved that girl with all my being,' she said. 'I didn't ask her to come here that night. She should have stayed at home.'

Freya lifted her head and looked at Anna. Tears were now running down her face, and streaks of phlegm had gathered at the corners of her mouth.

'I told him that it was stupid to think we could get away with it,' she continued. 'But he wouldn't listen. He said that nobody would believe us.'

'Are you talking about your husband?' Anna asked.

She gave a slight nod. 'He means well. He thought he was protecting me. But the guilt has been weighing me down. I've found it hard to talk about Holly and to look my sister in the eye. And I know it can only get worse. That's why I've been drinking. It's how I get through the days.'

Anna felt a sudden wave of compassion for the woman. She was being eaten up from within by something she couldn't control. She looked pathetic, diminished, like she was standing on the edge of a precipice preparing to jump.

'So what happened on that night?' Anna said. 'You'll feel better once you tell us.'

Freya shook her head. 'I doubt that. I know I won't need to pretend any more, but I will have to face the consequences. And the harshest punishment will be having to accept that Rebecca will never want to speak to me again.'

Freya reached for the vodka bottle and poured some more

into the glass. She grimaced as it burned a track down her throat.

'I suggest you start by telling us why Holly came here,' Anna said. 'We know she had an argument with her mother over selling her story to the *Sunday Mirror*. She went straight home afterwards, but only stayed in her flat for about fifteen minutes before leaving again and coming here.'

Freya wiped her eyes with the backs of her fingers and took a deep breath.

'When she turned up we were watching television and thinking about going to bed,' she said. 'We weren't expecting her, but it was typical of my niece. She would often arrive unannounced and at all times of the day or night.'

'So why did she come so late?'

'She was upset and didn't want to spend the night at home by herself. I made her a cup of tea while she told us what had caused the argument with Rebecca and Theo. She fully expected us to support her. But I told her that seeking to get her own back on Nathan Wolf was stupid and would cause enormous collateral damage, especially to her mother's chances of becoming Mayor of London. She threw a tantrum then and got really angry. She threatened to tell Rebecca that I had known about her affair with the MP.'

'So how did you react to that?' Anna asked her.

'I was furious. I couldn't believe she was behaving so badly, and so out of character. She was clearly obsessed with taking revenge against Wolf and nothing else mattered to her. I told her that she needed to calm down, but she became even more aggressive. She started screaming and said she finally realised that Wolf had treated her like a prostitute for the past year and she wasn't going to let him get away with it.

'She didn't understand why her mother and I weren't as keen as she was to see him brought down. Robert tried to persuade her that going to the papers wasn't the way to do it, but she got hysterical and swore at him. And when he went to put an arm around her she became even more distressed. She threw her cup on the floor and started yelling that if she couldn't make Wolf suffer then she didn't want to go on living.'

Freya suddenly choked on her words and had a coughing fit. Anna grabbed the glass she'd been drinking the vodka from and went to the sink to fill it with water. But by the time she put it on the table in front of her, Freya had stopped coughing.

'What happened next neither of us saw coming,' Freya went on. 'It was so quick and I—'

She stopped suddenly in response to the front door being slammed shut. It was loud enough to make Anna jump, and it made the partition walls around them shake.

Seconds later Robert Gregory came storming into the kitchen. When he saw his wife a shadow of disbelief flashed across his face.

'Oh, fuck, what have you told them?' he yelled.

'I'm so sorry,' Freya managed before bursting into tears.

Robert snapped his gaze towards Anna, his expression belligerent. 'I told her not to answer your questions until I got here. Can't you see she's drunk? She doesn't know what the hell she's saying.'

'I accept that she's had a drink, Mr Gregory,' Anna said calmly. 'But she's still sober. And so far she's explained how your niece came here on Tuesday night and started kicking off. Before you so rudely interrupted us she was about to reveal how and why Holly ended up dead.'

Robert looked from Anna to Freya and his face creased up, as though in reaction to a sharp, unbearable pain.

Then he closed his eyes, his shoulders dropped and he slumped against the doorframe.

'It was no one's fault,' he said, his voice suddenly low and brittle. 'You really have to believe that.'

CHAPTER FIFTY-FIVE

Sophie was staring at her phone, willing it to ring. It lay on the kitchen table in front of her, moisture from her own hand glistening on the screen.

Bruno had told her that he would call back within the hour to set up a meeting.

'I'll tell you then what I have planned for you and the girl,' he'd said.

As she waited, Sophie's heart hammered against her ribcage, and she felt a cold terror in her chest.

She did not want to imagine how far Bruno would go in his bid to exact revenge against her. But she knew he wouldn't pull any punches. He had waited a long time for her to be at his mercy, and he probably couldn't believe his luck that he'd been able to snatch Alice. She was now his leverage, his key to making Sophie do whatever he wanted her to do.

In hindsight it had been stupid to allow her to go out by herself. He must have been watching the flat, either alone or with an accomplice, waiting for the right moment to strike.

And suddenly there she was. All alone. A naïve, unsuspecting twelve-year-old.

Sophie wondered how Bruno had abducted her. Was it along the street or did he wait until he saw her walk into Gloria's flats? And was she dragged into a car or van, or did he somehow manage to entice her in even though she had been told many times never to go off with strangers?

In London child abductions in broad daylight had increased alarmingly in recent years. But even some of those that were witnessed were not reported by passers-by. The kidnappers were often mistaken for the parents, and sometimes people just turned a blind eye because for whatever reason they did not want to get involved.

Sophie desperately wanted to call the police, but she didn't dare. She was convinced that Bruno hadn't been bluffing when he'd warned her that if she did she would never see Alice again.

The man was a monster who was as dangerous now as he was ten years ago. And she had no doubt that he was just as slippery. He would have made sure of two things before coming anywhere near her flat – that he had a solid alibi for today proving that he was elsewhere, and that he could not be identified on any CCTV footage within miles of Shoreditch.

Sophie couldn't help conjuring up images in her mind of Alice and Bruno together. It was all too easy to believe that he had already harmed her. Perhaps she'd been beaten or sexually assaulted.

Or maybe he had even raped her!

She closed her eyes, squeezed out more tears, felt the adrenalin fizzing through her body.

The waiting was becoming too much to bear. She picked

up her phone and called Alice's number. But it didn't go through. Her phone was switched off again.

Oh, please God, don't let the bastard hurt her.

Another five minutes passed.

Then ten.

Twenty.

Thirty.

The phone finally rang, and anxiety trembled in Anna's throat when she answered it.

'Is that you, Bruno?'

'Are you still alone?'

'Yes, but let me talk to Alice. Please. I want to know that she's all right.'

'All in good time,' he said. 'I take it you're ready to meet.'

'I am. Where do you want me to go?'

'There's a taxi waiting for you downstairs. The driver has been told to take you to Shoreditch Park, the entrance where Bridport Place meets Grange Street. Remember what I said about the girl. If anyone follows you then you'll never see her again.'

CHAPTER FIFTY-SIX

Robert pushed himself away from the doorframe and entered the kitchen. He crossed to the table where he pulled out a chair and sat down next to his wife, who had managed to stop sobbing and was trying to compose herself.

He put an arm around her shoulders, leaned close, whispered in her ear. In response, she shook her head and said out loud, 'No, I won't let you take the blame. It's time now to tell the truth.'

Freya then turned to Anna. 'What happened to Holly was a terrible accident. After she told us she didn't want to go on living if she couldn't get her own back on Wolf, she became hysterical. She grabbed one of the carving knives from the block on the worktop, then held out her left arm and went to cut her wrist.'

As Freya spoke, she gestured towards the knife block on the worktop, and Anna saw that one of the knives was missing.

'But the only wound she suffered was to her throat,' Anna said.

Freya nodded. 'That was because I rushed forward and tried to take the knife away from her. But she wouldn't let go of it. She yelled for me to let her die and acted like she was possessed. We struggled and then she fell forward onto the floor just behind where I'm sitting and . . . and . . .'

Freya couldn't continue. Her chin dropped onto her chest and the tears came again.

'Holly fell on the knife,' Robert said matter-of-factly. 'Neither of us realised this until we saw the blood pooling on the floor. I turned her over and saw the knife was embedded in her throat. It was awful. Freya started to scream and I pulled the knife out and tried to stem the blood.

'I didn't know she was dead for about a minute. And that was when I looked up and saw that my wife was on the house phone. She said she was calling for an ambulance, so I rushed over and stopped her. I told her that Holly was gone and that there was nothing anyone could do for her. I also explained how bad it looked for us and that I didn't think anyone – including Rebecca and Theo – would believe our account of what had happened.

'So I convinced Freya that we had to cover it up. If we didn't there was a chance we could both be charged with murder and go to prison. It was my idea and I take full responsibility.'

Anna threw a glance at Walker and was glad to see that he was still recording the conversation on his phone. Then, to Robert, she said, 'What happened next?'

Before replying, he took a hanky from his pocket and gave it to his wife, who used it to soak up the tears on her face.

'I told Freya that we had to dispose of Holly's body and make sure that no one found out that she'd come here,' he said. 'It was me who came up with the plan because my wife was too upset to do anything. I suppose it's fair to say that the survival instinct kicked in. I had to do what I could to save us, no matter how extreme.'

'So tell me what you did exactly,' Anna said.

'I made Freya go upstairs to the bedroom while I took Holly's clothes off,' he said. 'It was a nasty business but it had to be done because I knew we'd have left traces of us all over them. I put the clothes into a bin sack along with her bag. I then wrapped the body in more bin sacks and carried it out to my car, the Toyota, and placed it in the boot. Once that was done I went back into the house and cleared the blood off the floor with paper towels. I gave it a proper clean the following day.'

'Did you go straight to Barnes Common?' Anna asked.

He nodded. 'I know the area well because I drive past it on the way to and from the office. I chose the spot opposite the old cemetery because I knew I'd be able to carry the body into the woods without being seen from the road.'

'What did you do with her stuff?'

'When I drove away from the common I stopped next to a number of street bins and dropped her clothes, bag and phone into them.'

'What about the knife?'

'That went in as well.'

'But you kept Holly's driving licence.'

'That's right. I came across it while I was checking her purse and it suddenly occurred to me that I might be able to use it to incriminate Wolf, who I knew would be suspected of killing her. After all, it was his fault that Holly came to our house. So I used a tissue to flick some of Holly's blood on it.

I decided I would visit him in his home or office and plant it there. As it turned out it was much easier than I expected it to be. I just slipped it into his jacket pocket as I walked out along the hallway. I know it was wrong, and I don't feel good about it, but I hated him for the way he had treated Holly. As far as I was concerned the bastard was responsible for everything.'

It was a lot for Anna to take in, and it certainly wasn't how she had expected the case to end. She was inclined to believe that what she'd been told was the truth – that Holly had died as the result of a tragic accident.

But the pair would need to be formally interviewed again under caution, and the house, along with Robert's car, would be subjected to a rigorous forensic examination.

The decision on what charges to bring would be up to DCS Nash and the CPS. The Gregorys had admitted perverting the course of justice and withholding and planting evidence. But there was every chance that if their story was believed they would not be charged with murder or manslaughter.

Anna told Walker to call the office and tell the team what had happened, and to arrange for uniforms and forensic officers to come straight to the house. Then she read the couple their rights and told them she was arresting them in connection with the death of their niece.

CHAPTER FIFTY-SEVEN

Sophie was familiar with Shoreditch Park. It was only a twenty-minute walk from the flat, and she had taken Alice there a number of times over the past three years.

The private hire cab was waiting on the paved area in front of the block. Panic filled her lungs as she got in. The driver glanced at her in the rear-view mirror and confirmed their destination as the junction of Bridport Place and Grange Street. He didn't speak again until they got there just under ten minutes later. She paid him the fare and climbed out.

She was left standing outside an entrance to the park she had never used before. Behind her, vehicles were parked along both sides of Bridport Place and ahead of her, beyond the railings, was a large expanse of grass dotted with planted trees and criss-crossed by pathways. In the distance a skyline of high-rise flats and office buildings.

There were few people about. Sophie saw a couple of dog walkers in the distance and a woman pushing a pram along one of the paths. It wasn't until she stepped through the open gate that she spotted Bruno. He was sitting on a bench to her left and looking right at her.

And he was alone. There was no sign of Alice.

He stood up as she approached him. He was wearing a black hooded sweatshirt over jeans, and his hair was shaved close to his scalp. He had lost weight since she saw him three years ago when he'd followed her to the bar in Puerto de Mazarron. But he was still an imposing figure, with broad shoulders and solid arms.

His lips curled into a thin smile when Sophie got up close.

'You need to show me what's in your bag and pockets,' he said. 'I want to make sure you're not carrying any kind of recording device.'

'Are you serious?'

'I'm cautious.'

He held out his hand for her bag. She gave it to him and watched him rifle through the contents. He made a point of switching off her phone before he got her to empty her pockets.

Finally he patted her down and his hands on her body made her blood freeze.

'Tell me where Alice is, Bruno,' she said. 'I need to know.'

He sat back down on the bench and invited her to sit next to him, but she remained standing.

'Why are you so worried about the girl anyway?' he said. 'It's not like she's your kid. She belonged to that tosser you were shacked up with while I was in prison, the one who thought he could scare me off when he saw me following him in Southampton.'

'I adopted Alice after you killed her father,' Sophie said, and it took a lot of will power not to lunge at the bastard and scratch his eyes out. 'She's got no one else, and I love her like she's my own.'

His gaze drilled into her, steady and unflinching, his eyes filled with malice. It made her wonder yet again how on earth she had ever fallen for him.

'Sit down, Sophie,' he said, his tone harsher. 'There are things I want you to know.'

'All I want to know is where Alice is,' she said.

He nodded. 'First you'll hear me out. I've waited ten fucking years to get a load off my chest.'

She sat down, but as far away from him on the bench as possible.

'That's better,' he said. 'Now we won't attract attention. We look like any other married couple enjoying a summer's day in the park.'

'Get to the point, Bruno,' she said.

He licked his lips. 'First I want to know if you remember what I told you when you came to see me in prison.'

'How could I forget? You said you were going to make me suffer for not providing you with an alibi.'

'That's correct. And I really meant it. It's why I haven't stopped looking for you. I swore to myself that one day I would pay you back.'

'Can't you just forget me and get on with your life? I'm sorry I did what I did, but at the time it felt like I never had a choice. I needed to get away from you because I was being bullied and suffocated. I saw an opportunity and took it. You got your revenge when you forced us to move from Spain and then killed James.'

'That's not enough, Sophie. It was because of you I spent seven years in a shithole Spanish jail.' He touched the scar below his left eye. 'Every time I look in a mirror I'm reminded of how bad it was.'

She wanted to tell him that it was no more than he'd deserved, but she held it in.

'It was also because of you that I never got to have any kids,' he said. 'If I'd known you were a sterile bitch back then I wouldn't have married you. But I did. And I looked after you while I tried to build a business for our future. But you showed your appreciation by betraying me. All you had to do was tell the police that I was with you that night. But instead you decided to stab me in the back. And there's no way I can ever forget or forgive it.'

'It's fair enough that you want to hurt me, Bruno. But you need to leave Alice out of it. She's only twelve, for Christ's sake. What happened between us has nothing to do with her.'

'Then you shouldn't have got her involved, should you?'

'What do you mean? I didn't . . .'

'You let her go wandering the streets by herself,' he said. 'And that was irresponsible. She didn't know what hit her when she strolled past our van and the door opened and I pulled her inside.'

Sophie felt a jolt, like a bullet hitting her chest.

'It happened in the blink of an eye,' he said. 'She didn't even have time to scream before I had her mouth taped up and her wrists tied, and she got even more scared when she saw my face. She's since let it be known that she recognised me from three years ago when I trailed you into your bar.'

'Have you hurt her?' Sophie asked.

'Not yet.'

Sophie felt completely helpless. She was in no position

to threaten him or call his bluff. He had her over the proverbial barrel.

'Aren't you curious to know how I tracked you down?' he said.

She couldn't speak so she nodded.

'Well, you can thank your old friend, Lisa,' he said. 'She met a colleague of mine at a funeral and your name came up. She claimed she hadn't been in touch with you but he didn't believe her. So he snatched her phone when she wasn't looking and lo and behold your number was on it. So he used our cop contacts to locate the signal. Then he came to Shoreditch and it didn't take him long to find and follow you.'

'I had the feeling that someone was watching me,' Sophie said. 'But I thought it was my imagination.'

'Well, he did a good job keeping tabs. I was in Spain so I told him to watch you until I got back. I didn't want to lose you again. And this morning is when I arrived. He drove me here and we parked in front of your flats. When the girl walked out he told me he'd seen her with you. I didn't recognise her at first because her hair's shorter and a different colour to what it was three years ago.'

Sophie chose not to tell him that Lisa had already been in touch with her. She didn't think it would serve any useful purpose.

'But you've done well to have stayed under the radar for so long,' he carried on. 'I had no fucking idea that you were living in London. Tracking you down in Southampton was much easier.'

'How did you do it?' she asked him.

He shrugged. 'After I confronted you in Puerto de Mazarron that day my intention was to make your life hell over the following weeks. I'd arranged for a bunch of guys to kidnap your bloke and turn him into a cripple. And then you were going to be gang-raped. But you vanished before I got it organised. Your landlord wasn't happy. I left him my number and told him I would make it worth his while if he found out where you'd gone. A few weeks later he rang to let me know that James Miller had asked him to post a parcel with some belongings in it to a courier depot in Southampton.

'I found out what time it was due to arrive, flew over, and waited for him to turn up. And sure enough he did. Then he saw me in the park and threatened me. He had balls, I'll give him that. But when he got physical I had no choice but to shaft him. It pissed me off because I'd wanted him to lead me to you. And if you've wondered what happened to the parcel, I dumped it.'

Sophie was battling a whirlwind of emotions. Anger, fear, shock, curiosity. She hated the fact that he was clearly enjoying himself, getting off on her despair, playing a vile game for his own satisfaction.

'You should know that before I arrived at your place today my intention was to abduct you and then make you wish you had never been born,' he said. 'But catching hold of Alice allows me to take your punishment to a new level and to make sure your suffering is not short-lived.'

'What's that supposed to mean?'

'It means that Alice will be my guest for a couple of days and I'm going to have some fun with her. I even plan to share her with a couple of the guys who work for me and are into young flesh.'

As Sophie listened to him speak, a cold line of sweat formed on her brow and her spine grew rigid.

'I'll send you photos and maybe even a video,' he said. 'And for you they won't make pleasant viewing, but that's the whole point. Then after I've had my fun it'll be your turn. I'll free Alice and you'll take her place. How does that sound?'

Sophie shook her head. 'You can't do it, Bruno. It's sick.'

'But I can and I will.'

'Then I'll go to the police. You'll be arrested.'

He grinned. 'I don't think you'll dare risk it. If I hear the filth are looking for me she'll die a horrible death. But I'll still come after you. So think carefully before you do something you'll regret. You can't stop the girl from losing her virginity and suffering a few bruises. But you can save her life.'

Sophie lost it then and hurled herself at him. She managed to grab his shirt front and pull on it. But he jerked his body back before she could get to his face.

And then he reacted with ferocity, jumping to his feet and seizing her shoulders with both hands.

'Listen to me, you slag,' he seethed. 'You need to get it into your head that this is payback for what you did to me. It's been a long time coming and I'm gonna make the most of it. There's no way out until I'm done with you.'

He let her go then and stepped back, his face a mask of rage and hatred.

'If you try to follow me I'll throttle you and then I'll go and take it out on Alice,' he said. 'So just go home and wait for me to get in touch.'

Bruno pulled up the hood of his sweatshirt, shoved his hands into his pockets and walked briskly towards the gate.

Sophie watched him pass through it before she gave in to the urge to go after him. She would plead with him to change his mind, beg him to forgive her.

'Bruno, stop,' she cried out. 'Please.'

He stopped and turned, waited for her to catch up. But when she reached him he didn't give her a chance to say anything else. He rammed his fist into her stomach and as she doubled over, he brought it down hard on the back of her head.

Sophie's legs gave way beneath her and she hit the pavement with a heavy, painful thud. She blacked out briefly, and when her senses returned Bruno was gone.

CHAPTER FIFTY-EIGHT

News of Robert and Freya Gregory's confessions was greeted with surprise and a measure of relief by Anna's superiors.

She was still at the house in Fulham when she took calls from DCS Nash and the Commissioner himself. She told them what the couple had said and made it clear they needed to be formally interviewed back at headquarters before charges could be brought.

After the pair were whisked away in separate police cars, a forensics team arrived at the house. Anna told them to start with the kitchen, where Holly allegedly died, and the boot of Robert's Toyota, where he said he put the body.

Before leaving the house, which was now a crime scene, she got the SOCOs to spray the kitchen floor with Luminol. Within minutes the SOCOs got a result. The Luminol started emitting a blue glow when it highlighted latent bloodstains at the spot where Freya said Holly fell on the knife.

*

Anna had to settle for another sandwich lunch, which she ate while addressing the team back at headquarters.

At first there was widespread disbelief that Holly Blake's death had been accidental. But after Anna ran through what Robert and Freya said, most of them came to accept it as a plausible account of what had happened. After all, the files were full of cases where people had been accidentally stabbed to death during violent altercations.

Anna dished out various tasks. She wanted another trawl of the CCTV footage from cameras around Barnes Common, with the aim of spotting Robert's Toyota in the early hours of Wednesday morning. She also wanted every aspect of their lives looked into, including their financial position, employment situation, social media activity and circle of friends.

At three p.m. Anna started to formally interview Robert Gregory, who had been assigned a duty solicitor. His wife remained in a holding cell to allow time for the vodka she'd drunk to pass through her system.

Anna half expected Robert to retract some or all of what he'd told them back at the house. But instead he repeated it almost word for word. At the end of the interview she told him that he would be held in custody and charges would follow.

Anna then took part in a conference call with DCS Nash and the Commissioner. She gave them a full briefing and it was agreed that Nash would consult the CPS about what charges to bring against the couple.

DCI Walker was despatched to the Royal London Hospital to inform Holly's ex-boyfriend that he was no longer a suspect in her murder. While he did that, Anna broke the news to Nathan Wolf. The MP's relief was palpable, and he was moved to tears.

'So who did kill her?' he demanded to know.

'I can't reveal that information at this stage,' Anna said. 'But you and everyone else will know in due course. I'd like to thank you for cooperating with us, Mr Wolf, and I apologise for the ordeal we had to put you through.'

'You've not heard the last of it, Detective Tate,' he said. 'What has happened to me is an absolute disgrace. I intend to sue the Met for the part it's played in destroying my life and my reputation.'

Anna simply responded by telling him he was free to go and then left it to DC Sweeny to show him out of the building and arrange transport for him. She then faced the grim task of going to Pimlico to make Holly's parents aware of what had happened before the news broke.

Rebecca was understandably devastated to be told that her sister and brother-in-law had confessed to accidentally killing her daughter. She kept shaking her head and saying that it wasn't possible.

'If it was an accident then why didn't she tell us?' she said. 'It doesn't make any sense.'

She collapsed on the sofa and Theo did his best to console her, even though he was in tears himself. Anna felt like crying along with them so she thought it best to leave them in the capable hands of the Family Liaison Officer, who was still on the scene.

An hour later Anna was summoned to Scotland Yard to take part in a press conference at which DCS Nash announced that two as yet unnamed people were being questioned about Holly's murder. He also said that Nathan Wolf had been cleared of any involvement in the killing.

Anna left the Yard straight after, believing that the day wasn't going to throw up any more surprises.

But it did.

On the way back to Wandsworth she answered a call from DC Sweeny, who said, 'Something has happened, guv, to suggest that Freya and Robert Gregory might not have been totally honest with us.'

CHAPTER FIFTY-NINE

Sophie had been home for a couple of hours, and yet the pain was still gnawing at her head and stomach.

Bruno's fist had struck her with the force of a pile driver and she was lucky that he hadn't broken any ribs. It appeared that no one witnessed the attack or if they did they chose not to come to her aid as she struggled to get to her feet. The walk back to the flat had been a real ordeal and she attracted lots of strange looks from other pedestrians who probably thought she was drunk or high on drugs.

After arriving home she cancelled the taxi to the airport and the trip to Spain. And then she sobbed her heart out because she knew that she and Alice probably wouldn't be going anywhere together again.

Now she was sitting on the sofa with a cigarette in one hand and her phone in the other. The television was on, but only because she couldn't stand the heavy silence that surrounded her.

She had stopped crying, but inside her head she was screaming for an end to the agony and uncertainty. At the same time it was proving impossible to rein in her imagination. Shocking images of Alice being abused flashed through her mind. She was lying on a bed and Bruno was on top of her. She was on the floor, handcuffed to a radiator, her face bruised and bloodied. She was tied to a chair while pleading with Sophie to come and save her.

Sophie drew deeply on her cigarette and tried to decide what to do. One voice was telling her to call the police and tell them everything. Let them go after Bruno and bring Alice back safely. But another voice was telling her that such a course of action would only end in disaster.

Bruno would kill Alice before or after the police turned up at his door. And he'd deny even knowing who she was. He would have covered his tracks, made sure it was just Sophie's word against his, and that there were people who'd claim he was somewhere else when she said she was with him in the park.

But she just could not see herself doing nothing while knowing that Alice was at the mercy of a cold-blooded monster. And there was no guarantee that he would keep his word and let her go. In fact the odds surely had to be against it. Wouldn't it be safer for him if he killed them both? That way he'd get his sought-after revenge on Sophie, and Alice wouldn't be around afterwards to pose a threat.

As if Sophie's thoughts were not chaotic enough, another face was suddenly hurled into the mix.

Detective Anna Tate.

There she was, just six feet or so in front of Sophie,

staring out of the TV screen. It was a press conference that had apparently been recorded a short time ago. Tate was sitting behind a table with two other police officers.

Sophie leaned forward and tuned in to what was being said. It was the man to her right who was speaking. On the card in front of him were the words *Detective Chief Supt Nash*.

'And so I can confirm that the two individuals who were arrested in connection with Holly Blake's murder have now been released. They are Mr Ross Moore and Mr Nathan Wolf. Two other people are about to be charged with the murder.'

As Sophie listened to the words, her eyes remained firmly fixed on Detective Tate. She appeared calm, unruffled, and Sophie suddenly wondered what the woman's reaction would be if she discovered what had happened to her daughter.

This thought caused Sophie's heart to trip and the air to lock in her chest.

Was that it? she asked herself. Was Alice's real mother the solution to the terrible dilemma she faced? Would the detective be able to help her get Alice back?

Desperation drove Sophie to conclude that Tate was indeed her only hope. She stubbed out her cigarette in the ashtray on the table and opened up the emails on her phone. She found the one from the head of Alice's school who had told her that Tate's private detective had been in touch with her. Sophie scrolled down to his name at the bottom of the message. Jack Keen. Beneath it was his mobile number.

She wasted no time ringing it, and when he answered, she said 'My name is Sophie, Mr Keen. The head of Oakfield

School gave me your number after you contacted her about the Chloe Tate age progression image. Well, I'm the person who's been taking care of Chloe for the past three years since her father was killed. Before that I was with them in Spain. I now need you to get Detective Tate to call me right away on this number. I need to speak to her urgently because Chloe is in trouble.'

CHAPTER SIXTY

Doubt was cast on Robert and Freya's story by something overheard by Custody Officer Noel Jackson. He was waiting to speak to Anna when she arrived back in the office.

'It happened when we were taking the husband up to see his lawyer and his wife was on her way to see the medic because she'd complained of feeling sick,' Jackson said. 'By chance they passed each other in the corridor. I was accompanying Mrs Gregory and her husband took the opportunity to lean towards her and mouth the words "Stick to the story." I don't think he realised I saw him.'

'Are you sure that's what he said?' Anna asked.

'I'm ninety per cent sure, ma'am, because the movement of his mouth was exaggerated and that kind of thing happens all the time between perps.'

There were two ways to look at it, Anna decided. Either Officer Jackson was mistaken because he wasn't a qualified lip-reader; or Robert Gregory was desperately concerned that his wife would change her story under pressure during the formal interview.

The couple had claimed that Holly's death was an accident. And they had managed to convince Anna that they were telling the truth. But now she had to consider the possibility that they had lied.

'Where is Freya now?' Anna asked.

'Back in the cell,' DC Sweeny said. 'The doc gave her something for her stomach and he reckons she's ready to be interviewed.'

'The question is, how do we approach it?' Walker said. 'She's bound to repeat what she said back at the house. And if the story is made up then they'll both be sticking to the script.'

Anna thought about it and said, 'We need to get to the bottom of this before we charge them.'

Walker nodded. 'So how do we go about it?'

Anna grinned. 'We do exactly what we did when we got her to open up. We exploit her fragile state of mind and tell her a whopping great fib.'

Minutes later Anna and Walker were facing Freya and the duty solicitor across the table in the interview room.

Freya looked a mess and was clearly struggling to maintain her composure. Her face was swollen and the shadows beneath her eyes had become darker. Anna could tell that she was an emotional wreck, unable to control whatever was eating away at her conscience. Anna knew from experience that it would make the woman's defences easier to breach. For that reason she wasted no time with a warm-up act.

'I want to begin by informing you that since we last spoke there has been a significant and surprising development, Mrs Gregory,' she said. 'You see, your husband was overheard in the corridor a little earlier telling you to stick to the story. I'm sure you can remember it clearly. Well, because of that we decided to interview him again and half an hour ago he finally admitted mouthing those words and went on to give a different account of what happened to your niece in your home on Tuesday night.'

The shock was evident in her expression. Her jaw dropped and she shook her head.

'That can't be right,' she said. 'You're lying.'

'I'm afraid not, Mrs Gregory. What's more, in your husband's latest version of events he places the blame for Holly's death squarely on your shoulders.'

Once again Anna was stepping over the ethical boundary in the full knowledge that it might backfire on her. But she felt it was a risk worth taking if, as she now suspected, the couple hadn't told the truth.

'There's really no point holding back now,' she said. 'We know that you and your husband concocted a story that you believed we would fall for. And we probably would have if Robert hadn't made a stupid mistake by not trusting you to say what had been agreed.'

Freya broke down for the second time that day and when she eventually stopped crying, she said, 'It's true what Robert told you. It wasn't an accident. I stabbed Holly. But she might have survived if Robert had let me call an ambulance.'

Much of the story the couple had told earlier remained the same. Holly had turned up at their house unexpectedly and they'd got into an argument during which their niece grabbed a kitchen knife.

'It's true she threatened to kill herself,' Freya said. 'But I didn't struggle with her and she didn't fall on the knife.'

'So what happened?' Anna pressed.

Freya squeezed her eyes shut, but it failed to stem the tears.

'She was waving the knife in front of her face and telling me how much she wanted to die and how much she hated her mother and how she'd never forgiven her for what happened to her father. And she didn't give a shit if what she was going to do to Nathan Wolf would destroy her mother's chance to become Mayor.

'She then held the knife against her own throat and I instinctively grabbed it from her. In response she spat in my face and told me that she hated me as well for always siding with Rebecca. And she accused me of being jealous of my sister because I had no children of my own and that was why I'd acted like she was my daughter. She said it was pathetic.

'Then she thrust her face forward and dared me to kill her, to end her suffering, she said. And before I knew it, I was lashing out with the knife. It was like I was possessed. I stabbed her in the throat and she fell to the floor. I immediately regretted it and tried to call for an ambulance when I saw that she was still breathing. But Robert stopped me. He said I wasn't thinking straight and that if Holly lived she would tell the police that I had tried to murder her and I'd spend years in prison.

'So I didn't try to save her and to my shame we both sat there in the kitchen and watched her die.'

'And how long did it take?' Anna said.

'I'm not sure, but I think it was about forty-five minutes.'

CHAPTER SIXTY-ONE

After Freya's revised confession, Anna re-interviewed her husband and it didn't take long for him to come clean as well.

It was an outcome that shocked every member of the team. But it was also a relief because if it hadn't been for Officer Jackson they might not have uncovered the truth.

Freya was charged with murdering her niece and Robert with being an accessory. They were also charged with perverting the course of justice and withholding evidence.

By the end of the process, Anna was exhausted. She decided to hold one final meeting with the team and assign a list of jobs to the night shift. Then she planned to go home and have a celebratory meal and drink with Tom.

But everything changed when she took a call from Jack Keen. The excitement in his voice was evident as soon as he began to speak. He told her about his conversation with the woman named Sophie.

'She says she lives in Shoreditch and that the girl she calls her daughter is twelve and named Alice. She's the same girl who was spotted outside the school in Bethnal Green and the hair salon in Shoreditch High Street.

'But the woman also reckons that Alice is really Chloe and they've been together for ten years. She's been the child's sole carer since her father was murdered in Southampton three years ago. She refused to give me her address or second name.'

'I don't understand,' Anna said. 'If she's genuine, and not a prankster, why would she reveal all this?'

'Because she says the child is in trouble and she needs your help. She's given me her number and you're to ring her right away.'

'What does your gut tell you, Jack?'

'That you should call. I think this could be the woman we've been looking for.'

Anna felt uncertainty beat in her heart as she went into her office and closed the door behind her. She took a slow breath to try to control her emotions before making the call.

'Is that Sophie?' she asked when a woman answered.

'It is. I take it you are Detective Tate.'

'I am. Jack Keen has told me that you have information about my daughter. Is that true?'

'Yes.'

'You told Jack that she's in trouble. What do you mean by that?'

'I'll tell you when you come to my flat, Miss Tate. But please understand that I wouldn't be asking for your help if I wasn't desperate. Alice, or Chloe, needs you for reasons I'll explain when you get here. I can't involve the police in an official capacity so you cannot tell anyone about this.'

'How do I know this isn't some vile prank?' Anna asked.

'You won't know for sure until we talk face to face,' Sophie said. 'But I beg you to take me seriously because if you don't you'll regret it for the rest of your life.'

Anna filled her lungs and held her breath as Sophie gave her the address of her flat in Shoreditch.

'Come now,' Sophie said. 'And please come alone.'

Anna picked up her bag, and on her way out of the office she told Walker to take charge of the briefing.

'There's something I have to do,' she said.

'Is everything all right, guv?' he asked, a look of concern on his face.

She shrugged. 'I'm not sure yet, Max. But if I need help I'll call you.'

It took Anna forty minutes to get to Sophie's flat. It would have taken longer if she hadn't used the siren and blue light to whizz around traffic hold-ups along the way.

Before getting out of the car she rang Tom to say she'd be home later than expected. As usual he took it in his stride and said he'd delay making dinner.

Sophie buzzed her into the small, insalubrious block after she pressed the flat number on the security buzzer at the entrance. Emotions were running high in her head as she mounted the stairs to the first floor. She wanted to believe that she'd done the right thing in coming here and that it meant she was closer to finding her daughter. But she was bracing herself for disappointment.

The first thing she was going to demand was proof that this person calling herself Sophie had been acting as Chloe's stand-in mother for all these years. If that wasn't forthcoming then she saw no point in wasting any more time.

Anna reached the first floor and Sophie's flat was right in front of her. The door was open and the woman was standing just inside with one hand behind her back. She was middle-aged, with long black hair and an attractive face.

Anna stopped abruptly and for several seconds the two stared at each other.

Was it really true? Anna wondered. Was this the person who had shared the house in Southampton with Matthew three years ago and then fled the city with Chloe after he was murdered in the park?

'Is my daughter here?'

'No she isn't, but this is her home.'

Anna stepped forward. 'Before we talk you need to convince me that this is not a hoax or even a genuine mistake. I have to be sure that the girl you call Alice is really Chloe.'

'I expected you to ask that,' Sophie said.

She brought out the hand she'd been holding behind her back. In it was a photograph which she held up for Anna to see.

Anna took one look and it was like being hit with icy water. The picture showed Anna holding baby Chloe in their back garden on her first birthday. It was one she hadn't seen in years because Matthew had taken it on his phone and had never got around to printing it.

'I've got more photos to show you,' Sophie said. 'Lots of them are of me and your ex-husband, who told me his name was James Miller. I met him ten years ago when he came to Spain, where I was living and working. He said he went there with his daughter to start a new life after his wife died. I had no reason not to believe him and I didn't know that he'd lied to me until I read your story in the *Evening Standard*.'

Anna continued to stare at the photo, her throat too tight to speak.

'Come in,' Sophie said. 'I want to get this part over as quickly as possible.'

Sophie led Anna into a small kitchen and pointed to the table.

'Sit down, Detective Tate,' she said. 'In a moment I'll tell you why I need your help. But first you need to satisfy yourself that my Alice is your Chloe.'

Sophie disappeared into another room, leaving Anna struggling to get her mind around what was happening. When she reappeared she was holding a photograph album. She placed it on the table.

'Start with that,' she said. 'While you look through it I'll make you a cup of tea. Or would you prefer something stronger?'

As Anna looked up, there was a tightness in her chest and her hands were shaking. She wasn't sure what to make of the woman, or whether to believe that she had only just discovered that Chloe's mother was alive. Was that actually conceivable? Did Matthew really manage to convince her that he was a widower with a two-year-old daughter?

'So what's it to be?' Sophie said. 'Tea, coffee or wine?'

Anna shook her head. 'Nothing for me.'

She sat at the table and turned her attention to the album. And as soon as she opened it she knew that the ten-year search for her daughter was over.

CHAPTER SIXTY-TWO

For Anna each turn of the page was a painful reminder of how much she had missed.

The first few photographs featured Chloe before her father abducted her. Anna remembered taking one of them herself. It showed Matthew sitting in an armchair with his sleeping daughter on his lap. But after that the snapshots were of their new life in a place called Puerto de Mazarron in Southern Spain. Beneath most of the photos was a date and many of them also had a caption.

Alice's first paddle in the Med.

Day at the beach.

Christmas morning 2009.

Her first day at school.

Mixed emotions gripped her as she ploughed through the album with tears in her eyes.

It was a relief to see that Matthew had taken good care of their daughter. From the photographic evidence it seemed that Chloe had enjoyed growing up in Spain. While there she'd grown into a beautiful little girl with a dazzling smile.

But it was impossible for Anna not to feel jealous and resentful. It should have been her with Chloe when she first paddled in the sea, and on the day she started school. Not some stranger that her good-for-nothing father had shacked up with.

'For your information we never got married,' Sophie said as she sat down opposite Anna at the table. 'That's why I kept my name. It's Cameron, by the way. Sophie Cameron. And I don't have an important job like you. I'm a cleaner and for Alice and me these past few years have been a struggle. But we've got by.'

Anna lifted her eyes from the album and looked at her.

'So you were with him from 2009 to 2016,' Anna said.

Sophie nodded. 'I was. And in all that time it never occurred to me that you might be alive. That's why reading your story in the paper came as such a shock. I'd never heard of you before then, and I knew nothing about the abduction, probably because it didn't attract much coverage in Spain. And for what it's worth I'm really sorry. If I had known I would never have got involved with him. What he did to you was unforgivable, and even now I can't believe that he made his own daughter believe that her mother was dead. But I have to say that he treated me well and I loved him. For seven years we were happy together. After he died I took responsibility for Alice and brought her here to live.'

'So why didn't you call the *Evening Standard* as soon as you saw the story? The first part was published five days ago.'

'I wasn't sure what to do, or whether to do anything at all,' she said. 'I couldn't – can't – bear the thought of losing Alice. She's all I have. My plan was to take her away on a holiday and think it through. I appreciate that you're her real mother, but I've been with her virtually every day for the past ten years.'

Anna felt her blood heat up, and she wasn't sure if it was because she suddenly hated the woman or pitied her.

'So now tell me why you did decide to get in contact with me,' Anna said. 'What kind of trouble is Chloe in?'

Sophie's eyes grew intent under dark brows as she answered the question.

'She's been kidnapped, Detective Tate. And the man who has her is threatening to kill her if I involve the police. Which is why I called you.'

CHAPTER SIXTY-THREE

Sophie watched as the detective's features hardened with shock. It was clear that she hadn't expected to be told something so serious.

'Who has her?' Anna said. 'And where is she?'

Sophie shook her head. 'I don't know where she is, and that's why I need your help to find her. But I do know who took her. His name is Bruno Perez and he's my estranged husband. It was because of him that we had to leave Spain three years ago, and he's the man who murdered Alice's father.'

Sophie told her story. She began with her marriage to Bruno and how it quickly became an abusive relationship. She explained how she was instrumental in him being sent to prison and how soon afterwards James Miller walked into the restaurant where she worked, with his little girl.

'We started going out and within months we were living together,' Sophie said. 'But he wasn't the only one who harboured a secret from the start. I didn't tell him about Bruno, or that I was married. I thought it would scare him away. Despite the deceptions on both our parts we were happy for seven years and I came to love Alice as though she were my own daughter.

'James invested in a bar and it did well. But when Bruno was released from prison he somehow found out where I was. He turned up one day three years ago and reminded me that he was going to make me suffer for what I'd done to him. That was when I confessed everything to James, but he continued to keep his secret from me.

'That same night we decided the safest option was to leave Spain and return to the UK, and that's what we did. James found a rented house in Southampton, where he used to go to university.'

Sophie then gave a detailed account of what took place there, how Bruno tracked them down and how he stabbed James to death in the park.

'I didn't go to the police because I knew they would never be able to prove it was him,' Sophie said. 'Plus, I didn't want Alice taken away from me. So we fled the city and came here. And life was good until a few days ago when I read your story and then received a call from Alice's headmistress, who'd been contacted by your detective.'

Sophie then told Anna how at the same time Bruno found out that she was living in Shoreditch.

'Michael Taylor works for Bruno and he's the one who stole Lisa's phone and used it to find my number,' she said. 'He then used it to track the location of my mobile.'

She went on to describe what had happened this morning. How she discovered that Alice hadn't turned up at her friend's house, and then the call from Bruno to say he'd abducted her. When she relayed the conversation she'd had with him in the park, Anna bit into her top lip and tears swelled in her eyes.

'I've tried ringing Alice's mobile but it's switched off,' Sophie said. 'So please tell me what we can do to find her before he does bad things to her.'

For half a minute the silence stretched between them. Sophie knew that whatever happened next there was no going back to her cosy life with Alice. But she didn't want to dwell on that yet. What mattered now was getting Alice back.

Anna stood up suddenly and took her phone out of her pocket.

'Do you have Bruno's address?' she said.

'No, I don't. But he probably lives south of the river. That's where his family own some wholesale businesses, which are fronts for all sorts of crooked activities that I didn't know about until after we were married.'

'What about his phone number?'

Sophie shook her head.

'This bloke Michael Taylor. Do you think he was there when Alice was snatched?'

'According to Bruno he was.'

'Then there's a chance he's still with him. Tell me what you know about him.'

'Nothing at all really. I haven't seen him for years.'

'What about your friend Lisa? Would she have his number? Or if not, maybe she knows someone who does.'

'I could call.'

Anna nodded. 'Do it now. I know you're worried that Bruno will find out that you've involved the police but my guess is he's bullshitting. And we can't afford to hang around.'

'But what if you're wrong?' Sophie said. 'He won't hesitate to kill her. I know him.'

'It's a chance we have to take. He's made it clear that he wants to hurt her to punish you. So God only knows what he's already done. We need to move now and we need to move fast.'

CHAPTER SIXTY-FOUR

Anna began with a call to Walker to enlist his help. He was still at MIT headquarters and so had immediate access to all the Met's systems and databases. She quickly put him in the picture and he was stunned. He started to ask her questions but she told him there was no time to answer them.

'Just get the team working on it,' she said. 'And alert DCS Nash. The bloke who has Chloe sounds like a right nut job. We have to assume that he's prepared to carry out his threat. His name is Bruno Perez and it's believed he lives somewhere in South London. Run a PNC check. He's served seven years in a Spanish prison and was released three years ago. So I'm willing to bet he has a record here. I've never heard of him or his family but they're apparently involved in some wholesale rackets so check with the organised crime unit. I want to know his current address, phone number and whereabouts. Plus the names of his closest associates, especially a man named Michael Taylor who works for him.

'I also want an armed response unit put on standby. And get someone to trawl CCTV in and around Bridport Place, which runs alongside Shoreditch Park. We're looking for a man in a black hooded sweatshirt who was there just before lunchtime today.'

Anna hung up and looked across the kitchen to Sophie, who was still on the phone asking her friend Lisa if she could get a number for Michael Taylor. As she watched her, questions spun around inside Anna's head. She wanted to know all about Chloe. What were her likes and dislikes? Had she suffered any illnesses? Did she ever ask about her real mother? Was she told that her father was murdered? Was the age progression image a true likeness of what she looked like now?

'Lisa doesn't know Taylor's phone number or where he lives,' Sophie said, coming off her mobile. 'But she says she'll make some calls.'

'Can she be trusted?'

Sophie nodded. 'She's the only person I do trust.'

Anna tried to focus on what else needed to be done. But it was difficult. She had to force herself to ignore the lead weight in her chest, and give up trying to process everything she'd been told. There was just so much, and it had shaken her to the core. The pictures, revelations, the fact that the woman who stood before her had raised Chloe from the age of two. It was overwhelming, surreal.

'I can tell that your mind has gone into overdrive,' Sophie said. 'I realise this must be a terrible shock for you.'

Anna tried to smile, but managed only a twitch.

'I'd convinced myself that one day I would find Chloe and that ten years of endless days and sleepless nights would come to an end,' she said. 'But I imagined that it would be very different to this.'

Sophie moved to the table and sat down. It looked to Anna as though she was at breaking point. Her breath was coming in short, shallow gasps and she was visibly shaking. Anna fought the impulse to feel sympathy for her.

'Are you being honest with me when you say that you didn't know that Matthew had abducted Chloe and that I was alive?' she asked.

'I swear it's true,' Sophie answered. 'He was convincing and at first I felt sorry for him. Perhaps later I should have guessed that something wasn't right because he never wanted to talk about you, and he had so few photos of his life before moving to Spain. I took him at his word and as it turns out that was a big mistake. But all I ever seem to do is make mistakes. I should never have married Bruno and I shouldn't have allowed Alice to go out by herself this morning.'

'Will you please start calling her Chloe?' Anna said, her voice sharp. 'That's her real name.'

Sophie nodded. 'I know. It won't be easy, though.'

'I don't care. It hurts every time you say it and makes me want to wring your neck.'

Sophie inhaled sharply. 'Look, we need to put the issues between us to one side for now. I can understand how you feel towards me, but saving the child we both love is all that counts.'

It struck Anna then just how much the other woman cared about Chloe. She was sure it wasn't an act, and that Sophie hadn't been lying to her. But that did not make it any easier to accept.

'I'm not able to have children and I desperately wanted to,'

Sophie said. 'So when your daughter came into my life she made a big impact. I felt complete, and I want you to know that I devoted myself to her. I've done my best to nurture and protect her.'

'Does she call you Mum?' The question came out before Anna could stop it.

Sophie nodded. 'She does. But I didn't tell her to and neither did her father. She fell into the habit.'

Anna swallowed. The more she heard the harder it was to take in. She felt desperation crashing over her like waves.

'What's she like?' she asked.

Sophie mustered a smile. 'She's a joy to be with. She's kind and considerate. She's also highly intelligent and she's got a mind of her own.'

Anna's heart flipped and she felt tears threaten.

'How do you think she'll react when she knows the truth?' she asked.

Sophie blew out a breath and shook her head.

'It will knock her for six. She'll need to be told the whole story and that will be a lot for a twelve-year-old to cope with.'

Anna was about to ask another question when Sophie's phone, which was lying on the table between them, pinged with an incoming message.

'It could be from your friend Lisa,' Anna said.

But from the look on Sophie's face when she opened it up, it clearly wasn't. Her eyes bulged and her mouth hung open.

'Oh fuck,' she said.

Anna snatched the phone from her. On the screen was a photo of a young girl with short blonde hair. She was sitting on a wooden floor with her back to a wall and her knees pulled up to her chest. And she looked terrified.

'It's Alice,' Sophie gasped.

Anna didn't need to be told that. She recognised the face from the pictures in the album and the age recognition image.

Below the photo was a message that read, '*Thought you'd like to know the fun is about to begin.*'

CHAPTER SIXTY-FIVE

The photo and message sent to Sophie had come from Chloe's phone. But when Anna tried calling the number it wouldn't connect.

She shook her head at Sophie as a twist of panic wrenched through her gut.

'It's turned off again,' she said.

Sophie covered her mouth with her hands, which muted the anguished cry that rose up from her throat.

Anna gripped her fear and reached for her own phone. She called Walker and told him about the photo and message.

'Please tell me you've got something, Max,' she said.

'I was just about to ring you,' he replied. 'Bruno Perez does indeed have a criminal record. He did a stint inside for GBH when he was in his teens. Then he got fines and community service orders for a range of offences before he buggered off to Spain, where he was banged up for a seven stretch.

'Since then he's kept a clean slate. But the organised crime team know the family. They're minor league and stick to one part of South London where they run an import-export business and own a wholesale firm and a couple of warehouses, one of which has been converted into flats. But behind the scenes they peddle drugs and stolen property.'

'So have you got an address for the guy?'

'We have. He's got a house in Peckham. Most of his family and associates live within a four-mile radius, including one Michael Taylor, who's got form for drug possession and theft. We don't have mobile numbers for them, which probably means they use burner phones. But I've got photos of Perez and Taylor and I'll send them to you. And for your information Taylor owns a transit van and it was picked up on a plate recognition camera in Shoreditch today.'

'Then there's a good chance that was the vehicle used in the abduction. Have you talked to Nash?'

'I have. He's still at the Yard and is keen for you to call him.'

'OK. Meanwhile I want you to mobilise as many units as possible and go in hard on the homes of Bruno Perez, Michael Taylor and everyone else whose names have come up,' she said. 'And send teams to their wholesale premises and warehouses. But move fast so Perez doesn't get wind of what's going down.'

Anna then sent the picture of Chloe on the floor to Walker with instructions to circulate it to all units. In response she received two photos from him of Bruno and Taylor.

Bruno looked a rough diamond with short, dark hair and slits for eyes. Taylor had softer features, glasses and a double chin.

She showed them to Sophie, who said, 'Bruno hasn't changed much. He's thinner now and his hair is cropped.

Taylor looks about the same as I remember him all those years ago.'

Sophie had recovered some of her composure but she was still shaking all over.

'I'm not convinced this is a good idea,' she said. 'What happens if she's not at any of those addresses? Bruno could be holding her in a place that nobody knows about. And once he's tipped off he's sure to kill her.'

'I'm aware of the risks but our options are limited,' Anna said. 'Besides, there's a good chance he believes he's scared you into not going to the police, so his guard is likely to be down.'

'So what do we do? We can't just sit here.'

'I don't intend to. I'm going back to MIT headquarters in Wandsworth and I'd like you to come with me. From there we'll be across everything that happens and we'll be close to where all the raids are taking place.'

They travelled to Wandsworth in Anna's car and on the way she fired off another text to Tom. She gave him a brief explanation of what was going on and warned him she wouldn't be coming home this evening.

She then phoned DCS Nash, who was still at New Scotland Yard. He had spent the last couple of hours dealing with the fallout from the Holly Blake case. But he told her that he was now fully focused on the hunt for Chloe and would soon be joining her at HQ.

'I've briefed the Commissioner and he's happy for us to deploy as many people and resources as necessary,' he said. 'Meanwhile, try to stay strong, Anna. I can only imagine what you're going through right now. This development is shocking beyond belief but rest assured that the whole of the Met is involved in this operation.'

A knot of dread was growing in Anna's stomach and she was gripping the wheel so hard her knuckles hurt. The photo of her terrified daughter on the floor kept leaping into her mind along with a rush of disturbing questions.

What was the bastard doing to Chloe?

Had he already caused her physical harm?

Would he really kill her if he discovered that Sophie had triggered a huge manhunt?

During the rest of the journey Anna pumped Sophie for more information about Bruno. And what she was told sent the blood rushing to her head. He was clearly a man on a mission to cause Sophie as much pain as possible. The guy bore a grudge that had festered for so long it had turned him into a killer.

Anna had come across other such men – and women – during her career on the force. And they all had one thing in common – they would rather die than fail to achieve their objective.

It should have been quiet in the office as the team started to wind down the Holly Blake investigation. But instead it was buzzing when Anna and Sophie got there. Some detectives were liaising with units involved in the raids, while others were busy digging up information on the Perez family and their associates.

Anna escorted Sophie into her office and got DC Sweeny to get her a cup of coffee and take a statement from her.

She then moved restlessly around the open plan office, monitoring the incoming feeds and radio chatter. She learned that Bruno Perez's home had been raided but he wasn't there. Police had stormed two warehouses but the only people in them were security guards.

Five other homes belonging to Bruno's family and associates had also been raided but there was still no sign of the man himself or Chloe.

Anna had to wait for over an hour before the news came through that Michael Taylor had been arrested as he arrived back at his flat. He'd been questioned on the spot and caved in when he realised the game was up.

He told officers that his boss Bruno had taken the girl to a warehouse in Deptford. It wasn't on the list of premises because the family had only just acquired it. Even as this news was coming through an armed response team was arriving at the scene.

Anna and Walker were just about to set off to join them when Sophie and DC Sweeny came rushing out of Anna's office.

'Bruno just called me,' Sophie yelled, holding up her phone. 'He's at a warehouse in Deptford and the police have just turned up. He said he's going to kill Alice unless I go there.'

CHAPTER SIXTY-SIX

Bruno's phone call to Sophie offered a glimmer of hope. Or so Anna thought until she arrived at the warehouse in Deptford. The scene that greeted them sent a fierce panic rushing through her veins.

It was a five-storey Victorian building, of the kind that were being turned into flats all across London. The forecourt and approach road were throbbing with the flashing blue lights of police cars, armed response vehicles and a fire appliance. The front of the building would have been in darkness but for the spotlights that were trained on it.

The focus of everyone's attention was the roof and the two figures standing on the edge of it. Bruno was behind Chloe with one arm around her neck, and Sophie screamed as soon as she got out of the car and saw them.

Anna's stomach turned over and she felt a surge of warm blood into her face.

The armed response team leader emerged from the crowd of uniformed officers to brief Anna and Walker.

'The guy saw us arrive,' he said. 'He was on the ground floor, where it seems he'd been planning to leave the girl locked up for the night. As we entered the building we noticed the lift ascending to the top floor. By the time we'd got there he'd gained access to the roof and taken her with him. Two officers followed him up and when they got there he was standing where he is now and threatening to jump off with the girl.

'He said he'd spoken by phone to Miss Cameron and had told her to come here. He's still demanding to speak to her, and, just so you know, he claims he hasn't touched the girl. He just wanted Miss Cameron to think that he was going to.'

'Then take me up to him,' Sophie said, her voice high and hysterical. 'It's me he wants. I'll try to talk him into letting her go.'

It was the only play they had and they all knew it. This was a classic hostage situation and no one could predict how it would turn out. There was no time to discuss it or to bring in a trained hostage negotiator.

So Anna took Sophie by the arm and said, 'I'm coming with you.'

A message was relayed to the officers on the roof, informing them that Sophie was on her way up.

The warehouse interior looked as though it hadn't been occupied for several years. There was a 'for lease' sign next to the entrance, and overhead strip lights revealed dust-covered floors and bare walls.

Anna, Sophie, Walker and the armed response leader bundled into the lift, which took them swiftly to the top floor. From there it was through a door and up a short flight of stairs to the roof.

There was an outside wall light and beneath it stood two armed officers. They were standing a mere seven yards or so back from Bruno and Chloe, who were now facing away from the edge but were still just as close to it.

The blood seemed to clot in Anna's veins when she laid eyes on her daughter for the first time in ten years. Chloe cried out for her mum, but it was Sophie she was looking at and not Anna.

Bruno's reaction was to smile as he shook his head.

'I warned you what would happen if you involved the cops,' he said to Sophie. 'I told you that you would regret it.'

'Please listen to me,' Anna said. 'Step away from the edge and—'

'No, you listen to me, copper,' he snarled. 'I'm not interested in anything you've got to say. I will only speak to my bitch of a wife. So don't open your fucking mouth again.'

His face clenched in murderous fury and he tightened his grip on Chloe's neck, which stopped her making another sound.

'You don't have to do this, Bruno,' Sophie said, taking a step forward. 'You've got your revenge. I've suffered big time for what happened all those years ago. Please, please let her go.'

'I'll be happy to,' he said. 'So long as you come over here and take her place. There's no way I'm going back to prison. I'm bowing out today and taking either you or her with me.'

'Let's talk this through, Mr Perez,' Anna said, but even as she spoke Sophie was rushing towards him.

Bruno held up his free hand, palm out, and told Sophie

to slow down. Then he turned his cold, shark-like eyes on Anna.

'If any of you take another step I'll jump and take the kid with me,' he said. 'This way she gets to live and you can tell the world that you saved her. And for your information I've not touched her. I'm many things, but I'm not a pervert.'

Anna and the other officers were forced to watch as the horrific scene unfolded.

Bruno beckoned Sophie forward with his hand. When she was close enough he reached out and grabbed her left arm. At the same time he loosened his hold on Chloe and thrust her forward with such force that she fell face down on the roof.

Anna hurried to her side and dropped to her knees beside her. She put her arms around Chloe and just touching her daughter sent a bolt of electricity through her body.

Chloe screamed for her mum and tried to break free, but Anna held her tight. She only stopped struggling when she heard Sophie's raised voice.

Bruno now had Sophie in a vicelike grip, with one hand around her neck and the other around her waist. His grin was wider, but what astonished Anna was that Sophie was also smiling.

'You're safe now, my darling,' Sophie said to Chloe.

Bruno took a step back towards the edge and Sophie twisted her head to look at his face.

'But please give me a couple more seconds,' she said to him. 'There are things I need to say.'

His smile vanished and he gave a little nod.

Sophie turned back to Chloe.

'You need to know that this is the man who murdered your father,' she said. 'He now intends to take my life and later you'll be told why. But that's not all I have to tell you. You see, your father told you lots of lies. Your real mother didn't die ten years ago. He took you from her because he wanted to punish her.'

Chloe had fallen silent, but sobs were still causing her shoulders to jump.

'Your real name is Chloe and not Alice,' Sophie continued. 'And your real mother has been searching for you since you were two years old. And at last she's found you, sweetheart. She is the woman who is now holding you and you must understand that she loves you just as much as I do. She'll look after you from now on and all I ask is that you don't forget me.'

Sophie's gaze shifted to Anna.

'And I want you to know, Miss Tate, that I'm really sorry for the part I played in your suffering. I'm so glad your daughter is back where she belongs.'

Sophie then did something unexpected. Rather than wait for Bruno to pull her over the edge, she took a deep breath and pushed him backwards. He maintained his grip on her and they both tumbled out of sight.

Anna jumped up and hurried across to the edge of the roof. She looked over and saw their two bodies sprawled on the ground far below.

Behind her Chloe screamed and Anna turned to see that her daughter was shaking her head violently from side to side.

'Oh, you poor thing,' Anna said as she hurried back to envelop Chloe in her arms.

'Please don't let my mummy die,' Chloe cried out. 'You have to save her. Please.'

Anna did not know what to say so she just held onto her little girl as the sobs racked her body and the tears gushed out of her eyes.

EPILOGUE

Eight Hours Later

It was the morning after and Chloe was still asleep, thanks to the sedatives the doctor had prescribed.

Anna sat beside her hospital bed, unable to take her eyes off her face. At last her daughter was getting some respite from the onslaught of pain, grief and confusion. But it was going to be short-lived. Soon she'd be awake again, and Anna would have to tell her that what had happened wasn't a nightmare.

Having witnessed the horror on the warehouse roof, Chloe had screamed and cried until the shock became so overwhelming that she had passed out in Anna's arms.

She didn't yet know that her adoptive mother was dead, along with the man who had killed her father. Bruno had died on impact with the ground. Sophie had survived for just an hour before succumbing to serious injuries to her head and neck.

Anna held onto Chloe's hand like her life depended on it. Her mind was a maelstrom of conflicting emotions. There was the joy at having her daughter back and the sadness at the death of Sophie Cameron, who had loved and cared for Chloe for so long and had then committed the ultimate sacrifice in order to save her.

There was also the seemingly insurmountable challenge she now faced of winning Chloe's love and trust. The search was over but the road ahead was going to be long and tortuous.

And it would start today when Anna began to answer as best she could the questions that Chloe was bound to ask.

ACKNOWLEDGEMENTS

I would like to say a special thank you to my editor Phoebe Morgan who has helped to make this book much better than it would otherwise have been. I'll be forever grateful. My thanks also to the rest of the team at Avon, including Molly Walker-Sharp, Sabah Khan and Helen Huthwaite who are doing what they can to make the Anna Tate stories a success.

Love DCI Anna Tate?
Then why not read the first book in the series to see where it all began . . .

Nine missing children.
The hunt is on.
But has time run out?
IN SAFE HANDS
A DCI ANNA TATE THRILLER
J. P. CARTER

A gripping thriller that will have you on the edge of your seat.